D0960490

THE FALLEN

ALSO BY T. JEFFERSON PARKER

California Girl

Cold Pursuit

Black Water

Silent Joe

Red Light

The Blue Hour

Where Serpents Lie

The Triggerman's Dance

Summer of Fear

Pacific Beat

Little Saigon

Laguna Heat

T. JEFFERSON PARKER

wm

WILLIAM MORROW

An Imprint of HarperCollins*Publishers*

This book is a work of fiction. References to real people, events, establishments, organizations, or locales are intended only to provide a sense of authenticity, and are used fictitiously. All other characters, and all incidents and dialogue, are drawn from the author's imagination and are not to be construed as real.

HarperCollins books may be purchased for educational, business, or sales promotional use. For information please write: Special Markets Department, HarperCollins Publishers, 10 East 53rd Street, New York, NY 10022.

FIRST EDITION

Designed by Stephanie Huntwork

Printed on acid-free paper

Library of Congress Cataloging-in-Publication Data

Parker, T. Jefferson.
The fallen: a novel / T. Jefferson Parker.— 1st ed.
p. cm.
ISBN-13: 978-0-06-056238-0 (acid-free paper)
ISBN-10: 0-06-056238-2
1. Police—California—San Diego—Fiction. 2. Ex-police officers—Crimes against—Fiction. 3. San Diego (Calif.)—Fiction. I. Title.

PS3566.A6863F35 2006
813'.54—dc22

2005047934

06 07 08 09 WBC/RRD 10 9 8 7 6 5 4 3 2 1

For Jim and Jeannie, four decades and counting . . .

ACKNOWLEDGMENTS

Thanks again to Dave Bridgman, retired San Diego Police Department firearms instructor, for his generous information about guns and the people who use them.

Also, thanks to Officer Jeff Gross of the San Diego Police Department, for his help with SWAT tactics and capabilities.

Many thanks to San Diego Police Department public information "officer" Dave Cohen, for his help with police department helicopters.

And special thanks to Lance Evers, for his insights into the world of professional wrestling.

Theirs are the facts; the errors are mine alone.

THE FALLEN

PROLOGUE

When the sixth floor of the Las Palmas Hotel caught fire Robbie Brownlaw was in the diner across the street about to have lunch.

It was a cool March afternoon in San Diego and Brownlaw's turkey burger had just arrived when he saw orange flames roiling behind the hotel windows. He took a bite of the sandwich and hustled outside. The sixth-story windows blew and an orange explosion knocked him back against the brick wall of the diner.

Robbie heard screams up there in the fire. He had never heard screams like these. Then he heard all the yelling as people spilled from the restaurants and offices, pointing up at the Las Palmas while debris clattered to the asphalt—a splintered chair, a flaming lampshade, a nightstand with the drawers hanging out.

Fire alarms shrieked competing warnings down the street. Brownlaw heard a guy screaming up on the sixth floor right through the ringing. Such fear. He looked up, still braced against the wall of the Sorrento Diner, heart pounding like a dryer with a load of sneakers.

Then he pushed off and ran toward the Las Palmas, weaving between the stopped and honking cars, past the smoking carcass of a television set with the wall mounts still on it that had crashed onto Fourth.

Brownlaw pulled up at the lobby door of the hotel and let the onrush of humanity sweep past him: a young man in a blazer with a nameplate on and a phone to his ear, a wide-eyed oldster on a wobbling cane, a cleaning lady still wearing yellow rubber gloves and glaring at Robbie as if he had caused this. Then two more old men in shabby suits, a gangsta in a wifebeater shirt swearing in Spanish, an Indian couple with three bawling children, a tall black man in a Sonics T-shirt, then a pretty young woman with a tangle of blond hair, a black eye, and a bathrobe around her.

Robbie headed up the stairs past an old woman with a Yorkie in her arms. He felt lucky and useful. The smoke was thick by the fourth landing and hot by the sixth. There was a weak moaning behind the first door he came to. It was locked but it took him just one kick and a shoulder slam to break it down. Inside he found a very old woman trapped under the mattress, which had apparently fallen onto her from the upended springs and frame. Only her neck and head and one arm were sticking out from under it. She looked up at him through the smoke as if he were God himself and Brownlaw told her she'd be fine as he bent and dug his fingers into the mattress and pulled it away. The old woman couldn't get up so Brownlaw just hauled her over his shoulders and ran back down the stairs with her.

By the time he got back up to the sixth story, he was coughing hard and his eyes burned and the sirens were wailing closer and all but one of the room doors had been thrown open.

Behind that door Brownlaw could hear the screams of a man, the same terrified, animal sounds he'd heard on the street. One kick later the door shuddered open and he was in. The smoke was thick but Robbie could see the guy kneeling at the glassless window with his back to him. He was wearing shorts and that was all. He was clutching the windowsill, bellowing at the city with wild fear.

When Robbie was halfway across the room the man turned and looked at him and Robbie realized it wasn't fear at all. The man wheeled and came at him fast. He was very big and had Robbie in a wrestler's bear hug in an instant. He lifted Robbie off the floor and swung him around the room. During those two rapid orbits Brownlaw stared from inches away into a face he would never forget or understand—a face of rage and desperation whose depths he could not measure. Pitiless eyes. He tried to groin the guy with his knee but the man was so tall that all he got was thigh. His gun was in his shoulder rig, which was under his sport coat, but his arms were pinned. He could not draw breath.

At the end of that second rotation—he was pretty sure it was only two—Brownlaw felt the big hands lock around his arms and fling him out the window.

The air was cool and he felt absolutely alone. His first thought was that he could stop his fall using pure willpower.

And it seemed to be true. He focused all of his will on staying up. *Up! Up! Up!* Raising his arms, Robbie clawed the sky and felt his body suspended in the great liberty of air. He wasn't falling at all, but moving forward with good speed, and for an instant he wondered if he might collide with the building across the street. Or maybe even crash through a window, land on his feet, and get back to the Sorrento before the waitress took away his lunch.

Then Brownlaw came to the end of his outward momentum. There was no hesitation, no moment of suspension. Just a heavy pivot of weight and down he went.

Fast, then faster. He had never felt such speed before, nothing close to this. Faster still. Robbie Brownlaw, on his back now with his arms spread and his hands reaching for nothing, watched the top of the Las Palmas rise up into the gray clouds and felt his ears bend forward in the awesome velocity of descent. He understood that he was now in the hands of something much larger than himself, if he was in any kind of hands at all.

He thought of his young wife, Gina, with whom he was ferociously in love. He understood that the power of their love would be a factor in the outcome here. It seemed impossible that their days together were about to come to an end. Something like relief flowed through Robbie and as the clouds rose away from him he tried to figure his estimated time of arrival. Sixteen feet per second? But is that only at first? Surely you accelerate faster. How high is a story in an old hotel? The phrase "two more seconds" came into his mind.

But in spite of Robbie's belief that he would live to love Gina for years to come, a more convincing idea now flashed into his brain: *This is it.*

He suddenly believed in the God he had doubted for all his life, his conversion completed in a fraction of a second.

Then he let go. He felt insight and understanding: He saw that his first five years of life had been happy, that his childhood had been filled with wonder, his teenage years were a search for freedom, his young adulthood had been a storm of confusion and yearning for love, his twenties a happy grind of Gina and friends and Gina and friends and Gina and Gina and Gina, and Robbie plummeted through the screams of sirens and alarms and onlookers and crashed through the faded red awning over the entrance to the Las Palmas Hotel like an anvil through a bedsheet and hit the sidewalk with a cracking, echoless thud.

My name is Robbie Brownlaw, and I am a Homicide detective for the city of San Diego. I am twenty-nine years old. My life was ordinary until three years ago when I was thrown out of a downtown hotel window.

No one knows it except my wife, but I now have synesthesia, a neurological condition where your senses get mixed up. Sometimes when people talk to me, I see their voices as colored shapes. It happens when they get emotional. The shapes are approximately two by two inches and there are usually between four and eight of them, sometimes more. They linger in the air midway between the speaker and me, about head high. They fade quickly. I can move them with my finger or a pen if I want.

Shortly after my fall I used graph paper and colored markers to make a chart of which words and word combinations triggered which colored shapes. This was time-consuming and not always pleasant, due to some very painful headaches. I also observed that blue triangles generally came from a happy speaker. Red squares came from a deceptive one. Green trapezoids usually came from someone who was envious—green really is the color of envy, just like we were always told.

But as the weeks went by, I noticed that identical words and sentences could sometimes trigger very different shapes and colors. I was afraid that I had posttraumatic swelling in my brain and worried that my synesthesia would worsen to the point where I'd spend the rest of my life drooling at invisible shapes while people tried to talk to me.

I spoke my fears to Gina one night and noticed that when she told me

I "shouldn't worry about it," her words came to me as the black triangles of dread. I looked them up on my chart just to make sure. It was then that I began to understand that the colorful shapes are provoked by the *emotions* of the speaker, not by the words themselves.

So I have what amounts to a primitive lie detector, though I'm not certain how reliable it is. I think a remorseless psychopath could fool me, or even an accomplished liar. Who knows what colors and shapes they might cause? In my line of work, people will lie to you about the smallest and most trivial things.

Synesthesia is considered a gift by synesthetes—the people who have it—but I'm not convinced that it is. There's a San Diego Synesthesia Society, and for over a year now I've been thinking about going to a meeting. I browse their Web site and note the date and time of the next meeting, but I've never attended one. I'm curious, but a little afraid of what I might discover. The condition is hard for me to talk about, even with Gina. Although she's tolerant and wonderfully opinionless about how others view the world, it annoys her that even her white lies announce themselves to me as bright red squares. It would annoy me, too.

When I was thrown out of the window I hit hard. You have no idea how hard cement really is until you land on it from six stories up, even if your fall is largely broken by a canvas awning. During the fall I came to believe in God. It is true what they say about your life flashing past when you believe that you are about to die, but it is not your entire life. Obviously. I should have died, but only a few bones broke, and I'm in perfect shape again, other than the large scar on the back of my head, now hidden by hair, and the synesthesia.

One benefit I got from that fall was two very quick promotions. As soon as I proved I was in great health and could do the job, doors opened right up. From Fraud to Sex Crimes to Homicide just like that. Everyone expected me to die from the fall. All of the media coverage made the department want to reward its unlikely hero. The reporters nicknamed me "the Falling Detective." And my superiors sincerely felt that I deserved a little something extra for all I'd been through. Anyway, I'm the youngest detective in Homicide, but nobody seems to resent me for it. I'm part of

Team Four. Our case-cancellation rate last year, 2004, was eighty-eight percent, which is considered excellent.

I got the call from our lieutenant at four that morning. An anonymous caller had tipped us to a body in a car near Balboa Park. Patrol had confirmed a black Ford Explorer parked in the trees near the Cabrillo Bridge, which spans Highway 163. The lieutenant told me there was a man slumped dead in the driver's seat. Blood, sidearm on the floorboard, probable gunshot.

I called my partner, McKenzie Cortez, then poured a cup of coffee. I sat for a minute on the bedside in the dark, snugged up the sheets around Gina and kissed her.

In the weak light of the breakfast nook I wrote her a note saying I'd be careful and I loved her. Spouses worrying about their loved ones getting killed on the job is what ruins a lot of cop marriages. And I like Gina to have something nice to wake up to. She works as a hairdresser at Salon Sultra downtown, which is top of the line. She cut Mick Jagger's hair when the Stones played L.A. not long ago. Just a trim, actually. Mick flew her up to his hotel in Beverly Hills in a helicopter. Paid a thousand for the cut and gave her another five hundred for a tip.

The drive from my house in Normal Heights took twelve minutes. It was a cool, clear March morning. There had been rain the night before, more than enough to leave shallow black puddles along the freeway. The stars were bright in the sky and the car lights sharp in the dark. The moon looked dull and cold as frozen steel, like your tongue would stick to it. When I see the wide-eyed grimace of the man in the moon I wonder if that's what I looked like on my way down from the sixth floor. The videotape they played on the news wasn't quite clear enough to show the expression on my face. At least that's what Gina tells me. I've never watched it.

There were two PD cruisers and the Ford Explorer parked off of the dirt road under the Cabrillo Bridge. The bridge was built to suggest a Roman aqueduct. It is a graceful old structure, rising up majestically from the greenery, built in 1914 for the big United States–Panama exhibition. That morning it looked stately and uncaring in the March dawn. One end of the bridge led directly into Balboa Park, while the other became Laurel Avenue. Under the bridge ran the highway. All around the great caissons rose the lush trees overflowing from the park. The air smelled damp and dense. Three cars sat in a small grassy swale shaded by big Canary Island palms and the ivy-covered stanchions of the bridge. One cop had pulled his cruiser broadside to the SUV and left his headlights on. The raindrops on the Explorer glistened in the beams.

The driver's-side window was nothing but a pile of shattered safety glass, most of it on the grass. A few pebbles lay on the door, by the lock. The guy was collapsed on the driver's side the way only a dead man can be. Like he'd been poured into an odd shape, then begun to harden. Head against the window frame at a weird angle. Left arm against the door, palm up. Right hand closed and resting against the center console. Autoloader on the passenger floorboard. Keys still in the ignition. A brushed-aluminum briefcase on a backseat. Blood all over the windows and the cloth seats and dash and console and headliner. Seemed like gallons of it. I walked around to the other side to make sure I was seeing who I thought I was seeing.

"It's Garrett Asplundh," I said.

"Yes, sir," said the patrolman. "DMV confirmed. His car, I mean."

Garrett had been one of our Professional Standards Unit sergeants until a few months ago. PSU is part of Internal Affairs. PSU are the cops who watch the cops. Garrett Asplundh was mysterious and a little feared. His young daughter had drowned in a swimming-pool accident about nine months ago, and it destroyed his career and his marriage.

I didn't know him well. Just after my fall, he had come to the hospital and we talked awhile, mostly about fly-fishing, which we both enjoy. Odd that two men in such circumstances would choose to talk about fishing. We agreed to fish Glorietta Bay together but never did. Cops don't hang out with PSU. Asplundh was quiet and neatly handsome. Dark eyes, smile lines on his cheeks. Within the department he was considered a man on the rise. He easily drew Gina's attention in the hospital that day.

Just a few months ago, Garrett had taken a lower-stress job as an investigator for the San Diego Ethics Authority Enforcement Unit. I say "lower-stress" because Ethics Authority personnel aren't cops any longer, though most Authority officers are formerly sworn officers or agents. Some carry weapons. The Authority was created two years ago to keep politicians, city administrators, and businesspeople from breaking laws in order to make more money and gain more power. The Ethics Authority watches city personnel the same way the PSU watches the cops.

"You think suicide?" asked the officer.

"Tape it off," I said.

McKenzie Cortez came across the damp, springy grass, hands jammed down into the pockets of her coat. Jeans and construction boots and her hair under an SDPD cap. Her breath made a little cloud in front of her mouth, not a common thing to see in San Diego.

"What's up, Robbie?"

"Garrett Asplundh."

"Really."

She walked past me to the Explorer, looked in. I saw her right hand trace a quick cross upon her front side, then return to the warmth of the pocket. She stared awhile, then came back to me.

"Looks like he might have pulled his own plug," she said.

"Kinda does."

"You don't sound convinced."

"Seems like he'd have done it sooner."

McKenzie nodded and looked at me. She's a few years older than me, half Anglo and half Latina. She is strong and intelligent. Single, proud, unfazed by risk. Her face is pretty but rudely scarred by acne. She's tough and unhappy.

"Let the GSR decide," she said.

The hand of a suicide by gun will be peppered with gunshot residue, mostly the barium and antimony contained in gunpowder. It's easy to lift off with tape. But if the hands are clean, you might have a homicide. A tricky bad guy can shoot someone up close, then put the dead or dying person's hand around the gun and fire it somewhere the bullet can't be found, so it looks like a suicide. But this happens in books and movies much more than in real life and death.

There were no known witnesses, although one elderly motorist stopped to tell us that he'd driven past here around nine the night before and seen a red Ferrari parked down by the side of the freeway. It was pulled over not far from where the black Explorer now stood. He also saw a man moving in the trees, just barely visible. I had one of the officers detain and run a records and warrants check on the motorist, but he came back clean. Retired Navy. He sat in the back of a prowl car with a look of authority while the check went through.

The anonymous caller who had reported the Explorer and possible victim was male and spoke English with an undetermined accent. The conversation was partially recorded by a desk officer at headquarters.

McKenzie and I watched the crime-scene investigators sketch and measure and photograph and video the scene. Glenn Wasserman, one of our best CSIs, brought me a small paper bag with a cartridge casing in it, a nine-millimeter Smith factory load by the look of it.

"Up on the dashboard," he said. "Almost fell down into the heater vent."

"Nice grab," I said.

"It's Garrett Asplundh, isn't it?"

"Yes."

"I never worked with him."

I talked briefly with the first-on-scene officers. They'd handled the scene by the book: checked for signs of life, called Dispatch with the possible 187, taped off the scene using the convenient tree trunks, and waited for the Homicide hordes to arrive. They confirmed that the passenger's door had been like it was now—closed, with the window up.

The Coroner's team pronounced and removed the body. They just opened the driver's door and guided Asplundh onto a plastic body bag atop a lowered gurney. Before they zipped it up, I pulled his wallet from his coat pocket. I noted the currency and credit cards, the driver's license and "City of San Diego Employee" ID. I noted that his birthday was in November and that he would have turned forty years old. I slid the wallet back in. I saw the cell phone clipped to his belt. I saw that his necktie was almost completely drenched in blood. A small portion of it was still light blue. There are few places where blood looks more startling than on a necktie.

They zipped him and covered him with a blanket. I thought of how he had once seemed large and been feared. And how the death of his daughter and the ruin of his marriage had left him smaller. And how, soon, not one recognizable molecule of him would be left.

I reached into the Explorer, slipped the automatic garage door opener off the sun visor and put it in my pocket. Then I walked alongside Asplundh to the Coroner's van. Hoped his soul would be well taken care of. After all, he was once one of us.

Over on the passenger side of the Explorer I hoped to find good footprints but found none at all. The grass was healthy and wet and too springy to hold an indentation for long. But a second vehicle had been parked here very recently. And it had left dark green tracks coming down the hillock, just as the Explorer had. The tracks of the second vehicle were deeper and darker than those of the Ford, and I wondered if its driver had perhaps gunned it in reverse to back up the side of the swale. With the grass wet from the rain, it might have taken a four-wheel drive to back up that hill.

I bent down a little and looked straight through the passenger-side window to where Garrett's head would have been when he was alive. Sitting there. Talking, maybe. Looking ahead. Hard to imagine he was unaware of the shooter.

Then I looked beyond him, trying to estimate where the bullet might be if it had continued in an approximately straight line. It would have shot across Highway 163, bored through several yards of tree foliage unless it clipped a branch and veered off, then lodged in the rising slope of earth toward the far end of the bridge. But the chances of an approximately straight line of flight were not good, given the skull and glass the bullet had to pass through. The chances of the bullet's being in one piece were not good at all. I made an unhopeful note to have the CSIs look for fragments.

I climbed the gentle embankment down which the Explorer had traveled to get to the secluded, shaded swale. It was easy to pick out the tire tracks that had been left by the vehicle. Easy, too, to see the second set that came down the embankment and stopped right next to it.

I waved to Glenn, pointed to the tracks. He worked his way up the hillock toward us, shooting digital and video. For a moment we stood at the top. I looked out at the cars charging by on Highway 163.

"Asplundh was a kick-ass cop, wasn't he?" asked Glenn.

I nodded.

"What a turnaround," said Glenn. "From Professional Standards to this."

We went back down for a closer look at the Explorer. Another CSI was examining and photographing the tires before they towed it off to the impound yard to be dusted for fingerprints and combed for hair and fiber.

"Look at this," she said.

I came around and knelt and looked at the shiny green rock caught in the tread of the left rear tire.

She photographed it. Two angles, three shots from each. Then she shot some video, explaining what she was shooting. Then she pried the rock out and dropped it into a small paper evidence bag. I took the bag and stared down, holding my flashlight beam steady. It wasn't a rock at all but half a small glass marble. It was bright green. I remembered that size from when I was a kid.

"We called them minis," I said.

"Right," she said. "Smaller than a shooter."

It looked like it had lodged in the wide tread of the SUV tire, then been sheared off to a half sphere. There was a fragment of something pale and red-orange embedded in the glass. Part of the cat's eye, maybe. Or some other kind of inner design. The sheared surface around it, recessed into the tread, was pitted.

"Fifty bucks he shot himself," said McKenzie.

Odd words for her to use, because the lavender ovals that spilled out of her mouth and hovered in the air between us meant she was feeling genuine sympathy for Garrett Asplundh. I nodded as the ovals bobbed like corks on a slow river, then dissolved. McKenzie likes to talk tougher than she feels. After three years I don't pay a whole lot of attention to the colors and shapes of other people's feelings, unless they don't match up with their words.

"I don't think so," I said. "He used to be Professional Standards. One of the real straight arrows."

"Straight arrows can't bend," said McKenzie.

We walked around to the other side of the vehicle. I pulled on some gloves, then swung open the right rear door. In spite of the cool early hour, the flies had already found the blood. I squared the aluminum case on the seat in front of me, pushed the thumb buttons, and watched the latches jump. One yellow legal pad with neat handwriting on the top page. Two pens, two pencils, and a tiny calculator. An address book. A datebook. A small tape recorder, a digital camera, and a .45 automatic Colt pistol in a heavily oiled leather holster. With a pencil I poked and pried around the items, looking for something hidden or loose or out of place. But all of it was splendidly organized into cutouts in the foam that lined both the bottom and the lid.

Cops and their guns, I thought. Pretty much inseparable, right up to the end.

"Look how organized he was," said McKenzie. "Must have cut the foam himself to get it all neat like that."

I put the automatic garage door opener in the briefcase, closed it up, and locked it in the trunk of my car.

A tall, slender man in a long black coat came skidding down the hill-side, well away from the crime-scene tape, feet turned sideways and lean-ing back for balance. It took me a second to recognize him. It was Ethics Authority director Erik Kaven, a man feared in the same way that his in-vestigator Garrett Asplundh had been feared.

"He got the news pretty fast," said McKenzie.

Kaven sized up the scene and came toward us. His handshake was strong.

"Garrett?" he asked.

I nodded.

"Robbery?"

"Suicide looks more like it," said McKenzie.

"It wasn't suicide," said Kaven. He looked at McKenzie, then me. Kaven was tall and big-jawed, and his face was deeply lined. His gray-brown hair was thick, straight, and undisciplined. He wore a gunslinger's mustache that somehow looked right on him. I guessed him at fifty. He'd been a district federal judge here in San Diego before signing on to lead the new Ethics Authority two years ago. Kaven had made big news when he shot two bank robbers out in El Cajon one Friday afternoon. Two shots, two dead men. He carried a gun on the bench, and he'd just gotten off work. He'd been depositing his paycheck when the robbers' guns came out. His eyes were deep-set and pointedly suspicious.

"It wasn't suicide," he said again. "I'll guarantee it."

Garrett Asplundh's apartment was up in the North Park part of San Diego. Nice area, decent neighborhoods, and not far from the ocean. From the upstairs deck of Garrett's place I could see Balboa Park. The late-morning breeze was cool and sharp.

It was a two-bedroom place. Small kitchen with a view of the neighborhood and the power lines. Not much in the fridge but plenty of scotch in the liquor cabinet. The living room had a hardwood floor, a gas-burning fireplace, a black futon sofa with a chrome gooseneck reading lamp, and bookshelves covering three walls. I stood there with my hands in my pockets, like a museum visitor. I like quiet when I'm trying to get the sound of a victim's life. There was a lot to hear about Garrett Asplundh. He had been executed, for one thing. Either by himself or someone else.

The books ranged widely, from *The World Atlas of Nations* to *Trout from Small Streams* by Dave Hughes, and they were arranged in no order I could see. Lots of photography collections. Lots of true crime. No paperbacks. No novels. An entire shelf of books on aquatic insects. Another shelf just for meteorology. Another for Abraham Lincoln.

There was a small collection of CDs and DVDs, some commercially manufactured and some homemade. One of the DVDs was entitled "The Life and Death of Samantha Asplundh." It wasn't in a plastic box, but rather a leather sheath with the title tooled onto the front. Some good work had gone into creating that container. I wondered if Samantha was the daughter who died.

The first bedroom had a computer workstation set up at a window. There was a padded workout bench, weights in a rack, and a stationary cycle. Facing another window was a small desk for tying flies. The walls were covered with black-and-white photographs of a woman and a little girl. I mean *completely* covered, every inch, the edges of the pictures—mostly eight-and-a-half-by-elevens—perfectly, spacelessly aligned. The pictures seemed artful to me, but I know nothing about art. The woman had lightness and depth and beauty. The girl was innocent and joyful. I could sense the emotion of the photographer. If he had been able to talk honestly to me about those two subjects, I'd have seen yellow rhomboids pouring out of him, because yellow rhomboids are the color and shape of love.

"Must be the ex and kid," said McKenzie.

The other bedroom was similarly sparse. Just a tightly made full-size bed, a lamp to read by, a chest of drawers, and more black-and-white photographs of the woman and the girl. A few of them had Garrett Asplundh in them. He looked drowsy and dangerous. He was a lean but muscled man, and I remembered that he was reputed to be a superb boxer and martial artist.

"He was obsessed with his wife," said McKenzie.

"I don't remember her name."

"Stella. The girl drowned in the pool while the mom was supposed to be watching. Or maybe Garrett was, I don't remember. But Mom couldn't handle it and left him. That's what I heard."

"Yeah. That's about what I heard, too."

"I wonder why all black-and-white. No color."

"Maybe it's the way he saw things," I guessed.

"Colorblind?"

"No. All one way or the other."

"You mean no gray," said McKenzie.

"None."

She shrugged. "Chick had a pretty face."

I wondered why there were no cameras here. No tripods, lights, lenses, cases, battery packs, motor drives, canisters of film. No evidence—except for the digital camera in his aluminum case—that Garrett Asplundh had taken a single picture since his daughter died.

I sat at the desk in front of the window and pulled out one of the left-side drawers. It was full of hanging files, all red, each labeled with vinyl tab and handwritten label. I flipped through the "Medical" but didn't find anything of interest. I checked the "Phone" file because I always do. Nothing unusual. In "Utils" I noted the gas and electric, as well as monthly checks made out to Kohler Property Managers for rent on the North Park apartment. Oddly, there were monthly checks made out to another management company—Uptown Property Management—for eight hundred dollars. Nothing written on the memo lines to indicate what the payment was for. Eight hundred dollars is a lot of money, month in and out. I'd seen Uptown Property Management signs around, mostly down in Barrio Logan and Shelltown and National City. Not really your uptown properties at all. I made a note to call them.

The "Sam" file contained only two documents—birth and death certificates. She had died of drowning at the age of three years and two months. Her official history was a folder with two pieces of paper in it. I wondered at the tremendous loss of this little girl if you projected in all the years she had to live and everything she might have become.

Next I got out the "Explorer" file and compared the Explorer's plate numbers with the ones I'd written down. The same. The SUV had been purchased new from a local Ford dealer. Three years of financing provided by Ford Credit. I wondered how much money Garrett Asplundh was making as an investigator for the city Ethics Authority.

The drawer above had my answer: stubs from City of San Diego payroll checks issued weekly for $1,750—give or take a few dollars and cents. That was before deductions for income tax, Social Security, and a Keogh account. Ninety-one grand a year wasn't making Asplundh rich. I was making eighty-one, counting overtime, as a first-year dead dick.

Behind the pay-stub folder were two folders marked "Entertain 1" and "Entertain 2." I opened "Entertain 1" and scanned through the receipts—high-line restaurants, the Del Mar Thoroughbred Club, exotic car rentals. Lots of nights out. Some of it was charged to a credit card in Asplundh's name. Some of it was paid in cash.

A right-side drawer was full of light blue hanging files, all related to fly-fishing: "Dream Trips." "Casting." "Strategy." "Misc." I fanned through the

"Misc" file and saw clips from some of the same goofily intense magazines I read. Technical stuff—graphite modulus and flex ranges. Esoteric stuff—"Delicate Presentations" and "Mono Versus Fluoro." Favorite articles—"Harrop's Top Baetis Patterns" and "Nymphs for Pickerel."

"Look," said McKenzie. "Garrett liked to dress."

She stood in the doorway with hangers in each hand. "Dude was wearing Armani and Hugo Boss. Dude's got shoes in the closet that cost three hundred a pair. He had a suit on last night, when he got it."

"Investigating ethics," I said.

"Yeah, you gotta look sharp to know right from wrong. Black from white. No grays. I wonder how much they were paying him?"

"About what we pay a lieutenant."

"Must have had a kick-ass expense account." McKenzie eyed the suits, then whirled back into the short hallway.

The closets in the weight room / office contained golf clubs, fly-fishing gear, and more file cabinets.

Back in the kitchen we listened to the messages on the answering machine.

Someone named Josh Mead had called about Garrett's rounding out a foursome at Pala Mesa in Fallbrook on Saturday, left his number.

A recorded voice tried to sell him lower-cost medical insurance.

A woman who identified herself as Stella said she had waited until eleven. She said she hoped he was okay, would try him later. Her voice sounded disappointed and worried.

"Not very friendly, is she?" asked McKenzie.

"She sounds anxious."

The secretary for John Van Flyke of the Ethics Authority called with some expense-account questions about last week's pay period. Van Flyke was Garrett's direct boss, the supervisor of the Ethics Authority Enforcement Unit. We cops thought Van Flyke was quirky and overly serious. When he was hired, the *Union-Tribune* had showered him with praise because he could help Erik Kaven get tough on San Diego corruption. Van Flyke had not allowed himself or any employee of the Enforcement Unit to be photographed for the articles. He reported directly to Kaven and was allowed to recruit his own staff. I had no idea where the Ethics Authority Enforcement Unit offices even were.

"I was introduced to Van Flyke once," said McKenzie. "He stared at me like he was guessing my weight. Drummed his fingers on the table like he couldn't wait for me to leave. So I left."

"Where?"

"Chive Restaurant down in the Gaslamp. Another macho fed, just like Kaven."

Stella called again, said she could meet him at ten o'clock tonight in the bar at Delicias in Rancho Santa Fe.

Garrett, said Stella, *if you've been drinking, don't even bother. I thought we might really have something to celebrate last night. I'd appreciate a call if you can't make it this time. I'm trusting you're okay.*

"She doesn't seem real concerned about him," said McKenzie.

"I think she sounds worried."

While McKenzie played the messages again I found Stella's phone number and address in Garrett's book. She lived downtown. Legally, Stella wasn't next of kin, but she was the one we needed to talk to. Death notifications are my least favorite part of Homicide detail but I couldn't ask McKenzie to do it alone because of her bluntness.

Asplundh's garage was like the apartment—neat and clean. It was big enough for one vehicle, two tall shelves of boxes, and a small workbench. Two pairs of eight-foot fluorescent bulbs cast a stiff light on everything. I sat on the metal stool at the workbench. It felt like a place where a guy would spend some time. On the bench was a shiny abalone shell with a pack of smokes in it, and a book of matches on top of that. In the cabinet over the bench were stacks of fishing magazines, boxes of flies and reels and tackle, a mostly full bottle of Johnnie Walker Black. In the drawers were the usual hand tools you'd expect to find and a five-shot .38 revolver, loaded and good to go.

I had the thought that if Garrett Asplundh were going to kill himself he'd have done it right here. But my opinion was that Garrett hadn't done himself in. He must have parked down there near the bridge because he was meeting someone. Someone he knew. Someone he trusted. That someone had killed him. And if someone else had driven him away, that meant at least two people were involved. Which could mean conspiracy, premeditation, and a possible death penalty.

Ballsy guys, I thought.

Head-shoot a city investigator in his own car. Leave him in a public place and don't bother to make it look like anything but murder.

Don't bother to take the wallet, briefcase, or car.

Didn't bother—I was willing to bet—putting the gun into Garrett's trembling hand and firing it into the night so we'd find GSR and work the case as a suicide.

No, none of that. They were too confident for that. Too matter-of-fact. Too cool. They had put a cap in Garrett, then cleaned up and had a cocktail at Rainwater's or the Waterfront.

I wondered when was the last time that Garrett Asplundh had sat where I was sitting. I looked across the workbench to the wall to see exactly what Garrett saw when he sat here—late at night, I guessed—as sleep escaped him and the endless loop of memories played through his mind over and over and over again.

I couldn't tell you what Garrett had seen. Maybe it was a picture. Possibly a photograph. Maybe one that he had taken. Maybe a postcard. Or a poem or prayer or a joke. Or something cut from a magazine.

All that was left were four white thumbtacks, four by six inches apart.

"No matter how long you stare, it's still four thumbtacks," said McKenzie.

"Makes me wonder what was there," I said. "A lot about Garrett makes me wonder. There isn't enough."

"Enough what?"

"Enough anything. There's not enough of him."

McKenzie gave me a puzzled look. Not the first time.

"What I wonder is why a cop would want to work for the Ethics Authority in the first place," she said. "Why spy on the city you work for? Why sneak around? What, to feel important?"

"It goes back to watching the watchdogs."

"Sooner or later you have to trust somebody," said McKenzie. "Otherwise there's no end to all the layers of bullshit."

"Well said."

I stood for a moment in the garage, facing the street. The March afternoon was rushing by and it was going to be a killer sunset. From a beach it would look like a can of orange paint poured onto a blue mirror. I thought of Gina and how much she wanted a place on the sand, and of the savings account I'd opened for that purpose. We were up to almost twenty thousand dollars in five years. Multiply by ten and we'd almost have enough for a down payment. At the current rate, I'd still be less than eighty years old. My Grandpa Rich is eighty-five and still going strong.

I turned and looked up at the neatly stacked boxes on the shelves. Everything Asplundh did was neat. I pulled down one box and set it on the workbench. It was surprisingly light. McKenzie cut the shipping tape with my penknife. Inside, individually wrapped in tissue paper, like gifts, were small blouses, shorts, dresses, coats, sweaters. A pair of tennis shoes with cartoon characters on them. A pair of shiny black dress shoes. Barrettes and combs for hair. Even a doll, a pudgy baby doll with a faded blue dress. None of it was new. It all looked like it was made for a three-year-old, which was the age of Garrett's daughter when she drowned. There was a black felt cowgirl hat stuffed with tissue to keep it shaped. Stitched into the crown in bright colors were buckin' broncos and ponies and a saguaro cactus and a campfire. *Samantha* was embroidered across the front in pink.

"Memorial in a box," said McKenzie.

"When my Aunt Melissa died, Uncle Jerry couldn't figure out what to keep and let go," I said. "He kept most of her stuff."

"Little doll," said McKenzie. "Man, tough call. You don't want to see it every day, but you can't just toss it out like it doesn't matter. You can't look at it, but you can't let it go."

Stella Asplundh slid open two dead bolts and one chain, cracked the door, looked from McKenzie to me, and said, "He's dead."

Four black triangles tumbled into the space between us. Black triangles are dread.

"Yes, ma'am. Last night."

"Was he murdered?"

"We don't know yet," I said. "It's likely."

The black triangles derealized and vanished.

She was wearing a loose black sweater, jeans, and dark socks. She was a beautiful woman although she looked disheveled and unhealthy. The elevator clanked down behind us.

"Come in."

Her apartment was a Queen Anne Victorian down in the Gaslamp Quarter, once a red-light district and now a place for restaurants and clubs. She was on the fourth floor, above an art gallery and two other flats.

We sat in the unlit living room on a big purple couch with gold piping. The walls were paneled in black walnut and the windows faced north and west. I could see the darkening sky and the rooftop of another building across the street, which reminded me of falling from the sixth floor of the Las Palmas. The room smelled faintly of cinnamon and a woman's perfume.

I explained to Stella Asplundh what we had found.

She watched me without moving. She said nothing. Her hair fell loosely around her face and her eyes were black and shiny.

"So much," she said quietly.

"So much what?" asked McKenzie. She had gotten out her notebook and was already writing.

Stella looked down, brushed something off her knee. "He went through so much."

"We have . . . we *had* an unusual relationship. It would be very difficult to explain. We were going to meet last night in Rancho Santa Fe—neutral ground. He didn't show. That's never happened before. In the twelve years I've known Garrett, he never stood me up. That's why, when I answered the door just now . . ."

"You knew something had happened," said McKenzie, head bowed to her notepad.

"Yes, exactly. Excuse me for just a moment, please."

She rose in the twilight and walked past me. A light went on in a hallway. I heard a door shut and water running. A toilet flushed. After a minute McKenzie set down her notebook and pen and went into the hallway. I heard the knock.

"Ms. Asplundh? You okay?"

Stella answered, though I couldn't hear what she said.

I stood and went to a small alcove hung with photographs and mementos. Mostly there were pictures of Stella, Garrett, and a cute little girl. A police commendation hung beside a day-care diploma for Samantha Asplundh. A master's degree in psychology for Stella Asplundh hung next to a photograph of ten college-age women in bathing suits standing in front of a swimming pool. The engraved plate said SAN FRANCISCO MERAQUAS, PAN AMERICAN GAMES SYNCHRONIZED SWIMMING CHAMPIONS 1983.

The toilet flushed again, and the door opened. They were talking quietly. Then they came back to the half-lit room, McKenzie with a hand on Stella Asplundh's arm.

Stella sat again and stared out the window. The streetlamps went on down on Island and a car horn honked and honked again. A pigeon flashed by.

"We can come back," I said.

"If we have to," said McKenzie.

"No," said Stella Asplundh. "Ask your questions."

"It's brave and good of you," I said.

Stella nodded but looked at neither of us.

"Was he worried?" I asked.

"Always."

"Enemies?"

"Hundreds. When he was a cop he policed other cops. For the Ethics Authority he policed the city government and the politicians and the businesspeople they have dealings with."

"A long list."

"Everybody, really."

"But who in particular?"

She looked at me, then back to the window. "He never really told me details."

"Some of the circumstances suggest suicide," said McKenzie. "Do you think he would have killed himself?"

"No. He was more full of hope the last time I saw him than at any time since Samantha drowned. He came close to killing himself last July when it happened. But no. Not now."

"Why not?" I asked.

Stella Asplundh's eyes shone in the dark. I knew they were trained on me. "We were trying to reconcile. We had both been through so much. We fell apart. But we'd begun to come back together. I really can't explain it, other than we once loved each other very much and we were trying to love each other again."

"What was the purpose of the neutral ground?" I asked. "The Rancho Santa Fe date?"

"Garrett could become emotional. If he was drinking it was worse, and he was often drinking."

I said nothing and neither did McKenzie. Nothing like silence to draw out the words.

Stella looked down at the couch. Her hair fell forward. "We were separated. I moved out of our house four months ago, November of last year. Garrett got his own place, too, because we'd sold the house where it happened. You can't live where there are memories like that. But I still would see Garrett, because I thought it was best for him. Unless we saw each other every week, or two weeks at the most, he'd become anxious and extremely irrational. We would sit in a restaurant or a coffee shop. Maybe just walk. He just needed . . . the company."

"Your company," said McKenzie. "Did you ever go to his apartment?"

"No. Never."

"Did he come here?"

"He never came inside. He would . . . I saw him down on the street several times. Looking up."

"He stalked you," said McKenzie.

"That's the wrong word," said Stella.

"What's the right word?" asked McKenzie.

Stella Asplundh sat still in the dark room.

"Were you afraid of him?" asked McKenzie.

"A little. And afraid for him, too."

"When was the divorce final?" asked McKenzie.

"It wasn't. I had the papers drawn up but never had the . . . courage to serve them."

After all that, I thought, she couldn't quite let go of him. And he obviously couldn't let go of her. As if I'd needed more evidence than his shrine of photographs.

"What time were you supposed to meet in Rancho Santa Fe last night?" asked McKenzie.

"Nine."

"At Delicias restaurant?"

Stella nodded and took a deep breath. She radiated an intense aloneness.

"When was the last time you saw Garrett?" I asked.

"Last Thursday evening. We met down at the coffee shop and talked for almost two hours. He was very hopeful. He said he had stopped drinking. He said he was still in love with me and ready to move on with our lives."

Darkness had finally fallen. March afternoons race by, but the evenings seem to last for hours.

"Do you know what Garrett would have said about his own murder?" asked Stella Asplundh. "He would have said it wasn't a murder, it was a piece of work."

I agreed but said nothing.

"Let's not jump to conclusions, Ms. Asplundh," said McKenzie.

"You don't understand very much, do you?" Stella asked gently. She bit her thumb and looked away. Tears poured down her face but she didn't make a sound. I'd never seen anyone cry like that.

A few minutes later Stella showed us to the door and we rode the slow elevator back down. On Island, lights twinkled in the trees and the streetlamps glowed. Over on Fourth the hostesses stood outside their restaurants.

A pretty woman in a white VW Cabriolet pulled over to talk with a guy. I wondered why she had the top down when it was cool like this, figured the heater was cranked up.

"I like the Cabriolets," said McKenzie. "But they're a little doggy in the horsepower department. I spun one out on a test drive once, totally freaked the sales guy. What did you think of the almost-ex?"

"Wrung out," I said.

"Yeah. Like a vampire sucked her blood."

Before going home we stopped by my office to hear the recording of the anonymous tip. It was made at 3:12 on the morning of Wednesday, March 9.

DESK OFFICER VILLERS: *San Diego Police.*

MALE VOICE: *I heard a gun fire near the Cabrillo Bridge on Highway 163. There is a black vehicle such as a truck or sporting vehicle. Maybe a murder, I don't know.*

DESK OFFICER VILLERS: *Your name, sir?*

MALE VOICE: *This will not be necessary.*

DESK OFFICER VILLERS: *I need your name, sir.*

The caller's voice was male, middle-pitched, and slightly faint. His words were clear but accented. There was a hesitation before he hung up.

"Arabic?" asked McKenzie.

"I think so," I said. "Eddie Waimrin can tell us."

Waimrin is one of two San Diego police officers born in the Middle East—Egypt. He's been our point man with the large and apprehensive

Middle Eastern community since September of 2001. I tried Eddie Waimrin's number but got a recording. Patrol Captain Evers told me Eddie had worked an early day shift and already gone home. I told him I needed help with the Asplundh tip tape and he said he'd take care of it.

"Did Garrett kill himself?" asked the captain.

"I don't think so."

"Garrett Asplundh was tough as nails. And honest."

"I know," I said. "We talked to a guy this morning who saw a red Ferrari pulled over to the side of Highway 163 that night. Not far from where we found Asplundh's vehicle. Said he saw someone moving in the trees. Maybe Mr. Red Ferrari saw something. Who knows, maybe he pulled the trigger."

I could hear him tapping notes onto his computer.

"Tell the *U-T,*" said Captain Evers. "Maybe they'll run a notice or something."

"That's my next call."

"Let me see what I can find out, Brownlaw."

I called a reporter acquaintance of mine who works for the *Union-Tribune.* His name is George Schimmel and he covers crime. He's a good writer and almost always gets his facts right. During my brief celebrity three years ago, I'd given him a short interview. Since then George has told me many times he wants to do a much longer piece or, better yet, wants me to tell my own story in my own words. I've declined because I'm not comfortable in the public eye. And because of certain things that happened, and didn't happen, during that fall from the hotel. I feel that some things are private and should stay that way.

"So are you ready to sit down and give me a real interview?" he asked, as I knew he would.

"Not really, but I could use a favor."

I told him about the red Ferrari parked off to the side of the southbound 163 on the night of the murder. I gave him Retired Navy's name and number.

"What was the very last thing you thought about?" he asked. "Before you hit."

"Gina, my wife."

"That's so human, Robbie. I mean, wow."

"Thanks for the red Ferrari."

"I'll see what I can do."

By the time I got home Gina had already left. Her note said that she'd be with Rachel, probably downtown or in La Jolla. Just dinner was all, and maybe one drink after—she'd be back early. Rachel and Gina are best friends. Their chairs at Salon Sultra are next to each other. They pretty much carry on like they did before Gina and I were married but Rachel resents me. At times Gina feels torn between her best friend and me, which is understandable. Rachel drunkenly hit on me one night just before we got married. I drove her home and didn't tell Gina about the offer, just that Rachel was too drunk to drive herself. Rachel has ignored me since then, which is pretty much what she did before that.

I heated up a pot pie and opened a can of asparagus for dinner. I drank a beer. After dinner I opened another beer, sat down at the tying table in our garage and tied some fishing flies. I've been working on a little pattern to catch the wild rainbow trout in the San Gabriel River above Pasadena. The San Gabriel is my closest river for trout, actually more of a stream than a river. The fish can be picky, especially in the evenings. I've invented two flies to attract the fish: Gina's Mayfly and Gina's Caddis. Come late springtime—another month or two—and I'll be able to see if they work. Part of the fun of tying a fly is fooling a fish with it. The other part is sitting in my chilly garage with the radio on in winter, imagining the currents and pools and eddies and riffles of the San Gabe on a summer morning, and picturing my little fake bug bounce along on the surface above the fish. There is a specific joy to coaxing a wild thing from the river and into your hand, then back into the river again. I can't explain it. Gina good-humoredly says the whole thing is boring and pointless. I certainly value her opinions and understand that fly-fishing isn't for everyone.

Later I worked the digital camera out of Garrett's Halliburton case and looked at the pictures he'd taken. There were only two. One was a close-up of Samantha Asplundh's headstone. It was red granite, simple and shiny. The other was a shot of Stella, with her hands up, protecting her face from the camera. She wasn't smiling. I put the camera back and looked at the tape recorder, saw that there was no cassette in it.

Then I surveyed Garrett Asplundh's datebook. His next-to-last appointment on the day he was murdered was with HH at HTA in La Jolla. Five P.M. There was a phone number.

His last appointment was with CAM at Imp B. Pier at six-thirty. The Imperial Beach Pier, I thought. Odd place for a meeting. Another phone number. I sat in our little living room and leafed through his datebook. Garrett Asplundh kept a busy schedule.

I called the La Jolla number and got a recording for Hidden Threat Assessment. I called the CAM number and got a recording that told me to leave my name, number, and a brief message. I didn't.

It was odd to flip ahead in Garrett's datebook and look at the appointments he'd never make. One caught my eye because it was underlined twice: *Kaven, JVF & ATT GEN.*

It was set for next Wednesday, March 16.

Our crime lab director called just after seven to tell me that the gunshot-residue test on Garrett Asplundh had come back negative. They'd tried everything for residue—fingers, thumbs, hands, shirt cuffs, jacket sleeves. Left and right. No GSR at all. But lots of it on and around his right temple, because the gun had been discharged close to his head. They'd found gunpowder burns, tattooing, the works. Two inches close, is how it looked.

He also told me that the Smith & Wesson nine-millimeter autoloader in the Explorer had been reported stolen in Oceanside, San Diego County, back in 1994. It yielded no latent fingerprints and had been recently wiped with a product such as Tri-Flow, a popular protectant for firearms.

"Cool customer, to pack a stolen gun and his own wipes," said the director.

I thanked him and called McKenzie and told her she owed me fifty bucks.

Gina got in late and hungry so I whipped up an omelet with bacon and cheese and made some guacamole for the top of it. She stood in the kitchen and told me about her evening and drank a vodka on the rocks while I cooked. When Gina is excited about something she can talk for paragraphs without a comma, but that night she didn't have much to say. Her soft red hair was up but some of it fell over her face and down her neck and I kissed her. I smelled perfume and smoke and alcohol but tasted only my wife. There is no other taste like it. I actually thought about that taste as I fell from the Las Palmas, though, to be honest, I thought of millions of things in a very short period of time.

She giggled softly and pulled back. She smiled. She has green eyes but the corners were slightly red that night.

"Wow, that omelet looks good!" she said, swaying on her way to the breakfast nook.

By the time I got the pan soaking and the dishes rinsed, Gina was in bed. I lifted the covers and settled them over her shoulders. I remembered doing very much the same just that morning after the lieutenant had called about Garrett. Her snoring was peaceful and rhythmic. I held her close. After a few minutes she gasped and turned her head away from my chest, breathing deeply and rapidly, as if she'd been running.

I placed a hand on her hot, damp head and told her she'd be okay, just a bad dream or maybe a little too much to drink. I lifted a handful of hair and blew on her neck. A minute later she was snoring again.

The next morning I parked in front of the San Diego Ethics Authority Enforcement Unit headquarters, a stately two-story Edwardian on Kettner. The day was bright and cool and you could smell the bay two blocks away.

"I can't believe they fight bad guys from here," said McKenzie. "It used to be a bakery."

"The family lived upstairs," I said. "Italian."

"Yeah, and the owner, he'd park the black Eldo with the whitewall tires right out front. He made his son wash it every single day."

I looked out at the former residence that now housed the Ethics Authority Enforcement Unit. Although we call ourselves America's Finest City, there is a long tradition of collusion and corruption here in San Diego. Some of it once reached high enough to taint an American presidency—Richard Nixon's. Some of it is low and squalid and oddly funny—a mayor in bed with a swindler, councilmen charged with taking bribes from strip-club owners in return for easier rules on what the strippers can do. There is probably no more greed and graft here than in most other large American cities, but our mayor and council thought it was time to meet the problem head-on, so the Ethics Authority was formed and gunslinging Judge Erik Kaven was named director.

About a year after the Authority was established, Kaven hired John Van Flyke away from the DEA in Miami to run the Enforcement Unit. Van Flyke had never lived in San Diego and had visited just once, I'd read. He had no family here. This was exactly what the city wanted—an ethics enforcer with no vested interests in the city. Van Flyke was never photographed by the papers or videotaped for the TV news. His staff appeared in the media only rarely. All we knew about him was that he was forty-two years old, single, secretive, and incorruptible. George Schimmel of the *Union-Tribune* had nicknamed him "The Untouchable." McKenzie had quipped that no one would *want* to touch him.

The downstairs lobby was small and chilly. It offered two chairs and a dusty, unsteady glass table with sailing magazines on it. An elderly woman sat behind a large desk with a clean blotter pad, a ringed desktop calendar, and a gleaming black telephone on it. There was also a small vase with faded paper poppies. Her hair was gray and pulled into a tight bun. The cowl collar of a faintly green sweater came up nearly to her chin. She wore a headset with a very thin speaker arm extending from ear to mouth. She pushed a button on the phone console.

"Detectives Cortez and Brownlaw are here," she said. Her voice was clear and strong, and it echoed in the old former residence. "Yes, sir."

She pushed a button on her phone and looked at me. The lines in her face were an unrevealed history. Her eyes were brown with soft blue edges. The nameplate near the edge of her desk said ARLISS BUNTZ.

"Up the stairs and to your right," she said.

"Thank you."

It was odd climbing stairs to an appointment. It struck me as old-fashioned, and I couldn't remember the last time I'd done it. Our footsteps echoed up around us in the hard, drafty building. I know that the federal government would require an elevator for handicapped people in a public building, but I saw no sign of one. I wasn't sure what I thought about the Ethics Authority's ignoring the rules.

I looked down over the banister at the uplifted face of Arliss Buntz.

Van Flyke was tall and well built. Dark suit, white shirt, yellow tie. He was big-faced, like many actors or professional athletes are, and his red-brown hair was combed back from his face with brisk aggression. His hand was dry and strong.

A quiet young man in a shirt and tie appeared with a tray and coffee for three. He had suspenders over his shoulders and an automatic holstered at his hip. He handed McKenzie her cup with a brief smile, then left. The room was washed in sharp March light and through the windows you could see taller buildings and a slice of bay and a palm tree. McKenzie flipped open her notepad and propped it against her knee.

Van Flyke sat forward and studied each of us in turn. His hands rested on two green folders. "Have you run the GSR test?" His voice was deep but soft.

"Yes," I said. "Negative."

"No chance of suicide?"

"Very little."

"How many rounds left in the gun?"

"Eight," I said. "We recovered an empty from the dashboard of the Explorer."

"Did they take anything?" he asked.

"He wasn't robbed," McKenzie said, writing. "Not that we know at this point."

Van Flyke lifted his cup of coffee and looked at McKenzie. His brow was heavy and his eyes were blue and set deep. "This is difficult. Garrett was a very close friend. He was my best investigator. I was hurt by what he and Stella had been through with their little girl. Truly hurt. You didn't know him, did you?"

"We're getting to know him," said McKenzie. "If we knew what he was doing for you, it would help a lot."

"I'll bet it would. Witnesses?"

"Maybe," I said.

Van Flyke's expression brightened, like a dog catching a scent. "Oh?"

I told him about Mr. Red Ferrari standing off in the bushes.

"What time?"

"We're not at liberty to discuss that," said McKenzie.

Van Flyke deadpanned her. "Here's something we can discuss."

He handed each of us a green folder.

"Garrett was looking into two different areas for me," said Van Flyke. "One was the antiterrorism watch—Homeland Security R&D contractors, mostly out in Spook Valley. Right now there's more money than sense out there. About seven billion federal dollars, nationwide, just looking to get spent. Spook Valley is after its share. Erik—our director, Erik Kaven—believes it's a potential hot point. Garrett was also looking into the Budget Oversight Committee—Abel Sarvonola's group. Dull stuff, but big money. Lots of hands out, lots of paths that cross."

"Thank you," I said. "We appreciate this."

I got the Homeland Security file. It started with a long list of companies addressing security problems. Most dealt in information, security, and biomedical technology and software, but there were also makers of personal flight modules, solar-powered biohazard warning systems and "hit-stop" handguns. Names, phone numbers, addresses. Typewritten and handwritten notes followed—I assumed they were Garrett Asplundh's.

I traded files with McKenzie. Now I was looking at a list of departments and commissions, boards, committees, councils, and authorities. This was Abel Sarvonola's brew for sure. His powers as Budget Oversight Committee chairman were well known enough to be joked about at money-conscious PD headquarters. *When does a dollar disappear on its own? As soon as it's Abel's.* And so on. His appointment to the Budget Oversight Committee was part-time and paid only a small per diem when the committee was in session. Sarvonola was a big part of the La Costa Resort development in north county back in the seventies. There had been talk of Teamster pension funds and mob involvement in the building of that swank resort, but Sarvonola had come through it very clean and extremely rich.

I saw that in addition to being involved in the many arms of San Diego's government, Garrett Asplundh also knew the players in San Diego's biggest industries—hospitality, development, entertainment, and consumer technology. There they were, the sports owners, financiers, tech billionaires, land developers, biomedical-research companies, and old money that ruled the city. This was the powerful private sector that the Ethics Authority was entrusted to keep from getting too chummy with the various branches of the city bureaucracy.

"Why would an Ethics Authority investigator rent a Testarossa at four-fifty a night?" asked McKenzie.

"An occasional expense for cultivating his sources," said Van Flyke. He raised a heavy brow as if entertaining his own answer.

"Cultivating his sources," I said.

"Of course. Or, in some cases, maybe he was trying to foster an impression of corruptibility."

I heard McKenzie's pen racing to get those words down. I hadn't thought of using Ethics Authority investigators that way—trying to lure someone into doing something illegal. Such law-enforcement tactics are proactive and dangerous. But I knew that Van Flyke's days at the DEA had certainly taught him how to orchestrate an entrapment that would stand up in court.

"You let your investigators do that?" asked McKenzie.

"I give my investigators trust, respect, and independence."

Van Flyke's remote blue eyes went from me to McKenzie and back to me again. "He was a good man."

Neither McKenzie nor I spoke.

"A person's life can change so fast," he said quietly. "A pivot. A moment. An event that takes a fraction of a second but lasts a lifetime. Garrett comprehended that. It gave him depth and understanding."

He sighed and looked out the window.

"Are you talking about the death of his daughter?" I asked.

"Of course I am."

In the back of each folder was a list of complaints filed, fines issued, convictions won, or indictments handed down based on Garrett Asplundh's investigations. Most of the offenders were city contractors, some were city employees themselves. There were fines for violations of the Business and Professions Code, the Government Code, and the Civil Code. A city Building Department supervisor was discharged for taking a bribe. A city Purchasing Department employee was reprimanded for the "appearance of favoritism." I didn't see anything worth killing a man over, but I hadn't been fired or called down.

"Were his current investigations heating up?" I asked.

"Yes," said Van Flyke. He had returned his attention from the window and now stared at me. "Garrett was making progress in both areas. I printed and attached Garrett's notes to the end of each file. You can get a feel for where he was, how people were reacting to us."

"Are those his complete notes?" I asked.

"Yes. Everything he submitted."

I watched a hawk with something in its beak fly into the palm tree outside. The fronds shimmered in the winter light and the hawk disappeared into them. I thought for a moment. I pictured Garrett's apartment. It still seemed to me that something was missing. There just wasn't enough, not for a man as orderly and intensely focused as Garrett Asplundh seemed to be. For someone who, as his ex-wife had said, *went through so much.* I thought about the checks made out to Uptown Management. The hawk dropped out of the tree, spread its wings, and rose straight over us. I saw the stripes on its tail and the gleam of its eye.

I asked Van Flyke about the underlined entry in Garrett's datebook for next Wednesday, March 16. From my notes I read it back to him: *Kaven, JVF & ATT GEN.*

"That would translate as Director Kaven, myself, and a lawyer from the state attorney general's office. Garrett was going to present his findings. Together we were going to decide which cases to intensify and which ones to drop."

"If the attorney general was involved, Garrett must have had some serious evidence," I said.

"Not necessarily," said Van Flyke. "The meetings are semiannual and routine."

"The underline looked more than routine," I said.

"I can only tell you what I know," said Van Flyke.

"Did you issue him a laptop computer for work?" I asked.

"Of course," said Van Flyke. "We all got new ones about two months ago."

"We haven't found it," said McKenzie. "It wasn't in the Explorer or his apartment."

Van Flyke stared at her. "It's not here either. Maybe he was robbed after all."

McKenzie scribbled.

"His last two meetings were with HH at a place called Hidden Threat Assessment in La Jolla and with CAM at the Imperial Beach Pier," I said.

"HTA is a Spook Valley company," said Van Flyke. "HH is Hollis Harris, who started it. CAM at the Imperial Beach Pier? I have no idea about who that might be."

"May we see his workplace?" I asked.

"Sure."

Van Flyke wrote his cell number on the back of a business card and handed it to me. Then he led us out of his office and into what once must have been a bedroom for the Italian bakers. There was a partition through the middle of it. A desk and an empty chair on each side. Garrett's desk had a framed black-and-white photograph of Samantha and a coffee cup with a picture of a rainbow trout on it. On the wall was a pictorial calendar of San Diego. This month's featured site was the pretty Casa del Prado building at Balboa Park, which stands just a few hundred yards from where they'd found Garrett Asplundh's body.

I shook hands with Van Flyke and thanked him for his time. McKenzie did neither.

She went down the stairs ahead of me. Arliss Buntz was standing now, as if she'd been waiting for us to come down. Her headset was still on and her sweater still pulled up for warmth. Her blue-brown eyes locked on to mine.

"He was a man headed for trouble," she said.

"How do you know that?" I asked.

"Look at his high ideals!"

She sat and pivoted her chair, giving us her back as she bent to open a drawer.

"What do you mean?" I asked her.

"He was too good for the people around him," she muttered without turning.

McKenzie drove while I called Hollis Harris and CAM. Hollis had heard about Garrett's death and agreed to give us one hour of his time. CAM's computer-generated message told me once again to leave a name, number, and short message, but again I didn't. I wanted CAM live. Lots of people won't return calls to Homicide detectives, but very few will hang up on one.

I called Gina to make sure she was up and doing okay. She answered halfway through the greeting. She apologized for last night. Said she'd had one too many. Rachel got fully toasted. I told her not to worry about anything and maybe we could go out to dinner that night and I loved her.

McKenzie kissed the air as she gunned the car toward the freeway.

Spook Valley is a nickname given to a cluster of La Jolla companies specializing in nuclear-weapons technology, strategic defense, border control, industrial security, and military surveillance. Many of these are secret, or "black," programs, funded directly by the CIA or the Pentagon or the Department of Homeland Security. Some of the companies started back in the early 1990s, but a lot of them have sprung up since 2001. I thought of John Van Flyke's figure of $7 billion of R&D money from Homeland Security alone and what share of it came to San Diego.

Spook Valley isn't spooky at all. It's everything Southern California is supposed to look like—swaying palms and twisted coastal pines and jaggedly beautiful beaches under blue sky. The green hills tumble down to the Pacific like spilled loads of emeralds. The architecture in La Jolla is a vivid mix of Mediterranean, Spanish Colonial, Spanish Revival, Craftsman, Prairie, California Rancho, postmodern, contemporary—you name it. Even the "Tuscan" monstrosities have caught on here, though they look overweight, hunkered on their tiny but expensive lots. But the Spook Valley companies cling quietly to the top-secret shadows while the rest of La Jolla basks in the light, and everyone comes together at the fancy restaurants on the bluffs to watch the sun go down.

We drove past the Hidden Threat Assessment building before spotting the number, so McKenzie spun a U-turn and bounced my mushy Chevrolet take-home into the parking lot.

"Look at all that mirrored glass," said McKenzie. "They don't even put their name on the building, just HTA. And check over there—the Enzo. That's six-hundred fifty horses you're looking at. Sick. Oh, man, now that's a car."

It was a red Ferrari and the license plate read H-THREAT. I wondered if it had been parked briefly alongside Highway 163 the night Garrett was shot. I wondered how many red Ferraris there are in San Diego.

Hollis Harris met us at the security desk in the gleaming lobby. He was about my age. Thirty tops. He was small, slender, almost bald, and dressed in black—shoes, trousers, belt, golf shirt, watch. His face was trim, and his gaze was open and opinionless.

We stopped at a coffee-and-sandwich cart. Harris got a triple espresso, black.

"I'm trying to cut back," he said.

"How many a day?" asked McKenzie.

Hollis ducked his head and frowned. "Three? Okay, four, but four max."

"I'd be bouncing off the walls," she said.

"Maybe that's why I only sleep five hours a night."

"How do you feel in the mornings?"

"Actually," said Harris, "great."

His fourth-story office was large, uncluttered, and bright with late-morning light. The floor was buffed maple, and his curved desk was stainless steel. Most of the fixtures were stainless steel, too. There were windows on two sides and white walls on the other. A huge painting took up most of one wall—it showed the back end of a Ferrari speeding away from you. A collection of photographs of Hollis Harris with various celebrities graced the other.

We sat at a suite of stainless and cream leather furniture in front of one of the big picture windows. Harris clapped his hands softly twice and a sun filter descended from the ceiling. As it lowered I watched the vivid optics of the Soledad Highway and San Clemente Valley soften and retreat.

"I'd talked to Garrett Asplundh several times over the last two years," said Harris. "At first he was interested in HTA's financial relationships with the Department of Homeland Security and the CIA and some of the casinos in Las Vegas and San Diego County. And, of course, with the City of San Diego. So I opened our books to him, everything from contracts to payroll. I didn't see him for three months."

"I take it your accountants had done their jobs," said McKenzie, looking from her notepad to Harris.

"Our books are as clean as this floor," said Harris. "HTA makes good money and there's no reason to cheat, lie, or steal. I don't have the time or interest for that."

I was reading through Asplundh's notes on HTA while Harris talked. "Garrett said you—HTA—donated a hundred and fifty grand to the Republican Party in 2003, trying to get the governor recalled."

"We did," said Harris. "We also donated a like amount to the Democratic Party, to help them field a good candidate of their own. We're not a political company here. But we do believe in the state of California. I was born in this state. Lived here all my life. It means something to me."

I looked into Hollis Harris's steady eyes. "Garrett met you here at five o'clock the day before yesterday—the day he died."

"Right," said Harris. "We talked about developing Hidden Threat Assessment software for the Ethics Authority."

"What exactly is 'hidden threat assessment'?" asked McKenzie.

Harris sat forward on the edge of the cream-colored sofa, like he was getting ready to jump up. "The heart of it is a software system that lets databases talk to each other in real time. I got the idea back in high school. My dad worked for TRW and he was always complaining that the information was out there but he couldn't get it in time. *The information is out there but I can't get it in time.* So I designed him a program for my computer class and got an A on it. I sold it to TRW for half a million dollars when I was eighteen. That was enough to begin this company. We've gone bankrupt twice and bounced back twice. I've lived everywhere from ratty downtown hotels to mansions in La Jolla. Mansions are better but ratty hotels save you time on upkeep. Work ruined my marriage but I won't make the same mistake again. I have a wonderful young son. Last year this company did over forty-five million and we're on track to beat that this year. By a lot."

"How did you write a program like that as a high-schooler?" asked McKenzie.

Harris shrugged. "I don't actually know. It's a knack. When I deal with coded information it becomes aural to me. Musical. I hear it. I hear ways that sounds—they're not sounds actually, they're megs and gigs and beyond—can be harmonious and advantageously cadenced. As soon as you stack information like that, massive amounts of it can be digitally fitted and synchronized. Then it can flow, literally, at the speed of electricity. It's not all software. You need some special machines to run an HTA program. I designed them. It's hard to explain."

"Guess so," said McKenzie.

I was half tempted to tell Hollis Harris that I could see the shapes and colors of emotions behind spoken words. But only half. It's not a parlor trick. If news of that got back to headquarters on Broadway it would hurt me sooner or later. My advancement has been greased by my apparently miraculous recovery from the fall, and by my minor and unasked-for celebrity. I may be "different" enough to see shapes and colors when people talk, but I'm not different enough to admit it to anyone but Gina.

"How does it assess threat?" I asked.

"It finds hidden connections between people that could be threatening," said Harris. "It finds them instantly, in real time. Say that Person A applies for a job here. We run him through a basic HTA protocol. HTA discovers that his ex-wife's former roommate's brother is a convicted embezzler and that Person A and the convicted embezzler now share the same home address. It takes ten seconds. And guess what? We don't hire Person A. We show him the door. From casinos to the federal government, everybody needs HTA. I call HTA 'a symphony of information.' But it's more like twenty symphonies, crammed into the length of a sound bite."

"Impressive," said McKenzie.

"Impressive, Ms. Cortez?" asked Harris, smiling, then swallowing the last of his espresso. "It's almost unbelievable. We're currently running at five degrees of separation. We'll be up to eight degrees by the end of next year. We're doing a job for Border Patrol right now—you put your index finger into the scanner down at the border in San Ysidro or TJ, and guess what? I've got the following databases digging into your past like earthmovers on speed: Homeland Security, INS, the DEA, the Border Patrol, the San Diego Sheriff Department, the San Diego PD, the Interagency Border Inspection System, and the Automated Biometric Identification System—and that's not all. Let me take a breath and continue: the Treasury Enforcement Communications System, the Deportable Alien Control System, the Port of Entry Tracking System, the National Automated Immigration Lookout System, and the San Diego User Network Services system. I get winded when I talk about my work, so let me take another deep breath and keep going: the Computer Linked Application Information System and the National Crime Information Center of the FBI, and I'm going to have these bases talking to each other as fast as electricity in a phone line. I'm going to be able to tell everything about you—physical, financial, criminal, social. I'll have the name, address, and Social Security number of the doctor who pulled your tonsils when you were four, and I'll know exactly how much your cell phone bill was last month, and I'll have the name and address of your allegedly secret lover by the time you get your finger out of the scanner. If you are a threat, you will be exposed. If you *might* be a threat, you will be exposed. If you are only the reflection of a shadow cast by the memory of a possible threat, you will be exposed. Now that, Detective Cortez, is impressive."

Harris was short of breath. "I know that sounds like bragging, Detective. It is."

And sure enough, the orange rectangles of pride wavered in the air between us, then dissolved.

"Will you run an HTA on Garrett Asplundh for us?" I asked.

Harris looked at me but said nothing.

"Maybe he already has," said McKenzie. She smiled, a rarity.

Harris went to his desk and opened a drawer. He returned with a manila folder and handed it to McKenzie. "Yesterday, after I heard what had happened, I ran an HTA on Garrett. It's hard to get a lot on law-enforcement professionals because their employers have been playing this game for years. But the deeper background comes out. So Garrett was kind of skimpy by HTA standards. It came to one hundred and eighty pages of intelligence, all in this envelope. I included a CD for you also. I read it last night and saw nothing in there that might pertain to his murder. But I'm out of my element in that world. Your world. It may contain something you can use."

"Thank you," said McKenzie. "We appreciate it."

"Garrett wanted an HTA program for the Ethics Authority?" I asked.

"Yes," said Harris. "But they can't afford it. I explained to him that I could create the system, install it, train the users, and update it for two years for four hundred thousand dollars. Garrett's budget for system upgrades was eighty thousand. He told me I should offer my services at cost to help protect this city that had brought me such prosperity. I agreed, which is exactly what the four hundred thousand was—my cost."

"How did Asplundh take that news?" asked McKenzie.

"I never knew with Garrett. I could never read him. I could tell he was preoccupied that afternoon. He wasn't all here. Usually with him there was this focus, this intensity. When I saw him in this office . . . no . . . his attention was somewhere else."

"Did he say anything about that, about being distracted?" asked McKenzie.

Harris shook his head. Then he looked at each of us.

"What time did he leave here?" I asked.

"It was five-fifty."

"How was he dressed?"

"Black two-button suit, white shirt, gold tie. Hand-stitched brogues. Nice clothes."

"The tie was gold?" I asked.

"Gold silk."

Not blue. Not soaked in his own blood.

Harris looked down at his watch, sighed, stood. "I'm sorry. I'm out of time for this now. Maybe something in that HTA book will lead you in the right direction."

"How fast is the Enzo?" asked McKenzie.

"Top speed is two-seventeen, it goes zero to sixty in three point six-five seconds and ripples your face in first."

"Did you drive it Tuesday night?"

He looked at her, smiled. "I drove it home to Carlsbad around six. I took it out again to get drive-through with my son at about six-forty. He's five. We were home with our burgers by seven. Reading in bed by eight. I didn't drive the Enzo again until morning. I'll let him vouch for me if you'd like."

"That's not necessary right now," said McKenzie. "Does it feel odd driving a six-hundred-thousand-dollar car into a drive-through?"

He looked at her thoughtfully. "Yes. And it's a long reach up to the window, too."

Out in the parking lot she ogled the car. I must admit it was a beautiful machine. My dream car has always been a Shelby Cobra. Gina bought me a day at an expensive driving school in Arizona for my birthday one year. I listened to a lecture, then spent the rest of the day with an instructor in a souped-up stock car that hit 160 on the straights. Speed is marvelous, though I'm less enthused about it since my fall. It seems ungrateful to risk your life for a medium-size pleasure. That night at dinner Gina presented me with a small Shelby Cobra model that I still keep in a place of honor on my fly-tying table.

Before getting into the Chevy I tried CAM again and got an answer.

"Carrie Ann Martier's office."

"Robbie Brownlaw, San Diego Homicide."

"Please hold."

It was a woman's voice. She sounded assured and professional. I walked away from the car and waited almost a full minute. McKenzie eyed me from across the lot.

"Mr. Brown?"

"Brownlaw."

"Yes? How can we help you?"

"I want to talk to Carrie Ann Martier about Garrett Asplundh."

"I'm Carrie Ann Martier. But I'm not sure that I can help you."

"I don't need your help. Garrett does."

There was a long silence. "Okay."

"How about tonight at six-thirty, the foot of the Imperial Beach Pier," I said. "I'll wear a Chargers cap."

"Spell your name and give me your badge number."

I did both.

"Be alone," she said.

"Okay."

Silence, then she hung up.

The fog rolled in around six as I drove toward Imperial Beach. To the west I saw the Silver Strand State Park campground, where not long ago a seven-year-old girl was taken by her kidnapper. Later he killed her. Her name was Danielle. I thought of her every time I made this drive, and probably will for the rest of my life. A lot of people will. I was thrown from the Las Palmas about three weeks after her body was found.

I didn't need the Chargers cap. I stood alone at the foot of the Imperial Beach Pier and watched the waves roll in and the lights of the city coming on in the twilight. A public sculpture of acrylic surfboards glowed faintly in the fog. Imperial Beach is the southernmost city on our coast. You can see Mexico right across the Tijuana River. In some odd way, you can sense an end of things here, the end of a state and a nation and the Bill of Rights and a way of living. Then you think of Danielle and wonder if it all means what you thought it did.

Six-thirty came and went. I called Gina again and we talked for a few minutes. She said she felt bad about last night and I said I was sorry about breaking our date for tonight. Funny how two people can live together, have no children, but have so little time together. Sometimes it seems like I hardly see Gina. I'm not so sure she misses my company the way I miss hers, but then I don't know how she could.

I retrieved a message from Samuel Asplundh, Garrett's older brother and next of kin, who was due to arrive in San Diego this evening.

I retrieved a message from Patrol Captain Evers saying that they had collected three more witnesses who had seen a car parked off to the side of Highway 163 the night Garrett was killed. All said the car was red. One said it was a sports car, like a Mustang or maybe a Corvette. Another thought he saw a man loitering in the bushes nearby, which is what Retired Navy had told us early that morning.

Next I returned a call from Eddie Waimrin, our Egyptian-born patrol sergeant. He told me that the accent on the taped call to headquarters was probably Saudi. He said the speaker was almost certainly foreign-born. I asked him to put out feelers for Saudi men who drove red Ferraris, on the not-so-off chance that the caller was Mr. Red Ferrari himself.

"I know one for sure," he said. "Sanji Moussaraf, a student here at State. Big oil family in Saudi Arabia. Big, *big* dollars. Popular kid. I've got his numbers for you."

"Maybe you should talk to him first," I said.

Three of the nineteen September 11 hijackers were living here when the doomed jets took off. One of the hijackers had inquired about attending a flight school here. Several of the first arrests in connection with that attack were made right here in San Diego—two of the arrested men were held for nearly three years before being deported in 2004. There was some local trouble right after the suicide attacks, too—spray-painted insults on a local mosque, curses shouted at people who appeared to be of Middle Eastern descent, vandalism at restaurants and businesses, some very intense police questionings in the days and weeks that followed.

Eddie Waimrin—who speaks Egyptian, Arabic, Lebanese, French, and English—was often called in to conduct interviews and to translate words and customs. He came to this country when he was eleven years old, sent by his father to keep him from the strife and poverty of Egypt. Since then Eddie has brought his father, mother, and two sisters to the United States. He's an outgoing officer, quick with a smile and active with the Police Union.

Since San Diego's large Middle Eastern population has been watchful and very cautious ever since September 11, I didn't want to spoil a good source if Eddie Waimrin had a better shot at getting information from him.

"I'll see what I can do," he said.

I thanked him and punched off.

I was about to call Carrie Ann Martier when light suddenly hit my eyes and a woman's voice came from the fog.

"Brownlaw?"

I slid the phone onto my belt.

"Robbie Brownlaw, Homicide?"

"Put the light away."

The beam clicked off and a woman stepped into the faint light of the pier lamps. She was small and pretty, mid-twenties. She had shiny straight blond hair not quite to her shoulders, and bangs. She wore a black down jacket over a white T-shirt, jeans and suede work boots. A small suede bag hung cross-shoulder so you couldn't pull it off and run.

I showed her my badge and thanked her for coming. "You didn't have to and I appreciate it."

"I don't know if I can help you and I don't have much time."

"We can walk," I said.

"I'd rather not."

"Then we'll stand. Did you see him night before last?"

"We met here, at six-thirty."

"What was the purpose of the meeting?"

Carrie Ann Martier sighed and looked out at the surf. "Let's walk."

You couldn't see the end of the pier in the fog. You couldn't see the waves either but you heard them thrashing against the pilings underneath. I felt their strength and it unbalanced me in a way I did not enjoy. Overhead the light fixtures were studded with nails to keep the birds from nesting and the nails threw toothy shadows onto the stanchions. Through this joyless scenery walked Carrie Ann Martier, wholesome and fresh as a model for a vitamin supplement.

"You know he was a detective for the Ethics Authority," said Carrie. "Well, a city employee was dating a friend of mine and my friend got beaten up. Pretty badly. This was a month ago. She wouldn't file a complaint with the cops because she's from a good family and the guy's married. She didn't want the scandal. I took one look at her and went to Garrett because he's a watchdog, right? I talked to him. Someone had to. Two days later she received four thousand dollars in cash, a very nice set of pearl earrings and a note of apology in her P.O. box. Garrett told her that the jerkoff had 'listened to reason.' "

"Who's the employee?"

"Steven Stiles, the councilman's aide."

I remembered the name from Garrett's handwritten notes.

"And your friend?"

"Ellen Carson."

I didn't remember hers.

"Were you a witness?"

"No. I saw her after it happened. Bad."

We continued out over the invisible ocean. There were a few bait fishermen with their rods propped on the railing and their lines disappearing into the fog. I could feel the tiny drops of moisture on my face. A fish slapped in a plastic bucket.

"Tell me more about Ellen," I said. "What does she do? What's her profession?"

Carrie Ann Martier, hunched into her jacket, took a long and sharp look at me. I could see that she was deciding something. "She's a student at UCSD. And a working girl, part-time. High end, fast dollars."

"Which is how she met—"

"Stiles."

"Are you a student, too?"

"English major, prelaw. And no, I'm not a working girl. I do proofreading for McGrew & Marsh here in San Diego—we publish automotive-repair books."

I watched the red squares of deception tumble from Carrie Ann Martier's mouth. I'd already guessed that she was "Ellen," but it was nice to get a second opinion.

"Those are good books on car repair," I said. "I bought the Volkswagen one years ago. The proofreading was excellent."

"Oh. Good."

"What was your meeting with Garrett about?"

"A videodisc. Evidence of other men enjoying the company of Ellen and some of her coworkers. It was the third collection Ellen had given me for Garrett."

"How many other men?"

"I don't know. I've never seen them."

More red squares, bobbing in the air between us. I was barely aware of them. But I was very aware that Garrett's interest in the videodisc could only mean one thing. "City people?"

She nodded. "That's what Ellen and her friends say. All sorts—City Hall, cops, fire, politicians, administrators. And also the guys who do business with the city—contractors, service people, company owners."

"That's a bomb waiting to go off."

"I think it did, with Garrett. That's why I agreed to meet you."

"I need to talk to Ellen," I said.

"No. She can't risk that. It's your job to put people like her in jail. She did her part for you, Mr. Brownlaw. Don't ask for more."

"I don't care what Ellen does in her spare time. I care who killed Garrett Asplundh and I need to talk to her."

She fixed me with a cool stare. Funny how she could appear so clean and fresh, but hard. "I knew you'd pull that."

"It worked on you once," I said. "And maybe it will work on you again because you liked Garrett. And you knew he was a good man trying to do the right thing and it probably got him killed."

"My time is valuable. Are you prepared to pay me for it?"

"No."

"Garrett Asplundh did."

I had to dodge the red squares.

I smiled at her because I really admire hustlers. Something about the courage to tell a lie and not know if you can get away with it. You run across some great hustlers in fraud, which I enjoyed immensely. Maybe because I could never tell the smallest fib without my face lighting up. Mom and Dad would just laugh and shake their heads.

"Actually, he didn't pay you for your time, *Ellen.*"

Her stare went from cool to cold. "Fuck yourself, cop."

"Well, okay. But what's the difference between talking to Garrett and talking to me? Besides that someone blew his brains out two nights ago after he met with you?"

"He was cute and sad and a totally great guy."

I thought about that. "I'm not cute or great, but I'm sad sometimes. One out of three, though, that's three-thirty-three, and if the Padres could—"

"I hate people like you."

I shrugged but didn't take my eyes off her because I figured she might make a break for it.

"Look, Carrie," I said. "Or Ellen or Marilyn or Julie—I don't care what your name is. I don't care how you make a living, though I hope you get health care and a decent retirement plan."

She sighed, pulled her little suede bag around and unzipped it. "Your judgment means nothing to me. I do the same thing your wife does but I get paid cash up-front and I can say no anytime I want."

"Oh, man, do I have to respond to that?"

Her lips began a smile.

"Help me out here," I said. "Help Garrett."

"Okay, o-*fucking*-kay. Just get me out of this fog and buy me drink, will you? I'm freezing. And to tell you the truth, maybe I need to talk to a cop."

"Why?"

"Because I'm really kinda scared, Robbie."

She pulled a pack of smokes from her little bag, offered one to me. I shook my head.

"Light?" she asked.

"Sorry."

"Men were better in old movies."

"Our stock is down."

"Then, here. Learn something useful." She pulled a lighter from her bag and held it out to me.

I smiled but didn't move.

"What?" she asked. "What's so funny?"

"Okay, whoever you are. I'll learn something useful."

I walked to her slowly but grabbed her wrist fast and gave it enough of a turn to smart.

She yelped.

The lighter fell to the wooden beams of the pier and I watched it roll to a stop. She watched it too.

I picked it up and she didn't try to kick me and run. Sure enough, it was a lighter. But the other end was a pepper sprayer. I'd heard about them from some of the Vice officers.

"Come on," I said. "Let's get that drink. I'll drive."

She flexed her wrist. "I wasn't going to use that on you. Swear to God, man—"

"I think you were."

"Give it back."

"I'll give it back later."

"Garrett would have lit my cigarette."

"Maybe that's why he's dead."

At the Beachside she drank Irish coffees and I had a beer. I asked her what her name was and she said Carrie Ann Martier worked just fine. She said she grew up in San Diego, rich family, though her father was a bastard and her mother was kind but insane.

"Schizophrenia, with a paranoid subtype," she said. "Not a good combo when you're married to a sneak like him."

She told me Steven Stiles, an aide to Ninth District Councilman Anthony Rood, had punched her in the body twice and stiffed her because he couldn't get it up. This was back in February. Two bruised ribs—he really laid into her. His wedding band had scraped her skin, which she found "highly ironic," along with the fact that it was the day before Valentine's Day. She leaned toward me and waited until I leaned toward her.

"And, Mr. Brownlaw," she whispered, "nobody treats Carrie Ann Martier like that."

She said that after getting hit, her ribs had tensed with pain every time she breathed or talked. Laughing was worse, but sneezing and coughing took the cake. She missed two weeks of work. She told me she'd gone to Garrett because Garrett wasn't a cop and she knew he'd be interested in city employees and contractors buying girls. She wasn't about to go to the police and she still was not willing to file a criminal complaint, though her ribs still hurt every time someone told her a good joke, which wasn't often.

She said she'd made the discs for Garrett with a video cam hidden in her flop. She used a room at the Coronado Oceana Hotel, had "good relationships" with security out there. Two girlfriends had similar recording setups, not because Stiles had beat them too, but because they were "pissed off at Jordan" and thought they should be able to show a solid connection between Jordan's phone calls, which they'd recorded on the sly, with actual men paying for actual sex.

"Tell me about Jordan," I said.

"You don't know anything, do you?"

I shook my head. Actually, I knew a little. Vice had been working up a case against Jordan Sheehan for months.

Jordan was the "Squeaky Clean Madam," said Carrie. She got the name because years ago she actually started a maid service called that. She had made some good money, gotten popped for illegals, labor violations, and back taxes. She did her time, and when she got out she discovered that sex paid more than custodial skills and she didn't even have to buy mops and vacuums if her girls were pretty enough. Now she ran fifty or sixty girls, more for conventions and special events like the Super Bowl. She had some kind of investment-counseling business as a cover, some fakey name like Sheehan & Associates or something. She had associates, all right. Jordan's girls dressed like corporate receptionists, they looked like the girl next door, they had to have good manners and pretty smiles, and they cost a lot. Hotels couldn't even spot them if they rotated right. Pure class and plenty of rules, she said—nothing kinky, nothing rough, no toys, no drugs, no pain or threesomes. Never in a car. They were not allowed to wear risqué clothing. No "CFM shoes" and no pierced body parts except the ears. No swearing, no smoking. No girls over thirty. Every girl had a pager. You never talked to Jordan because the madam was like the top of a pyramid and beneath her were the "spot callers" who told you when and who the john was. Jordan lined them up by the dozen. She had this way about her, pure and simple. Jordan owned men. Jordan could turn a priest into a paying customer in five minutes. The girls did their own marketing, too; they didn't just wait around for the pager to go off. Jordan told them to drive VW Cabriolet convertibles so the guys could get a look at them. The fleet manager at Mission Center VW was a friend of Jordan's and would make them deals on the Cabriolets. It was just automobile advertising, like for pizza or exterminators, only for women. Jordan got the idea from Ida Bailey, the old madam in the Gaslamp who used to parade her girls around in carriages so the guys could see the choices and pick. So you got fifty total foxes zooming around San Diego, and guess what happens when you whistle or wave, man, they pull right over and make you a deal. An hour later you're a grand poorer but you've been Squeaky Cleaned. Jordan got four hundred per contact, the "meet tax." The girls got what they bargained for over that. A thousand was "industry standard" for a Squeaky Clean but sometimes you had to take less. If you were with a city guy, one of Jordan's "special clients," then you got a lot less, just the tip, but some johns thought twenty bucks was a tip. If you tried to cheat on the meet tax Jordan had this huge guy called Chupa Junior with a tiny shaved head and tats all over him and he is not nice. Why cheat though? Could make an easy thousand plus on your lunch hour—you'd be surprised how good lunchtime could be—and afternoons, too, with the flex hours a lot of men worked. And a good night you got home before the sun came up with three or four grand in your purse, sometimes more.

"Except me," she said. "I go straight to the ATM and deposit my winnings. That's where the trouble starts for working girls—they spend faster than they save and some nights you don't work at all. Sometimes a whole week you won't work. But you wouldn't believe the stuff they buy. Jewelry and electronics and clothes and trips and dope—they party like crazy when they're off duty, just like everybody else. But not Carrie Ann Martier. Nope. I shop catalogs for my work clothes because I look good in anything. I shop Costco for bulk stuff because I'm sole proprietor of my own business. I happen to think that's funny. And so what if I have two gallons of hair conditioner under the sink? I'm saving for a place in Maui and I'm going to get it before I'm thirty. *I am going to get it.* After that, it's aloha Squeaky Clean Madam. I'm leaving the life. I'm going to surf and garden and learn to make my own sushi."

"Wow, that's quite a plan," I said. "Good luck."

She shrugged and a faraway look came to her eyes, which were blue. "Whatever."

"No, I really mean it."

She studied me. "I think you'd pop me in a second if you could get a raise or a promotion out of it."

I sipped the beer. She had a point, though it had nothing to do with money or status. The law was just the law. Sometimes a cop could look the other way, for the greater good, you know. Sometimes not. I thought back to the white VW Cabriolet I'd seen outside Stella Asplundh's place and the red one coming from the HTA parking lot earlier that day. Both driven by attractive young women.

"Why were your friends mad at Jordan?"

"For raising their meet tax to six hundred."

"Why'd she do that?"

"To make room for the younger girls. The younger ones get a little lower contact charge to get them started and locked in. Young is what the johns want. Cost of business goes up the older you get. Six, seven, eight hundred per meet. Pretty soon you're either working all for Jordan or you're not working."

"So you and your friends sneak the videos and make some discs. You give copies to Garrett for his investigation because you got beat up by a politician's aide and Garrett has made it right for you. But what about the two other girls? What were they going to do with their copies? Blackmail Squeaky Clean for the higher taxes?"

"It isn't blackmail if you're being ripped off."

I thought about two young working girls trying to run a hustle on their own madam. It sounded perilous. "Does Jordan know about the videos?"

"She couldn't. If Jordan even suspected we'd done that, she'd have pulled the plug on us by now—she'd never call. Or worse."

"Chupa Junior?"

She looked at me and drank the last of her second Irish coffee. "Yeah. There's talk. Always talk, you know? Then something happens. One day a girl is working, then she's gone. Maybe she crossed Jordan. Shorted her one too many times. Tried to get the johns calling her direct. Made a scene. Disappointed or pissed off somebody important. Chupa shows up here. Chupa shows up there. Like something out of a nightmare. It makes you wonder."

"Have you ever met Jordan Sheehan?"

"Not face-to-face. Not many of the girls have, unless she recruited them personally. Those are mostly the spot callers. Maybe that's why Squeaky Clean is still in business. She lives in La Jolla somewhere, running her little investment company. Ha, ha."

"How old are you?"

"Why?"

"I'm curious," I said.

"Trying to figure what I'm worth?" She squared her shoulders, frowned, and shook her head once. Her shiny blond hair flared with light, then settled back into place.

"I'm twenty-nine," I said.

"You're not selling."

"That must be kind of weird. Selling yourself. I don't mean any offense by that."

"You can't offend me, Robbie. You'll wear out someday, too. We'll both end up in the same trash pile."

I thought about that, about everybody ending up in the same condition. I'd often had that thought and could never figure out if it was a reason to cry or to smile until I was thrown from the Las Palmas. Somewhere on the way down I realized that the fact that you're going to die is a reason to smile. Every second you live, you're getting away with the biggest prize there is.

"You look familiar," she said. "TV or something?"

"No."

"Magazine?"

"No."

"I've seen you. I'm sure."

"A lot of people think that. I've got a common face. Sorry."

She looked at me hard again and nodded. She began a smile, then turned it off.

"I can take you back to your car," I said. I paid up and we walked into the foggy night.

"I checked you out with the PD. And with some of my friends who do a little business with the PD once in a while. You came back clean. Bet you never thought a whore would run a check on you, but I didn't know what I was going to run into on that pier tonight. Maybe someone who enjoyed Squeaky Clean girls. Maybe someone who knew what Garrett had. Maybe they figured I'd be better off quiet, too. That would make one less person to tell this wretched little story."

I liked the way Carrie Ann Martier, or whoever she was, tried to take care of herself. I liked her aloneness and her bravery. Her foolishness worried me.

"Don't try to run a number on Squeaky Clean," I said. "You can't win."

"I'm not suicidal."

"Why don't you just get out of this business?"

"Stay off my side, Robbie."

I drove us back to the pier. It wasn't more than a few blocks. The acrylic-surfboard sculpture still glowed in the darkness, its colors dampened by the fog. I could tell that Carrie Ann was looking at my profile, trying to locate a memory to go with it.

Her car was a yellow VW Cabriolet convertible, in keeping with her employer's wishes.

"When do I get my lighter back?"

I dug it out of my coat pocket and gave it to her.

"You remind me of Garrett," she said.

"I'm not cute and sad and a totally great guy."

"Yes you are. Even if you did get thrown out of that hotel. You lied to me. You're the Falling Detective. You're famous."

Gina didn't come to the door when I walked in. Lots of lights on, but no music. No sounds from the back. No smell of cooking. The house had an odd feel, like something had changed. I stood in the living room for a moment.

"Gina?"

I hustled into the bedroom but she wasn't there. The bed was made and it almost never was. There was an envelope on my pillow and a letter inside. I read in Gina's cheerful, big-looped handwriting:

Dear Robbie,

This is the hardest thing I've ever done. I hate myself and you deserve an explanation. I feel like my heart is shrinking down to almost nothing and I don't know why. I often feel so unhappy. I do love you. It's not that I don't. But I need some space right now, so I'm with friends from Sultra. I need some time to think and to work through the problems inside me. I wish I could take out the unhappy parts and fix them and put me back together whole and happy like when we first got married. Hard to believe that was five years ago, isn't it? I'm going to come back tomorrow while you're at work to get a few more things. Please don't come by the salon looking for me. I think I'd just cry and make an even bigger mess of things and if Chambers saw that he might toss me out and get someone lower maintenance. You know how Chambers is. I drove through Taco Bell so there's two tacos and a Burrito Grande in the fridge for you. You got a little box of fishing stuff from The Fly Shop so maybe that will help take your mind off things. It's on the kitchen table. I'm sorry I'm putting you through this. I'm so, so, so, so sorry. Maybe someday we'll still be the best friends in the world and we'll look back at this and laugh.

Love,

Gina

I stood there and read it two more times. The very first thing I thought was what a surprise this was. What a huge and horrible surprise.

My second thought was no. This was not a surprise at all. You saw this coming. You knew something was wrong and you did nothing about it.

I lay down on our bed and wrapped her pillow around my head. Clamped my arms across it. Listened to the throb of blood in my ears and smelled her perfume and imagined her face. For a long moment I felt like I was falling from the Las Palmas again, only slower.

"No," I said. "This cannot happen."

I jerked upright, sat there for another minute, then tossed the pillow against the wall.

I called Rachel and got her machine. I said if Gina was there, I wanted her to know I loved her and understood how she felt and was looking forward to talking to her about it. I tried to think of something optimistic and soothing to say before I hung up but I couldn't think of anything except I love you and don't worry, Gina, we'll get over this hump.

I opened a bottle of brandy we'd gotten for Christmas one year and poured a coffee cup almost full. I forced down a couple of big gulps, then poured the rest down the drain and opened a beer.

I put the dinner Gina had gotten me in the microwave and mistakenly set it for two hours instead of for two minutes. By the time I realized what I'd done, it was severely overheated. It sat before me on the breakfast-nook table billowing steam and bubbling. I thought of calling my buddy Paul, but he was working swing shift, repaving Interstate 5 up near Carlsbad. I thought this would be a good time to have a brother or a sister.

I thought of calling my mother and father but didn't want to make them anxious about a misunderstanding. They lived down in El Cajon, just east of San Diego. My father is a sales representative for Pacifi-Glide, a subsidiary of Great West Consolidated. They manufacture sliding tub and shower doors. My mother has worked as a secretary in the San Diego School District for twenty-four years, ever since I started kindergarten. They're not old people, but I saw no reason to upset and alarm them. My father had a heart attack last year, though it was considered minor and stress-related. Besides, things between Gina and me were going to work out. Why get other people worried?

After dinner I sat at my table in the cold garage and tried to tie some flies. But I kept wondering why Gina was so unhappy, and I couldn't concentrate on the tiny hooks and feathers. How long had this been happening? Five years ago, when we first got married, she was happy. She was only nineteen then, but she was almost through the College of Beauty and had a job waiting for her when she got out. I was twenty-four and had just started working fraud. We got married in June at the Pala Mission out on Highway 76, because Gina is Catholic and St. Agnes Church in San Diego was booked up that day. We rented a place here in Normal Heights and all we did for two straight years was work hard, party, and make love. Between her friends and mine we always had something fun to do. Sometimes I might have spoiled things for Gina's crowd because they wanted to do drugs. I didn't mind but I didn't want to watch them do it or see them drive a vehicle while acutely impaired. Rachel would occasionally pass joints under my nose and smile tauntingly, but mostly she pretended I wasn't there. I tried to take up cigarettes as a way of fitting in but they made my mouth and fingers stink. Most of Gina's friends were pretty and nice. In general, hairstylists are a talkative people. They are curious and have an eye for the unusual. They don't stick closely to the facts. They are tremendous gossips. Many of the men were gay, though not all of them.

I sat there at my fly-tying table, drinking another beer, fingering the new packets of feathers. The new #3 Metz Brown Capes looked good, though I would have liked the higher-quality #1. Cops are always on a budget, unless they're on the take. I dropped them back to the tabletop, shut off the garage light, and went back into the empty house.

So when did it start to go wrong?

I remembered a night about a year ago, when Gina had discouraged me from going to a party with her. It was a loft party in Little Italy thrown by a producer of surfing movies. She came home just before daylight. She was jittery and chilled in her flimsy clothes and I could tell she'd taken some kind of stimulant, which she denied. I wondered why someone as chipper and verbal as Gina would want more stimulation. I made her some herbal tea and as she sat at the table I wrapped a blanket over her shoulders. She threw it off and said, You're smothering me don't smother me, don't *smother* me. She stormed off to the shower and when she came out, told me she only meant smothering her with the blanket. We made incredible love, one of our top ten, at least for me. She was extraordinarily passionate and cried after. I think she had begun to slip away.

Later that morning at roll call I overheard some of the night-shift patrol talking about the party at the movie producer's loft in Little Italy. "Babes and buns and boobs all over the place," is how one patrolman put it, out of earshot of our female officers. They'd shaken down some of the louder partiers on the street outside, popped one for coke, one for ecstasy, and one for Mexican brown heroin. *Hey, Brownlaw, isn't your wife a redhead that cuts hair downtown?*

Since then, scenes similar to the smother scene have played out more than once. I admit it. None has been quite as surprising as that first one, and our reunifying lovemaking happens less often. But Gina and I are durable. We've always eased back together from these sudden fights and everything is fine for a long time. We have never slept in separate beds except for two nights when she visited her parents in Nevada.

So tonight would be a first.

I thought about Gina while I rinsed the dishes. Thought about her while I showered. Thought about her while I drove to the store for a six-pack and some pretzels. When I couldn't think about her anymore, I got the Asplundh murder book from the trunk of my take-home and sat at the breakfast table.

First I leafed through the Hidden Threat Assessment of Garrett Asplundh. Although the HTA report was 180 pages long and contained the names of hundreds of people, living and dead, who had had contact with Garrett Asplundh, no one, including Garrett, had set off a "Threat Alarm" on the HTA software.

A fuzzy picture emerges when thousands of facts about a person are collected but given no real degree of importance. It's like cutting a photograph of someone's face into small pieces and arranging the pieces at random. I learned, for instance, that Asplundh had had a hernia operation at the age of six and that his twice-divorced surgeon had filed bankruptcy a decade before the operation. I learned that Garrett had gone to the University of Michigan on a football scholarship. He played safety and was later drafted by the Detroit Lions but never signed. And I learned that the pool in which his only child drowned had been built by a company owned by a man named Myron Franks. Franks's son, Lyle, was a convicted felon in the state of Arizona—attempted murder.

I was interested to find on page 156 that then–Vice detective Garrett Asplundh had arrested Jordan Sheehan for drunk driving way back in 1990. Fifteen years ago. He was also listed as a visitor at the Federal Women's Detention Center in Westmoreland, where Sheehan had done time for tax evasion.

I was also interested to see that Garrett had interviewed for a job with the DEA in Miami roughly one year before he interviewed for his job with the Ethics Authority here in San Diego. Both interviews had been with John Van Flyke.

I found out that Garrett's older brother, Samuel Asplundh, was a special agent assigned to the FBI office in Los Angeles and that he had been Garrett's best man at his marriage to Stella.

All interesting, but I believed that the motive for Garrett's murder lay somewhere in his recent work, not in his past. So I forced myself to read through the pages, searching for something that might shed light.

I learned many facts but nothing jumped out at me.

I kept thinking about the eight hundred dollars a month that Garrett Asplundh had been paying to Uptown Property Management. I had already made a noon appointment with Al Bantour, the manager of Uptown. If Garrett Asplundh was paying eight hundred a month for what I thought he was—a small, secret place, off the radar of anyone he knew—maybe I could find the discs he'd been given by Carrie Ann Martier, and the intelligence he'd gathered on the city's wayward personnel, and the laptop issued by the Ethics Authority.

I thought that Garrett knew his shooter. I thought Garrett had agreed to meet him—or her—and while he was waiting, he was taken out. I thought the shooter's name would be right there, in the trail of Garrett's recent investigations. I thought of what Stella had said when we asked about enemies.

Hundreds.

I closed the murder book, wondering if Carrie Ann Martier was working right now.

At midnight I walked around the house. I grew up in this home, so every space and corner is packed with memories. Gina and I were very fortunate to be able to buy it from my parents several years ago, before the real estate market really topped out. We couldn't have done it without my folks' help—they wanted a low-maintenance condominium, so they made us a good deal and carried the paper at a low interest rate. It's small and old but in good repair because both my father and I are handy with household tools. It's grown in value.

Our Normal Heights neighborhood is fairly nice and convenient. It got its name from a teachers college, or normal school, that used to be here. I went to elementary and junior high just a few blocks away. Hit my first home run at the Little League field. Hung out with Gary and Jim and Rick. Fell in love with Linda when I was ten and Kathy when I was eleven and Janet when I was thirteen. They all lived within a mile. After Gina and I were married she lobbied hard for a high-rise condo downtown by the bay, but the rents are astronomical down there. The one she wanted was twenty-eight hundred a month. The rent on our first place here in Normal Heights was fourteen hundred plus gas and electric but you got trash pickup and a garage. Two years later I was happy to buy my childhood home, though I understood Gina's lack of enthusiasm. It is not a high-rise by the bay.

I tried to imagine this place without Gina in it and it was difficult because I knew that she would come back and we would take care of whatever was bothering her. Gina teases me sometimes about trying to fix the unfixable. Once I dropped a dinner plate, which shattered badly, but I glued it back together. It took hours, gathering the shards and wondering which tiny triangle or sliver fit with another. The repaired plate was ugly and incomplete and useless and really kind of funny. Actually, it worked okay collecting runoff under a potted plant out on the back patio.

Gina called around one o'clock. She was crying and I had trouble making sense of what she said except that she was sorry. I told her I would come get her but she refused to tell me where she was. I heard no voices or noise in the background. She sounded very alone.

She said she was sorry again, and then she hung up.

7

The man who threw me out of the Las Palmas Hotel is named Vic Malic and he lives in a rented room in the Gaslamp Quarter. It's not far from the former Las Palmas, which was rebuilt as an Execu-Suites.

After his arrest Vic was overwhelmed with grief at what he'd done and he waived his right to a trial, pleading down to charges of aggravated assault, arson, public endangerment, larceny, and destruction of property.

He was somber and repentant during the proceeding and he explained himself with apparent honesty. He had been under terrible stress at the time. He was recently separated from his wife of six months, had gone bankrupt, and had just been denied his World Wrestling Federation certification, which would have allowed him to work. Apparently he had hurt a fellow wrestler during his tryout match, resulting in an unofficial blackballing of his career. He was down to his last sixty dollars. He had consumed nearly a liter of gin on the day he set the hotel on fire. He had no idea the natural gas submain that ran behind the sixth-floor rooms would blow. He had fully intended to jump out his window when the flames got bad enough but he had lost his courage after seeing me rip through the awning below. A suicide note had supported his story. In the end Vic had walked downstairs, looked down at me, and surrendered to a fireman.

I noticed him in the courtroom one day at lunch. The deputies had legcuffed him to a table in Courtroom Eight, then gone off to have lunch in the cafeteria. This was an accepted practice until a man on trial for stabbing a fourteen-year-old girl to death had slipped out of his cuffs and walked outside a free man. Now the San Diego accused are never left alone at lunch.

Anyway, I was walking by the courtroom and saw him through the door window, examining a sandwich that looked tiny in his huge hand. I went in and Vic hung his head and tried to turn away, though the leg cuffs didn't leave him much wiggle room. It was my first time alone with him. I wasn't sure what I was going to say, and the huge fury I had hoped to feel never came to me.

We talked for just a minute. It was very strange to be close to him again, close to that face that had been burned into my memory in such vivid detail. For a moment I smelled fire, and my heart beat wildly. He could hardly look at me. He asked if I could ever forgive him and I said sure, I forgive you right now, for whatever it's worth.

"I've got no grudge," I said. "But you shouldn't take out your problems on other people. Even a child knows that."

He was shaking his head, still looking down. "No. No, I'll never do that again. I swear to God. Never, ever."

When he told me that, it was approximately two months after throwing me from the window. And when he spoke, his words were accompanied by an outpouring of pale blue ovals. Since the fall I had been seeing a lot of pale blue ovals when people spoke and I was just beginning to understand that they meant sincerity.

So I believed him. I also know that insane people can be very believable and there was some doubt as to Vic Malic's sanity. Two psychiatrists gave depositions, one for and one against him, but the actual condition of Vic's mental health remained vague and disputed.

The next day, by coincidence, I had to be in court on another case. I'd bought a roach-coach burrito and was looking for a place to eat it in private and walked by Courtroom Eight to find Vic chained to the table again, fiddling with another tiny sandwich. So we had lunch together. He was an oddly gentle conversationalist, very curious and nonjudgmental. We talked mostly about the pro-wrestling circuit and his hope of getting that certification someday. Vic had begun a fitness program in his cell and he was already up to a thousand sit-ups and five hundred push-ups a day. He looked strong.

During the hearing, old Judge Milt Gardner listened with his usual wrinkled calm. Vic's public defender noted that there was no loss of life, only two minor injuries besides my own—which was, thank God, far less damaging than it first appeared—and the aging, long-out-of-code Las Palmas was actually being wooed by Execu-Suites at the time of the fire. Vic's apology to me and the court was lengthy and very moving. He said so many nice things about me I sort of wished he would stop. Gardner questioned Vic in depth, and I never sensed dishonesty in him. I never saw any shapes and colors that didn't match his words.

Vic was given seven years in the state prison up in Corcoran. A few months in, he helped expose a ring of correctional officers who were staging fights between the inmates and betting on them. As an almost-professional wrestler Vic was heavily pressured to fight, but he turned state's witness instead. It was an ugly story, went on for weeks, made the papers and TV.

He was released two and a half months ago, the day before Christmas, for good behavior and for helping to crack the fight ring.

I met Vic at the Higher Grounds coffee shop around the corner from his place. He lives on the fourth floor of his building, and though he's invited me, I've never had the courage to go up and see how he lives. I like him, but I still can't imagine being in the same room with him again, four stories up from the pavement. I've met him once a week for coffee, always on Fridays like today, for a couple of months now. It was Vic's idea but I agreed to it. He needs me more than I need him and that's okay, though we quickly run out of things to say.

"Hello, Vic."

"Hi, Robbie, how's it hangin'?"

"The usual, you know."

"And how's Gina?"

"Great as ever."

"Tell her I said hi."

Vic and Gina have never met but Vic always asks about her. I keep waiting for the red squares of deception or the black rhombuses of anger to spill out, but they never have.

I thought of Gina's letter and the unhappiness and pain it contained.

"How's the book?" I asked.

"Sold eighteen this week."

While in prison Vic wrote *Fall to Your Life!* It's about his difficult life and how he turned it around after setting fire to the hotel and throwing me out the sixth-floor window. It's all about having a can-do attitude. He self-published the book as soon as he was released and he sells it at the tourist places around town. He arrives in a sputtering ancient pickup truck with a small card table, a folding chair, a change box, and a box of books. The cover of the book is a picture of me falling from the hotel, used with the photographer's permission. I appear oddly calm—faceup, legs and feet out, and though you can't see my exact expression, I seem to be looking up at something small and puzzling.

I get uncomfortable looking at that picture. I've tried to imagine what I was thinking about when it was taken. But again, it all went by so quickly there's no way to tell. I could have been thinking about anything from the way the back of my mother's blouse used to crease in alternating directions as she walked away from the Normal Heights bus stop each morning, to the flag atop the bank building above me that was rapidly getting smaller as I fell, to my first Little League home run. Gina made me a copy of the video that was shown widely on local and national news, but I still hadn't gotten up the courage to watch it. She has suggested more than once that viewing it might make me "whole" again, but I honestly don't want to see it. I'm not a hundred percent proud of some of the things I thought of on my way down and would prefer to keep those difficult memories to myself.

"Here," he said.

"No, I wasn't—"

"Come on, Robbie, I know you don't need it, but take it."

We agreed a month ago, when Vic started selling the books, that we'd share the proceeds. I told him I didn't want money from his work, but he insisted and I could see that it was morally imperative for him to pay me. He suggested a seventy-five / twenty-five split, with the larger portion going to him. I figured that was fine since I didn't want his money in the first place.

Fall to Your Life! sells for ten dollars even, so Vic handed me forty-five. Our best week, which coincided with a street fair in Little Italy, was one hundred and ten dollars. Seemed like everybody in San Diego bought his book that weekend.

He smiled.

"Thanks, Vic."

"Well, you know. I still got NBC, the *Union-Trib,* and the *Reader* interested in doing a story on us. *Esquire* is a maybe."

"I've got nothing to tell them, Vic."

"I know. I respect that."

"Any word from the federation?"

"I sent them the newspaper articles about me, so we'll see. I think my publicity would be good for wrestling. You know, a guy getting his act together. They're always looking for another angle."

We took our coffees outside and stood by the brick wall. The cold front was still hovering over the city and the fog moved down Fourth Avenue like something dreamed. I looked north in the direction of the Salon Sultra then checked my watch. Gina would be coming in to work in just a few minutes.

"Robbie, did you hear about the Ethics guy who got shot?"

"It's my case, Vic."

"Oh, man. A former cop. A city employee. Anything to do with a government agency is scary if you ask me."

"What have you heard?"

I asked because Vic lives downtown and he talks to a lot of people on the street, many of whom treat him like a celebrity. I've watched him from a distance, standing tall above his audience. They're mostly the lost and lonely and destitute, but they're an oddly curious bunch. They love to know and to pretend they know.

"Micro says the guy busted him once."

Micro is a small man named Mike Toner, who rotates between the homeless shelters and the jails and the churches and the sidewalks.

"For what?"

"Panhandlin'. Not really busted, just ran him off his corner. Micro recognized him from the picture in the paper. The guy, his daughter drowned and it ruined him."

"I guess that's true," I said.

"He shouldn't have let that get him down," said Vic. "Look how you pulled yourself back up. And me."

"I'd rather get thrown out a window than have my little girl drown," I said. I don't know how I knew this, not being a father, but I did.

Vic nodded, lost in thought. "I saw the *Union-Trib* article. It said there was a broken-down car, maybe a guy who saw something."

I silently thanked George Schimmel. "We're hoping someone will step forward. Keep your eyes and ears out, Vic."

"I'll do anything to help you."

A black VW Cabriolet convertible picked its way down the avenue. The top was down in the chill and the woman driving it wore a black leather coat. She had a string of pearls around her neck and a pair of dark sunglasses. She gave us a tired smile. I wondered what the life was like once you got past the cool clothes and cars—men, cash, rubbers, AIDS, drugs, danger, vice, jails, bonds, lawyers, madams, pimps, sleep all day, then do it again.

"Seems like half the pretty women in San Diego drive those little convertibles," said Vic. "Man, they really get your attention."

"Yes, they do."

I watched her drive away and thought again of Carrie Ann Martier and the place in Hawaii she was going to buy no matter how much it cost her.

"Thanks for the royalty," I said.

"Thanks for the coffee, Robbie."

"Next Friday?"

"Sure. See you then. Robbie? You saved me, man. I love you. I really do."

I walked north to Market then toward San Diego Bay. From half a block away I watched Gina go into the salon. Her head was down and her steps were quick and short. That made me feel slightly better. If she had come striding along the sidewalk, chin up and smiling at the world, I might have run down to the Execu-Suites, gone to the sixth floor, and jumped out again, away from the awning. Not really, but my heart hurt just watching her go through that door because I knew her heart hurt too.

I wanted to go after her but I didn't. Sometimes, no matter how bad you want something, you just have to wait.

The Salon Sultra door is made of mirrored glass and when it closed behind her it completed the building's larger reflection of Market Street and Gina was gone.

McKenzie met me outside Uptown Management over on Fifteenth. Al Bantour was a slender man in an old blue suit. Sixties, gray hair and eyes. He mouthed an unlit cigar and gave us a canny once-over as McKenzie explained what we needed. He smiled around the cigar, then explained that yes, Garrett Asplundh had a place at the Seabreeze Apartments down in National City. Too bad what happened. Garrett was the last guy in the world he thought would get murdered. When the cops are getting killed it's a bad situation, most bad. Bantour said the on-site manager at the Seabreeze was a guy named Davey, and Davey ought to have an extra key. Any problems, just call. Wasn't I the guy who got thrown out of the hotel?

We headed down I-5. Light traffic and the fog still thick out over the ocean.

I told McKenzie about my meeting with Carrie Ann Martier, about the sex videos made for Garrett, the Squeaky Clean Madam, her spot callers, and the girls in convertibles. McKenzie shook her head and exhaled in disgust. She told me she'd run across Squeaky Clean Madam's enforcer and he was a real cool guy.

"Cool, like he'd cut your nipple halfway off to teach you respect," she said. "Cool, like he'd break some ribs and toss you into Glorietta Bay to watch you suffer. Six-four, three hundred. Half of him's tattoo. One of those big dudes with too small a head but he shaves it anyway. He's got a carjack crew that works San Diego and TJ, and he runs cockfights out in east county. And an occasional gig for Jordan Sheehan because he likes pretty girls. Chupa Junior. Short for *chupacabra.* And 'Junior' because his daddy was just like him."

I'd heard tales of the *chupacabra.* It meant "goatsucker" in Spanish. It was a vampirelike creature with huge red eyes and a row of spines down its back. They were reputed to stand five feet tall and suck the bodies of goats, sheep, and other animals almost completely dry.

I thought about Carrie Ann Martier versus three hundred pounds of Chupa Junior and hoped she wasn't foolish enough to run a hustle on her boss. She couldn't win that one.

I thought of Gina again. I imagined her at work now, standing beside her chair, arms raised, shears and comb in hand, snipping away. Last year for her birthday, I bought her a pair of Hikari Cosmos scissors, among the best money can buy. They had molybdenum-alloy blades that were said to be able to "melt" through hair. The Rylon glides were for accuracy from pivot to point. They cost twelve hundred dollars. They fit her small hands particularly well without the inserts she sometimes had to use. I'd had them inscribed along the inside of the tang, which is where the cutter rests his or her finger. It said *Hugs and Kisses, Me,* though because of limited space the words were hard to read. She somehow left them at the Mick Jagger trimming up in Beverly Hills not long after. The next day she'd made a dozen phone calls to the hotel but had never gotten them back. She was crushed. She couldn't believe she'd just forgotten to put them back into their case and box. I couldn't either so I scanned eBay for them and sure enough, there they were, with "genuine hair from Mr. Jagger." I tried to quickly trump all bids by offering five hundred dollars over the asking price of thirty-five hundred, so long as I could authenticate the engraving first. I was willing to travel at my own expense and would of course pay in cash. The owner of the shears and hair turned out to be in Culver City. When I got to a squalid apartment I felt bad for the young maid who had found or more likely stolen them. Her muscular husband suddenly demanded seven thousand so I thanked the woman, put the shears in my pocket, and headed for the door. When the husband charged me I finally lost the temper I'd been trying so hard to keep and I punched him sharply in the solar plexus, pulled his shirt over his head, and pushed him to the floor. He was balled up and gasping when I walked out. I'd committed more than one crime in all of this, including assault and battery, and I drove home to San Diego with my stomach in a knot.

McKenzie interrupted my thoughts. "Hollis Harris called me yesterday afternoon. Asked me out for a drink after work and I said yes."

"McKenzie, that's good."

"You don't think he's yuppie scum?"

"I liked the cut of his jib. And I could tell he was showing off for you."

"Me too. But I didn't think he'd call. I gotta give him some credit, leaving a message on some lady cop's answering machine, asking her out on a date. We had drinks at Dobson's. You get a lot of attention when you walk in with Harris. For some reason, when I'm on duty I can stare people down. Anybody. But when I'm just me I want to look away. What the hell. Drinks led to dinner and I had the lobster. Whew, good. Did you take Gina out?"

"We stayed in."

"Sounds nice."

"Really was."

We'd gotten to the Seabreeze Apartments by then, in the heart of National City. Built along the waterfront south of San Diego, National City used to be a railroad town but now it's all ships. Huge Fifth Fleet Navy vessels tie up to the massive shipyard piers for repair and maintenance, thousands of men and women scurrying over them. Every ship is a small, self-supporting city. Booms and cranes bristle into the sky, welders' torches join steel to steel, and at night the bars are edgy and rough.

The Seabreeze was three stories, gray, built in the fifties. One outside wall was claimed in black spray paint by the Ten Logan 30s. The foyer had dusty windows and a glass door with a metal handle that scraped when I pulled it open. There was a wall of mail slots with the names mostly missing or marked over. Jazz came from a downstairs unit that said MANAGER on its open door. An amused-looking black man stared at us from the doorway, then slowly raised his hands.

"I didn't do it."

We both badged him. "Here to see Garrett's place."

"Bet you are. Two-oh-five, upstairs. He was Jimmy around here. Didn't know nothing about any Garrett until the picture in the paper. Elevator's busted."

"We'll need a key," I said.

"Oh, no you won't. Just knock."

"And who's going to answer it?" asked McKenzie.

The man smiled. "You tell me."

His laughter followed us up the stairs. The carpet was worn away on the steps and landing and the air smelled like disinfectant and mildew.

Garrett's unit was the last on the left of a short hallway.

McKenzie popped the holder on her hip holster and stood left of me. I knocked and stood to the right.

"Who's there?"

A woman's voice.

McKenzie frowned. "Detectives Cortez and Brownlaw, San Diego Police. We'd need to talk to you."

I heard a chain latch click, then a dead bolt thunk back.

The door swung open. She was just a girl, young and pretty. She wore jeans and sheepskin boots and a plaid flannel shirt with the sleeves rolled. Brown eyes and fair skin and her cheeks had a blush to them. Dark hair, up and disorganized. She looked like Stella Asplundh.

"We'd like to talk about Garrett," I said. I told her our names again.

"Okay. I'm April Holly."

She stepped back to let us in, then closed the door. McKenzie badged her and April Holly looked at me uncomfortably.

The apartment was neat and sparsely furnished. Hardwood floor and an old red sofa that looked comfortable. There was a small gas-burning fireplace with a tidy little flame running the length of the logs. Two bedrooms off a short hallway. Framed photographs on the wall, black-and-whites that looked like Garrett Asplundh's. There were no high buildings to the west, so a swatch of Pacific showed in the distance.

"What am I supposed to do?" she asked. "I can make coffee. You can look around. Or—"

"Just sit down," said McKenzie. "You don't have to entertain us."

April Holly pointed at the red sofa, then clunked softly into the small dining area and brought a chair over for herself.

"You know that Garrett's dead," I said.

She nodded. "I saw the papers. And TV. He told me his name was Jimmy Neal. I saw him the night it happened."

McKenzie glanced at me as she got out her notepad and pen.

"I want you to tell us about that," I said. "But first, April, can you tell us who you are and why you're here?"

She blushed and looked away. "Gee, that's kind of a lot, isn't it?"

"It might help us find out who killed him," I said.

She continued to look away from us. Down at her boots or maybe the floor.

"You know . . . um, basically what it is . . . I ran away from home and was heading for some trouble and Jimmy, he was all, 'You're ruining your life, April.' So he made me come here and basically get my act together."

"Were you working for Jordan?" I asked.

April shook her head and blushed. She wouldn't look at either of us. I was heartened to see her shame because so few people have it anymore.

"I was about to," she said quietly. "But Jimmy said no way. He wouldn't let me."

McKenzie looked at me again, then scribbled.

"How old are you?" asked McKenzie.

"Eighteen."

"Tell us about Garrett and how you met him," I said.

When she finally looked back at us her eyes were shiny with tears. She wiped them with her palm. "Why would anybody want to kill that man? He was the most gentle and kind man I'd ever met. Ever."

"Talk to me, April," I said.

April spoke for almost half an hour before we asked her another question. Her colors and shapes were true. She was fairly intelligent but naive. She didn't seem to harbor illusions about herself. She didn't make a lot of excuses, which, you learn very early as a cop, is what criminals do, with endless energy and creativity. She felt bad about some of the things she had done, which is something that criminals almost never do, because they're too busy blaming someone else.

Home was a crammed-in tract in Temecula, a bustling little city north of San Diego. Dad was long gone, Mom involved with boyfriends, little brother a petty thief and drug user. April knew her effect on men, but the boys her age were immature and totally random. At a party one night a friend's father had gotten her aside and offered her a hundred dollars to take her clothes off out in the pool house but she said no. This was a year ago. Later some of the tough chicks at school said you could get men at the mall to give you two hundred bucks if you'd get in their car and do oral. Use a rubber, never take off so much as your bra, it was over in five minutes and if you did it five or six times a week you had enough for just about anything you wanted. April had said no to that, too, though she'd hung out and watched her friends hustle and had come close to trying it. This was last June, after graduation. By fall she'd had it. Always thought of that Thanksgiving as the most miserable day of her life. So she ran away to San Diego and hostessed in the Gaslamp for a while but that paid minimum and Hooters was hiring but she wasn't twenty-one yet and it seemed like every time she turned around some guy was hitting on her, guys a lot older than her, half of them with wedding rings on, made her wonder why anybody got married in the first place. Then, you know, she needed some work on her teeth and she got pneumonia and didn't have health insurance for the antibiotic and her car tanked and she heard about the Squeaky Clean Madam from one of her new friends, Carrie Ann, and . . . well, yes, she had actually met one of Jordan's spot callers and got "approved," and Carrie took her over to meet this guy Jimmy, who she didn't know until two days ago was really named Garrett Asplundh, and he paid her five hundred bucks to come back to this apartment and they talked for pretty much the whole night and when they were done April wasn't going to be a Squeaky Clean anymore, she was going to live here, get a straight job, which she did, and save up for a better car and her own place.

"Did you have sex with him?" asked McKenzie.

April shook her head. "Never."

"Did you accept gifts or money from him?"

"Well, yeah. I did. All this."

April admitted how unreal it might sound but Jimmy had something that went straight into her heart and saw everything she was and made her be totally honest with herself and the world around her.

"He never asked you for sex?" asked McKenzie.

April shook her head again. "No. I would have, too. I wanted to please him. Because I think he'd have done anything for me. He was like a good father. He had standards and you wanted to live up to them."

He had ethics, I thought.

"And now?" she said very quietly. "I can't believe they killed him. I just can't believe it."

"Tell us about the last night you saw him," said McKenzie.

"He came here about seven-thirty. I was done at the camera stand at six so I'd been here maybe fifteen minutes."

"Camera stand?"

"Oh, *duh.* I work at SeaWorld. The stand for disposables and film and videotape and stuff."

"What did Garrett want? Why did he come here?"

"He was checking up on me. Usually every other day. At least three or four times a week. We'd try to make it at a mealtime but couldn't always. I mean, we both worked."

"Just checking up on you?" asked McKenzie.

"Yes, just checking up, believe it or not." There was an edge to her voice as she glanced at McKenzie. Like she was talking back to her mother.

McKenzie looked at me. By now she is impressed by my "instincts" about whether or not people are being truthful. I was waiting for the red squares of deception to roll out of April's mouth but they didn't come. No symbols or colors at all, which is how most conversations go. So I nodded.

"What?" asked April.

"Nothing," I said. "Go on."

"He was random that night," said April. "He was all, 'I can't have dinner with you and I can't stay long.' I'm all, 'I'm fine, I'll be okay. I've got some laundry to do and this cute guy from the freeze stand—that's at SeaWorld, too—he's going to meet me out at the movies.' And Jimmy was fine with that."

"Whatever," said McKenzie, frowning. She wasn't buying April's story.

"Whatever nothing," said April.

"What time did he leave here?" I asked.

"Around eight."

"Where was he going? Why the hurry?"

She shook her head. "He didn't say. But I got the feeling he was looking forward to something. Like he was going to do something he really wanted to. Like he was eager."

McKenzie's pen shot across the pad.

"What was he wearing?"

"That's hard. Jimmy was a really cool dresser."

"Close your eyes," I said. "Picture where you were in this apartment. And think of what you talked about."

She closed her eyes. Took her time. Then, "Hmmm. Oh, *duh,* black suit and white shirt, and he changed his necktie before he left here. At first he had on a gold one, which I remember because it's the color of my new Mazda. I'm pretty sure it's still here, in Jimmy's room. But before he left, he put on a light blue one. Very cool."

We sat for a moment without talking. I remembered Garrett Asplundh's pale blue tie, drenched and splattered. I listened to a car passing down on the avenue, bass loud enough to quiver the Seabreeze windows and the singer's voice sharp with anger over his bitches. I was trying to fit the singer and Garrett Asplundh into the same world but it didn't work. Maybe that's why Garrett was dead. Though maybe the singer was dead, too.

"He said lots of things," said April. "He told me about his daughter that drowned and his wife. He told me about being a cop before he was an Ethics guy. I called him 'E-man.' Anyway, he talked about making yourself. About how good things make you stronger and bad things make you weaker. About what's true and what's not and how you can tell them apart. And the scams people will run on you. About creating character and the cost of behavior and losing people you love. Jimmy knew all about that. I didn't understand everything or agree with everything. He was trying to figure out his own stuff, not just mine. He was hard on himself and on me, too. But it was all good. And once he told me something that I thought was so poetic and true. It was about him. He told me he was afraid of losing himself in the spirit of the chase."

"Afraid of losing himself in the spirit of the chase," I said.

"Yes," said April. "Those were Jimmy's exact words. I remembered them like you remember lines from a song you really like."

"Why were they true about him?" asked McKenzie, without looking up. I could see that she was writing carefully, to get those words just as Garrett had said them.

"Well," said April, "because he was looking for something extremely important."

"Like what?" asked McKenzie.

"I have no idea. I don't know if *he* even knew. He always told me not to let the questions become the answers. Don't let the path become the woods. And I think what he meant about the spirit of the chase was that the spirit was leading him away from what he wanted. It's like, the faster you chase, the further away you get from your goal. But he couldn't help himself from chasing, you know?"

"I like that," I said.

McKenzie sighed and sat back.

April looked at each of us. "My turn to ask you a question. Why do you think Jimmy would help someone as lost as me?"

"Why do you think?" said McKenzie.

"Because he was lost, too. It was the first thing I noticed about him. That's why it was so good to see him looking forward to something that evening. Whatever it was. Whoever it was. And that's why when I saw the news the next day it felt like somebody had ripped out my heart and thrown it off a cliff."

I thought of something my mother told me once when I was a teenager.

Robbie, a person needs three things to be happy: Someone to love. Something to do. And something to look forward to.

Maybe he was looking forward to his twice-monthly date with Stella, I thought. Did he always look forward to it that much, or was there something else?

"Had you ever seen him eager like that before?" I asked. "Looking forward?"

April thought for a moment. Knocked the toes of her boots together softly. "No. I think he was onto something special."

April showed us the kitchen and her bedroom. Her room was girly and not very neat. She'd brought home a big cardboard stand-up of a killer whale jumping out of the water and it took up most of one wall. She'd bent out some of the bottom teeth to hang necklaces on. Her bed was pink and there were clothes everywhere.

The second bedroom was Jimmy's. She said he'd asked her not to go in there, and though she'd stuck her head in a few times she had never gone in and looked around. Not that there was much to see.

I pushed open the door. Just a card table and two folding metal chairs over by the window. A gold tie over one of the chairs. On the card table was a printer, a CD burner, and a laptop. On the wall under the window was a picture of what looked like a stream or river.

Pay dirt, I thought. The other half of Garrett Asplundh.

McKenzie sat, looked down under the table, and pushed the "on" button of a surge protector with her toe. The machines whirred to attention, green lights blipping. She had worked fraud a few years before I did, where she had specialized in computer crimes. And she'd taken special department classes in computer forensics. She can figure out or bypass a password in a matter of minutes.

She opened the laptop and smiled.

"Oh," said April. "He brought the laptop with him that evening. He did that pretty often, left something here and picked it up later."

I asked her if anyone else ever came over and asked for Garrett, or maybe to pick up something for him.

"No. He was always alone."

McKenzie glanced up at me, then back down to poke at the keyboard with curious authority.

"You have no idea what's on that laptop? No idea what Garrett did in here?" I asked.

"None. That was Jimmy's stuff. I didn't mess with Jimmy's stuff. That was the first rule of the house."

"What was the second?"

"He said if I ever turned a trick, I was out."

"Now what are you going to do?" I asked.

"I'm taking over the rent as of the first. Got a roommate maybe coming in from the park. You're welcome to take these things if they'll help you."

I thanked her, even though the computer and peripherals weren't hers to give away.

"I'd like to ask you one favor," she said. "Please get me invited to the funeral if there is one."

"I'll do that," I said.

April excused herself, said she had to get ready for work but to make ourselves at home.

McKenzie watched her go then looked up at me. "I'm in."

Garrett Asplundh and Carrie Ann Martier had kicked ass and taken names and put it all on his laptop. He had Captain Chet Fellowes from Vice with three prostitutes. Three different girls, three different times. It was surreal to see the naked, ununiformed version of a superior I'd worked around during my almost ten-year career. It was interesting that Fellowes didn't pay, though he was very specific and sneering about what he wanted the girls to do.

Garrett also had a young Motor Patrol officer on film, though he did pay—one hundred dollars. I knew little about him other than his name was Mincher or Mancher or something and he was a recent hire.

There was also a fire department sergeant whose name I didn't know but whose face I recognized. And City Councilman Anthony Rood and his aide, two-fisted Steve Stiles.

All caught on video, having the times of their lives with Squeaky Clean girls. Some paid and some didn't.

"This is bad," said McKenzie.

"Bad enough to get you in serious trouble," I said. "If you did the wrong thing with it."

There were three men that neither McKenzie nor I could identify, though a couple of them looked familiar to both of us. One looked eighty. One looked terrified. One was young and dark-haired and wore a shiny wedding ring and a dog-tag necklace that dangled into Carrie Ann Martier's face as he looked down at her with an air of entitlement.

We skipped through most of the videos. It doesn't take much to get the point across. The money part—when payment was required—was direct and explicit. The action itself was strenuous and somewhat comic. It's odd for a man to watch recorded fornication with a woman beside him, partners or not. None of the comments I might have made to a buddy seemed appropriate.

It saddened me again to see Carrie Ann Martier with the married councilman. He paid nothing. She rolled her eyes at the camera as he did his thing. She got a two-hundred-dollar tip from him when it was over and Rood told her he had a decent apartment she could rent cheap if she needed a place to live. *Maybe trade some partying for some rent,* he said.

April came into the room, fresh in her SeaWorld uniform. Luckily, a print file was on-screen by then. She looked so innocent and young and I suddenly fully understood what a good thing Asplundh had done for her. She handed me a key and asked me to give it to Davey on our way out.

"I hope you get whoever killed Jimmy," she said. "I'll do anything to help. You can call me anytime if you have more questions."

"Call us if you think of anything," I said. I wrote down her cell phone and driver's license numbers. She took my card with a nod and walked out.

I sat back down next to McKenzie in front of the laptop.

Garrett had collected more than just dirty videos. Print files on his laptop included names and numbers, addresses, job descriptions, biographies, even financial and medical information on the johns. I wondered if he'd hit up Hollis Harris for a few free hidden threat assessments to help protect America's Finest City. Holding together these informational paragraphs were Garrett's own comments and notes and questions, easily identifiable in a large, bold typeface. Some of the pages looked like the Bible with Christ's words in bold type that my parents gave me when I was twelve and baptized. There were thirty-two print documents and some of them went on for almost a hundred pages.

Into one file Garrett had scanned phone bills from the Squeaky Clean girls, apparently trying to close the loop between them, the johns, the spot callers, and the madam herself.

Tough job, because none of Jordan Sheehan's six phone numbers appeared in any of the girls' bills, although the numbers of three spot callers did. But there was no way to prove what any of them were talking about without a wiretap, and Garrett had noted caustically that *Abel Sarvonola says the city doesn't have the money to buy the Ethics Authority one piece of phone-intercept equipment, but it can pay for empty seats at Chargers games.*

He rambled on about the wiretap problem for a while, then this interesting paragraph:

Think about it for one second, Stella. Sarvonola says no money for Ethics. Just like there was no money for fire protection while half the county burned and the firefighters didn't have enough batteries for their walkie-talkies. And don't forget we've got good honest city workers with a failing pension after some of them paid into it for thirty years. These are just more examples of the collapse that's coming, Stella. The crash that nobody will talk about.

"He's pissed at Sarvonola," said McKenzie. "Because the Budget Oversight Committee calls the money shots at City Hall. And Abel Sarvonola rules the Oversight Committee."

"Because Sarvonola values a losing football team over the Ethics Authority," I said. I'd always thought that the Budget Oversight Committee was too eager to please the wealthy businessmen who profit so hugely from our city.

Garrett angrily went on to note that his attempts to get any SDPD Vice recordings between the Squeaky Clean Madam and her business associates had been denied, twice, by Captain Fellowes, whom we'd just seen on disc.

"He's even pissed at us," said McKenzie. "His old employer."

"You can't have cops doing stuff like that," I said.

But my comment made me think again of decking the muscular husband after claiming Gina's engraved Hikari shears. I had broken the law, too.

Another line in Garrett's voluminous notes caught my eye, largely because I'd seen part of it before:

Could lay all or most of this out at the 3/16 meet with Kaven, JVF & Att. Gen, though the backfire could consume us all.

"What do you think he meant by this?" I asked McKenzie. I turned the monitor to face her.

"He means if the state attorney general gets involved, the cure may be worse than the disease."

That put Garrett in an interesting situation, I thought: He wanted to clean up the dirt without hurting the city. Could you really do that? That was the trouble with corruption. The bigger the players who went down, the bigger the headlines got and the worse the city looked. So it was always the little ones—the ones mixed up in things they didn't necessarily ask for, the ones who wouldn't be missed—who were sacrificed. And the big fish eased back under their rocks to let the storm blow over.

I closed the document and scanned down the menu of videos again. One of the available videos caught my eye because it was so short.

JS Live was listed at just eight seconds long.

So I clicked play and rubbed my eyes and sat back.

First a blond woman, fortyish, sat down at what appeared to be a restaurant bar and smiled at the camera. She wore a lacy white blouse under a black blazer and her straight thick hair was cut just above her shoulders.

"Oh, Garrett, what's this?" she asked brightly. Her smile was generous. Pretty teeth and lips. She fingered her hair behind one ear, revealing an earring the shape of a crescent moon with a small jewel on the inside of the curve.

She was still smiling as her hand left her hair and came toward the camera.

"My window on the world," said a man, probably Garrett.

"You must think I'm a real idiot."

Then everything got noisy and the picture went black.

I played it back again.

"Squeaky Clean herself?" I asked.

"That's her," said McKenzie. "Jordan Sheehan."

I played the fragment several more times.

"Didn't take her long to find the hidden camera," I said.

"Eight seconds," said McKenzie. "That was the Onyx Room, by the way."

"Never been."

"The tourists haven't discovered it yet," said McKenzie. "But you gotta be cool to go there. Not some happily married guy who likes to stay in at night."

I thought of Gina again, maybe on her lunch break by now. I thought of all the men who'd like to take her out for that lunch. Her boss, Chambers, was boldly homosexual, which made me feel only slightly better. Watching the videos had filled me with a fresh wave of longing for Gina and made her departure even sharper and more punishing. For the first time since she'd left, I believed it was possible—though I believed it only for one terrifying moment—that I'd never see her again.

"Maybe Hollis can drive you there in his red Ferrari," I said.

"Robbie, I have to confess, that car turned me limp in one block. Luckily, I recovered walking into Dobson's."

"He didn't carry you?"

She smiled. "I don't think he's strong enough."

Her cell phone beeped and she put a hand on my shoulder and stood.

McKenzie and I rarely banter about personal things like this. I think that viewing the lewd material had left us both a little thankful for each other's unlewd company, as if we'd come through something difficult together.

I heard her writing as she listened, thanked somebody, and rang off. I looked at the picture of the river tacked to the wall under the window. It took me a minute to really see that picture.

"Finally," she said. "Verizon Security. Those 212 calls made on Garrett's cell phone the week he died were to Trey Vinson of New York, New York. Never heard of him. But I got his stats from warrants and records."

While McKenzie made the call, I checked Garrett's e-mail directory and found Trey Vinson.

Garrett had his e-mail and two phone numbers and the name and address of his company in New York City—Jance Purdew Investment Services. I knew them from my days in Fraud. They were one of the big credit-rating agencies on Wall Street, up there in size with Moody's and Standard & Poor's. Jance Purdew helped keep investors from getting ripped off by unscrupulous issuers of stocks and bonds.

I opened three of Garrett's longest files and did a word search for "Trey" and "Vinson."

I found just one reference, from a document last updated on Sunday, March 6, two days before Garrett was killed.

Vinson's name appeared in a brief paragraph that followed ninety pages of City of San Diego financial reports and disclosures, some of which went back to 1995, and eighteen pages of budget abstracts.

City cooked the books. Now up to Vinson. Diminished to negative. If he holds we're alive, if he folds we're not.

McKenzie clipped her phone back to her belt and told me Vinson had come up clean on the warrant check.

I told her Vinson worked for a big rating agency and pointed to his name on the screen.

She read over my shoulder. "If the city cooked the books and Vinson found out, that would kill our credit. No credit, no bonds, no money. Bankruptcy."

"But he might hold," I said.

"Why?"

"Pressure? Money? The wonderful San Diego weather?"

I knew from my brief stint in Fraud that a city's credit rating governed the amount of interest that would have to be paid to investors. If a city's rating was high, it could successfully issue municipal bonds and pay a relatively low rate of return. But if the rating was lower, the city would have to offer higher interest to attract bond buyers. To a city the size of San Diego, the difference between an A and a B rating on, say, a $100 million bond could be $3 or $4 million. I knew also that the city had issued roughly $2.5 *billion* in municipal bonds in the last ten years. If the city was caught "cooking the books," the penalties, fines, and refinancing costs would send us deep into bankruptcy.

I stood and let her tap her way out of the programs. I looked again at the picture of the river. It was a photograph on photographic paper, not something cut from a magazine. It was in color, though I was reasonably sure that Garrett had taken it. It was held up with tape now but there were holes in each of the four corners.

Really all you could see was rippled water. No bank or rocks or horizon or anything to give size or perspective. Just four by six inches of yellow-green ripples. It could have been a close-up of something else. Or an abstract painting. But I knew why Garrett had taken it because I could just barely discern the fish lying beneath the shimmering surface. I had to look slightly to the side of the animal, like viewing a shape in the dark. Just a faint vertical tail line was all that gave it away, but once you had seen the line, you saw the fish.

"What?" said McKenzie.

"It's a picture of a fish."

"No fish I can see."

I pointed to it and she looked at me.

"I wonder if that's what Garrett used to look at from his workbench out in the garage," I said. "Remember? The tacks on the wall where something used to be?"

She nodded. "All those hours looking at something that's not even there."

"It's there."

"Okay, Robbie. Okay, Garrett. Okay, fish dreamers. You guys see what you want to see. In the meantime I'll just try to live a normal kind of life. It bugs me that Garrett's secret girl looks a lot like his wife."

"Bugs me too."

"How about lunch?"

"Would you mind just dropping me off at Gina's work? She'll bring me to headquarters."

McKenzie gave me an analytical look. "Sure. Say hi for me. You two have a good thing, Robbie. You're lucky."

I walked through the Sultra doors trying to look casual while my heart beat hard in my ears. I strolled to the reception desk and waited while Tammy talked on the phone. I smiled across the travertine floor at Gina, who smiled faintly back, her Hikari Cosmos poised over an older woman with her hair clipped into sections. Gina looked almost unimaginably beautiful. One chair over, Rachel glanced at me as if she were fed up.

I sat in the waiting area and waited for Gina to finish. My heart kept beating extra hard. I didn't expect her to just drop everything and run over to me, though I wouldn't have minded. I didn't stare at her but rather looked up from my hairstyle magazine every few seconds as if imagining a certain cut on myself. Tammy asked if I were a walk-in, not remembering who I was.

It took Gina quite a while to finish the cut, another while for the dry and style, another while for the woman to leave the chair and head in my direction. Finally Gina looked at me again for the first time since I'd walked in, held up a be-right-with-you finger then walked quickly off toward the bathrooms in the back.

I set down the magazine and waited. I looked out the white shutters to the street. The sun had broken through and now threw soft, cool light onto the travertine. I wondered what to say to Gina. I wondered what she'd say back. I wondered how she could possibly take so long in the bathroom. I waited another few minutes then went back to see if everything was okay.

A woman came from the bathroom and I waited another minute, then opened the door slightly and called her name. Just an echo.

So I tried again.

Silence is silence no matter how long you wait.

"Give her some space, Robbie. It's all you can do."

Rachel pushed the door all the way open and swept into the women's room, the door closing behind her with a faint feminine breeze.

Down the hall I saw the rear exit door ajar and felt like a world-class fool. I went out the back way, too.

I walked back to headquarters, looking around for Gina as I went, but knew I wouldn't see her. It took forty minutes and nothing registered. I didn't see, hear, or smell anything. It's interesting how quickly forty minutes can pass, how quickly they can drop from the memory of your life.

The next thing I knew the seven concrete-and-blue stories of police headquarters stood before me and I realized that if Gina was really gone, this job would be just about my whole world.

I found my captain in his office, eating alone and looking out his window. His name is Jim Villas and he has my respect. He's a career San Diego cop, started when he was twenty, just like I did. He's late fifties now, a grandfather and an accomplished handball player.

Captain Villas always wears his uniform on Fridays. He grew up a street kid and began as a street cop and he's proud of that. He was picking a crumb off his navy trousers when I knocked on the doorjamb.

"May I close the door, sir?"

"Sure. Come in, Robbie."

We talked for a minute about the cool, foggy weather and about an upcoming handball tournament. Then he asked me what was up.

"Captain Fellowes has been enjoying himself with working girls," I said. "Some of Jordan Sheehan's girls got him on video and Garrett Asplundh ended up with it."

Villas stared at me for a moment. "This is not an early April Fools' joke."

"It's not."

"You're positive it's Fellowes?"

"Unless the video has been tampered with. I don't think it has. Fellowes it is, sir, nothing on but his socks and a sneer."

"How did you get it?"

I told him about Garrett's secret National City apartment, April Holly, the spare room, the laptop. I told him about the other cop and everyone else I'd recognized.

"Councilman Rood and his aide?"

I nodded.

"Who else knows?"

"McKenzie. Possibly the girls in the video. I'm not sure if they knew who their clients were."

"And Fellowes was the only one who appeared to be getting his fun for free?"

"The other men paid different amounts. The Vice captain got his for free."

Villas stood and went to the window. The view was north toward Balboa Park. "This Sheehan woman, she's the one Vice calls the Squeaky Clean Madam?"

"Yes, sir. That's also what people on the street call her."

"If a Vice captain is involved, that could explain why nobody's touched her. Does Fellowes know he was recorded?"

"I've got no way of knowing, sir. Nothing on the discs suggests that."

"Are they dated?"

"Yes. His last romp was two weeks ago."

"Is there any mention of Fellowes in Asplundh's notes or journals?"

"Yes, sir. He said the captain had become 'flabby, dull, and an easy mark.' "

"Sounds like Fellowes, actually," he mumbled.

Captain Villas dug a finger under his shirt collar and worked his neck around, like the shirt was too tight. He shook his head, sat back down. For a long while he looked out in the direction of Balboa Park.

"Okay," he finally said. "I'll handle it. Keep it to yourself for right now. This is not going to make your life easier, Robbie."

"My life is fine."

"I'll have to talk to Internal Affairs and Professional Standards."

"I understand, sir. And I need to talk to Fellowes."

"Why?"

"If he knew he was on video, that's motive."

Villas just stared at me. "What, Garrett takes him for a little ride to tell him what he knows, and Fellowes blows him away? Calls Mincher or one of those other guys to give him a ride home?"

I shrugged. It sounded very possible to me. It had the one thing that a successful premeditated murder needs: audacity.

"That's one of the ugliest things I've heard all day," said Villas.

"Asplundh wasn't killed for what he had," I said. "He was killed for what he knew."

"Yes. Okay. Talk to Fellowes."

Back at my desk, I briefed McKenzie and called Captain Fellowes's office. I got his machine and left a message that I wanted to talk. I had the feeling Fellowes would not be eager to see me or anyone investigating the murder of Garrett Asplundh.

Next I called Sally, a friend over at City Hall who works for Human Resources. She knows everybody. She's usually happy to help me because years ago I frightened her young son with a "don't do drugs" lecture and walked him through the county jail after she'd caught him with marijuana. It seemed to help the boy because she'd never found any drugs since. At any rate, I asked Sally if she could discreetly determine if Ninth District Councilman Anthony Rood had made a public appearance on the nights of either March 7 or 8. Ditto his aide, Steven Stiles. I could tell by her hesitation that she had instantly connected one of the dates with the murder I was investigating. I asked her to please keep this to herself and she said she would.

I also called Abel Sarvonola's office and made an appointment to see the chairman of the Budget Oversight Committee. His secretary sounded pert and happy but Abel and his wife were vacationing in Las Vegas. The secretary made an appointment for me on Wednesday, Abel's first available date.

Then I tried Trey Vinson of Jance Purdew Investments in New York City. His secretary told me that Mr. Vinson was on the West Coast now and I said that was great, because I was too. After asking several questions about my reasons for talking to Mr. Vinson, she unhappily set up a time for us to meet.

Stella Asplundh called a few minutes later. Her voice was soft but clear. "I read in the paper that Garrett was found in his car near the Cabrillo Bridge," she said.

"Just north of it, off the 163."

"That is significant."

"Please explain."

"That was where he proposed to me ten years ago. It wasn't at night and we weren't in a car. It was springtime and we'd taken off our shoes to walk in Balboa Park. We crossed the bridge and wandered down through the trails. Garrett said we needed a bridge like that one. I said, 'What are you talking about?' and he said, 'To connect you to me and me to you, something solid and beautiful and useful. Like a marriage,' he said. He had a ring in his pocket. I almost knocked him over. Since then, a couple of times a year, we'd go back to that spot and look at the bridge and remember things. Sometimes during the day. Sometimes at night, in our car."

We were both quiet for a moment.

"You were supposed to meet at Delicias in Rancho Santa Fe," I said.

"At nine o'clock."

"So why would he park at your special place by the bridge before going to meet you?"

"I talked to him earlier in the day," she said. "On the phone, I mean.

He said he was going to say a prayer at the bridge. I didn't mention it to you before because I didn't realize that's where you'd found him."

"A prayer at the bridge? Explain that."

She paused. "We were trying to start over. It was important to us. I told you."

"Is there anyone else he'd take to your special place?"

"No," she said. "I hope not."

"Who knew that Garrett proposed to you under that bridge?"

Another silence. "My mother and father. I told several friends back when it happened. It was romantic."

"Did you tell any of them that you two still went back to that spot sometimes?"

"I . . . yes. I'm sure I must have."

"Did Garrett?"

"How could I possibly know that?"

"Did Garrett ever go there without you?"

"He said he went there alone sometimes. To remember and to think."

I pictured Garrett in his SUV at his special place under the Cabrillo Bridge. Was he alone? Garrett would be seeing Stella later. He was hoping for a reconciliation with her. After the death of their daughter, the heartbreak of their separation, and months of heavy drinking, he was finally catching a break.

Or so he thought.

I spent the early part of that Friday afternoon at my desk with the coroner's report on the death of Garrett Asplundh. McKenzie sat across the aisle with her own copy. The day was cool but clear, and the city was beautiful as I looked downtown to the new ballpark and the glassy condos and the silver-gray water of the bay.

The city has changed a lot in my twenty-nine years. When I was a boy there was no Gaslamp Quarter, just a rough borough of bars and porn shops and tattoo parlors and cheap hotels overrun with sailors on leave and a lot of down-and-out people. I remember an inordinate number of wig shops. The hairpieces looked so strange in the dirty windows, displayed on the sleek, faceless mannequins. The joke was, you didn't stroll through this part of downtown, you ran. When I got older, I thought it was interesting to find that this area had always been rough and tumble. Back at the turn of the century it was nicknamed "The Stingaree," and it was filled with saloons, opium dens, and gambling houses. Wyatt Earp ran a place called the Oyster Bar, while upstairs in the same building was a brothel called the Golden Poppy. Ida Bailey was one of the locally famous madams, from whom Jordan Sheehan had borrowed and updated a marketing strategy—parading her girls around town in the latest mode of transportation. The cops were slow to shut Ida down because some of them were her best customers. Funny how history was repeating now. Same truths, different people. They named a restaurant after Ida. There was plenty of trouble in the Stingaree but until a few years ago, no gas lamps. They were put there by the city for character.

There was no "East Village" either. Just big warehouses and weekly hotels and odd businesses that seemed to be dead or dying. Trash in the street blowing in the bay breeze. Plenty of homeless people and services to get them back on their feet, or at least out from under other people's feet. Our current police headquarters was built right in the middle of it, like a church in the middle of a pagan village. With the ballpark now in and millions of dollars committed for redevelopment, San Diegans say that East Village will someday be the crown jewel of downtown.

As I looked down at the city it struck me that a lot of the Gaslamp and East Village was built with municipal bonds sold on San Diego's high credit rating from Jance Purdew Investment Services.

Garrett Asplundh had been questioning the truth behind those ratings. Garrett Asplundh had helped a call girl get satisfaction from a city councilman's aide who had hurt her. Garrett Asplundh had helped a girl get on her feet without having to make a living on her back.

And someone had murdered him. Now it was official.

The cause of death: "Gunshot to the head. Cardiac failure due to massive brain trauma."

The murder weapon was likely the nine-millimeter Smith & Wesson semiautomatic recovered from the front floorboard of the Explorer. But since the fatal bullet had passed through Garrett's head and the driver's-side window of the vehicle and lodged or landed in a still-unknown location, there were no tool marks to check against the weapon.

I knew that our chances of finding that bullet were very small.

Time of death was between 8:00 P.M. Tuesday, March 8, and 2:00 A.M. Wednesday, March 9.

Photographs of the blood spatters and free histamine levels in Asplundh's blood suggested he lived for nearly ten seconds after he was shot.

And in that brief time, there had been a struggle.

Or at least contact. Garrett had lashed out with his right hand and come up with three brown wool fibers from either a jacket or sweater. One fiber strand was stuck to his palm, and two were caught in a fingernail that had been clenched tight enough to break and snag the material. I looked at the close-up photo of the finger and broken nail, at the fibers caught in the line of the break.

For a moment I considered one of the photographs of Asplundh slumped in a blizzard of his own blood. And I wondered at our human instincts for holding on to life. They were the same instincts that led me to claw the air on my fall. It's pure biological impulse and has nothing to do with the odds.

"Ten seconds," said McKenzie. "I wondered about that, with all the blood."

"Wouldn't you love to match up those fibers and get this guy?"

"They probably won't get us far, with so many brown sweaters and jackets in the world," she said.

I had a thought. "But wouldn't it be cool if a little of the nail was left in the garment? Look how jagged that break is. Maybe Garrett left something of *him*self behind. It could snag right into the weave and you'd never know it was there."

McKenzie gave me a tolerant look. "Maybe."

I noted that, contrary to Stella Asplundh's worries, Garrett's blood-alcohol content was zero.

His blood type was B positive.

His heart appeared normal for a thirty-nine-year-old man. His veins and arteries were unobstructed. His kidneys and pancreas were normal. His liver was slightly enlarged, likely the result of prolonged heavy alcohol use.

The medical examiner's report told of the same hernia operation that was mentioned in the hidden threat assessment run for us by Hollis Harris.

"Funny he wasn't drinking that night," I said.

"Why?"

"They say here he had some liver damage from heavy drinking. Every drinker I've known drinks every day. When they're sick they drink. When they're in the hospital they're pestering you to sneak them a bottle. They drink when they're nervous or happy or down or celebrating or thinking or washing away sorrows or just washing the car. You know, drinkers *drink.* But that night he didn't."

"Stella said he'd quit," said McKenzie. "Maybe he was telling the truth."

"For his last night alive, he was."

"What else do we know about him that night?" asked McKenzie. "We know he met Harris at five P.M. Then Carrie Martier at six-thirty, from whom he got a nasty DVD. Then April Holly at seven-thirty. He was supposed to meet his ex at nine, but he never showed. He was wearing a gold tie when he got to April's and a blue one when he was shot."

I thought for a moment. "According to Harris, he was scattered and unfocused."

McKenzie considered. "And later April said Garrett was looking forward to something or someone. We've got a big window here. M.E. says time of death between eight and two the next morning. That's a lot of time to do a lot of things. To do a lot more than just change your tie."

"Why did he change the tie?"

"For Stella, don't you think?" said McKenzie. "If you're going to take eight thousand artsy pictures of your hottie and put them on your wall, you're going to make sure you look sharp when you see her. If you're going to reconcile, you want to look your best."

For Stella, I thought. For your ex. The woman who bore your daughter and later almost sued you for divorce. The woman who was the object of your desire, object of your artist's eye, object of your obsession.

Still your hottie. Reconciliation.

"Stella said he was going to the bridge to say a prayer," I said.

"For what?"

"For what would happen between them later that night."

"You'd figure he'd go alone," said McKenzie.

"Sure, alone."

"Okay, Robbie, but Garrett was an ex-cop. He was a good investigator. He was bright and alert and suspicious and ready. And sober. But he sat there behind the wheel and somebody drives up and leaves that extra set of tire tracks we saw. And Garrett takes it point-blank."

"He got fooled."

"Big time. He trusted the shooter."

The M.E.'s report noted that Garrett's left arm had once been broken just above the wrist, something that had eluded Hollis Harris's lightning-fast hidden threat assessment.

His weight at death was 204 pounds, adjusted for the loss of two of his estimated five and a half liters of blood.

McKenzie and I sat at our own desks, lost in different chapters of

Garrett's murder book. She waited until the other detectives were gone and Captain Villas's door was shut, then came over and leaned down close.

"Villas will have to tell the chief about Fellowes. The chief will have to tell Professional Standards. They'll have to interview us. They'll want the discs and we should have our stories straight about making copies or not making copies."

"I'll burn them."

"Just for us?"

"Just for us, McKenzie."

"Gotcha."

A minute later Sally from HR called and told me that Councilman Anthony Rood and his aide, Steven Stiles, had hosted an "exploratory fund-raiser" aboard the aircraft carrier *Midway* the night Garrett was murdered. Her sources had told her that both men arrived onboard about six o'clock and left around midnight. Rood had nailed down pledges for eleven thousand dollars and found "substantial support" for a run at a California assembly seat.

A few minutes after that, Ethics Authority Director Erik Kaven called. His voice sounded like his face looked—craggy and lined and suspicious. I pictured his Wyatt Earp mustache and his bright, distrustful eyes. I recalled that he had killed the two bank robbers with a total of two shots.

He wanted to know how the investigation was going, and I told him it was going well.

"Are you getting full cooperation from Van Flyke?" he asked.

"Yes. He's been helpful."

"Garrett was a smart man. Smarter than his boss. But Garrett had an Achilles' heel that occasionally hurt him as an investigator."

"What was that?"

"He had a higher opinion of human nature than was realistic."

"I can see how that could get in his way."

"I would hope so."

Kaven hung up.

Later that day Glenn Wasserman met us at the impound yard to show us what he'd found in the Explorer. The vehicle sat in a clean bay under strong incandescent lights. The window blood was black and thick enough to throw shadows onto the dash. Industrial air conditioners hummed along and gave the air a cold, clean feel, and anybody who worked here always wore at least a sweatshirt under the lab coat.

Glenn is a pleasant-faced twenty-five-year-old with two sons already and twin girls on the way. He grew up in Normal Heights like I did, though the four-year age gap kept us from knowing each other well. His handshake was strong and cool.

"After the GSR came up negative and I knew we had a homicide, I worked with two scenarios," said Glenn. "One was an unknown assailant. The other was a known assailant. I'm leaning toward number two. Here's why."

He led us to the passenger side. I saw the silver fingerprint dust on and around the door handle.

"You already know about the gun that was found in here," he said. "Wiped clean. Not so much as a friction ridge."

"No surprise," said McKenzie. "This guy is every kind of cool."

"What about the cartridges in the magazine?" I asked.

"Clean."

"The spent one?"

"Clean again. You bring a Tri-Flow wipe for prints, you don't forget to wipe the cartridges you load."

Glenn nodded at the Explorer. "While I was working on this vehicle, I realized it has automatic door locks. With the ignition on and the vehicle put into gear, all five doors lock. So if Asplundh came down the swale and parked near the bridge, then shut off his engine to wait, all four doors and the rear lift gate would have been locked. Could he have opened them while he waited? Sure—for someone he knew. Could he have gotten a good look at them through the passenger's window? Maybe he could, if he had the engine running and his heater and defroster on."

"The engine was off when patrol got there," I said. "Everything was off."

"Exactly," said Glenn.

I pictured Garrett sitting alone in a locked and cooling car. I thought of the second set of tire tracks leading down the hillock from above.

"Maybe Garrett's killer was already in the vehicle with him," I said.

"And the second set of tracks was the pickup car," said McKenzie.

"That's consistent with some other things we found," said Glenn. "Now here, the door handle of this vehicle is painted black. And the paint continues up the backside, where you'd put your fingers to pull it open. A handle like that is one of our potential honey pots. It's a perfect print trap. But guess what? No prints again. No partials and no overlaps. I think it was wiped by our shooter on his or her way out."

Glenn used a hankie to pull out the handle and swing open the door. He pointed at the numbered pink tags taped to the radio, ashtray, vanity mirror, console, seat-belt buckles, automatic door and window controls, even on the door-lock button in the far rear cargo section.

"We lifted partials from all over this vehicle," he said. "Most of them are Garrett's, but some aren't. Nothing big enough to run through the print registries. We got a decent thumb from the radio on/off button—not Garrett's. We got two partial fingers from the cover of the vanity mirror on the passenger-side sun visor—not Garrett's. Probably not the shooter's either, if he or she was careful enough to wipe the inside of the door handle. Prints can keep a long time, especially in cool, damp weather, so these could be weeks old."

Glenn folded his handkerchief and pushed it back into a pocket on his lab coat.

"Hair and fiber," he said. "We're lucky the interior is upholstery instead of leather or vinyl. It won't clean up very well, and it grabs and holds more than leather. Upholstery is a hair and fiber trap, and we got plenty. Ditto the floor mats."

The passenger seat was marked with numbered yellow tags held in place with pins. Eight in all—three on the back and five on the bottom. I saw more yellow tags down on the floor mats.

"Yellow tags two, three, and six all locate apparently female hairs," said Glenn. "Naturally blond—three, seven, and eight inches long, respectively. Straight."

He pointed to a tag on the seat back. One on the floor mat. Another on the driveshaft hump in front of the center console.

"Kind of spread out," said McKenzie.

"We know Asplundh got a hand on his killer," said Glenn. "Grabbed the shooter hard enough to break a fingernail and trap some fibers. Maybe he struck or tried to grab the head first. Maybe when he clutched the coat or sweater that left those brown fibers, it shook the shooter violently. Either way, that could explain the spread of hairs if the killer was a woman."

"Or they could have been floating around in there since Garrett's last date with a straight-haired natural blonde," said McKenzie.

"Sure," said Glenn. "And there is some indication that the hairs could have been in here longer. Two of the three were intertwined with very small debris—lint and dust and dander particles. The kind of material that builds up in carpet or flooring or floor mats."

He pointed to the other two tags on the seat back. "Here and here—more brown wool fiber, very similar to that found caught in Garrett's fingernail. This automotive upholstery is wonderful for collecting things."

"None of those fibers were found on the driver's side," I said.

"Right, so check Garrett's closet," said Glenn. "I'll bet you he didn't have a loosely woven sweater or jacket. Or at least one that he wore very often. He was wearing a well-made suit when he died. The worsted wools and blends like that, the weave is much too tight to shed. Scratch one of your suit coats with a thumbnail sometime and see what you get."

Glenn used his hankie to shut the door. "Come over here. You'll like this."

We followed him to a workbench. Glenn knelt down and keyed open a steel filing cabinet, then stood back up with a paper bag in his hand. The bag was labeled with the date and case number. From inside it he took a small white envelope. He snapped a paper towel from a roll on top of the bench and laid it out, then opened the envelope and tapped it to the towel. He stared down.

"Make of this what you will," he said. "We found it up front, between the driver's seat and the console."

It was a gold earring in the shape of a crescent moon. Sitting inside the curve of the crescent was a blue sapphire. There was a dry black smear on the moon.

Beside the earring was the backing piece, bent out of its likely original round shape.

McKenzie and I traded looks.

"We found the backing in the rear of the Explorer, by the utility compartment," said Glenn. "It got quite a ride. Maybe that's how it got bent, too."

"You found the earring on the driver's side, not the passenger's side?" asked McKenzie.

"Yes," said Glenn. "A struggle could easily account for that."

He packaged up the earring and backing, put the envelope into the bag, and returned the bag to the file cabinet.

"A hit chick wearing gold and sapphire earrings?" asked McKenzie.

Glenn shrugged. "Women kill."

"Not like *this.* We have standards. We have style and finesse."

He smiled.

I thought of Jordan Sheehan's straight blond hair and crescent-moon earring. I wondered if she was a person who could blow the brains out of a man sitting next to her in a car. A man she'd met with, smiled at, joked with.

"Come on back to the lab," said Glenn. "We'll fire up the microscopes and get a good look at the hair and fiber."

"I'll leave that to you two," said McKenzie. "I got an actual date tonight."

"Always have cab fare and be in before midnight," said Glenn.

She deadpanned him, then turned to wink at me and walked away.

I spent an hour in the crime lab looking at the hairs and fibers through Glenn Wasserman's scanning electron microscope until my eyesight began to blur.

I was pleased to see in the very fine autopsy photographs that a visibly large piece of Garrett Asplundh's right index fingernail had been torn away and could possibly still be imbedded in a garment worn by his killer.

Back at my desk, it took me five minutes to call up the Squeaky Clean video clip from Garrett's laptop and confirm that Jordan's crescent-moon earring was very similar to the one found in Garrett's Explorer.

I called Glenn to see if he could do a visual comparison of the latent fingerprints in the Explorer with Jordan Sheehan's ten-set in the PD file.

"Isn't she too squeaky clean to leave a print?" he asked.

"You tell me, Glenn."

On my way home, I stopped by John Van Flyke's Ethics Authority office unannounced and received a flinty look from Arliss Buntz. She admitted that Mr. Van Flyke was upstairs in his office, but unavailable. I asked her to let him know I was there but she didn't. I sat at the rickety little table and picked up a very outdated sailing magazine.

I heard her forcefully open, then close a drawer. I heard the rattle of papers on her desktop. I turned and looked at her.

"You thought Garrett was headed for trouble," I said.

"I saw it the moment he walked through those doors."

"Why? What did you see?"

She fixed me with her old gray eyes. "That he had standards."

I thought about that. *He had a higher opinion of human nature than was realistic.* Van Flyke appeared at the top of the stairway and motioned me up. I walked up the stairs, listening to my footsteps on the wood and the sudden loud ringing of Arliss Buntz's telephone. I noted again how sounds carried in this drafty old Edwardian building. I wondered if the Italian baker and his wife ever got much privacy. I wondered why America's Finest City couldn't afford a better office for its own Ethics Authority Enforcement Unit.

Van Flyke swung his office door shut.

"We found Garrett's laptop," I said. I told him what we'd found on it.

"It's ugly stuff," said Van Flyke.

"You knew?"

"I was his boss."

"What were you planning to do with it?"

"We wanted Garrett's Squeaky Cleans to gather all the evidence they could gather. Then we'd see where we stood. Delicate matter. You do things just wrong and the big boys get away. You do things just wrong and the feds or the state gets into the mix and you lose control of your own battlefield. Garrett, Director Kaven, and the attorney general's office were going to meet next Wednesday, in fact, to figure out where to go with certain investigations. Certain situations. That meeting has been rescheduled."

"Does Kaven know what Garrett had on disc?"

"Not yet."

"Will you take the evidence to the grand jury?"

"Kaven will insist, and I'll concur. That's how we'll keep things out of the State of California's hands."

"Did any of the johns know what Garrett had on them?"

Van Flyke shook his head. "Not that I know of. We were waiting. Ethics does its best work when people have just enough rope to hang themselves."

"Did you know about Garrett's safe house?"

"No."

I could tell by his expression that he didn't. And by the fact that no red squares tumbled into the air in front of him. I gave him the basics about the apartment, but not the address. And I told him nothing about April Holly.

He looked at me from under his bushy brows. "I'd like copies of everything on the drive, at your convenience."

"That will take a little time, Mr. Van Flyke."

"Take whatever time you need, Brownlaw."

I looked at the sparse walls of John Van Flyke's office. No pictures. No paintings. Just a bachelor's degree in psychology from Ohio State and a commendation from the Drug Enforcement Administration from three years ago. The frames hung close together on a wall of freshly painted plaster, not far from a window with a peek of the blue Pacific.

"Garrett interviewed with you for a job in Florida early last year," I said.

Van Flyke stared at me with his deep-set eyes. "Yes. We'd met at an FBI digital-evidence seminar at Quantico two years ago. He contacted me later, said he wanted to raise his daughter somewhere other than Southern California. I brought him out for an interview and ended up offering him the job—a small pay increase, but he'd be with a good bunch of people at DEA. He brought Samantha and Stella out with him. They seemed to enjoy Miami. He asked for a week to make his decision, then called and declined."

"Why?"

"Stella decided she wanted to stay in San Diego after all. Garrett had this theory that Southern California wasn't the best place to raise a daughter, though I told him Miami has its problems, too. Does it ever. Anyway, Garrett always seemed willing to accommodate his wife."

"She seems . . . emptied."

"She's still heartbroken over the daughter," said Van Flyke. "Now this."

"If they'd have moved to Florida—"

"I'm sure that's crossed Stella Asplundh's mind a million times," said Van Flyke.

I wondered what it would be like to have that dark fact inside you, ready to flash into your thoughts when you least expected it.

"What brought you to San Diego?" I asked.

Van Flyke nodded. "Garrett recommended me to Kaven and he liked what he saw."

"So Garrett returned the favor you tried to do for him."

Van Flyke shrugged, tapping on his desktop with his fingers. "A man's life can change in a moment, don't you think?"

"Yes," I said.

"Something divides it into what went before and what comes after."

I had the odd feeling that Van Flyke was talking to himself as much as to me.

"You, Brownlaw, should understand that. What I'm trying to explain is that when I came to San Diego last year for the first time, it took me all of about an hour to see I wanted to live here. There's no place like it. This is the best big city in the country. I've seen them all. I still can't figure out why Garrett would want to leave."

I couldn't either, but I've always loved my city, blemishes and all.

"Just so you know," I said, "I got a message from Garrett's brother, Samuel. He came down from Los Angeles yesterday. He's FBI and next of kin. Interesting combination."

"I know, I know, and I think so, too. Sam and I have been in contact," said Van Flyke. "How long until you get me those hard-drive files?"

"Monday afternoon," I said.

"I'm having lunch with Sam Asplundh at Panchito's, one o'clock. Drop off the files there, would you?"

At home that Friday evening, I logged on to the FBI Drug Fire site and ran the serial number of the gun used to kill Garrett Asplundh.

The gun was originally sold in 1985 by the Oceanside Gun Rack to Carl Herbert, sixty-five, also of Oceanside. Oceanside is just a few miles from here. The gun was a Smith & Wesson Model 39 chambered for the Parabellum nine-millimeter cartridge. It is a double-action, self-loading pistol with a four-inch barrel, an aluminum-alloy frame, and an eight-round magazine. It weighs twenty-six and one-half ounces and carries a total of nine cartridges when the chamber is loaded.

I've fired several of them in my life and found them to be good, solid reliable sidearms, though I believe the nine-millimeter has insufficient stopping power for modern-day law enforcement. I carry the same 45-caliber Colt automatic used by my great-grandfather in the Pacific Theater in World War II. It has stopping power galore. I've drawn it only once on duty.

When I had come home that night, I was very disappointed that Gina hadn't called. After her escape through the rear exit of the salon, I'd hoped that she would want to talk. Sometimes Gina reacts like a particle with the same polarity as me. I reach out and she moves away just ahead of my touch. I used to wonder if that meant we're too much alike, but I don't see many similarities between us, which I believe is one of the many reasons I love and am delighted by her.

My throat had tightened as I slowly opened her side of the closet and saw so much empty space.

I especially missed her shoes because they were dainty and chipper and colorful as wildflowers, and some of them were frankly provocative. I stood there wishing I knew what she was thinking.

I opened the floor safe, which is on my side of the closet, and saw that all of her jewelry was gone. I'd never been able to afford lots of jewelry for her, but what few pieces I'd given her had been of good quality and quite beautiful. I shut the lid and spun the combination dial. I felt more fearful, knowing that she'd taken her jewelry.

I had called her cell and left a brief message. It's hard to sound casual when your heart is racing. I called Salon Sultra but Tammy said she'd gone home for the day and didn't offer to take a message.

So I sat at the computer with a worried heart, to which the Drug Fire history of the Smith & Wesson Model 39 was a welcome distraction.

According to the FBI, Carl Herbert was a retired Navy lieutenant. He had purchased the gun in May of '85 and used it in what he described as self-defense in August of the same year. He had fired at a "suspected gang car" that was cruising his street very early one morning. He missed. The car had sped away, but its driver—a young man delivering newspapers—called police a few minutes later. Apparently Mr. Herbert had bought the gun because there had been gang activity on his street and he was fed up with the noise. He was arrested and charged and later pled down to firing a gun within city limits. The nine-millimeter shell casing, however, was recovered by Oceanside PD and logged on to the regional Drug Fire registry. Drug Fire is an FBI database containing a computerized dictionary of casings fired in crimes. It was actually created for gang and drive-by shootings, where often the main evidence is ejected casings. Each casing—like each human fingerprint—is unique, because it displays unique marks from the gun that fired it. A match is a match, one of the most powerful pieces of evidence that can be presented in a courtroom.

Carl Herbert's Model 39 Smith was quiet until February of the next year, when his Cadillac was broken into and the gun stolen. Herbert reported the theft to Oceanside PD.

About a year later, the Model 39 got hot.

In April of 1987, it was used in a San Diego gang shooting. This was determined by the four empty casings left behind at the scene. Two young men were wounded in the Barrio Logan area of the city, but no fatalities. No arrests were made.

A month after that, it was used again in a National City convenience-store holdup. Two shots fired, no injuries, and no arrests.

In July the Model 39 was back on home turf and used in a drive-by shooting in Oceanside. One dead. No arrests.

Then the gun went quiet for almost two years. Like it had taken a vacation from crime or done time.

But in June of 1989, it was used to kill a drug dealer in Fresno, California. No arrests.

In December of 1994, the Model 39 left behind six casings in an Oakland, California, shoot-out that killed two members of the Mexican mafia. Four arrests were made, but the weapon was not discovered.

In September of 1999, it was used in a Houston armed robbery in which five shots were fired but nobody was hit. Two arrested, but no Model 39 in possession.

In January of 2001, it was used to kill a suspected drug-cartel enforcer in New Orleans. A midlevel cocaine trafficker named Arthur Leder was arrested, tried, and convicted of the murder. Carl Herbert's Model 39 was a star witness.

After the trial the weapon was impounded and archived as homicide evidence by the New Orleans Police Department, which is where everyone thought it was until our crime lab ran the casing in Garrett Asplundh's Explorer through Drug Fire.

What a bloody history for a twenty-six-and-a-half-ounce piece of metal. I wondered if there was a deeper, secret history that might contain even more murder and suffering, unwritten because empty casings had been picked up by shooters or overlooked by investigators or recovered but simply never checked against the Drug Fire database. I wondered if Herbert's Model 39 had ever been used to poke, prod, pistol-whip, or intimidate.

And of course I wondered how it had escaped from the New Orleans Police Department property room and traveled two thousand miles back to its hometown to murder Garrett Asplundh.

I searched the Web for New Orleans PD and found the site. Their "Law Enforcement Only" page offered a professional number and e-mail address to help other agencies, so I left a brief message. As I suspected, there was nothing in the site about the PD property section, so I tried the Web with combinations of "New Orleans," "police," and "property" and came up with dozens of real estate offerings. Some of them were reasonably priced for a police officer. I tried the online *Picayune* and found what I was looking for. The dateline was October 30 of 2001:

DRUGS, GUNS, CASH TAKEN IN
POLICE BUILDING BREAK-IN

In an embarrassing reversal of fortune for law enforcement, New Orleans Police yesterday confirmed that a warehouse used for storing felony trial evidence was broken into over the weekend. Illegal drugs, cash and firearms were taken.

The New Orleans Property Annex on W. 8th St. was entered sometime Saturday or Sunday night. Employees coming to work on Monday were alerted to the break-in when they found a rear entrance door ajar. No alarm sounded, police said.

It is believed that over $12,000 in United States currency was taken. Also believed missing is an undetermined amount of heroin. An unknown number of firearms, mostly handguns confiscated and presented as evidence at criminal trials, is also believed missing.

"We've got some egg on our face," said Sgt. Gordon Mauer of the New Orleans Police Department. "This was a sloppy, hurry-up job. But it shows how determined some criminals can be."

There have been no arrests in connection with this weekend's break-in.

Then, three days later:

PAIR ARRESTED IN P.D. ANNEX BREAK-IN;
DRUGS, GUNS AND MONEY RECOVERED

Two men were arrested yesterday on suspicion of burglarizing the downtown police Records and Property Annex last weekend.

Arrested were Manuel Cisnos, 25, and Ed Placer, 34, both of New Orleans.

Three pounds of heroin, eleven firearms and $14,000 in cash were recovered in one of the suspects' apartments, according to police. The suspects surrendered without incident.

Police are hopeful that most if not all of the evidence property stolen from the downtown facility will be recovered.

"We're hoping we got them before they had time to sell the stolen evidence," said New Orleans Police Sgt. Gordon Mauer. "We still haven't had time to tally what we found against our list of what was missing."

Two days later:

POLICE SAY NEARLY ALL EVIDENCE
RECOVERED WITH ARREST OF TWO MEN

New Orleans Police believe that almost all evidence recently stolen from a downtown police storage facility has been recovered.

"We're only missing two handguns and a half ounce of heroin," said police Lt. Mike Hines. "Which is impressive, considering what was taken."

Arrested on suspicion of last weekend's burglary of . . .

I looked for follow-up stories regarding the missing weapons but found none. By then the story had ceased to be news. I logged back on to the New Orleans PD "Law Enforcement Only" page and asked about the two missing handguns.

Then to the FBI VICAP site for more information on Manuel Cisnos and Ed Placer.

Cisnos was a junkie and small-time burglar until the annex break-in. One fall for possession of heroin, one for breaking and entering, one for possession of stolen property, one for assault and battery. He was a small, light man with a sharp face and thick black hair. He'd spent three of his seven adult years in some kind of lockup. And two years in juvenile facilities for drug violations. He'd been convicted of the annex job and sentenced to eight years. With good behavior he'd be getting out soon. His next parole-eligibility hearing would be May of this year.

Placer was a petty thief and "rare-reptile dealer" who had done time for assaulting a U.S. Forest Service ranger, illegal possession of a protected animal species—California mountain king snakes—and drunk driving. He'd turned prosecution witness against Cisnos, blaming the younger man for planning the burglary and convincing Placer to help. Placer was six-four, 260, and at the time of his burglary arrest had long brown hair. His booking mugs made him look surly and intelligent—not someone who actually could be talked into burgling a police facility. I figured he'd told a true story but conveniently swapped roles with Cisnos. He'd done nine months in a New Orleans Parish work camp and was released in late 2002.

His last known address was his mother's home in San Diego.

Finally. A little pinch of pay dirt.

Maybe the Model 39 was one of the two unrecovered guns. Maybe Ed Placer had hidden it, dug it up when he got out of prison, then headed west to see Mom and Garrett Asplundh.

I requested his ten-set from the FBI for comparison with the partials taken from the Explorer.

Then I called downtown for a records and warrants check, which gave me more or less what the Drug Fire search had given me. Placer had been clean since his release. They had the same address for him as the Bureau did.

The Louisiana Probation and Parole Field Service Law Enforcement Only Web site explained Placer's unusual privilege of being allowed to leave a state while still paroled for a felony. The mother in San Diego—Placer's only living relative—was part of the reason. The other part was the special arrangement made with the New Orleans district attorney's office during the prosecution of Cisnos.

Placer had arrived here roughly one year ago and registered with the California Parole Board as required.

I figured it was too late to get anyone at New Orleans PD who could access Property Annex records, but I left messages for Gordon Mauer, Mike Hines and Assistant Chief Dale Payne.

I hung up and called Gina's cell phone again and was told that the subscriber's number was no longer in service. I tried the salon again, but there was no answer. I called Rachel, got her voice mail, and hung up.

Fuck.

McGinty's Pub on India Street downtown is Gina's and my favorite Irish bar in San Diego. It's not the oldest, biggest, or most popular, but we have spent many a Friday evening there having drinks and sometimes dinner before heading out to party with our friends. For an Irish pub, McGinty's is an oddity because it sits in the middle of Little Italy. Gina's maiden name was Brancini but her mother's maiden name was O'Hara, so maybe an Irish pub in the middle of Little Italy is perfect for us. Me, I'm German-English and one-eighth Irish from my mother's side. McGinty's is a friendly little place, just a few blocks from the Ethics Authority Enforcement building, where Garrett Asplundh was employed.

I walked in and had to duck through the ribbons attached to festive green and silver balloons bouncing against the ceiling. And the streamers of green crepe paper wavering down. St. Patrick's day was next week, so McGinty's had all the standard decorations, plus posters promoting a lucky green pint and Harp-battered fish and chips for $9.99.

I squeezed into the last open stool at the bar and sat down in front of a giant brandy snifter half filled with small green marbles. They were minis, like I collected as a boy. Smaller than shooters and just a small fraction the diameter of boulders.

Mike the bartender came over, and I asked him for a beer and the fish and chips.

"Gina coming?"

"Not tonight. She's out with friends."

I stared at those marbles.

"Been a while since I've seen you two," Mike said.

"We've been busy, all right."

"Garrett Asplundh yours?"

I nodded.

Mike shook his head as he dried off the pint glass. "Cold work, Robbie."

"Yes, it was."

In the glittery green marbles, I saw the shattered glass of the Explorer's window. And Garrett slumped down into the space between the seat and the door like something that had leaked.

"Take some marbles if you want, Robbie. They're promotional. Little shamrocks and Irish lasses inside, see?"

He handed me a few. Sure enough, there were dark green shamrocks inside some, and little lasses with curly orange-red hair inside others. The images were suspended in the middle of the glass, like a cat's eye. The girls looked like Gina.

I detached myself from the marbles for a moment. "You know, Mike, how about a Johnnie Walker to go with that beer? That was Garrett's drink, I believe. In his honor."

"It sure was—Johnnie Walker Black on the rocks. Doubles. I'll lift one to Garrett if you're asking me to join you."

"On me, Mike."

"Not in my bar it isn't. On me."

The double scotch hit me hard because my stomach was empty and I'm not a drinker. It made me feel unbalanced in a harmless way, suddenly light and amused in spite of what was happening with my wife. I'm always amazed how Gina at 110 pounds can drink so much and appear normal. I outweigh her by eighty pounds, match her drink for drink on a Friday night, and wake up with my brain wrapped in sandpaper while she goes to an early workout at the gym. I'm lucky to drag myself out of bed by noon.

I ate the fish and chips and ordered a shepherd's pie to top it off. I'm one of those tall, wiry guys who eats a ton and doesn't put on weight. Alcohol makes me even hungrier. The pint vanished ahead of schedule so I asked for another.

"So, Mike, where do you get the promotional marbles?"

"Mexico. Fourth year in a row we've put them out. People take them by the pocketful. Had a fresh load brought up Tuesday, I think it was. Why?"

"I like them."

"You're not alone," said Mike. "But we lost half of our new shipment before they even got here. Truck tipped over and something like fifty cartons of them spilled. Five thousand of them is what I heard. Talk about losing your marbles."

"Now that's interesting."

"It's different anyway. I kept picturing guys sliding around on them and falling. You know, like a slapstick routine."

"I keep seeing cars running them over and getting them caught in their tire treads," I said.

"That could happen," said Mike.

"When did this spill take place?"

"Tuesday, it was."

Garrett's last night, I thought.

"And exactly where, Mike?"

"Right around the corner, Kettner and Hawthorn."

About halfway between here and the Ethics Authority Enforcement building, I thought.

"What time did it happen?" I asked.

"Let's see. I'd been here three hours when Donovan came in and told me about it. So the spill must have been, oh, seven o'clock or so."

I put that into Garrett's timeline on the night he died. It was well after he'd left Hollis Harris at HTA, "preoccupied" and "distracted." It was one and a half hours after he met Carrie Ann Martier at the Imperial Beach Pier and received another sex video. It was one hour before he left his not-quite-secret National City apartment, wearing the blue necktie he'd changed into. And two full hours before he was going to meet Stella in Rancho Santa Fe for a date that was supposed to be a new beginning for them.

I made a note to check with our Traffic Division and get the exact time for the accident. I was certain that because of the downtown location, the marble spill would have been reported to us.

What it looked like was that Garrett's vehicle had picked up a spilled marble a half block from where he worked at the Ethics Authority Enforcement office sometime after seven that night.

And sometime soon after that, Garrett Asplundh's plans for the evening had taken a turn drastic enough to make him miss a date with the ex-wife he still loved and was trying to reconcile with.

"Did you see Garrett that night?" I asked.

"No. No Garrett that night. The week before."

Which tallied up with a blood-alcohol level of zero.

I ate the shepherd's pie, ordered another beer and took it back to the dartboards. I played a long time, though I don't remember my opponents or any bull's-eyes I might have thrown.

Later I sat at the bar again and considered the green marbles. I took a handful of them and put them in my coat pocket. A pocketful of Ginas and lucky shamrocks. I got one more of Garrett Asplundh's doubles and drank it quickly. I felt suddenly horrible, like I was a big-screen TV with the vertical hold slipping over and over. Mike had one of the busboys take me home and I fell onto the bed sometime around midnight after checking the machine for messages, but nobody had called.

An hour later the light blasted on and Gina stood in the bedroom doorway. She was wearing her faux fox jacket and dangling her purse straps in both hands, like she was trying to decide whether she was staying or going.

"I missed you," I said. "Are you okay?"

Her face collapsed and tears like diamonds fell from her lovely green eyes. "I missed you so much, Robbie. I'm so sorry I hurt you."

"Here."

I threw back the covers and wavered across the floor and took her in my arms. My world was still swirling but somehow my world was right.

It was the most longing and needful love we ever made.

I woke early but Gina was already up. I listened for the sounds of her making coffee or perhaps the early-morning TV she sometimes liked to watch. Gina is not a quiet person in the kitchen and the silence pulled me from the bed to the living room, then the kitchen. The note she left on our breakfast table said:

Dear Robbie,

I want you to remember me like I was last night.

Good-bye.

Gina

The card she wrote it on had a picture of a fish on it. We didn't have such cards in the house so I knew she'd bought and probably even written it before coming over.

I could deny one good-bye, but two were inarguable.

She really was gone. I felt my face get hot and a quick spike of malice in my heart. I was glad there was nobody else in the house to see my foolishness and my anger.

I didn't have the spirit to do much more than read the *Union-Tribune* that day. My hangover was tremendous. It took me an hour to read the front page, an hour for sports, an hour for business.

On the front page of the business section was a picture of Jance Purdew Investments rating analyst Trey Vinson. I remembered his name from Garrett Asplundh's notes. Garrett had written something about the city cooking the books and things were now up to Vinson. Mr. Vinson had been photographed the day before as he asked questions of the Budget Oversight Committee. He was a young man with a sharp, piercing expression. He almost looked angry.

The caption read:

"Trey Vinson of Jance Purdew Investments grills the Budget Oversight Committee yesterday at City Hall regarding San Diego's financial-disclosure statements. A lower rating from Jance Purdew could cost San Diegans millions of dollars."

I not only remembered Vinson's name from Garrett's notes. I recognized his face from Garrett's video. He was the dark-haired, anxious little man with the shiny wedding ring whose dog tag dangled into Carrie Ann Martier's face.

Ed Placer lived with his mother in Logan Heights, south of downtown. It was a decent neighborhood. The house looked pugnacious compared to those around it, with wrought iron over the windows and a private security sign stabbed into a lawn of tan crabgrass.

"Cozy," said McKenzie as I pulled up and parked. It was Monday morning.

Ed Placer answered the door and immediately recognized us for what we were. I badged him, said we were working Burglary, and watched his hands. McKenzie introduced herself while his dark eyes roamed her, then locked on to mine. He was surprisingly tall. Jeans, cowboy boots, and a faded short-sleeved shirt worn untucked, which always makes me uneasy. His hair was short now, and he had a mustache and a smirk.

"We've got some questions about the loot from the annex," I said.

"I told everything in court."

"We can keep this friendly and short," I said.

"Short's good."

"Then pretend you're a gentleman and invite us in," said McKenzie.

We had decided on the drive over that even though this was just a knock and talk, we'd do it inside the house. Because Ed had been violent with law enforcement. Because he was large. Because, if he'd used Carl Herbert's stolen Model 39 to murder Garrett Asplundh, he could try something similar on us. And because we wanted to see the rare reptiles.

"Invite you in?" his eyes roamed McKenzie again. "You, sure. But maybe Junior here can stay outside, play in the street or something."

When I'm challenged in the way that Ed Placer had just challenged me, I feel a quick jolt of fury crack through my body. It's like lightning. If I wait just a second or two, it almost always fades.

So I took a deep breath and stared at him.

"Raise your hands, Ed," I said. "I'm going to pat you for weapons."

"Oh, hell, let's go inside."

"Good boy," said McKenzie, and we were in.

I patted the sides and front of his waistband, spun him around and checked his back. I cuffed him, then turned him back to face me.

"That's probably a good idea," he said. "I was feeling a strong desire to kick your ass."

"Lost your big op," I said. I felt that flicker of anger again, but that was one of the reasons you cuff creeps.

"My partner only looks like a nice guy," said McKenzie. "That's all I'm going to say. Where are the rare lizards anyway?"

"I've got all sorts of specimens. Want to see them?"

"Sure."

"Where's your mother?" I asked.

He smiled. "Sleeping. Want to see her, too?"

"Critters first," I said.

"Ever held a cobra in your bare hands?" asked McKenzie.

Ed smiled. "It can thrill you. I've got a more-or-less tame one back here if you'd like to try."

"Maybe," she said, with an odd glance at me.

We were in the living room. It was dark and close, with slouching bookshelves and defeated furniture and yellowed curtains and dust balls on the dulled hardwood floor and a television playing a soap opera in colors not found in nature.

"What's that smell?" I asked.

"Mouse piss," said Ed. "I have to raise my own mice. They stink. Snakes hardly stink at all."

"Ever held a rattlesnake?" asked McKenzie.

"Routinely. They have to be held behind the head or they bite you. Come back here. I'll show you."

The room was good-size. All four walls were covered by shelves, which ran six high, from floor to ceiling. Above each shelf was a bank of lights. The lights shone down into glass terrariums in which small, brightly colored snakes writhed and climbed and slithered and fell in hypnotic tangles.

In some containers there were lizards piled up in the corners, jumping and scampering over each other, their claws faintly audible against the glass.

Other cages housed hundreds and hundreds of wriggling white mice. Every now and then, one would bounce up like a piece of popcorn.

Ed moved between McKenzie and me.

"These are mostly juveniles, which remain active this time of year," he said. "The breeding pairs are out in the garage, where I can keep the temperature quite cool. If the adults don't overwinter properly, they don't reproduce. It's hormonal."

"Which handguns did you sell back in New Orleans?" I asked. "Out of the eleven that you and Cisnos took."

He turned away from McKenzie to look at me. "A Sig .38 and a Ruger .22."

"You're sure?"

"Don't I sound sure?"

"Yeah," I said. "You do."

"I have a good mind for snakes, lizards, and guns. That's about it, unfortunately."

I thought about that. "I'm interested in a Smith Model 39."

"The nine-millimeter autoloader," said Ed. "We got two of those from the warehouse. Great handguns. I could have made one phone call and moved them within an hour, but I got distracted."

"By the dope."

"Yep."

He turned his back on me to speak to McKenzie. "Hey, Cortez, you want to hold a cobra?"

"Not really."

"Scared?"

"Yes."

"I don't have one anyway. It's illegal in this state. Then how about a baby king snake? They're not even venomous."

"I get nervous around babies."

He glanced back at me and shrugged.

"So you never saw the Model 39s again?"

"Not after they dragged me out of that apartment. We had the guns spread out on the couch. Guns are fun to look at. Manny had already traded off the Sig and the Ruger for some speed to cut the smack. Otherwise we'd have just slept the whole time."

McKenzie had stepped up to look closer at the snakes.

"You want one, Cortez? I'll sell you one cheap. They're easy to take care of."

"How much?"

"I've got some nice Arizona mountain king snakes. Six weeks old and eating real good. Beautiful markings, really red reds. I can go a hundred for a male. Females are more. They all come with certificates of captive breeding, which keeps Fish and Game from busting you. Buy two, mate 'em and make yourself some money. My regular prices are triple that."

"So why do I get a discount?"

"Because you're so sexy."

"Yeah, I really am, aren't I?"

"We should go out."

McKenzie has almost-black eyes. When her disgust and her acne scars get together, she looks volatile.

"Never mind," said Ed Placer.

"So, Ed," I said, "what do you do around here at night?"

"Sleep, like most people."

"I'm thinking of last Tuesday."

He turned around. "You're not Burg. You're Homicide."

"I confess."

He eyed me without noticeable emotion. "The Ethics dude. He got it with a Smith 39?"

"It looks that way."

"Bet it messed him up pretty good. Newspaper said shot in the head."

I stared at him. Some men can look a cop right in the eye after killing someone and convincingly deny it. Not many, but some. Ed Placer held my stare, then disengaged without hurry.

"I was home."

"With your mom."

"Right."

"Did you go out for dinner?"

"I cooked frozen pizza. I cook every night. Mom does the dishes. She's schizophrenic, heavy meds, but she does the dishes up real clean."

"Did you go out after dinner?"

"I drove down to the store for a half gallon of vodka and some orange soda. That's what we drink around here. Mom and me."

"Which store and what time?"

"Right Spot Liquor. Eight, maybe. Take the clerk a picture of me. I go in a lot."

"Then where?"

"Right back here. Watched TV. Lights out by midnight."

I kept waiting for colored shapes to appear because few criminals can converse this long without lying. Ed struck me as manipulative, evasive, and dangerous, but I saw no signs of deception when he spoke.

"You have a girlfriend, Ed?" I asked.

"Used to. She got too serious."

Beyond Ed Placer I could see McKenzie shaking her head.

"Easy to see why," said McKenzie. "She saw all your snakes and lizards and bouncing mice and wanted you for the rest of her life."

"She actually liked them," said Ed. "I gave her a pair of Chiricahua kings and a bearded dragon, to show her there were no hard feelings."

"That was sweet."

"Did you know Garrett Asplundh?" I asked.

He gave me a surly look. "No. Ethics Authority. What the hell is that for? In a place that's got no ethics?"

"They keep the city free from corruption," I said.

"That'll be the day," said Ed. "My neighbor shot his neighbor's dog for trying to kill his cat. The guy that did the shooting was a San Diego police officer. No charges filed. Not even shooting a gun inside the city limits. Maybe the Ethics Authority should look into that."

"Great idea, Ed," I said. "Now let's meet Mom."

"She sleeps until noon."

"It won't take long."

"Take these cuffs off."

"Get Mom," I said.

McKenzie and I waited in the dusty, sun-starved living room. Ed went into one of the bedrooms and shut the door. I heard his voice. I couldn't hear what he was saying but it sounded low and soothing. I popped my holster snap, swung my sport coat back behind it, and rested my hand on the Glock. McKenzie moved to the other side of the room and did the same.

"Depressing," she said, looking around the house.

"I had a schizophrenic aunt," I said. "Her house was sloppy, too."

"Maybe when you have voices in your head, the dirt just doesn't matter."

"She died young."

"You just get swept away in the delusions," said McKenzie.

"Uncle Jerry was good to her."

The disconnected chatter was the nervous tic of cops with their hands on their guns.

Ed's mother came down the hallway. She was short and gray-haired and dressed in a blue robe. Behind her walked Ed, his hands behind his back and an embarrassed expression on his face.

"Why, hello, I'm Virginia Placer. How do you do?"

I smiled and introduced myself and McKenzie. Virginia reminded me of my aunt. Very pleasant and seemingly in the moment, but also gone. Not a thousand miles gone, just gone a little sideways, living in a world similar to ours but not the same.

"What brings you to San Diego today?" she asked.

I explained that we were just following up some leads on a case we were working. We wanted to talk to her son because of some of the trouble he'd had back in Louisiana. And we wanted to talk to her, just to make sure that she and Ed had been home last Tuesday night.

"Oh, my," she said. "I'm afraid that's impossible to say. I believe we were home, because that's what we usually do. But I have no specific memory of that night."

"Mom? Hawaiian-style pizza, with the pineapple and ham? And later I ran to the Spot for some booze and orange soda? Remember, the big orange bottle, I dropped it, and we were both surprised it didn't break?"

She looked at him with an openness and innocence that made me sad.

You could almost see the fingers of her memory reaching back in time, feeling for something to hold on to. I know how medications can make you lose your memory. After my fall my head hurt so bad they gave me pain pills that made me unaware and forgetful. The pain was better than the haze.

"Yes. I recall those things very exactly now. Yes, yes, Officers, Ed is right. We were amazed that the bottle didn't break, because orange-soda plastic is very, very thin."

Her words were totally convincing. And the red squares of deception never spilled out. But I wondered if delusional people could fool me, so long as they were fooling themselves. Then I wondered if my primitive lie detector was as good as I thought it was. I found it almost incredible that Ed Placer and his schizophrenic mother had answered questions for over half an hour but never tried to fool us.

"Ed *is* right," said Ed. "Maybe you can leave now. Mom, you can go back to bed if you want."

"Good-bye," she said. "What a pleasure it was to meet you."

McKenzie and I said likewise as Ed came toward me and turned around. I keyed open the cuffs, stepped back, and slipped them into the case on my belt. I stashed the cuffs without taking my eyes off of Ed. You never want to lose visual contact with a guy like him.

"So, Brownlaw, how do you think one of those Model 39s got from New Orleans to San Diego?" Ed asked. He offered me a disgusted smile.

"I give up."

"Pretty obvious," he said. "New Orleans cops grabbed a few choice pieces for themselves. Maybe for a throw-down. Maybe for their bed-stands. Maybe as a present for a buddy or to make some money. Retail new is what, seven, eight hundred? But some bad guy ended up with it. Stole it, maybe."

He stood there rubbing his wrists. "Or—and this is where the possibilities get fun—maybe your Ethics killer is a cop. Wouldn't that be a kick?"

"Yes, it would be."

He held open the door. "Detective Cortez, call me if you ever want to handle my cobra."

"And you stay right by that phone," said McKenzie.

I was called in by Professional Standards as we drove back downtown from Logan Heights.

"Those guys give me the crawls," said McKenzie. "Kind of like Ed back there."

"I'll tell them that."

"Keep it between us," she said. "Like the nasty DVD you burned. Fellowes with his damned socks on. Christ."

"You'll be next for Professional Standards," I said.

"Yeah. They'll separate us like criminals so we can't match our stories. I hate being treated like that by the people I work with."

Professional Standards is part of the Internal Affairs Division. These would be Garrett's people, the ones who get paid to watch the watchers. A lot of the Professional Standards officers don't work out of Broadway headquarters, so we everyday cops don't even know what they look like. One of their captains is Roger Sutherland, who is rarely seen around headquarters but who now sat at a conference room table with my boss, Captain Villas, and Assistant Chief Bryan Bogle.

Bogle shut the door behind me as we sat. The table was rectangular and not large. I was seated along one side. Sutherland sat directly across from me, Bogle to my left, and Villas to my right. Two small tape recorders sat in front of Sutherland.

"Thanks for coming," said Sutherland. Which was faintly comic because any SDPD officer who refuses to answer the questions of Professional Standards can be fired. There is no such thing as Fifth Amendment rights. A convicted criminal has more rights than an officer before Professional Standards. It is widely known in the department that Sutherland attended law school at night but could never pass the California bar. Maybe in compensation, he often seems vigorously bound to the letter of the law. He switched on both recorders.

I nodded and waited.

"Fill us in on the Asplundh investigation, will you?" he asked.

I did. Sutherland flipped open a notepad and pulled a pen from his coat pocket. He's a big man, and the pen looked small in his hand. I wished that Villas had warned me about this interview, but I was obviously not supposed to be warned. Assistant Chief Bryan Bogle leaned back with his hands behind his head, staring past me out the window.

There was a lot to tell. McKenzie and I had come up with hundreds of pages of information gathered by the victim, six hours of incriminating video, and an interesting though incomplete timeline of Garrett Asplundh's last hours. He had enemies to spare. The CSIs and crime lab had worked their usual magic. We had decent latents, a woman's earring, a broken marble, and a gun possibly stolen by someone in law enforcement and brought here all the way from New Orleans to murder Garrett Asplundh. We had a Spook Valley genius, a clever madam, Chupacabra Junior, and a Wall Street investment analyst.

I told them we liked the Squeaky Clean earring. And that the lab couldn't match the Explorer latents with Jordan Sheehan's file prints, but that didn't mean she wasn't there. Whether she pulled the trigger or not, what was her jewelry doing in Garrett's car?

We'd see her later today.

"Detective Brownlaw," said Sutherland, "I understand you recognized some of the men in Mr. Asplundh's sex video."

I looked at each of them in turn. "Yes, sir. One john was Captain Fellowes. Another was a Motor Patrol officer named Mincher. Also, Councilman Rood and his aide, Stiles. I recognized a fireman but don't know his name. And a couple of paving contractors who get a lot of city jobs. I recognized them from a fraud case I worked years ago."

Sutherland looked down at the table and shook his head.

Bogle still stared through the window.

Villas exhaled loudly.

"Detective Brownlaw," asked Sutherland, "who knows the content of these sex videos, besides you and McKenzie Cortez and Captain Villas?"

"John Van Flyke—Garrett's boss at Ethics Enforcement. And Carrie Ann Martier, the woman who compiled them. And two of her work friends. It's possible that Stiles has seen a portion or was told about it by Garrett. Martier got an apology and some money not long after she told Garrett about getting beaten by Stiles. I think Garrett was behind that. He must have used something . . . convincing."

"Have you or your partner spoken to Stiles?"

"Not yet."

"To anyone on the sex video?"

"Just Carrie."

Sutherland and Bogle traded some quick eye work. I looked out the window and thought about my wife again.

"Say nothing about these videos," said Sutherland.

"No, sir."

"Not one word."

"It would be bad."

"Bad? It would be unfair to this department and terrible for this city," said Bogle. "We need to find internal solutions."

"I know."

I knew it, but it still didn't mean much to me. The truth is I've never been interested in the political side of law enforcement, or in other men's ambitions or in palace intrigues. Even less so since the fall from the Las Palmas. All I really wanted since I was six years old was to be a cop. That's because a cop found me after I'd been chased and bitten by a dog on the way home from first grade and become lost in an unfamiliar neighborhood of Normal Heights. I was stuck down in a thorny juniper hedge where I thought I could get away from the dog. I was terrified and blubbering and bleeding and the dog was growling at me but the cop scared it away and helped me out and gave me a ride home. He called Animal Control right there from his patrol car, and they captured the dog, tested it for rabies and saved me from a series of painful abdominal injections. It may be a corny story but it's true. Later, when I was thirteen, I read *The New*

Centurions by Joe Wambaugh, and it only made me want to be a cop more. When Roy Fehler got shot in the gut the second time, I cried for his bad luck. I met Mr. Wambaugh at a party once and he's a good guy. I'm just a cop and that's all I'll ever be, because it's all I want to be.

I could tell that these men were playing on a different field than I was. They were thinking ahead, thinking around, thinking big, thinking of themselves. Spin. Proaction. Damage control. Acceptable losses. Bureaucratic triage.

"I'm just trying to find a killer," I said.

"Don't say anything about these videos to anyone," said Sutherland. "We're going to have to figure out the best way to handle it."

"Yes, sir. I just hope we don't have to cover for whoring cops very long. Fellowes has no right to those girls just because he looks the other way when he's finished."

"That's true," said Villas.

There was a pointed silence then, as Sutherland, then Bogle, looked hard at Villas.

"Let me ask you something, Brownlaw," said Sutherland. "You've spent the better part of a week looking at the life of Garrett Asplundh. You've talked to his ex and his boss and some of the people he was working with. Do you like what you've learned about him?"

"He seemed to have had integrity," I said.

"He did. He was one of us. I mean *us,* Professional Standards. He knew what standards were, believe me. He knew them in his heart. In the end he wasn't able to stay with us, because of other things in his life. But Garrett knew things. He understood things. He knew how the city works and how this department works and how people behave. He knew everything about everybody. And never once did Garrett go outside these walls with what he found. He always came back here with it. Internal solutions for internal problems. Van Flyke understands that. As does Director Kaven."

Three looks in my direction. Brass is allergic to the idea of scandal. If the brass is a bun boy—that's an officer who has worked his way up through desk jobs instead of working the streets—he'll get hysterical at the mere possibility of scandal. Sutherland was just such a man.

For a moment I tried to distract myself, which wasn't hard. I realized again, for the millionth time since Saturday morning, that Gina had left me, probably forever, and I tried to blame myself for sleeping too drunkenly to wake up and stop her. But really, I doubt that it would have mattered. And the anger I felt at her and at myself that morning was still there inside me. I wondered if she went in to work today. I wondered what she would do if I showed up at the Salon again.

I must have distracted myself quite well, because the conversation took a sudden turn.

"How are you feeling these days, Detective?" asked Bogle.

"Oh, fine. Thank you."

"No problems with equilibrium?"

"None at all."

"What about vision or hearing?"

"All fine, sir. The doctor checked me out in January. Full physical. I'm healthy."

"That's really good, Robbie," said Bogle. "I'm glad to hear that."

"Tell us about the book," said Sutherland. *"Fall to Your Life!"*

That was a surprise. I explained that Malic had written it to explain what he did and to help other people realize they can overcome problems and start new lives.

"And that's you on the cover?" asked Sutherland.

I nodded.

"We're told he shares the profits with you," said Sutherland.

"I get twenty-five percent. It comes to two-fifty per book."

Sutherland checked back through his notes. "You know, Detective, you signed a confidentiality agreement when you went to work here. You're not allowed to publish information about the San Diego Police Department unless it's submitted to us beforehand."

"I didn't write anything, sir."

"You granted an interview to Mr. Malic, though, didn't you?"

"Not formally. We got to know each other during the trial. I told him some personal things. Not much, really. And nothing about the department except that everyone here was pulling for me after the fall."

"But interviews are very specifically covered under that CA you signed," said Sutherland.

"Come on, Roger," said Villas. "It's a dumb book but it shows that Robbie is a good officer and that reflects well on all of us. Who cares if he makes some beer money off of it?"

Sutherland lowered a bored stare at Villas.

"IRS might," said Bogle.

"Well, then let Robbie worry about the IRS. He's a big boy. Robbie, don't forget to report your millions in royalties come April," said Villas.

"What's the point of this?" I asked.

"Robbie, these guys were just a little worried," said Villas. "Because of the book. They thought you might be tempted to somehow use or profit from what Garrett had found out. I told them you would never use your experience here for personal gain. But they don't know you like I do. They just wanted to hear it from you."

"I would never use what I learn here for personal gain," I said. "I don't operate that way."

Sutherland and Bogle nodded without enthusiasm.

"If Fellowes knew that Garrett had him caught on video," I said, "that could be a motivation."

"Fellowes didn't shoot Asplundh," said Sutherland. "That's ridiculous."

"I have to talk to him, sir. And I can't pretend that Garrett didn't have him on tape with the girls. You don't have to worry about Chet Fellowes telling the world about our internal problems. He *is* our internal problem. One of them anyway."

Sutherland looked at me with a hostile calm.

"You might not want to tie Robbie's hands like that," said Villas. "If he tells Fellowes that Garrett had sex tapes, maybe that's enough. Let Fellowes sweat it, not knowing if he was caught or not."

Sutherland looked to Villas, then back to me. "Talk to Fellowes. Acknowledge the existence of the discs but not *who* is on them."

I nodded and stood.

"I want the discs and all copies of them on my desk in ten minutes," Sutherland said. "Forget you ever saw them. It's eleven-forty now, and you are dismissed."

Dale Payne, assistant chief of New Orleans Police, returned my call just after lunch. I was at my desk, thinking about what Sutherland and Bogle had said, wondering why fear was the number one motivator in our bureaucracy.

Payne spoke with the unhurried pace and sly humor of many southerners. In my earlier message I had told him briefly about the murder of Garrett Asplundh, and that I wanted to know what his department had done with the guns recovered from the Property Annex burglary of 2001.

"We put some of 'em back in the annex," he said. "I mean, we made some changes to that annex first. Installed a real good alarm system. Don't know why the old one never worked right. And we got new locks on the doors and windows. We've got an officer at the desk twenty-four/seven now. I don't think we're going to get burglarized again, Detective Brownlaw, but I never get tired of surprises. Some agencies wanted their evidence back, though. Got tired of us givin' away their goodies, I think."

I gave him the serial number for Carl Herbert's Model 39 and asked him where it was supposed to be.

"Let me see what I've got here," he said.

I could hear the tapping of his keyboard, a slow "nope," then more strokes.

"Well, okay, here it is," he said. "That Smith nine-millimeter is still here, safe and sound in the newly fortified Property Annex."

"No, it's here in San Diego, and it was used to kill a man."

"My computer says we've still got it."

"You don't."

"Let me check before we get our panties in a bunch. I'll call you right back."

I sat back and looked out the window. Half of my mind was still upstairs in Sutherland's conference room and the other half was in New Orleans, where Dale Payne was searching for a weapon he wouldn't find.

Five minutes later he called back.

"Well, I don't know why we can't keep track of that gun," he said. "But apparently we can't, because you're right—it isn't here. I've got the intake forms right here in front of me, the ones we filled out after the guns were recovered and the trial was over. And they say we kept that gun right here. But it isn't right here. Not unless it changed itself into some other kind of weapon."

I wondered if we could be off by one numeral or letter on the Smith & Wesson factory serial number.

"Do you have other Model 39s?" I asked.

"Yeah, but the numbers aren't even close."

I thought for a moment. "The agencies that wanted their weapons back after the burglary—do you have a record of who took what?"

"Well, yes, that'd be the release forms. Let me see. Okay, one of our sheriff departments figured they could hold on to their own evidence better than we could. Not that they *said* that in a direct fashion. Then the DEA and ATF—they wanted theirs back, too. We signed out four guns."

"But you kept the Smith nine that ended up here?"

"This is really damned unacceptable, Detective Brownlaw. I'm going to make some inquiries, you can bet on that."

"Can you send me copies of the intake and release forms?"

"I'll fax them right over. Good luck on your case, Detective. I'm sorry I couldn't be the kind of help you needed."

"You may have been more help than you think."

When the faxes came through a few minutes later, I was wondering what I thought I'd find. I don't know what I was expecting. There was one intake form for each weapon returned to the annex after the trial—a total of eleven forms.

New Orleans Sheriffs had taken back a Taurus .38. The release form was signed by a Sergeant Willis Simms.

DEA agent Bob Cramer had signed out a Colt Python. ATF agent Barbara Keene had reclaimed an M16 and a sawed-off Remington 1100 and signed the release forms.

All three of the release forms were signed by Lieutenant Darron Wight of New Orleans PD.

Clearly it was New Orleans PD that had lost the weapon—or, worse, a Property Annex insider had stolen it for use or sale.

I sat for a moment as something far back in the detail heap of my mind began to stir. New Orleans. New Orleans. I'd been there once with Gina for a brief vacation. It was pretty and hot and I gained weight on the delicious food. I really wanted to take a swamp tour and we saw alligators, cottonmouths, snapping turtles, and nutria, though Gina with her fair skin was uncomfortably hot.

From my duplicate of Garrett's laptop hard drive, I called up one of his voluminous files of information on the johns that Carrie Ann Martier and her friends had entertained. I used the "edit" icon to search the files for "New Orleans."

Nothing in the first or second files. Nothing in the third.

But in the fourth I found what I had so dimly remembered. There was in fact a reference to New Orleans.

Officer Ron Mincher had been employed there before coming to SDPD.

I called one of my friends in Personnel and got her to check Mincher's file for his hire date here and his years of employment at NOPD. It's nice when department clerks will do you a favor now and then. I'd signed a copy of *Fall to Your Life!* for her son.

Mincher had been hired here in December of 2002. He had been an officer in good standing with the New Orleans PD until he quit Louisiana in November of 2002 and made his trip to the Golden State.

I checked the New Orleans PD intake forms that Payne had faxed over. The Model 39 had been booked back into the Property Annex two months before Mincher had quit and headed west for the Golden State. It was there for his taking.

I called Captain Villas and asked him if he could find out if Ron Mincher had worked Tuesday night, March 8. If the inquiry came from Villas, it would have weight and little suspicion around it. If the request came from me, it had little weight but tons of suspicion.

He rang me a minute later and said that Mincher had gotten off at five that afternoon.

I called back Dale Payne in New Orleans and asked him if Lieutenant Darron Wight was still in good standing with the NOPD.

"Why, sure," he said. "Darren's moved himself up to captain."

"Did he have help with the release transactions?" I asked.

"What kind of help, Detective Brownlaw?"

"Well, would Darron Wight have been working alone on the weapons releases? Wouldn't a lieutenant have some help?"

"I see what you're getting at. Yes, he'd have had some help."

"Was it Ron Mincher?"

"I remember Ron. He's out your way now— Oh, damn, I see where you're going with this."

A moment of quiet then, as the possibility sank into Dale Payne's mind. "I'll find out," he said.

I tried to picture the release transactions. I asked Payne if the annex was busy or quiet, large or small, windows or none.

"The annex, it's about fifty thousand square feet," said Payne. "And the room there where the intakes and releases take place, it's a big one. Little slots for windows, vertical slots. Lousy light. There's a counter and holding lockers behind it. There's a copier right there because the forms always need to be duplicated. There's chairs to sit and wait if you have to, and a water jug with a stack of paper cups."

"What about the officers who came to claim their weapons?" I asked. "Did they bring partners?"

"I couldn't tell you."

"But you'd have the names of any partners who were there, right? For instance, if Cramer's partner was with him, they both would have signed in, right?"

"Sure, yeah, that's right."

"Can you get me the full roster for those three release procedures? New Orleans PD, Sheriffs, feds, everybody who signed in. It's a lot to ask, I know. But somebody out there in New Orleans made off with that Smith and it ended up killing an ex-cop here in San Diego."

A moment of silence. "Detective, that's one tall order. We don't have the sign-in sheet on computer. It's just a pad on a clipboard, you know, so we have a good handwriting sample if we need it. The professional visitors sign in, and at the end of the day we strip off the sheet so there's a clean one for the next day."

"But what do you do with the sheet?"

"We keep it for . . . I'm not sure how long. I'll see if we have it. It's going to take a little time."

I drove down Broadway and past Petco Park and found a spot on Fourth in the Gaslamp Quarter. It was warm, and some of the restaurants were doing good business. I walked north, feeling betrayed by Sutherland and Bogle. Betrayed because they were more worried about the image of the department than the murder of an apparently good man.

John Van Flyke and a man who looked very much like Garrett Asplundh sat at a sidewalk table of Panchito's in the pleasant March sun. Van Flyke introduced me to Samuel Asplundh, who rose and shook my hand. Samuel looked somewhat like Samantha, too—his niece and namesake. He had a sharp, unhappy glint in his eyes and a half-finished beer before him. He wore jeans and a white dress shirt, a loose corduroy sport coat and cowboy boots. He said he'd be available to help the investigation in any way he could. I told him I would appreciate an invitation to any memorial service or funeral that Garrett might be given, and I knew a young woman who asked to be included also. He gave me the specifics right then and there and said my partner and I, and the young woman, would be welcome.

Stella Asplundh came from the restaurant. She looked the same as the first time I'd met her—exceptionally beautiful and almost completely spent. There was something about her that made me think of my fall. She had fallen too, and I wondered if some important part of her had not survived. She acknowledged me with a small nod.

Van Flyke stood and pulled out a chair for her. I noted the attentiveness with which he pushed it in. Then he sat and regarded me from behind his sunglasses, red hair brushed back from his big face, arms crossed. He seemed annoyed.

I handed him the copies of the hard drive that McKenzie had run from Garrett's laptop.

"Nice work, Brownlaw. Maybe I could tempt you with a job in Ethics Enforcement someday."

"I doubt it. But like you said, everything in a person's life can change in an instant."

"I said that?"

Sam sipped from his beer.

"Why don't you join us?" Stella asked.

Van Flyke turned his shaded gaze down the avenue.

"No thank you," I said. "I'm going to have lunch with my wife."

I headed up the avenue toward Salon Sultra. Even on Monday it's open and busy.

I waited at the reception desk while Tammy talked on the phone. Gina was not there and her chair was empty. My stomach felt funny. Rachel saw me midclip, excused herself from her client and waved me outside.

"Where is she?" I asked.

"She left town, Robbie. She's gone."

It took me more than a second to believe that. But in my heart I knew it was true. I felt the anger gather inside me again. I was surprised how fast it could form.

"She said she wasn't happy," said Rachel. "She thinks there's more."

"More *what*?"

"I'm just telling you what she said."

"You covering for her? Is there a guy?"

"There's no other man. She wanted me to tell you that."

I saw no sign of deception in her words.

"And what else did my wife want you to tell me about her?"

"Don't get pissed at me, Robbie."

"What else?"

"That was all, actually."

I stood there for a moment, watching the cars go past in the sun. A warm wind had blown away the fog and a couple of poppies had opened in a planter along the sidewalk. But my heart was hard with anger and my hands felt heavy and thick.

"I want to talk to her."

"I do, too. I think she's making a terrible mistake."

"Where did she go, Rachel? Don't give me the bullshit you're so good at giving. If she'd tell anybody, it would be you."

"I thought so, too. I feel betrayed. I'm really sorry. But, Robbie? You're going to be all right."

The orange triangles of pity bounced into the air in front of her. She pressed her face through them and kissed me on the cheek. She looked into my eyes, kissed me on the other cheek, then turned and pushed through the mirrored salon door.

Jordan Sheehan was a tall, full-bodied, and very pretty woman. She looked like she could endorse a high-quality detergent or a tooth whitener.

She met us at the front door of her La Jolla home that afternoon and shook our hands and asked us in. She was wearing a sleeveless dress, red with big white polka dots. Around her waist was a shiny red belt. She was barefoot and her toenails were the same glistening red.

Her house was up on a hill overlooking the Pacific. It was not impressively large. The building looked somehow Castilian, a tall rectangle with wooden shutters and window planter boxes that dangled bright purple bougainvillea down the white plaster walls. Beyond the house the ocean was blue and casually vast. The garage had been converted into guest quarters. It was a miniature version of the house, nearly lost in a jungle of trumpet vine that made the air sweet. A light blue Porsche was parked in the driveway.

Inside, the house was sunny and simple. It had slate floors and honey-colored maple furniture and cabinetry and big, bright oil paintings on the walls.

"My office is distracting—all phones and files, so let's just sit here in the living room," she said. "Can I get you something to drink?"

We both declined. I sat on a cushy white couch and set my briefcase on the floor.

The Squeaky Clean Madam walked barefoot to her kitchen and came back a moment later with a tray and three tall glasses.

"Do you like Arnold Palmers?" she asked with a smile. She set out decorative tile coasters, then drinks on the low table between us. "It's sun tea, with lemonade made of lemons from my garden. Now, what can I do for you?"

"When was the last time you saw Garrett Asplundh?" I asked.

"I saw him a week before he died, out at the San Diego Yacht Club. It was a black-tie fund-raiser for the Cancer Society."

"Did you talk?" asked McKenzie.

"Briefly. I've known him for years."

"Tell us about that," I said.

"He pulled me over for drunk driving fifteen years ago. I was in the midst of a bankruptcy filing and discovering that half of my employees had either lied to me or used fake papers to get their jobs. The IRS was crushing me. My boyfriend had made off with a lot of my money and my best girlfriend. I was twenty-five years old. So I went to the Hyatt, found myself a seat in the highest bar in the city and got myself more loaded than a girl should ever get. On my way home Garrett Asplundh pulled me over. I told him everything that was happening to me and he actually listened. He was so cute in that uniform and so seriously unhappy at all the bad luck I was having. I asked him to marry me and I really meant it, but he said I was too late and arrested me instead. A good thing. I was death on wheels that night."

"He was a patrolman back then," I said.

"And what were you, Detective Brownlaw, a freshman in high school?"

"Yes."

She sipped her drink. "Anyway, as I'm sure you and everybody else in this town knows, I did a night in the drunk tank and a year in federal lockup for tax evasion. It was a vile place. It was filthy and cruel. But I studied investment strategy and got lots of exercise. Garrett visited me twice during that time. Brief visits. He was looking out for me. He liked me and I liked him. When I got out, I moved back to Iowa for a while to be with my family. I felt like I was a hundred years old but I was only twenty-seven. Got my B.A. in business from the state college. Got married and divorced. Made some money with tech investments. Actually, a lot of money, which wasn't hard with the market going up twenty and thirty percent a year. But it wasn't just luck and I knew I could help people do the same thing. I came back here in 2000 and hung my shingle. It said 'Jordan Sheehan & Associates, Investments.' I was not able to become certified as a financial adviser because of my felony convictions, but I started making good money for my people, very quickly. Word spreads when somebody can make money for someone else. I saw Garrett Asplundh around. San Diego's a small town for being a big city. And we'd meet for coffee every few months. Just to keep in touch, you know? When I saw the news, I thought about him and I cried."

She watched me.

"We have the video of you finding his hidden camera," I said.

Then a small smile. "Oh, that. Garrett was trying to implicate me in some sort of pandering and prostitution conspiracy. I thought a trick like that was below him. That was the new Garrett."

"New?" I asked.

"He changed when Samantha died. That's what death does, isn't it? It changes the people who are left behind. After she died, Garrett seemed to become . . . what's the word? He became supercharged. He became driven. He became a . . . crusader. The casual, nice-looking young man was gone. He hardly ever smiled. He looked at you like he was booking you. I'll bet if you asked him why, he'd say it was a way of doing something for his daughter. And maybe doing something for his own guilt at what happened. Anyhow, I'm not sure what the hidden camera was supposed to catch, but I couldn't resist busting Garrett for his bad manners."

"He's got videos of your girls with all kinds of customers."

She looked at me with mild irritation. "They are not my girls. What makes you believe they're my girls?"

Three red squares slipped from Jordan Sheehan's mouth, betraying her lie.

"I know some of them," I said. "They talk."

"I've heard that from other people, you know. Everyone knows one of my girls. And yet not a single one of these girls has come forward and accused me. Or charged me. Or presented evidence against me. Why don't you just get them to file a complaint or whatever you call it, and be rid of me?"

"Because they're breaking the law and they know it," I said.

"Because of Chupa Junior," said McKenzie.

"Because of those sharp lawyers you provide," I said.

"Because they're afraid," said McKenzie. "And they don't want to bite the hand that feeds them."

Jordan nodded along. "Well, those are all valid reasons. But if I'm taking such good care of my alleged employees, maybe you should quit harassing me. Maybe you should go out there and do something about the crime rate in this city. There was a big *Union-Tribune* article about that in the paper just yesterday. The violent crime rate is up three percent."

"Chupa Junior doesn't take good care of people," said McKenzie.

"I'm thirty-percent owner of a San Diego nightclub called Indigo," said Sheehan. "Peter Avalos, which is his real name, does security work for me there occasionally. He is not a *chupacabra.* He is not a goatsucker. He's honest and operates within his own moral code. He is a bouncer. And by the way, we were working at Indigo the night Garrett was killed, so you can scratch both of us off your list."

No red squares.

"Neat moral code that allows for car theft and cockfighting," said McKenzie. "You ever seen what those birds do to each other?"

Jordan looked at me. "We've all done things we regret. For instance, Vic Malic regrets throwing you from the Las Palmas. He did that. It is a known fact. Now he's written a book about it, so other people—"

"Please, Ms. Sheehan," I said, "spare us the condescending nonsense, will you? We know you're running fifty or sixty girls around town in their cute little convertibles and pretty clothes. We know you charge a nice meet tax and you've got a bunch of spot callers to make the arrangements. Garrett had videodiscs of men buying sex from these young women. Some of these men are in positions of power. One of them is a Vice captain who gets his fun for free, and maybe that's why Vice hasn't shut you down. For now, that's between you and Vice. What we're interested in here is murder. We need to know if any of those men on Garrett's video knew what was happening. If they ever said anything about being recorded or blackmailed or harassed. We want to know who was onto Garrett, and we think you're in a good position to know."

Sheehan set her drink on the table. "Detectives, I have heard nothing of the sort. I have no idea what kind of smut Garrett had in his possession. And no idea how he got it. Why should I? I'm an investor and an investment adviser."

A few more red squares slipped from between her lips.

McKenzie shook her head and looked around the bright, pretty room. "That's how you got all this? A tax cheat giving investment advice?"

"People change. Or are you too jaded in your line of work to understand that? I have a license to run my business and a small clientele that is prosperous and satisfied with my service. I'm honest and I work hard. I make good money. Not a fortune, but I live well and set my own hours. I rent this house, because tax cheats don't get mortgage loans. I drive a late-model Porsche but my payments are substantial. I'm doing okay for myself. I've socialized with the chief of police and several high-ranking officers, Director Kaven of Ethics, most of the city council, and dozens of the business leaders of this city—from Abel Sarvonola on down. Prostitution? I don't have time to run a prostitution ring because I'm too busy working. And I can promise you, I'll *never* go back to lockup as long as I live."

The air was suddenly bobbing with red squares. They jostled each other, corners tipping against other corners, and made interesting geometric patterns against the white polka dots of her red dress.

I opened the briefcase and arranged my laptop on the table. I booted up and retrieved the eight-second video of Jordan and Garrett. Then I pointed the screen toward Jordan and hit "play."

Oh, Garrett, what's this?
My window on the world.
You must think I'm a real idiot.

Jordan watched the clip with a grin on her face. I replayed it and stopped when she'd smoothed back her hair and revealed the earring. She held the iced-tea glass close to her lips but didn't drink. After her last line, she looked up and smiled at me.

"I should have been in pictures," she said.

"You'll be TV-movie material when Vice gets done with you," said McKenzie.

"Can I please cast you as the beautiful detective?" asked Jordan. "And you, Robbie, as the intelligent, honorable man who finds out that the Squeaky Clean Madam really isn't a madam after all?"

"I'll talk to my agent," I said. Then I pulled out a copy of the crime-lab photo of the inside of Garrett's car and set it on the table beside the laptop, facing Jordan.

She leaned forward, smoothed her hair behind her ear just like she was doing on Garrett's unhidden video. She looked at me to see if I'd caught the coincidence, smiling when she saw that I had. Her smile was inclusive and playful.

"This is the inside of Garrett's Explorer four to seven hours after he was shot," I said. "The dark liquid you see so much of is his blood. The pink and yellow tags were put there by the CSIs, to mark where certain pieces of evidence were located."

Jordan set her drink down, leaned back, and fixed me with a very cool stare. "Is this necessary?"

"Yes," I said. "See this arrow here? The perspective is foreshortened, but it indicates the space between the driver's seat and the console. Well, you can't see the yellow tag, but it was put there to mark where they found this."

Next to the Explorer picture, I set a digital photo of the crescent-moon earring with the sapphire in the curve and the misshapen backing.

I watched her closely. She looked from the picture to the screen of the laptop, then back to the picture.

"That's funny," she said.

"I missed the joke," I said.

"No, no," she said quietly. "I meant no disrespect to Garrett. What I meant was, I lost that earring—or one just like it—at a party in San Diego back in January. I didn't notice until I got home that night."

"Convenient," said McKenzie.

"You can buy those at Macy's for a hundred ninety-nine a pair. I did. The box said 'Made in China.' Mine couldn't have been the only pair sold in Southern California."

"How was the party?" I asked.

"Very nice," said Jordan. "I was honored as one of Fifty San Diegans to Watch, by a local magazine. Because I got ditched by my best friend and boyfriend years ago, then thrown in prison, then went on to run a successful company, I'm newsworthy. Everyone is impressed by success, aren't they? I don't really want to be kept an eye on, but we celebrated at the Hotel del Coronado. Did you know that *The Wizard of Oz* was written there?"

"Everybody in San Diego knows that," said McKenzie. "Have you ever been in Garrett's Explorer?"

"Yes. Late February he gave me a ride back from the Cancer Society party."

"Why?"

"He wanted to talk. Our twice-a-year get-together, like I said earlier."

"What did you talk about?" asked McKenzie.

"Garrett said he was happy with the Ethics Authority work. Said it was less pressure than being a cop. He had apparently helped a young woman avoid a life of prostitution and was pleased about that."

"She told us you sent her on a call," I said.

"No, Robbie. I did not. I told Garrett the same thing."

"Then one of your spot callers sent her," said McKenzie.

She sighed and looked out to the lazy gray Pacific. "You're such nice people, but I'm really getting tired of you. Maybe I've helped you enough? Terrific, then."

She stood and looked at the pictures again. "Wait here. I can offer you something that might help."

She left the room in a swirl of red and white polka dots. Her bare heels made a thunking sound on the slate. A moment later she was back with a small tan jewelry box. She handed it to me and I opened it. I looked down at the neat little crescent moon and the sapphire reclining in the curve. It was smaller and prettier than it had looked in the crime lab or on Garrett's video.

"The backing is different than the one you found," she said. "Look."

I pried the little insert out of the box and tipped it over. Sure enough, the backing to Jordan's earring was an ornate octagon with rolled edges. And the one in the picture was a circle.

"Dum da dum-dum," she sang. "See you later, guys. And thanks for everything. I hope you catch whoever did this to Garrett. I hope he spends a year in federal lockup. Then I hope you give him a shot like an old poodle and smile down on him while his lights go out."

Ninth District City Councilman Anthony Rood met with us in his City Hall office. He was a dapper young man, dressed in an expensive and well-tailored navy suit. His shoes and belt were black and magnificently polished. He used both of his hands to shake one of ours.

"I'm happy to meet you, Detectives," he said. "I scarcely knew Garrett Asplundh but I'll tell you what I know."

He stood behind his desk, smiling. There were plaques and awards and pictures of children on the wall in back of him.

"You might want to close that door," said McKenzie.

"Oh? Sure."

Rood returned and sat. "What can I do for you?"

"You can tell us what you know about the Squeaky Cleans," I said.

"Squeaky Cleans?" he asked. "I'm not sure what you mean."

The red squares of the lie spilled from his mouth. Sometimes the squares bounce and lilt in the air, like balloons. Sometimes they line up side by side like boxes on a shelf and don't move unless I touch them. Rood's stood at attention.

"Sure you're sure," said McKenzie. "Jordan Sheehan's girls."

Rood's face turned red. Not as red as the squares in front of him but still a full, vivid red.

"Mr. Rood," said McKenzie, "I've never seen a man blush so deeply. It's really kind of handsome on you. But don't tell me you haven't been with some of the Squeaky Clean Madam's girls, because we've got video of you in action. Yeah, that's right. It isn't pretty."

We let him stew. His expression went from shame to fear to petulance to resolve. The red squares diminished and were gone.

"I don't believe you," he said.

"Wrong words," said McKenzie.

I took a folded piece of paper from my pocket and handed it to Rood.

He opened it and the red flooded back into his face. He refolded the picture and flicked it back at me.

"So we need some answers," I said.

Rood nodded, placed his elbows on his desk, and squared himself in his chair. "I . . . am acquainted with some of the young women called Squeaky Clean girls. I've met Jordan Sheehan socially and know of no connection between her and the girls. The women have never told me of a connection between them and Jordan. It appears that the label 'Squeaky Clean Madam' may be of the police department's making. I have certainly never, *ever* paid money for sex—from alleged Squeaky Clean girls or anyone else."

"You tipped Carrie Ann Martier two hundred dollars on a video that I saw," I said. "Do you usually tip your lovers? Do you offer them apartments in return for sex?"

Rood's face looked painfully red. "If she was a working girl, then I was fooled. I was lied to and manipulated. Not only by her but—" He took a deep breath and let it out slowly.

"How did you meet Carrie Ann Martier?" I asked.

He looked at the ceiling. He looked at his hands. He looked into the space between McKenzie and me but he didn't look at us.

"Jordan Sheehan asked me if I'd be interested in meeting a friend who had expressed an interest in me. That evening after work, Carrie and I met at a bar in Del Mar. There was no offer of prostitution, no implication, no money. Carrie's a party girl, not a hooker."

"What's that going to matter to your wife?" I asked.

"Very little."

"It matters to us a lot," said McKenzie.

"What do you want from me? I only met Garrett Asplundh once. He seemed very intense and professional. I don't know anything about his life or his death—except what I've read in the papers. His daughter, the swimming pool, everything."

I waited for another rush of red squares but there was none.

Rood looked from me to McKenzie, then back to me again. He took another deep breath and let it out slowly. He bowed his head. "I had no idea that Carrie was a professional. I'm devastated."

Out came the symbols of the councilman's dishonesty, red squares marching in formation through the air toward me.

"I swear upon the graves of my children I didn't know."

The red battalion came at me. If the squares had had substance and weight, I'd have been knocked off my chair.

"Did you know that Garrett had you on video?" I asked.

"My God, of course not."

"Did you know that Stiles had been caught?"

"Steve? No, I had no idea."

The red flood kept pouring out. Rood's panicked gaze went back and forth between McKenzie and me again.

"What do you want from me? I've never been blackmailed before. I'm not sure of the protocol."

McKenzie smiled and shook her head. "You're funny, Councilman." She took out her notepad, flipped it open and clicked her pen three times. "Let's start with Tuesday evening, March eighth."

"I was at an exploratory fund-raiser aboard the *Midway*. I'm interested in running for a seat in the state assembly."

"I hope you win it and move to Sacramento," said McKenzie. "Maybe the Gubernator can keep you out of trouble."

"What did Jordan want in return?" I asked. "She introduced you to a wonderful woman who was very interested in you, even though you're married. All you had to do was tip her when it was over. So what did Jordan want from you?"

"What do you mean?"

"He means, she did you a favor," said McKenzie.

"No," said Rood. "I have no idea what you mean."

The red squares were dribbling out again.

"Think hard," I said. "Jordan needed something. She was interested in something. Something you could arrange for her. You'll think of it."

I sat and stared at him. McKenzie looked up from her pad and waited. "Robbie, let's just go downtown, get him his lawyer, and do this the old-fashioned way. This is too time-consuming."

"Shit, no," said Rood.

"What did she want, Anthony?"

He looked into deep space again. "I . . . really . . ."

"You really have no choice but to talk to us," said McKenzie. "It's either now or downtown with the bright lights on you and the newspaper guys dying to know what's going on."

"Oh, shit, no."

"She's right," I said.

"Jordan told me that she's very interested in . . . well, in helping the city she loves."

It took a moment for me to get it. "She wants an appointment."

"It seems so."

"To what?" I asked.

"The Budget Oversight Committee."

"Abel Sarvonola's financial watchdogs," I said.

Rood nodded. "The way the Oversight Committee is formed is that the mayor gets two picks. And each councilmanic district gets one. If I make the assembly and Steven fills my spot in the Ninth District . . . well, Jordan was hoping I'd influence Steven on her behalf."

McKenzie laughed. "That's a good one. A convicted tax cheat and madam on the Budget Oversight Committee. Making sure the city's budget is balanced and fair."

Rood was staring at his desk now. "I never saw what Jordan Sheehan could bring to the party myself."

"You know exactly what she can bring to a party," I said.

"With Carrie, I . . . avoided my problems. I admit it. My marriage was a wreck long before I met Jordan Sheehan, if that makes you feel any better."

"What did Stiles say about Garrett's murder?" I asked.

Rood looked up at me. "Steve was with me that night too, on the *Midway,* so you don't have to badger him. But what he said was that Garrett was bad for business and he got what he had coming."

I stood in Garrett Asplundh's North Park apartment and looked at the hundreds of faces of Stella and Samantha. It was odd to see Stella in the prime of her happiness, then compare her to the woman I'd seen a few hours earlier outside the Gaslamp restaurant. The difference in age couldn't have been more than ten years at the most. In some pictures less than two years. But what a drastic reduction. Samantha seemed to have smiled for most of her three brief years on earth.

I walked the room slowly, looking at the black-and-white photographs, dodging the weightlifting machines that took up so much of the space. I could hear McKenzie in the next room, opening and closing closets and drawers and talking on her cell phone.

I sat down at the workstation by the window and slid "The Life and Death of Samantha" into the DVD player of Garrett's home computer. I looked at the beautiful tooling on the custom leather cover, propped it up against the computer tower.

Then I rolled back in the chair, crossed my arms, and watched.

The video opened with pregnant Stella. Garrett slid into view on the couch beside her. It was a sunny living room. Beyond the windows were green hills and scattered homes. He kissed her and put his hand on her middle.

"Well, here we are," he said. "Two going on three. Three months to go and look at this! How are you feeling, Stell?"

She smiled. "Wonderful, but I'll be glad to have little Sam on the ground. That camera makes me feel silly, Garrett."

"Then I'll turn it off."

And so on. The next part was Stella closer to birth. Then closer still. Then a countdown of days. There was a nice pace and balance to it, and I could tell that Garrett had the same knack for video that he had for still photography. Stella became more beautiful and Garrett looked fuller and more energetic with each installment. Finally the birth, in which Garrett was presented tiny Samantha while a very pale Stella smiled with exhaustion and accomplishment.

"Oh, gosh," said Garrett as he smiled down on his newborn daughter. Then he looked up at the camera, his eyes running over with tears. *"Look!"*

McKenzie stood beside me, folding her cell phone.

"Tough to watch," she said. "When you know what happens."

I nodded.

"I just talked to Wasserman," she said. "He couldn't match any of the Explorer latents with Ed Placer's ten-set."

"I didn't think he would."

"No," said McKenzie. "Big Ed was home with Mom drinking spiked orange soda because his girlfriend got too serious."

"Found any loosely woven brown wool garments in the closet back there?"

"Not a one, Robbie. I think those brown fibers in the Explorer came from somebody else's wardrobe."

On-screen, newborn Samantha was wrapped in blankets and asleep, her head covered by a small pink cap.

"Mind if I watch?" asked McKenzie.

"Pull up a chair."

Nearly all of the video of Samantha's life was shot by her father. Garrett's clear voice described the settings and events, but you didn't see much of him. Stella was often on-screen with her daughter. There seemed nothing unusual about Samantha's growing up. She was a dark-haired, fine-featured girl, apparently an even physical mix between mother and father. Like a lot of children, she seemed to consist not only of her parents' features but also of independent, unrelated ones. There was video of her in the crib. In new outfits. Crawling. Playing with toys. Taking her first steps. Toddling with increasing confidence. Walking, running, laughing, mugging. Birthdays, Christmases, Easters.

Then the Fourth of July party at which she drowned. Garrett and Stella were the hosts, which I remembered from the papers at that time. The party video started with Stella and Samantha setting out Statue of Liberty napkins on a long outdoor picnic table. Garrett set the date and event—"The 2004 Asplundh Fourth of July Pool, Barbecue, and Fireworks Blowout."

Then a shot of the pool—no guests had arrived yet—with its still-clear water and the red, white, and blue ribbons tied to the trees and shrubs around it. The pool looked truly ominous because I knew what would happen that day. Samantha burst into the picture from behind her cameraman father, who shouted at her to *"slow down, honey!"* as the girl approached the pool.

Next were short scenes of people arriving, hugging, making drinks. I saw a woman who had to be Stella Asplundh's mother, and an old Professional Standards lieutenant who had retired later that summer, and John Van Flyke looking uncharacteristically festive in a Hawaiian shirt with a woody and surfboards on it.

Then a long left-to-right pan of adults sitting around the picnic table eating and drinking. Garrett and Stella sat side by side at the middle of the table. Garrett's brother, Sam, sat at one end with a woman who looked to be his wife. Whoever had picked up the video camera narrated: *Great party. Great people. Great country.*

The next scene was later—I could tell by the shadows—and it showed a shimmering swimming pool full of children and teenagers. They were yelling and screaming like kids in pools do. Water drops from a boy's great cannonball dive splashed onto the camera lens. Next it was dark and fireworks fizzed and popped in the middle distance. The video shooter was inside the house, shooting out. A little boy ran with a sparkler. Then, with the sudden speed of an unheard bullet, the scene became a small casket in a chapel with solemn light slanting down from a stained-glass window across which a dove flew with an olive branch. It was one of the most jolting series of images I'd ever seen.

"Jesus," said McKenzie.

"Yeah. Tough stuff."

"How could she drown with all those people there? I never understood that. It happens every summer. All the time. I just never get *how*. From a pool party to a funeral. Boom."

I played the sequence again. Then again.

"What are you doing, Robbie?"

"There's something in that first part, when the adults are eating at the table. Something caught me."

"Play it again."

I did. The dining sequence was one long pan, maybe eight or ten seconds. There was a table full of adults. It reminded me of the Last Supper, with all the activity and drama, people leaning this way and that. Ten different conversations seemed to be going on. Roger Sutherland was there—Garrett's boss at the time. His companion was a shapely brunette in a yellow sundress. The Professional Standards lieutenant who had since retired sat across from Sutherland. Garrett's other future boss was there, standing behind the table and looking on—Erik Kaven—tanned for summer and wild-haired as always.

The narrator said, *Great party. Great people. Great country.* Then the next scene was the pool with all the kids splashing and diving and yelling.

"What is it?" I asked. I played it again.

Great party.

"There's Garrett's brother, Sam, left end of the table," I said.

The camera moved right again, taking in Garrett and Stella and the others.

Great people.

The camera showed the right end of the table. And just as the narrator said, *Great country,* I thought I recognized the guy standing off to the side of it. He was wearing a straw hat and had his back to the camera. He was almost lost in the overhanging foliage of a pretty tree with yellow blossoms. But as he turned to the shooter, right before the sequence ended, I could just make out his profile.

"There," I said.

Funny how your mind catches up with itself in its own good time.

"Fellowes," I said. "The hat threw me. And you can't see his face until he turns."

"Hell," said McKenzie. "Our whore-loving captain of Vice. You're right. Is that his wife beside him?"

"Yes. Partying down with the Asplundhs on the day their daughter drowned."

The last twenty minutes of the disc were harder to watch than the first twenty. Some of Samantha's memorial service was recorded, part of the eulogy. Part of the burial was shown. There was a brief tour of her room, some close-ups on her collection of stuffed animals and the clothes in her closet. There were newspapers with the Asplundh tragedy recounted in increasingly smaller articles. Garrett said nothing at all. Silence. But the emotion came through the silence—exhaustion, heartbreak, and numbness.

The last five minutes featured a family portrait done by Garrett. Samantha must have been close to three years old. It was Garrett's usual black-and-white. His usual balanced composition and subtle emotions. The camera stayed fixed on it while he spoke off-screen. His voice was clear and soft and it sounded like he was speaking to someone who was right in front of him.

> *Sam, honey, I don't know where you are now, or if you're anywhere, but I wanted to say good-bye. Through all of this, I never really said that to you. I was afraid that if I did, I'd lose the last little bit of you, but now I know that can never happen. I love you more each day. I know that must sound odd but it's true. So I'm not afraid to say good-bye anymore. You know I'd give anything to have you alive and here. I would eagerly trade places with you. The world is a much different place to me without you. When I see the sun in the morning it gives no light, and when I walk out in this September heat I feel no warmth. I've learned that in the darkness you see no horizon. I can still feel your body on my lap from when we would read at night in the rocking chair. I can still feel your exact weight and temperature from when you'd crawl into bed between Mom and me. Oh, sweet Samantha, I still know the smell of your head and the clarity of your eyes and the brightness of your soul shining through them. You will never die in me. You*

will live, perfect and three years and two months and eleven days old, inside me. From now on I will find a way to protect you and I will never let you down again. I promise. I will make you proud. And someday when I go to my grave we will finally be together. When you reach for me, I will be there. Your hands will find not water but me. I welcome that day. Good-bye, daughter and perfect girl. Bye for now, Sam.

The video ended with a close-up of Samantha, framed by silence. I thought of Garrett sitting in his black Explorer by the Cabrillo Bridge in the rain.

We sat there in the slowly darkening room. For a moment I tried to imagine what Stella Asplundh must be going through, having lost her daughter and husband in the last nine months. Nine months, I thought—the time it had taken her to bring Samantha into this world. All I could imagine was a darkness that would not lift, a darkness that would drown all light in your heart.

"Sometimes I feel exhausted and lucky at the same time," said McKenzie.

"I know that feeling."

"And sometimes . . . I just feel wrung out and dried up as an old bag. You know what I'm glad of? I'm glad Hollis Harris is going to whisk me off in his ten-billion-horsepower red race car tonight and I'll forget about stuff like this for a few hours."

"I guess you two have hit it off."

She looked at me, then away. "He's a hyperactive Looney Tune but I do like him. Get a load of this—he wants me to teach him how to shoot."

"He's a lucky guy. And I'm happy for you, McKenzie."

I ejected the DVD and placed it back in its special leather case.

"He'll get sick of me in a week or two but we'll burn some fossil fuel along the way," said McKenzie. "Fire some bullets too, I guess."

"You never know."

"True. Maybe I'll get sick of him first."

"Why not be optimistic?"

I put the DVD in my briefcase. McKenzie stood on the porch looking out over the city while I locked the door of the apartment.

"You going to watch that thing again at home?" she asked.

"It will help me understand Garrett."

"It's hard to watch."

"Robbie, do you ever get sick of being a nice guy?"

I thought about that a minute. "I never put much effort into it."

"Just naturally a nice guy?"

"I guess. Maybe I got a little nicer after the fall, you know, just trying to be more considerate."

"You always say 'fall,' instead of 'being thrown.' Like it was an accident."

"No, it was no accident. I was there because I wanted to be there. I just got caught off guard."

"I didn't mean it like that," said McKenzie. "Either way, you're a nice guy, Robbie."

"Well, thanks."

Just then a late-model Corvette grumbled to a stop on the street outside Garrett's apartment building, then angled back quickly for a precise parallel park.

Sam Asplundh uncoiled from the driver's seat, pushed the door closed with his boot, and came down the sidewalk toward us. He was dressed the same as he was a few hours ago when I'd seen him with Stella Asplundh and John Van Flyke. When his coattail swung out, his Bureau sidearm was holstered in plain sight over his right hip.

"Brownlaw," he said, "I'm going to have a look around Garrett's place if you don't mind. Stella and I have to figure out what to do with everything in there."

He came up the stairs, brandishing a house key. "I'll be a good boy with respect to possible evidence."

I introduced him to McKenzie. He gave her a sly smile and a quick appraisal.

"What's your take on the murder?" he asked her.

"Enemies," said McKenzie.

"That's what three years in Professional Standards and three months in Ethics gets you," said Sam.

"How is Stella holding up?" I asked.

He looked at me and shook his head. "It's been tough. Her folks will be here later today, and that might help. She's a good person, you know, not just a pretty woman."

I thought it odd that Sam would comment on Stella Asplundh's good looks.

"Maybe you and I could sit down and talk about your brother and Stella sometime," I said.

"Break my heart, but I'll do it," said Sam. He took out a card and wrote his cell number on the back. "Anytime."

I drove back toward headquarters in the falling winter light. It would be spring in a few days. The breeze of a memory of Gina crossed my mind, and it made my heart feel like it was about to crash straight down through the floorboard of the Chevy, plummet through the earth, and come smoking out the other side of the planet.

"I hate what happened to that little girl," said McKenzie. "I try to imagine how Garrett felt but I can't. The video gives an idea but still, to actually be the one going through it. Then his total babe pretty much ditches him."

"I can't imagine it either."

I had just pulled into the headquarters officers' lot off Broadway when my phone rang. It was Captain Chester Fellowes, clearly unhappy that he'd reached me. He said he'd gotten my message.

His timing couldn't have been better. I'd wanted to talk to him since seeing him do the sock dance on Garrett's video, but I wanted to talk to him even more now that he'd shown up at Garrett's house the day his daughter died.

"This about Garrett?"

"Yes, sir."

"What makes you think I can help?"

"You were friends."

"Not really."

"I'd just like to ask you a few questions about him, sir."

A beat of silence.

"You in your car somewhere?"

"Yes, sir."

"We'll have to do this later. I'm only going to be here for about two more minutes."

"Fine, sir," I said. "We'll be up in one."

I thanked him and rang off.

Chet Fellowes was a large, poorly shaped man who gave off an air of self-serving intelligence. He had sloping shoulders, long arms, and small, quick eyes. He played for Bogle on the department golf team and was rumored to be a scratch golfer and a cheat.

I'd never been in his office. He sat behind his desk and watched McKenzie examining the Fellowes family photographs by the window. Behind him were college and academy diplomas, commendations, and awards. Fellowes slumped down and crossed his hands over an ample gut.

"Bad," he said. "Garrett Asplundh was, what, thirty-nine years old?"

"Yes," I said.

"And he wasn't robbed?"

"No. He was shot from about two inches away. They left his cash, cards, vehicle, everything."

"Prints on the gun?"

"Wiped clean with Tri-Flow."

"You bring your own Tri-Flow to clean up the gun, that's an execution."

"That's what we're thinking," I said. "Did Garrett make enemies here?"

Fellowes eyed me flatly. "You bet he did. Professional Standards, with an attitude like his? A lot of people, they really disliked him and I can't blame them. Like having a . . . what's the word? Being around Garrett was like having a hawk following you all around. When he went to the Ethics Authority everybody was relieved."

"Who in particular was relieved?" I asked.

He shook his head. "You two are way off if you're looking for a suspect in this department. Come on."

"Captain Fellowes, enemies are enemies," I said. "As an Ethics Authority investigator, he had come up with videodiscs of men buying sex from prostitutes. Some of those men are powerful in this city. Some are cops."

Fellowes's mouth hung slightly open. It looked like he had to halt facial movement in order to complete his thought.

I watched him closely.

"Who?" he asked.

"I'm not at liberty to discuss that," I said. "Captains Villas and Sutherland are fully informed."

His eyes shifted from me to McKenzie then to me again. Fury makes a small room smaller. I could sense the captain's anger spike, then settle down to a manageable temperature.

"I thought you probably knew about all of it, sir," I said. "Since you're a captain in Vice."

"Of course I knew about it."

The red squares of deceit spilled out of his mouth and floated out over his desk. His face was almost gray. "I'll take care of any problems within Vice. We take care of our own in Vice."

"And we'll find out who murdered Garrett Asplundh," I said.

My words seemed to hang in the air of Chet Fellowes's office. He shifted his big body in the chair. I was surprised by the level of menace that emanated from a man who looked hapless and uncoordinated. But Fellowes called on some inner strength while he considered me, and I could see in his eyes that he would be merciless if given the opportunity.

"We also wanted to talk to you because you were at the Asplundhs' Fourth of July party," said McKenzie.

Fellowes fixed her with a flat, small-eyed stare. "That's ancient history. You put things like that out of your mind if you can."

"Tell us about it," I said.

"Why? It has no bearing."

"You're sure of that?" I asked.

Again, a look from Fellowes that told me he would get me someday.

"That was a bad day," he said. "I mean, really—three years old. What a shame. Nothing we could do. A dozen adults all hovering over this pale little thing Garrett had fished from the pool."

"How did it happen?" asked McKenzie.

"About sundown everybody left the pool area to go set off some fireworks in the street. I remember Garrett standing by the gate that guards the pool, and he waited for all of us to file on through, and I was the last guy out, me and Phyllis, my ex-wife. And I clearly remember Garrett snapping that lock into place and spinning the combination dial and pulling on it once or twice. Then it was fireworks."

"Out in the driveway, right?"

"Yeah, over twenty people there, counting the kids. Stella had Samantha in her arms. I remember because I held my daughter at that age. Samantha was a real go-getter, I remember that, too. Running everywhere, laughing and playing, a happy kid. It was a nice evening. Real warm and kind of humid, and up and down the block you could hear the fireworks going off. Just little stuff, you know—Smokey Joes and Piccolo Petes and sparklers for the kids. The air smelled like sulfur. Twenty minutes, half an hour went by. And I saw Stella go into the house. She wasn't carrying Samantha anymore. A minute or two later she came back out, walking fast, head up, you know, worried about something. Garrett, then, he came out behind her, calling for Samantha. Some of the adults followed them into the garage, then around the side of the house looking for her. Phyllis and I stayed where we were but I kept looking back toward the house, and then someone yelled for Stella. I mean, really yelled loud. You knew something had happened. Then I heard Stella scream from the backyard. And this short kind of . . . uproar of voices, a bunch of people yelling at once. The only words I clearly remember hearing were 'breathing,' and '911.' Phyllis turned an ankle running for the backyard, which didn't help things any. When I got back there, Garrett and Van Flyke had Samantha laid out on a chaise by the pool. Garrett was already doing CPR. Stella had just gotten the gate unlocked so most everyone was still on the other side of the fence. Garrett had jumped it to get to his daughter. I think maybe some other men had jumped it, too. To help, you know. Sam, Garrett's brother, he was the one who pulled her out."

Fellowes unlocked his hands and leaned forward in his chair. He rubbed a hairy forearm and sighed. "Really, what's any of this got to do with Garrett?"

"I don't know yet," I said. "How did Samantha get back to the pool without anyone noticing?"

"Garrett put the chronology together later," Fellowes said. "He told me that when the fireworks started going off, Samantha didn't like the noise. She had told her mother to let her down so she could go get Dad. Garrett was in the house rinsing some of the dishes, shooting some video of the fireworks through the window, drinking a beer. He didn't see Samantha get down and come looking for him—she was hidden by the adults. And she didn't look for him in the house. Instead she scooted over to the side gate, pulled the string, and let herself into the backyard. Garrett told me that side gate was usually locked, too, but they'd taken off the lock so the party guests could circulate. Anyway, Samantha climbed the pool fence to get in. It was five feet high, made out of that rubberized chain link, so climbing it wouldn't have been hard for a determined three-year-old. Later we found her doll floating and the pool skimmer sunk to the bottom. You know, the long-handled ones you use to whisk off the leaves and stuff. She must have dropped the doll in earlier, then remembered where it was and tried to fish it out with the skimmer before going to get her father. If there wasn't so much noise from the fireworks, somebody might have heard something. Stella thought Samantha was with Dad. Dad thought she was with Mom. A brave three-year-old climbs a fence, tries to get her doll out of the pool, and it's over."

I imagined the tragedy unfolding as Fellowes described it. A hundred ingredients, a hundred things that had to go exactly wrong for it to happen. I tried to imagine how Stella felt, having had last custody of her daughter. And how Garrett must have felt, having missed her escape from the fireworks noise by so little—not by yards and minutes but by inches and seconds.

"It changed everything," said Fellowes. "Garrett and Stella fell apart. Garrett became very intense and humorless and driven to catch bad guys. Blamed himself for everything. I didn't blame him. I don't blame him for anything that happened then or after. But I couldn't be around him. I guess the end of our friendship was the least of Garrett's problems. Stella?

I see her around. She always smiles, puts on the face. But she looks empty if you ask me."

"How did it affect you, Captain?" asked McKenzie.

He sat back, looked at McKenzie and me with his quick little eyes. "You learn to turn it off, like a lot of other stuff in this business. I don't have to explain that to you two. Me and Phyllis split up a week later."

McKenzie and I took the elevator down. We were alone.

"Fellowes didn't know that Garrett had him on video," I said.

"Now he suspects. Be careful of him, Robbie. I don't like the look in his little eyes."

"Why didn't Garrett show Fellowes his evidence?" I asked. "Why collect if you don't use?"

"I don't know," said McKenzie. "There's enough on his hard drive to cause ten city scandals and ruin a dozen people. But he doesn't seem to have *done* anything with it."

"Maybe he thought there was more to know."

"Maybe he was just *about* to do something with it," she said. "The meeting Wednesday—he was going to lay it all on the state attorney general."

"Then his killing was proactive."

"Yeah," said McKenzie. "No matter what Van Flyke said about that meeting being routine. They knew Garrett was going to meet with the attorney general, and they couldn't let him do that."

"Who is 'they'?"

"I'm working on it, Robbie."

Ron Mincher worked the patrol shift that day, which ended at 6:00 P.M.

I waited for him near the walkway that leads from the locker room and showers to the officers' parking lot. I told McKenzie I'd talk to Mincher alone. One reason was that a Homicide team is unmistakably a Homicide team, whereas one detective can mean anything from a Police Union solicitation to an invite to join the bowling league. The other reason is, I knew she was eager to get to Hollis Harris and his fast red car.

Mincher came down the walk about quarter to seven, freshly showered and in his street clothes. He had his sidearm, ammo, belt, badge, and probably handcuffs in a small cloth duffel.

Seeing Mincher made me remember my own days on patrol. It was nice to leave the job behind when you got off work. When you make detective, you start taking it home with you. I thought of hustling down this same walkway, showered up just like Ron and in a hurry to get home to Gina. I could usually make Normal Heights by six forty-five or seven. Stepping through our front door was like stepping into heaven itself. No criminals, no BS, no lies. Just you and the beautiful woman you loved and six or seven hours with nothing to do but enjoy each other until you conked out, slept hard, and woke up to do it all over. I'd love to be young like that again.

Mincher held my eye as he approached. He was twenty-six, six feet and well built. His hair was brown, matched by a neat cop-style mustache.

"Ron, I'm Robbie Brownlaw from Homicide."

"I know who you are, sir."

"Don't need the 'sir' stuff. Talk a minute?"

"Absolutely."

"Let's take a walk."

He locked his duffel in a snappy yellow Ford pickup and we left headquarters on the Fourteenth Street side, then headed east on Broadway.

"I've got two things bothering me," I said. "One of them I have to do something about. The other one I'm going to let slide for now."

"What's on your mind?" he said with a very small smile. "Doesn't sound good."

Mincher had that same casual southern tone of voice that Dale Payne had.

"How are you liking San Diego?"

"Oh, it's fine. New Orleans was too humid."

"I'm working the Asplundh murder."

"Yeah, I know."

"He got it with a nine-millimeter Smith that went missing from the New Orleans Property Annex a couple of months before you left that city and came here."

Mincher looked at me. "Interesting coincidence," he said.

"But it ties into the other thing that's bothering me," I said. "And that is, Garrett didn't get killed for his money or his credit cards or his car or his weapons. He got killed for something he knew."

We walked along Broadway. I could smell the ocean and see the red trolley making its way south to the border. The city lights twinkled, and the new baseball stadium stood out beautifully against the black sky.

"And Garrett knew a lot of things," I said. "For instance, he knew you were buying Squeaky Clean girls."

Even in the streetlights I could see his face go red.

"One of them had a hidden camera. Garrett was working with her. It's all on DVDs, good quality. You weren't alone, if it's any consolation. I printed a still image that's right here in my pocket if you don't believe me. Want to see it?"

"Guess I better."

It was a full page, folded three times. He opened it, glanced at it, then folded it and put it in his pocket.

He looked at me briefly, shaking his head. "You first."

"Talk to me."

"I'm a stupid guy."

We continued on but Mincher was lost in himself.

"Did Garrett talk to you about this?" I asked.

"No."

I waited for the proof of his lie but it never came. And again I wondered exactly what Garrett was planning to do with the discs he had collected from Carrie Ann Martier and her friends.

"He never showed you the videos?"

"Never."

"He never told you what he had?"

Mincher shook his head.

"Did you suspect you'd been recorded?" I asked.

"No. The girls were always so . . . professional."

"What did you do to get such a deal? You were paying a hundred for what usually costs a grand."

Mincher looked at me again. We turned south onto Fifteenth. "I'm getting myself into some huge trouble here."

"No, you're already in it."

"Who else do you have?"

"Fellowes, if that's what you're after."

"Oh, man," he said quietly. "He's not going to like this one bit."

"Did he proposition you?" I asked.

We walked awhile, and then Mincher nodded.

"Tell me about that."

He said nothing for a few steps. "Help me."

"Here's the only help I can offer you, Ron: You tell me everything you know, and I don't arrest you right here on the spot. Good enough? I'm armed and I've got my cuffs. Your stuff is back in that new yellow pickup. I'll subdue you right here on this street, cuff you, and walk you into the jail in front of the guys you work with. Then you'll have to tell your whole story anyway, to a defense attorney."

He stopped walking and stared at me. He was a little taller and heavier than me but I saw no fight at all in his eyes. I thought for a second he might actually run away. I'm not fast but I have endurance. I can run mile after mile after mile.

"I played for the golf team, is how I met Fellowes," he said. "He's a captain with weight, you know, and I'm a twenty-four-year-old new hire. We get along okay. He's always asking about my love life. I'm young and single and new to town and he wants to know how I'm getting along. He's too interested. At first I thought he might be hustling me. Then one day he says he knows some classy girls who like cops. And I was just the kind of good-looking young cop they'd love. You know the type of woman he's talking about—the cop groupies, right? So I didn't think much about it, but he kept talking up these girls, and one day four of us met in a restaurant up in La Jolla after work. Classy girls? They were two of the prettiest women I'd *ever* seen. They were bright and sassy and drove cool cars. A drink and an hour later, Fellowes and his date were gone. Another drink and another hour later, I was in the Valencia Hotel watching Allison take my clothes off. After, she said it was supposed to be four hundred for the room and six for her, plus whatever extra if I liked her, but for me a hundred would cover things this once. I only had eighty on me and she laughed and took it. I went home that night and thought about what I'd done and couldn't believe it. Ron Mincher doesn't do things like that. Ron Mincher was a good Southern Baptist. Ron Mincher's idea of a wild time was two six-packs and a poker game. Ask anybody. But I'd done it. I'd jumped on that whore just like I had good sense."

"And you were about to pay a lot more than eighty bucks," I said.

"Well, yeah. That night Fellowes came by my house and we took a little walk like we're doing now. He said there was more where that came from, girls prettier than Allison and they'd do just about anything to make me happy. All I had to do was look out for the girls in the little convertibles while I was on patrol. Discourage my patrol friends from bothering them. Never talk to them when they had dates. If there was some dispute with hotel security, tell hotel security you'd handle it, and make sure the girl got back to her car and out of there. Later I started fingering his own Vice teams for the girls so they wouldn't get pinched. Fellowes would let me know where the stings were being set up and I'd let the Squeaky Cleans know in advance. He said there were plenty of other whores to throw in jail. He said we weren't easy on prostitution like they are in some cities, but you can't shut all the girls down. So why shouldn't we get to decide who works in America's Finest City and who doesn't? It was like he was providing a service."

It made a perverse kind of sense. If you were Chet Fellowes, you could convince yourself that you were fighting crime by committing crime. And his underlying logic was sound: You can't stop prostitution, you can only control it.

"What about cash?" I asked. "Fellowes must have been on Squeaky Clean's payroll for more than just fun."

"I got a couple hundred a week. And two dates. After that it cost me the hundred."

"Sweet deal," I said.

"Until about ten minutes ago."

"What was Fellowes taking down?"

"I didn't ask," he said.

"Did you ever deal with Jordan Sheehan personally?"

"I've never met her."

"What about Fellowes?" I asked. "Did he ever talk about her?"

"He called her the 'head whore.' Didn't say much more than that about her. He said she'd make a great politician if she wasn't head whore."

"Did you run across Chupa Junior?"

"Heard of him."

"From the girls?"

Mincher had his head down, nodding. "He's like a nightmare to them. Something that can just happen when you don't expect it. Squeaky Clean makes a lot of money for her girls, and they make a lot of money for her. But she holds Chupa over their heads."

"Fellowes lets him operate?"

"Yeah," said Mincher. "We're the protection. Chupa's the fear."

"I'm going to make sure Fellowes gets his butt thoroughly kicked for this."

Mincher looked at me, then away.

We walked onto the headquarters grounds. The lights of the city were clear against the night sky. I could tell that this crisis had surprised Ron Mincher. It had come up behind him like a fast car on a dark night. All he saw was a wash of light in front of him and by the time he turned there was nothing to do but try to dive off the road. He was still blinking.

"Maybe this is okay," he said. "My soul was rotting. I tried to tell myself it was just consenting adults and all that. But you get brought up a certain way and it sticks. I knew what I was doing was wrong. But it was just so easy. And the Squeaky Cleans. Oh, *man.*"

"Forget about them right now. So what about this Model 39 that vanished from New Orleans Property Annex not once but *twice*?"

"I don't know a thing about it. I remember the annex got hit by some junkie burglars one night, but I thought we got all the stuff back."

"Most of the stuff. The Model 39 that was used to kill Garrett Asplundh was returned, signed in, then disappeared."

"No," Mincher said softly. "I've got my own weapons. I don't need to steal somebody else's. I'm not much of a gun guy anyway."

"What were you doing last Tuesday night, the night Garrett got it?"

We had come to Mincher's new yellow truck. He hit the key fob and the alarm chirped and the door lock snapped up.

"I worked that day, then went to the driving range out in La Mesa. Hit three buckets, had the chicken basket, and drove back downtown. I had some drinks at Dick's. I know one of the bartenders, Parry Songrath. He'll vouch for me."

"Until how late?"

"Only ten or so. I went to bed early because I like to get my workouts in before shift."

"You were alone the rest of the night?"

"Yeah."

"No Squeaky Cleans?"

He smiled. "No. And just when I could use an alibi."

On my way home I drove past the Salon Sultra. The lights inside looked warm and inviting in the cool March night. The stylists were snipping and curling and weaving and chattering but Gina's chair stood vacant, the light around it dim. I wondered how long it would take them to lease that chair. I knew there was a waiting list to get into Sultra. I knew that Chambers could replace her in little more than an instant. My throat went hard, like it had turned into steel. It hurt. I pulled over across from the salon and waited for that familiar flash of anger, but it never came. Instead a small, optimistic glimmer of hope came to my heart and I wondered if there might be something I could do to make Gina want to come back.

When I got home I called her parents—Vince and Dawn Brancini—in Las Vegas.

They're good people. Vince is a pit boss at Binion's, and Dawn is a wedding coordinator for Caesars Palace. I met Gina because they had all come to San Diego for a celebration just after Gina had turned eighteen and graduated from high school. They brought her best friend, Rachel, too.

I was twenty-three at the time, working my last month as a uniformed patrolman before my first plainclothes assignment with Fraud. It was a warm August night and I was walking in the Gaslamp and I noticed this young woman with wispy red hair wearing a black dress. She was walking uncertainly because of her high heels. I stayed behind her for a few steps, convinced that I was going to be needed. She was with another young woman and a middle-aged couple. They decided to jaywalk in front of the Rock Bottom nightclub. She stepped off the curb, turned her ankle badly, and fell. I saw it coming and caught her before she hit. She was light. I carried her inside the Rock Bottom and put her in a chair. I examined the ankle very gingerly and told her to ice and stay off it. I advised ibuprofen for pain. I was half in love with her by the time she blew me a kiss and promised to call as I walked out. I knew she wouldn't. I could smell her perfume on the collar of my summer-weight uniform later that night as I undressed in the locker room. The next day she left a message for me at the station and that night she and Rachel took me to dinner. Her ankle was slightly swollen and she limped. I took them to a very nice restaurant for dessert after but wouldn't let them buy alcoholic beverages, which Rachel found condescending and Gina found funny. My heart was one hundred percent hers by the time we said good-bye. The moment we met was a scene her mother loved describing later—this surprised young cop with a moaning/laughing redhead in his arms. She said it was her favorite "cute meet," which was saying a lot given her line of work.

Now on the phone Dawn sounded distracted. I could hear the pop of a cork from a bottle and the clink of glass hitting glass, then a gurgle. Then again. I told her Gina had packed some things and left because she thought there must be more to life.

A moment of silence. Then, "Oh, Robbie. Oh, damn. Are you . . . are you *sure*?"

"I'm pretty darned sure, Dawn. The closet's half empty, she quit her job and had Rachel tell me good-bye."

"But are you okay?"

"I'm fine but I need to talk to her."

"But . . . I can't believe she'd just— You mean she packed and . . . Are you *sure* she . . . ? Have you been fighting or maybe . . ."

Dawn usually has an orderly mind. She has hundreds of things to track and coordinate with every wedding. I thought about the two clinks of glass on glass and thought I understood what was wrong. The little coal of hope inside me burst into a small flame.

"May I speak with her?" I asked.

"She's not here, Robbie. There's no way she—"

"Put her on, Dawn," I said.

"What? No, Robbie, she's not—"

"Dawn, you and I have known each other for, what, almost six years? I can tell when you're fibbing or upset, and right now you're both."

A long pause, then a quiet, "God*damn* it."

"Exactly."

"I don't see why I—"

"So just put her—"

"Damn it, Gina, honey. Just come over here and talk to your husband, will you? I can't—"

Then a clacking sound as the cordless phone smacked a table or counter.

"I'll be gone by the time you make the airport," said Gina. Her voice sounded frail but determined. "Or by the time you hit Escondido if you try to drive here."

"I won't come, then. Just stay where you're safe. I won't bother you but I need to know one thing."

"Liar. Good-bye, Robbie. You shouldn't have called."

"Is there any—"

But she clicked off and when I hit redial I got a busy signal.

Of course I was lying. I called two airlines for their Lindbergh–to–Las Vegas flights that evening but the times were too soon and too late.

I filled up my gas-guzzling slickback and used the toll lanes on northbound I-15, which actually deposit you directly into the worst of the commuter traffic when they merge back into the freeway south of Escondido.

Slowly floating down this river of red brake lights toward Gina was one of the most frustrating things I'd ever done. My heart was beating like a runner's but my car was hardly moving. Once, when I was ten years old and a first-time skier, I tried to ski in a snowstorm on Mammoth Mountain. I launched down the beginners' run ahead of me and I flung myself into the swirling whiteness, goggleless and determined. I was soon blinded—I could see nothing but white—but I could feel the snow slapping against my face and the strong wind biting through my cap and I remembered to keep my knees bent and I got into a rhythm with my skis like the instructor had said and I headed into that storm until there was a lull in the white fury around me and I regained my vision to find that I'd been standing still the whole time. But now, inching along in the north-bound traffic, I didn't even have the luxury of my own illusions.

Five hours and thirty-seven minutes later, I pulled into the driveway of the Brancini residence in south Las Vegas. My heart fell when I didn't see her car, just the empty driveway and the open garage door. Dawn and Vince's two cars were in the garage. To my surprise, Vince sat in a folding chair behind his Cadillac with an electric heater glowing red at his feet. An empty chair sat beside him. Gina's car was nowhere to be seen. Good to her word, she had probably left here by the time I was stuck in the Escondido traffic.

I sat in the folding chair next to Vince and we talked for a few minutes. He poured me a cup of coffee from his thermos. I was surprised how cold it was out here in the Nevada desert. To the south the stars were bright and close.

Vince apologized for his daughter's "flightiness" and said he'd worried about things just like this when she'd announced her marriage plans at age eighteen. What could he have said or done? He had loved his daughter. He had liked me. Gina was happier than he'd ever seen her. Dawn was already talking gown material, floral motifs, and a way to trim the sit-down dinner costs.

"I've got a PI friend here in town," he said. "Between the two of us, we'll keep an eye on her."

"Did you call him already?"

"Soon as she left, Robbie."

"Where'd she go?"

"Don't ask."

I knew she had friends here from high school. I knew that some of them had found trouble. I knew that Gina had considered herself a candidate for trouble and that moving out to San Diego to marry me was part of making sure that didn't happen. She liked to call me her "big, square hero." Beneath all of Gina's gaiety and mirth is a heart closely attuned to what can go wrong. I think her lightness and darkness get strength from each other, like the roots and branches of a tree.

"I can't just let her go, Vince."

"No. But for now you have to. Go home. Do your job. She talks to her mother and me, kind of. I'll keep you in the loop. Things change, Robbie, and then they change again. You know what I'm saying."

That sounded both ominous and hopeful. I held my hands up to the glowing heating element and rubbed them.

"I love her," I said.

"You're lucky."

It was an odd statement but I knew he was right.

"Most people, they just drift apart, vanish on each other," said Vince. His words were soft and heartfelt and I wondered about him and Dawn. After all, Vince was sitting alone in a cold garage rather than in a warm house with his wife.

"This is fuckin' fucked," I muttered. I rarely swear and have no skill at it.

Vince laughed. "That's one way to put it. I'm sorry, Robbie. I don't know what I can do."

I sat for a while and looked at the stars. I could see the lights of the city a few miles north.

"How come you're sitting in the garage, Vince?"

"I miss the outdoors."

"I'm serious."

"Me, too. I grew up in Buffalo, you know? Sometimes I miss the woods and the stars and the cold."

"Well, you've got two out of three tonight."

He looked at me but said nothing.

"See you and thanks, Vince," I said.

"It's almost one o'clock. I made up the spare just in case."

"Love to Dawn."

"She wanted me to apologize for her not waiting up. Actually, she didn't think you'd race over here but I knew you would."

Vince gave me a big, strong Italian-style hug, which I appreciated.

"How's the head?" he asked. Vince is the one person who has never shown me any great sympathy for what happened at the Las Palmas. He seems to believe that it was a fairly common event in my line of work, the kind of thing that most cops have to endure sooner or later. I like that attitude, because it takes attention away from me.

"Hard as ever."

"You're a good man, Robbie."

"Who's the PI?" I asked.

"Get in your car and drive carefully," said Vince. "I'll call you when I've got something you need to know."

"I don't want to just drift apart, Vince. I don't want her to vanish on me."

"I don't either."

"You know, we have it pretty good. I can't understand what she wants. I was thinking, though, maybe I can do something that will make her want to come back."

"She doesn't know what she wants, Robbie. She's young. She'll figure it out."

I looked up once more at the glittering stars.

"The Mobil down at the corner's got the best prices," Vince said. "But stay away from the slots."

I was back home in bed around sunrise. I slept for two hours, showered, shaved, and went to work.

Chupa Junior—the Squeaky Clean Madam's bouncer with his own moral code—had been arrested at three that morning on suspicion of driving under the influence. While I'd been zooming through Barstow, Chupa Junior was blowing a .24 blood-alcohol count, over double his legal limit.

Patrol Officer Ron Mincher had left a message for me that Chupa had been busted, and thought I might want to see him. I was thankful for Mincher's tip but not surprised by it. He was a young man who'd gotten himself into some understandable trouble and now he was trying to get himself back out of it.

Chupa Junior glowered at me as I walked toward his cell. A normal man would have been in the drunk tank but Peter Avalos was six-four, three hundred, and not normal. I'd learned from his jacket that he'd been questioned and released in two murders before I came to Homicide. They thought he was good for them but couldn't get anyone to talk. They did, once, and she was found in Glorietta Bay one morning just like McKenzie had said, strangled and three ribs broken. Chupa had done his prison time for carjacking, armed robbery, and multiple assaults. Like a lot of creeps, Chupa had no problem selling out other creeps. He'd turned a few dollars informing for us, even slipped out of yet another assault rap when he snitched out a La Eme—Mexican mafia—boss, which could have gotten him killed and still might.

He was as big as Vic Malic, just shaped differently. Malic is a wrestler, all shoulder and back. Chupa was big in the legs and middle. His small, shaved head crawled with tattoos, and his black eyes stared at me with open violence. He was slumped on the metal bed and looked half drunk.

I was happy to have the bars between us. Two hours of sleep leaves the dreams still trying to get in and out of you. I felt wobbly.

"I'm Detective Brownlaw, Homicide," I said.

"Then get me out of here, big man."

"Jordan told me to say hello. She says you're a good guy, have your own sense of right and wrong, do some bouncing for her at the club."

"She's the one."

"Guess you drank a little too much last night. Wish I could have, but I was driving down from Las Vegas."

He looked at me as if he was sizing me up for a knife.

"I like the rooms at the Venetian and the rubdowns at Bally's," he said. "They use old fight men, really got the hands."

"My brother is a dealer at Excalibur," I said.

Chupa thought about this, as I knew he would. I wanted to give him something personal to keep him off balance and talking. Not that I would ever tell him anything truthful, because I could see that Chupa was already looking for a way to use this new information. One thing about genuine bad guys is, they never overlook an opportunity, and to them everything is an opportunity.

"What's his name?"

"Bill Brownlaw."

"Make good money?"

"It's all tips, but he does okay. The good-looking women do better."

"You and him got a little system going at the tables?" asked Chupa.

"I'd never mess with him or a casino."

He looked at me like he didn't believe me.

"Funny time of night for you to be driving in from Vegas," he said.

"You make better time."

"So what are you doing here, man?"

"Asking you about Garrett Asplundh."

A spark of pleasure twinkled in his black eyes. "The cop in the car with the brains all over?"

"He wasn't a cop. He was Ethics Authority."

"He used to be a cop. He popped me back in '98 for an assault I didn't do. Want to know how to tell I didn't do it?"

"Because the guy lived."

"Fuckin' right."

"You got dynamite in both hands, from what I hear."

He stood up and lumbered over. He moved like an elephant, with a tonnage that was slow but not unwieldy. His ears were stacked curves, like hourglasses, lobes big and round, with black hair growing from the canals.

"Why am I talking to you, man?"

"The Ethics guy. I want to know what he was up to with Squeaky Clean."

He clamped two big hands to the bars. The tats on his forearms were a black jailhouse jumble of Celtic letters, *chupacabras,* and demons that wrapped around to his underarms. One of the demons jammed his claw up a woman's dress as he drank the blood gushing from her severed neck. Chupa Junior burped beer at me.

"Why would I tell you?"

"I'm rich," I said. "I'm influential."

Chupa smiled. Small teeth, pale gums.

"I saw them together at the Indigo. That's Jordan's place."

"When?"

"Six months ago. I was working the door. Tried to pat him for guns on his way in and I thought he was going to tear my head off. Try to anyway. Could have gotten messy. Jordan pushed him past me, told me he was VIP. I said, 'Yeah, very important pig.' He gave me the mad dog, the look, you know, so I owed him."

In gangland's code of honor, you answer a mad dog with a bullet. If you don't, you're not respected.

"Yeah, you owed him a bullet, didn't you?"

He was already shaking his head. "Someone beat me to it."

"What did Jordan and Garrett do that night you saw them together?"

"Drank at a booth in the back. Watched the people dance. About an hour, then he left."

"Without her?"

"Alone, man. On the way out he came up behind me and whispered some shit in my ear."

"What, exactly?"

"I just ran out of memory. What a time."

We were on closed-circuit TV, of course. But I'd asked the sergeant at the Professional Visits window if I could offer the arrestee a small amount of cash to pay for material comforts in the jail. The sergeant had agreed.

"Here's twenty," I said.

"Forty."

"Don't get greedy, Junior."

I folded the bill over twice and watched his hand closely as it unlocked itself from the bar, reached through, and took it.

"He said if I ever touched another Squeaky Clean girl he'd put a cap in my ass and dump me in the bay," said Chupa.

"Wouldn't that just be *great*?" I asked.

He gave me a confused smile. It's funny how simple, straightforward sarcasm can throw a street-smart thug like Chupa Junior. But his smile quickly became genuine, full of mirth and violence.

"How many of those girls have you touched?" I asked.

He shook his head. "None. Don't know where that *pendejo* got his ideas."

"But everybody knows you smack the girls around when they get out of line," I said.

"Man, I'm going to tell you what I'm going to tell you. I don't know anything about Squeaky Clean girls. I don't know anything about Squeaky Clean except that her name is Jordan and she pays me thirty an hour to keep the Indigo smooth, quiet, and making money."

The red squares of deception rushed out of him. They were bigger than most I'd seen, and their sides were slightly dipped, concave, as if bowing from Chupa's enormous weight. They just kept coming.

"What are you looking at?"

"Nothing, Chupa."

"Call me Mr. Avalos."

I looked at him. I like tough guys who give you trouble better than the weaklings who roll over and tremble and stab you when you turn your back for one second. With guys like Chupa, you always know where you stand and what your mission is.

"You weigh three hundred?" I asked.

"What do you care?"

"I just wondered, how much did you drink to blow a point two-four?"

"Most of a case of Bud."

"Wow."

"Couple shots of tequila."

"Ouch."

"Some bourbon."

Chupa Junior gave me another flat, contained stare, then turned and went back to his cot. The flesh piled up on the back of his shaved neck like a folded set of bath towels. The steel bed squeaked with his weight.

"I worked the Indigo the night your boyfriend got his mind blown. Stayed around for drinks after. Girl named Dolly came home with me. She's one of the waitresses. Ask Jordan. She was there."

"I'll be checking that story, Chupa."

"You do that, man."

"Vice would love to make you a deal for Squeaky Clean," I said. "They'd make this DUI disappear in a hurry."

"Roll over on a friend for a DUI? What kind of man does that? Jordan's right. I got my own sense of right and wrong. Even if I wanted to lay her out for you, I couldn't."

"Why not?"

"Because I don't know what you're talking about. I've never seen a Squeaky Clean girl. Know what this Squeaky Clean shit really is? It's what the hos make up on slow nights to give themselves a little shine. Makes them feel like they're part of a secret organization and the organization has got this big mean fucker who'll rip 'em up if they don't follow the rules. *Chupacabra,* man, a goatsucker. It's made up. It isn't true. There's no such thing. It's the same as in the 'hood when you're a kid, man—there's always the monsters and the stories and the bullshit. It's *all* a bunch of bullshit, man. You ought to know that."

During the first part of Chupa's monologue, the air was vibrant with his concave red squares. By the time he got to the end of it, they were gone.

"I guess the Squeaky Cleans I talk to are just swamp gas," I said.

"And all you are is a sucker who laid out twenty for nothing. That's all you're going to get from me. Unless, you know, the situation is *perfect.*"

"Talk to me about perfect."

"Some night when everything's right, man, maybe I catch you alone in your car, reach in with a piece and do some window painting with your brains."

"That's a knee-slapper. Tell me another one."

"Cost you forty."

"My wallet's as empty as your future, Chupa. Enjoy the hangover."

I stopped by the office of *San Diego Monthly* magazine and bought the January issue, which had a photo spread on December's "Fifty San Diegans to Watch" party. If that was really where Jordan Sheehan had lost the earring that ended up in Garrett's Explorer, maybe I could figure out who had picked it up. The idea of a killer's being among the Fifty San Diegans to Watch intrigued me but seemed highly unlikely.

Back at my desk, I looked at the pictures and read the article. I had been named such a person back in 2003, having miraculously survived the Las Palmas fall and been promoted twice within six months.

Gina and I attended the party at the end of that year, and we were treated wonderfully by the publishers of the magazine, the other "Fifty," and the many partygoers. Gina pretty much stole the show away from me, for which I was thankful. She was at her best, simply beautiful, full of radiant nonchalance and smart-aleck attitude. When people found out she was a Salon Sultra stylist, many of them wanted to know what she would do with their hair. Stylists often run across this at parties, just as doctors are asked about ailments and stockbrokers for hot picks. So Gina delivered her hairstyle tips that night with plenty of chipper comments about *who* was cutting their hair now and *what* were they trying to accomplish—*No, no, no, don't answer that*—but nobody took offense and over the next week Gina actually got several calls from society-type San Diego women who wanted her to style their hair.

My parents were there, though they huddled together in a corner almost the entire night, dazzled by the local celebrity. That was the only time I'd ever seen my mother too nervous to smile for a picture. I'll never forget the pride in their faces as I was introduced as one of the Fifty San

Diegans to Watch, though Mom told me later she was really just glad I was still alive. Dad said it was one of the top ten events of his life, and we had a revealing discussion one night about the other nine. Gina and I celebrated privately after the party in a suite at the Hilton, which cost us almost four hundred dollars and was totally worth it. She had arranged for a bottle of Dom Pérignon to be there waiting for us but that was the least of the pleasures I remember.

I looked out the window of the Homicide room and thought about that night. Because of what had happened at the Las Palmas, I was no longer surprised by how quickly things can change. John Van Flyke certainly had that right. But I thought of Gina at that party two years ago, and I thought of her now, and I couldn't help but feel flabbergasted that something so large and precious and wonderful in her could have gone away in what seemed an instant.

The pictures from this year's Fifty San Diegans to Watch party looked very much like the ones taken two years ago. Society pages often seem to have repeating faces, or facial types. Among the fifty were an outfielder, a relief pitcher, a defensive end, four actors, eight lawyers, a dozen businesspeople, a new TV weatherman, and a painter.

I was not surprised to see that Abel Sarvonola, chair of the Budget Oversight Committee, was an honoree. The article said it was his third appearance on the list in as many decades. He was by far the oldest person pictured and he looked withered but eternal in his tux. His wife's hair could have used Gina's sensible touch.

I was surprised to find that councilmanic aide Steven Stiles had been named a "San Diegan to Watch." According to my sources within City Hall, his career was undistinguished and he was considered to be overly ambitious. He smiled broadly at the camera, his wife on his arm and a glass of bubbly in the other hand. I wondered if he was smiling like that when Garrett Asplundh asked him about hitting Carrie Ann Martier. I also knew that of all the men captured on the sex disc, Stiles and now Mincher were the only two who knew for certain they'd been caught. But the Fifty San Diegans party was held *before* Stiles had bruised Carrie's ribs. Could he have picked up the lost earring out of curiosity, then later skewed the crime scene by dropping it into the mix? It was a stretch, but it was possible.

The next two names that jumped out at me were Hollis Harris and Garrett Asplundh.

Harris was pictured with HTA comptroller Elsa Shnackenburg, who looked like a movie star. She stood half a head taller than Hollis, who seemed not to care as he smiled tiredly into the camera. The article said that "the 28-year-old Harris's Hidden Threat Assessment company will not only make the nation a safer place this year but will bring in over $45 million in sales for systems designed, built and maintained right here in America's Finest City." I pictured Hollis bending down to pick up an earring dropped by Jordan Sheehan. Why not return it to her right then? If he didn't know it was hers, why hang on to it? Why not turn it in to hotel security? More importantly, why would Hollis Harris kill Garrett Asplundh?

Garrett was pictured alone, and the article mentioned no companion at the party. He looked oddly nonfestive for such an event, more like a losing defense lawyer caught leaving a courthouse. I could make out Abel Sarvonola talking with John Van Flyke in the dark background of the photo. Neither was identified in the caption. What sense did Jordan Sheehan's earring make in the hands of Sarvonola or Van Flyke? None that I could see. Garrett disagreed with Sarvonola's political and budgetary policies, but was that enough to shoot someone point blank? Garrett was Van Flyke's employee and friend.

The article said, "Garrett Asplundh, former star investigator for the SDPD's elite Professional Standards Unit, was suddenly hired away by the city's Ethics Authority in an attempt to clamp down on corruption, collusion and crime. Does he have what it takes? Former boss and SDPD Captain Roger Sutherland once described Asplundh as 'the most principled man I've ever worked with.' And what will it take besides principles to monitor ethics in our bustling city of over a million people? 'Endurance,' said Mr. Asplundh, with just a hint of a smile."

Jordan Sheehan was pictured twice. In the first shot, she stood between a new Padres relief pitcher who was supposed to help us win the National League West and a TV actor who played a New York cop and lived part-time in Rancho Santa Fe. In the second she was part of a group that included Steven Stiles, the chef of the city's hottest new restaurant, and "visiting Jance Purdew financial wiz Trey Vinson."

I tried to picture scrawny, unimpressive Trey finding the fallen earring and saving it for his murder of Garrett Asplundh. It was hard to do.

McKenzie met me at ten for our interview with Vinson. I drove to La Jolla and found a place to park. We headed down the sidewalk toward Vinson's hotel. I could smell the ocean in the warming March breeze and hear the sharp cries of the gulls wheeling through the perfect blue sky.

"How was your date with Harris?" I asked.

"Fast. I drove us in his car to the range in Oceanside. Taught him how to handle Death and Destruction. Then dinner, drinks, dessert."

"Death and Destruction" is McKenzie's nickname for her sidearm, which is a Glock nine-millimeter. Under the old chief, we were told what weapons to carry, but now we have greater latitude. The Glock is a workhorse that rarely jams or misfires, though it is on the large side of "concealable."

"He's an okay guy, Robbie."

"Good."

"It's like I've known him a long time. Did you feel that way when you first started seeing Gina, like you'd known her forever?"

"No, she seemed totally alien to me."

"He asked me to spend the weekend with him and some friends out in Jackson, Wyoming. He charters a jet to get there, and his house, you can ski from the porch right to the lift. Leave Friday noon and be back Monday night."

I thought of my stationary Mammoth Mountain skiing adventure. "That would be nice, McKenzie. Have a ball."

"You need me, Robbie, I'm on that plane in five minutes and landing at Brown Field less than two hours later. I told him that could happen, and he's down with it. He knows what my priorities are."

"You're a good partner, McKenzie. I'll be fine."

"The big money makes me feel strange," she said. "The Enzo trees me because I'm a car chick, but all the other stuff makes me wonder. And the way they live—way busier than I'm used to. To Hollis and his friends, a weekend is a time to fly somewhere special and play. For me it's laundry and the cat. I get my car *washed* on Saturdays, you know—I don't go buy a new one."

When we walked into the beautiful lobby of the Valencia Hotel, I thought of Ron Mincher and Allison, and Mincher's comment that his soul was rotting. It couldn't have started in a nicer setting. There was an enormous vase in the entryway, overflowing with big tropical blooms and flowers. The floors were the shiniest gray marble I'd ever seen. The registration desk was small and neat and staffed by a neatly groomed man about my age and a pretty woman a notch older.

In person, dressed in tennis whites and inviting us into his ocean-view suite, Trey Vinson looked less pathetic than when he was fornicating with working girls on video. He still had an air of entitlement, the look of a man who believed he deserved everything around him. He wore his shiny wedding ring.

Vinson offered us something from a fruit basket, but we both said no. He took a red apple and reclined on a cream-colored chair. The apple popped when he bit in.

I told him that we were investigating the murder of Garrett Asplundh and had discovered Asplundh's notes. We found some of them intriguing.

I read to him:

"City cooked the books. Now up to Vinson. Diminished to negative. If he holds we're alive, if he folds we're not."

"Well," he said. "He got straight to the center of it, I'll say that."

"Center of what?" asked McKenzie.

"Being up to me. The city's bond rating. I'm the one who brings the information back to New York so Jance Purdew can formulate its ratings. I assess the municipality, talk to its accountants and legal teams, review its books, investments, holdings, assets, et cetera. My recommendation is heavily weighted."

Pop went his apple.

"So did San Diego cook its books?" I asked.

"A case could be made that it did," said Vinson. "It goes back almost ten years. A city's bond rating is based on the things I just mentioned. The city government must keep its books with accuracy and transparency. Disclosure is everything. Back then the city failed to disclose that its pension fund was one billion dollars underfunded. 'Underfunded' means that they had taken pension dollars owed to employees and used them to balance the city budget to get a high rating. I said one *billion* dollars, Detectives—not one million, not one hundred million or six hundred million. There were piles of errors and omissions in city financial reports. 'Egregious' is the word often used to describe those errors and omissions, and it's a good one. Well, that same pension fund is still underfunded by a billion dollars but now everyone knows it. And the city is bleeding red ink every day. Your PD needs new cars and new officers. The fire-rescue department needs hundreds of millions of dollars, unless you want another disaster like you had three years ago. The new library is on hold. But San Diego is trying to keep its rating up. I told them I could only be so optimistic on their behalf. I told them they were probably looking at a rating diminishment from 'stable' to 'negative.' I had no choice."

"When is your report due back in New York?" I asked.

"May fifteenth," said Vinson. He looked thoughtfully at the apple and took another bite. "I leave a week from Friday. I've got more meetings, but I don't see any way around the negative rating. Sorry. I know you guys need your bullets and guns."

I thought about the underfunded pension and the nondisclosure. "So when Garrett wrote, *'If he holds we're alive, if he folds we're not,'* he's saying that if you recommend to keep the old rating—"

"Right. If the City of San Diego is seen as stable, the bond rating remains attractive. If I diminish it to negative, it's going to either prevent the city from issuing bonds at all or cost San Diego many millions of dollars in higher bond-interest payments."

"How many millions?"

"Fifty million, plus or minus twenty. Lots can happen."

Vinson arched his apple core toward a black enamel wastebasket. It went long, bounced off a beautifully papered wall and dropped in. He got up, swiped a tissue from a desktop, and patted down the wall.

"Garrett Asplundh wasn't a financial wizard," said Vinson. "But he understood lying and its consequences."

"Meaning what?" I asked.

"He was one of the only city guys who wasn't trying to influence me to keep the rating high."

"It was his job to prevent that kind of thing," said McKenzie.

Vinson shrugged, checked his watch and sat down again. "Ethics people aren't immune to money and pressure. Believe me."

He cited several city and county governments for their craven dishonesty and eagerness to "pander" to ratings agencies. I thought pander was an interesting choice of words, considering what we were about to reveal to him. He said investment-rating companies like Moody's and Standard & Poor's and Jance Purdew saved investors billions of dollars a year by bringing undisclosed risks to the light of day. He said he loved San Diego but he couldn't compromise his standards or shade his findings. He'd be honest, and quite frankly, it was going to be a very difficult recommendation.

"So you don't know what it will be?" asked McKenzie.

"Isn't that what I just said?" He looked at her with a bored arrogance.

"Did you know that Garrett Asplundh had you on video with three of Jordan Sheehan's working girls?" I asked.

Vinson's arrogance went brittle. He stared at me. *"Jordan Whoosies whatsies?"*

I said it again.

"Bullshit."

"I've got a laptop here in my briefcase," I said. "A picture is worth a thousand words."

He stood, looked at McKenzie, then at me again. "What is this?"

"You and some working girls you didn't pay for. Here—you tell us what it is."

"Sit down, Mr. Vinson," said McKenzie.

Vinson sat irritably.

I brought out the laptop and showed him a few seconds.

"Enough," he said.

"Your part doesn't last long," said McKenzie.

"Just turn it off."

For a moment we all sat there in the beautiful room. I listened to the waves crashing below and watched a pelican float in a perfectly straight horizontal line across a window.

"What do you *want*?" he asked.

"Answers," said McKenzie. "Who introduced you to the girls?"

"It was never a crime. I never paid money. They were San Diego bimbos. Party girls looking for a good time."

"And you're a good time?" asked McKenzie.

I chuckled quietly, happy to add to Vinson's humiliation and glad that McKenzie wasn't grilling me.

He stared at McKenzie with an odd, glazed look of captivity. "I can't believe this is happening."

"Believe. Who introduced you?"

"I want my lawyer."

"You don't get one until we arrest you," I said.

He stood.

"Sit," snapped McKenzie.

Trey sat.

"Who introduced you to the girls?" I asked. "Someone did, because someone expected something in return. They weren't really free, and you knew it."

"I *didn't* know that," he said.

"Trey," said McKenzie, "we're your only chance. We don't want to ruin you. In fact, we want you to like us. We want you to go home and ask for a stable rating for our wonderful city. We want the goodies you can help us get—more ballparks and stadiums and downtown development. Ethics needs telephone bugs. We need new radio cars and helicopters and bulletproof vests. But we're more than happy to make your life miserable and ruin your career if you'd like. We want the big guys. Talk to us."

"Nobody asked for anything. I was never asked to do anything but my job. *Not one thing.*"

"But you understood, didn't you?" asked McKenzie. "You knew you didn't get girls like that for nothing. You knew you were being provided a service."

I listened to the waves crash. Down the hallway a door slammed with a muffled thud. I looked out the window and wondered if I'd have survived a fall from it.

"Robbie, let's just call New York," said McKenzie. "We'll e-mail Jance Purdew a clip of Trey's leading-actor performance. Just to show them how San Diego is treating their guy."

Vinson was pale and wet-eyed.

"I'll do it, Vinson," said McKenzie. "I don't like the pouty way you think you own the world. They can fire you for all I care. Christ, you punk—you're married."

"Abel Sarvonola," Vinson said quietly. "He said not to worry, these girls know how to have a good time. He said just go home happy and tell them things look good out here. Excuse me—I gotta use the bathroom."

That evening I walked through our house again, much as I had done after Gina first left. I felt different now. I knew for a fact that she was gone and did not want to come back. I also knew that my anger had passed. I still had that ticklish little ember of hope inside, though, a hope that I might be able to come up with some way to make her want to return. It was difficult for me to be here in a place bristling with her magnetic power, with so much of my life and our history stamped onto every object.

When my schizophrenic Aunt Melissa died, Uncle Jerry told me their house had suddenly developed "different weather." He said the drafts came from different directions, lightbulbs gave off substantially more or less light, that the house cooled on hot afternoons, and that rain came through half a dozen leaks in a roof that hadn't leaked in fourteen years. He bought buckets to catch the drips and an indoor thermometer to prove he wasn't going crazy. He recorded some "very strange" temperature patterns in the old North Park house. He said they gradually subsided, as did the lightbulb fluctuations and roof leaks, though three years of San Diego drought followed Melissa's death.

Standing in the bedroom I looked at our wedding picture on the bedroom dresser. By the expressions on our faces it seemed impossible that we had been photographed in the process of making a huge mistake.

I took a few minutes to browse the Web site of the San Diego Synesthesia Society, as I had done several times in the last year. Their next meeting was Wednesday—tomorrow—and I was tempted to go. I was also unnerved by the prospect. I wasn't sure what I would find in a roomful of people with conditions like my own, but I was curious. I'd read that most synesthetes were female and left-handed, like Gina. I was curious about the long-term effects of my condition. Did it slowly drive people crazy? Might my synesthesia gradually fade away? Could it get more acute?

When I called Vince, he would tell me nothing other than that Gina was in a good safe place and doing well. This troubled me in a way I couldn't admit. I knew that Vince wanted to help me but I knew he had to put his daughter first. Dawn came on to tell me that I should let whatever was supposed to be, be—things happen for a reason, and things were going to work out. This made me feel worse because it seemed like a loftier way of saying, Why don't you just give up?

I went to the garage and looked at my fly-tying table but had no interest in creating imitation insects to catch trout that I would put back in the river anyway. Instead I sat there and wondered how McKenzie was doing with Hollis Harris. I had an unprovable feeling that he was taking advantage of her in some way but I couldn't say what it was. She was a grown-up. She was smart. She was experienced in the world. She had a sharp tongue and could shoot a chest-size group at fifty feet in nine and a half seconds with her sidearm. I wondered if Harris had run a standard hidden threat assessment on her, maybe come up with something he could exploit. I knew that there were gang problems in the outer branches of her family tree. His money bothered me, as it bothered her. He could rent things that most of us committed a lifetime to buy. No risk. I hoped McKenzie wasn't one of them.

Well after dark I drove from Normal Heights back to La Jolla and parked across from Jordan Sheehan's place. The night was cool and clear and I could hear the waves and the barks of the sea lions down by the seawall.

It was a quiet neighborhood. An elderly couple walked a miniature dachshund in a red sweater. When they wobbled out of sight I ambled over to Jordan's driveway and slapped a piece of duct tape over the rear right taillight of the pale blue Porsche. I pressed it down against the cap so it would stay on.

I'd bought a bag of tacos and a large root beer from a drive-through, and after taping Squeaky Clean's taillight, I sat back in my big Chevrolet, ate, and waited.

Exactly for what, I wasn't sure. But logic told me that Jordan Sheehan was connected to almost everyone we had interviewed regarding the death of Garrett Asplundh. She was connected to the police through Fellowes and Mincher, to the city government through Rood and Stiles, to business through Sarvonola and Vinson. She was connected to the streets through her girls and their johns and Chupa Junior. She wasn't a work-at-home financial adviser who just partied with the city players for fun. Her connections were the very ones that Garrett Asplundh had been hired to keep clean, polished, and in working order.

An hour and a half later, around eight, Jordan came down the steps of her house. She wore a sunny yellow dress with a shiny belt and buttons that ended high enough to show her legs. Over it draped a silky gray overcoat. She unlocked the car and got in, and a moment later the powder blue Porsche revved hoarsely, then backed out of the driveway.

I let her get almost to the avenue, then turned on my lights and swung a U-turn. I let two cars between us. The taped-off taillight made her easy to follow and oddly enough, Jordan Sheehan was a conscientious driver who signaled her turns well ahead of time.

On the outskirts of town she picked up Interstate 5 north. I stayed four cars back and a lane over, my eyes keyed on the one-lighted Porsche. She got off at Lomas Santa Fe and doubled back south into Solana Beach, then Eden Gardens. Then east into the hills and up a grade.

There was just one car between us now—a gas-electric hybrid of all things—and I could see the Porsche eating up the incline ahead of us. I couldn't pass the hybrid without getting Jordan's attention, and the hybrid couldn't keep up with the Porsche. We were past the homes and offices now and the hills were dark against a darker sky. Far ahead she swerved right then took a left turn fast and disappeared into the darkness of the upper canyon.

I goosed the Chevy around the hybrid car and floored it up the grade. The gearbox kicked down into second, then third, and then the V-8 found its power band and the car ate asphalt. I broke the back tires loose around the turn that the Porsche had made so nimbly and tried to accelerate through it without making too much noise. Ahead of me I saw nothing but a vanishing white line and a glimmer of taillight moving beyond the hillside brush.

I let the incline slow me down and set the shifter for third. I followed a sweeping curve, still climbing, then straightened out briefly, then curved back the other way. Ahead I caught a flash of lighted windows and the shapes of buildings.

Squeaky Clean hit her brakes, signaled, then turned left into a wide entryway with a guardhouse and an ornate white gate blocking the way. The guardhouse was not lit. I saw her arm extend from the car window as I drove past, continued a hundred yards up the road, then made a sweeping U-turn and crept back down toward the guardhouse in second gear.

The gate was just closing and the Porsche was already far past it, moving into the neighborhood of huge, dramatically lit homes. I watched the little car make a right and vanish behind a house the size of a multiplex theater. When the gate settled into position I read the words formed by the white iron: EDEN HEIGHTS. I thought how different it looked from Normal Heights. The homes were several times larger and much more spectacular than in the old neighborhood where I lived.

I pulled off to the side of the drive, killed the lights. Twenty minutes later an exotic-looking roadster that McKenzie would probably drool over came flying up the road, then swerved into the entryway at the last second and stopped at the gate. The driver reached from the window and slid a white card into an electronic box set in a slate stanchion. Music and a woman's laughter floated into the night. The gate rolled back and the exotic car rolled through it as I guided my land yacht of a Chevy into Eden Heights.

Mr. Exotic went the same way Squeaky Clean had gone. I drove slowly toward that first turn. I had browsed just enough home and architecture magazines in my life to realize that places like this were where they got their cover shots. Everything was outsize and lit from the bottom. There was no wood construction, no stucco. Just stone, plaster, and glass. Majestic palms swayed overhead in the cool, gentle breeze. Fountains trickled within expansive courtyards. Each home sat on a big lot, recessed from the street, with a planted slope in front. Some of them faced the street and others faced one way or the other, like people trying to avoid eye contact.

I made the turn. More bashful mansions. At the end of the cul-de-sac, set off from the other homes by space and height as if it were royalty, sat a two-story Italianate villa with a grand circular drive designed around a big fountain spraying blue lighted water into the air. Squeaky Clean's car sat in the drive, tucked up close to the house. There were several other cars, too, and four of them were Cabriolets. Mr. Exotic got out of his roadster as I drove past. I recognized him—Anthony Rood, Ninth District councilman with an eye on an assembly seat, a soft spot for sports teams, and for throwing public money at depressed areas so poor people couldn't afford to stay. And a special friend of at least three Squeaky Clean girls. Still another girl now unfurled from the passenger side of his car. All I saw was the flash of a silver dress as I went by.

I came to the end of the cul-de-sac, made the turn, and parked out of sight of the house. I killed the engine. Behind me was the darkness of the hills and in front of me a hillock of brush from beyond which rose a bank of soft light from the house and grounds. I couldn't exactly cruise the place in my Chevy.

From the trunk I got my binoculars, a knit watch cap, and a dark windbreaker with SDPD on the back in yellow. I locked the plainwrap and climbed into the brush before putting on the coat and hat. I closed my eyes for a second, and when I opened them the night was lighter. It took me a while to make the crest of the hillock because of the stiff, high brush and the rocky earth. I stopped for a moment and looked up at the moon through the branches of a tall manzanita bush. I wondered if by some tiny chance Gina was looking at the moon too. A rabbit chose this moment to bolt, which sent my heart racing.

When I got to the top of the hill, the side of the mansion came into view. I was just about eye level with the first-story windows. I looked through the binoculars at the big patio behind the house and a swimming pool and a bubbling whirlpool. They were all enclosed by an elegant metal fence topped by ornate but intimidating spears. A man and woman buried to their shoulders in the boiling green water kissed urgently in a cloud of rising steam. A pool house stood dark, just a faint porch light burning outside. King palms stood around the pool, each tended by its own light like a painting in a museum. To my surprise, a pretty woman in a short dark dress and high heels came from the house with two drinks on a tray. She set the drinks on a small table by the whirlpool and went back inside.

All of the windows were shuttered, so I couldn't see into the house. Only the French doors through which Short Dark Dress had come offered me anything at all. Through them I saw a large, dimly lit room. Short Dark Dress stood behind a bar, rinsing a highball glass in a sink. I could make out a sofa and a floor lamp turned down low, a man and a woman sitting on the sofa talking intently, a big abstract painting on the wall behind them, and a pool table lit by a hanging Tiffany-style lamp. The balls were racked and ready but nobody was playing.

Suddenly Jordan Sheehan strode into the room with a cell phone held to one ear and said something to Short Dark Dress. Then, talking into the phone again, she walked past the couple on the couch and disappeared.

I moved up the hillside a few yards and found a place where I could sit and see the house. The couple in the whirlpool rose naked from the boiling green water, wrapped towels around their bodies, swept their drinks from the table, and hustled across the patio into the pool house. I didn't recognize either of them. In the binoculars I could see their dark footprints on the flagstone patio. The lights inside the pool house didn't come on.

I wondered what to do. Jordan would have at least one set of eyes on the road out front.

I could call for backup, but the arrival of police cruisers would only start a mass exodus.

I could go knock on the door and ask to come in. Whoever answered would be within his or her rights to tell me this was private property and to beat it. But they might let me in, and by law I would be able to observe everything and anything in plain sight.

Or I could enter the premises based on my reasonable suspicion that a crime was taking place inside and be prepared to argue probable cause later. People would scatter. I could chase one down or surprise somebody and make an arrest or two. But unless I saw the money change hands or could find a witness who had seen such a thing, there would be no case for court. I would have to justify my moving surveillance of Jordan Sheehan. As an officer acting alone, I'd be placing myself at risk. And I'd be setting up my department for lawsuits for illegal search and unlawful arrest.

Or I could come back some other time with paper and a half dozen plainclothes officers and we could serve the warrant and toss the place. But I wasn't likely to get a warrant based on what I'd seen—a suspected madam who was licensed by the county to do business as a financial adviser, a city councilman and his aide, a woman with a tray of drinks, two naked people kissing in a whirlpool. Does that sound like a brothel to you?

I unclipped my cell phone and called Captain Villas. He was not pleased to be interrupted at home but I explained to him, quietly, what I had done and what I was now watching from the bushes behind the mansion in Eden Heights. He said he'd inform the chief and I should keep it to myself for now. He asked me if I was alone and told me to be careful.

I stood and worked my way back around for a front view of the house. With my pocketknife I trimmed back some branches of wild buckwheat, then got out my notebook and sat down again. It was nine-thirty. A white VW Cabriolet rolled into the circular driveway and parked behind Rood's roadster. A redhead climbed out and my heartbeat spiked. She had Gina's bouncy red hair and fast walk and for a split second I thought I was seeing her. But her skin was darker, and she was fuller-figured than my wife. As she climbed the steps, Chupa Junior opened the front door. He was dressed in a shiny blue suit. They talked as he let her in. He scanned the street and shut the door. With the binoculars I could see the stylish grate-covered window in the handsome front door. Chupa's office window, I thought. I made notes and wished I had a silent camera with a long telephoto and a slow shutter.

I made more notes as the girls and johns came and went. Between nine-thirty and two in the morning, six men arrived alone and eight left. Four more Squeaky Clean girls came, parked, and entered the house. Seven left.

Among them were Carrie Ann Martier and one of her two friends who had cooperated to make Garrett's sex video. Chet Fellowes pulled up in a shiny SUV and climbed the steps around midnight. He looked nervous and hungry. Trey Vinson arrived at 1:00 A.M. and was gone by 1:25. I was surprised he had the courage to be here after what we had shown him earlier that day. By 2:30 there were only two cars left in the drive. Jordan Sheehan padded outside with her high heels in one hand, got into her blue Porsche, and drove away. A few minutes later the lights inside went out one by one, and Chupa walked from the house. He locked the door and lumbered across the driveway to a black BMW. The car dipped with his weight. The bass from his trunk woofer thumped into the night and his car disappeared downhill in a swirl of white smoke.

I took my time heading down the hill and out of Eden Heights. I made my way to La Jolla thinking about what I 'd seen. I didn't understand why such beautiful young women would sell sex to men who were married and not very attractive. It wasn't that the girls were starving or destitute or couldn't do anything else for a living. Could you really just put your mind somewhere else and pretend it wasn't happening? I parked short of Jordan's pretty home, walked briskly up the sidewalk to her driveway, and pulled the tape off her taillight.

When I got home I immediately checked for a call from Gina, but there was none. Rachel had called to ask how I was doing. She said she hadn't heard a thing and hoped I was okay. I didn't trust Rachel as far as I could throw her but it was nice of her to check in.

I sat in the darkness in our little living room and thought some more about what I had seen that night. I did some loose math in my head. Estimating one thousand dollars for each john I counted, minus the discounts for Fellowes and Vinson, the Squeaky Clean girls would have brought in somewhere around twelve thousand dollars. If Jordan Sheehan took four hundred per trick, that meant she made forty-eight hundred dollars. And this was based only on the men I had counted. The house had had paying customers in it before Squeaky Clean and I even got there. I figured that Tuesdays would be slow. What would a Friday night bring in—double that? More? And add to that the income of the Squeaky Cleans out in the streets in their shiny cute convertibles.

Because I was tired, my mind skipped along on minor thoughts: Did they have a laundry service? Was the house rented furnished? What did the neighbors think was going on so late at night? Was the brothel open only on certain nights?

For a moment I stood on my porch with the light off and looked out into the cool March darkness. The springtime that I felt coming seemed to be far away now. It seemed like the night could last forever. I wondered how Mom and Dad were doing out in El Cajon. I was glad they had each other.

A little while later, I sat on the couch and put "The Life and Death of Samantha" into the DVD player. I should have been exhausted by almost no sleep in the last forty-eight hours but all I felt was jittery and bleak.

I watched the adults eating and drinking and listened to their voices and the cameraman's voice: *Great party.* I saw Garrett and Stella at the center of the table, happy and expansive. And Garrett's brother, Sam. *Great people.* I couldn't help noting that even Fellowes looked leaner and better formed than he did now. *Great country.* Kaven's thick hair lifted in the breeze, and his smile flashed behind the big mustache.

I wondered which of the Asplundhs' party guests had shot and narrated this part of the video. His voice was clear and strong and I knew I'd heard it before but couldn't place it.

I watched the children playing and the splash from the cannonball and the water hitting the lens of the camera. Then the fireworks and the boy running with the sparkler. Then the awful hush surrounding the small casket bathed in the stained-glass light of the chapel.

I watched the party scenes again. I had the feeling I was missing something obvious. They took only a few minutes to flicker by in the bright July sun. Then I pictured Garrett Asplundh sitting in his black Explorer at his special place by the Cabrillo Bridge while the rain came down.

What a terrible difference eight months had made.

I woke up a few hours later to a room jolted by sunlight and the sounds of birds carrying on in the coral tree in our front yard. I was on the couch. I had the remote in my hand and a kink in my neck.

I had dreamed that Gina and I were living happily in a tree house in a forest of Saskatchewan. The house was near the top of the tallest tree and it was open on all four sides. It was small and fragrant, and you could see for hundreds of green miles. I was aware even in the dream that I'd never been to Saskatchewan and this made our lives there feel all the more precious and temporary. We had leaf blowers to keep the pine needles off the floor and we could point the blowers backward between our legs, just kind of sit on them, then jump right off into the sky and fly. The blowers were not loud, and they gave off the smell of cinnamon instead of gas exhaust. When Gina flew by she laughed and her dress blew up and I tried to catch her but couldn't. I don't know how the dream ended.

I checked her closet again but was unsurprised by what I found. I looked at myself in the bathroom mirror and wished I were somebody else.

Garrett Asplundh was buried on Wednesday morning, a week after he was murdered. The funeral made me thankful to be me again and I felt selfish and shallow for being so pessimistic the night before.

The memorial service was brief. Stella, who arrived with her parents and Sam Asplundh, did not address the mourners as a group. Garrett's long-widowed mother trailed behind them. There were two dozen SDPD officers, including the chief himself. The Ethics Authority showed up in force—from the director down to Asplundh's fellow investigators. Even Arliss Buntz was there, in a black dress and her once-green sweater.

John Van Flyke eulogized Garrett movingly, considering Van Flyke's superior and humorless personality. He said that Garrett, like many great men, had experienced deep joy and deep pain. He had seen darkness and light. He had overcome a million temptations in order to walk the straight and narrow. He had believed in the power of good. He had understood how quickly a man's life can change. *He was a great man.* Van Flyke's voice wavered when he said this, so he said it again. *Garrett Asplundh was a great man.* It took me a moment to realize I'd heard his voice just a few hours before. *Great party, great people, great country.* I hadn't realized until now how close he was to Garrett.

Van Flyke went on to say that Garrett Asplundh had left behind the memory of his daughter, a mourning wife, many close friends—and whoever was responsible for his death would pay once on earth and atone forever in hell.

The minister subtly winced at this last declaration but he said a powerful prayer for the souls of the dead and the living and of forgiveness in the name of Jesus Christ, amen.

Stella hid behind sunglasses and steadied herself on Sam's arm. Her hair was pulled back tight and she didn't say much. I wondered if she would recover from all of this, and how long it might take. To lose a daughter and a husband within one year seemed a punishment too large to absorb.

I was struck again at the resemblance between Garrett and Samuel. According to the information that Hollis Harris had given us, Samuel was three years older. He was slightly taller and heavier, too, judging by my memory of Garrett. But Samuel had the same trim, dark features, the same expressive eyes as his brother. I wondered why the attractive blonde from the Fourth of July video was not with him.

Ethics Director Erik Kaven was there, face lined and mustache drooping, but his eyes boring steadily into everyone around him.

The mayor, the fire chief, and five of the nine city councilpersons all attended.

Jordan Sheehan came late, stood just to the right of the assembled mourners, and left early.

Carrie Ann Martier did the same but stood completely opposite Squeaky Clean, to the left. They never acknowledged each other.

Captain Sutherland, who had interviewed me for Professional Standards, was there, along with several PSU officers I scarcely recognized—Garrett's old gang. Captain Villas was there, of course. Captain Fellowes of Vice gave me an oddly chummy look as he walked past me.

Abel Sarvonola, the Budget Oversight Committee chairman, fresh from Las Vegas, moved through the mourners with his usual entourage of whatever they were—advisers, bodyguards, sycophants. He was mid-eighties at least and he looked it. His suit looked hungry on him but his eyes were still sharp and his handshake had a strength that surprised me.

"I am saddened and angered," he said. "We cannot afford to lose the good men."

"It angers me too," I said. "Garrett spoke of you."

He blinked. His dark eyes glittered and he smiled. "I didn't realize he thought of me at all. We should talk."

"We have an appointment for this afternoon," I reminded him.

"Of course we do."

He shook McKenzie's hand and stared frankly into her eyes.

Councilman Tony Rood made it. He looked satisfied and penitent in the way you might expect a man fresh from a brothel to look. His girl-beating aide Steve Stiles was with him, straight-backed and thick-necked.

I stood in the shade of a Torrey pine with McKenzie, Hollis Harris, and April Holly.

Harris was plainly unsure how to behave around McKenzie and me. Cops can do that to people. He treated us with a formality that was gracious but forced, especially with McKenzie. I could see by the way he looked at her that he had been captured. Interesting what you can see in a man's eyes. But it wasn't like he could put his arm around her or hold her hand, though he did whisper something in her ear.

McKenzie was taken too. She kept it hidden much better than Harris did, but I could tell. Her entire posture was different and her complexion looked better. It was nice to see two people strongly drawn to each other.

I thought of Gina with the kind of hunger that knows it can't be fed.

I want you to remember me like I was last night.

I was beginning to think that I had nothing to offer her that would be enough to bring her back.

April was lovely and seemed older than her eighteen years. She looked wholesome and innocent and I saw again the value of what Squeaky Clean had tried to buy from April but Garrett had allowed her to keep. I wondered why the world was so eager to consume wholesomeness and innocence. When April paid her respects, I wondered if Stella knew of April's living arrangement in her husband's secret apartment. I made a note to find out. Garrett's women, I thought. He had an eye for beauty.

By the end of the service, Stella was looking slightly better than on the day we had told her of Garrett's death. There was a trace of resolve on her face. For a few minutes she was surrounded by a group of women her age, and they talked and touched each other comfortably. I thought they looked familiar and then it struck me why—the Pan Am Games synchronized swimming champions of 1983.

As I watched Councilman Rood and aide Stiles talking with Sarvonola and his group, I wondered again if Stiles had the cojones to take out Garrett, then toss Jordan's earring into the Explorer just to mislead us. There was something aggressive about him, his bullish physique and gelled-back hair and fashionable ultralight sunglasses. I'd made some inquiries with another councilmanic aide I know and trust, and she told me that Stiles was ambitious to hold public office and was in fact a school board member in his daughter's district. She said that Rood had his eyes on a California state assembly seat, and Stiles had his on the Ninth District council chair his boss would vacate. Convenient, I thought. I reminded myself that Stiles—out of all the men captured on Garrett's video—most likely knew before Garrett's murder that he'd been recorded. He'd certainly been confronted by Garrett. All his public ambitions could be shattered by that one thin disc, or that one deposition from Carrie Ann Martier. But what good would a murder have done Stiles at that point? Garrett had sprung the trap on him weeks earlier. Stiles had apologized and paid handsomely for his crimes. I could imagine Stiles's fury and helplessness as he was caught in his own web, but I still couldn't imagine him behind the trigger of Carl Herbert's Model 39.

McKenzie left with Harris. April Holly stood with me for a while then walked behind a row of graves to say good-bye to Stella. She drove off alone in a nifty gold coupe made possible by Garrett Asplundh.

I leaned against the tree and saw John Van Flyke leaning against his own tree on the other side of the grave. He was gazing out over the mourners just as I was. He looked tired. Kaven had long since gone.

I was about to leave myself when a trim young man walked across the grass toward me. He was dark-haired, wore dark sunglasses, and was dressed in a suit that must have been made for him. He had come to the service alone and I had seen him glancing at me and McKenzie several times. He stopped in front of me, took off the glasses, and looked me directly in the eye.

"I am Sanji Moussaraf."

"With the red Ferrari."

"My car was disabled on the freeway the night Mr. Asplundh was killed. I called the police. Are you Detective Brownlaw?"

"Yes."

"I recognize you from the burning hotel," he said. "I saw the article in the newspaper about Mr. Asplundh and decided I should come here to find you."

"Sooner would have been better."

"I didn't have the courage."

He was very young—nineteen or twenty. I saw sincerity in his eyes, and a spark of fear.

"Take a walk with me, Mr. Moussaraf. Tell me what you saw."

In his accented and slightly formal English, Sanji Moussaraf told me that his car had suddenly stalled on the southbound 163, and he'd guided it over to the side of the highway. He said it was like running out of gas, though he'd just filled up the tank that morning. He'd had trouble with the fuel filter once before and the car had stalled just like this. It was approximately 8:40 at night. It was raining. He called the Auto Club on his cell phone. They said a truck would be there within thirty minutes. He got out and raised the hood of his car but couldn't see much.

No colored shapes came from Sanji's mouth.

We walked along the narrow, winding road that led through the cemetery. The grass-cutting crew was removing flowers from the graves, which was too bad, because many of them looked fresh. I wondered if they ever kept a particularly nice arrangement as a gift for a loved one.

"So I got back in the car to wait for the Automobile Club," said Moussaraf. "And when I was sitting there I saw a vehicle come down the embankment from above. It was a black sport utility vehicle. It moved slowly. When it came to level ground, the driver turned off the lights and the engine. The vehicle was approximately one hundred and fifty feet from me. There were trees with dangling branches that made my vision difficult. Five minutes later another vehicle came down the embankment. It moved slowly also and it pulled up next to the black SUV. This vehicle was a white Hummer. It looked new. The chrome was very shiny. There was no license plate on the front. I thought I saw a temporary registration taped to the windshield but it could have been something else. The headlights then were turned off."

My heart sank a little. I'd had a fond hope that this alert young man had come up with at least a partial plate number. A temporary registration taped inside the windshield didn't help much, though San Diego–area Hummer dealers could shed some light on recent sales.

"I sat for a few minutes," said Moussaraf. "The rain increased. It was loud against the roof of my car. I looked at the two vehicles parked together in the grass. Because they were slightly behind me, I had to turn to see them. The trees still were between us. I saw an orange flash of light inside the first SUV. It was very bright and immediate. It was over instantly. It was thin and long like a comet. It appeared to be horizontal. My first thought was, someone had just fired a gun."

As I looked at Sanji, yellow triangles floated into the space between us. They come from fear. Which is what most of us would feel upon remembering the sound of a gunshot.

"Did you see the shooter?"

"A moment later I saw the shape of a man move between the vehicles. He wore dark clothing. He was very difficult to see."

"You're sure it was a man?"

Sanji nodded. "I am almost sure."

"Where did he shoot from?"

Sanji looked at me and frowned. "I cannot say for certain. The flash came from the passenger's side. Maybe the shooter was sitting there. Maybe he was outside the vehicle, but leaning in. I believed the flash was moving from the passenger side to the driver side, but this could have been an illusion. It was instant and brief."

"Did you hear a report?" I asked.

"The traffic on the highway was very loud. And the rain on the roof of my car. But I thought I heard something from the direction of the parked vehicles. A muffled pop."

"Then what?"

"I continued to watch. With the rain and the branches and the darkness it was difficult to see. This is when I saw the shape of the man moving between the vehicles. Then the white Hummer reversed up the hill. It slipped in the wet grass and the tires appeared to spin, but then very slowly it climbed to the crest of the hill and went over. The headlights were still off."

More yellow triangles.

"How much time passed between the flash and when you saw the man moving from one vehicle to the other?"

"Ten seconds."

I wondered why a shooter would wait so long. Any shooter I've ever known would have bolted into his car and up that hill in a heartbeat. Tossing in an earring to confuse the investigation? Wiping off his prints?

"How long between the time you saw him and when the Hummer reversed up the hill?"

Sanji Moussaraf wiped his brow with a pale blue handkerchief that matched his necktie. "Perhaps five seconds. Enough time to start the engine and put it in gear. Not long."

We stopped walking at the crest of a gentle rise. The graves stretched on for acres and acres around us and the grounds crews gathered up the flowers and tossed them into a pickup truck like trash from a sporting event. The Asplundh mourners seemed small and black and minor in this ocean of grass and stone. Van Flyke had left his tree and now stood with Sam and Stella and her parents. The morning clouds brooded above us in various shades of gray.

"As soon as I saw the flash I looked at my watch," said Sanji. "It was exactly eight fifty-two. My watch is a Rolex and accurate. I waited for perhaps a minute, maybe two, after the Hummer left. Then I got out of my car. I climbed the fence. There was a drainage ditch full of water and I jumped across it. I went to the SUV and saw that the window was broken and a man was in the front seat, not moving. It was very bloody. I ran to the fence and climbed it again. I cut my hand on the chain link. I got back into my car and tried the engine again but it would not start. I thought about what I had seen. The tow truck delivered my car to the mechanic's lot. The driver gave me a ride and I took a taxi home."

He showed me a small, jagged cut on the index finger of his right hand. We started back toward the mourners and Garrett Asplundh's freshly dug grave.

"But you didn't call until after three that morning," I said. "That's over six hours."

He glanced at me again and sighed. "I know it was wrong to wait."

"Why did you?"

"When I got home," said Moussaraf, "I stayed up late, drinking coffee. I thought about the immigration jail where I was taken after the September eleventh attack. It is called CCA because it is a private jail run by a private company called Corrections Corporation of America. I spent sixty nights there with no charges, no lawyer, no phone calls allowed to me, and no information about my status or future. Sixty nights, no exercise, no sun, no contact with my family or friends. My student visa was current and legal. I thought about the suspicion and disdain of the men who interrogated me about the San Diego–based terrorists. I was fifteen years old and my crime was that I attended the same mosque as one of the suicide hijackers."

A flood of yellow triangles swept past me and vanished.

"Did you know him, the hijacker?"

"No. I had met him exactly one time. But my name and phone number were found in his address book. I remembered him as being secretive and humorless. He asked me for money for a humanitarian relief project in Afghanistan. I refused. You can imagine the suspicion of the United States government, given the economic power of my family in Saudi Arabia. I thought about many things that night. Then I went to a pay phone and called the police."

"Did you follow the story in the papers?"

He nodded. "I knew it was important to talk to you. I suspected that what I saw could help your investigation. And Sergeant Waimrin said I could trust you."

"Better late than never," I said.

"Yes. I'm a junior now at San Diego State. I have an American girlfriend, though I know my family will not let me marry her. I have many friends here in San Diego. I was afraid to risk all that I have."

We continued back toward the mourners. Only a few remained. Apparently this was the kind of cemetery where they don't actually bury the coffin until all of the mourners are gone. The gravediggers sat on their Bobcats down the road a few yards, smoking and waiting. I watched as Van Flyke held open the limo door for Stella, her parents, and Sam, then closed it and walked back toward his car.

"There is one more thing," said Sanji. "I saw a new white Hummer drive down Kettner when I was at the mechanic's waiting for the taxi. It had what looked like a temporary license on the windshield. I cannot say that it was the vehicle from earlier. This is possibly coincidence, but maybe not."

"What did the driver look like?"

"I could see nothing through the darkened windows. But there was mud on the bottom of the body."

"Like it had climbed a muddy hill in reverse."

"Correct."

"What time?"

"Nine forty-four."

"Which way was it traveling on Kettner?"

"North, toward the airport."

Sanji pulled a small brown paper bag from his coat pocket. It was folded over once and neatly creased. "When the white Hummer was stopped at the signal, the driver rolled down his window and threw this out. Unfortunately, it was run over before I could get to it."

He gave me the bag and I opened it. Inside was a flattened paper Higher Grounds coffee cup, the small size, complete with the padded cardboard ring that keeps your fingers from getting scalded. The plastic cover lay on top, crushed and cracked, the vents stained with coffee.

"I wonder if you can obtain DNA from this material," said Sanji.

"Maybe. And fingerprints from the lid, if we're lucky."

The swimming pool where Samantha Asplundh drowned is small and looks harmless. It is rectangular, lined with blue tiles above the waterline, and overshadowed by two large pine trees that drop needles to the deck but make the air smell good. The former Asplundh home is located near La Mesa, which is east of San Diego and gets hot in summer. The backyard is shaded and secluded, which gives it charm. It is set downslope from and slightly to the side of the house and is all but hidden by a hedge of oleander blooming pink against the dark wood siding of the home. But the seclusion also suggests complicity in the terrible thing that happened here. The neighboring homes are set away and separated from the yard by large, sloping lawns behind chain-link or grape-stake fences, as if not wanting to get too close to a tragic place.

There was a For Sale sign in the front yard when I drove up. The home was now owned by Dr. Owen James, a dentist. His wife, Cindy, had given me a key for the padlock so I could get into the pool area.

She and two small children watched me from the house as I peered through the new chain-link fence at the pool. The fence was eight feet high and looked penal in this domestic setting. The bubbled plastic pool cover was littered with pine needles. The filter was humming and I could hear the water slurping into the catch.

I had no trouble picturing the Asplundh family here in this backyard. It looked very similar to the way it had looked in Garrett's Fourth of July video from last year. I shot a couple of pictures with the digital camera strapped around my neck.

I turned and waved to the dentist's children, then opened the lock and let myself through the gate. I toured the area slowly, trying to stand for a while in each of the places from which the Fourth of July party video was shot. I shot pictures from each place. I had no idea what I was looking for, other than a clearer idea of what had happened that day. And to pay respects to a little girl I'd never met and whose father I had just helped bury. But there was something more. I wanted to see this place for the same reason that I had wanted to watch and rewatch the pool scenes from "The Life and Death of Samantha"—because I had the feeling I was missing something.

I stood about where the picnic table had been and took a picture of the pool and one of the house. I thought of John Van Flyke's voice as he shot the hosts. *Great party.* I pictured the red, white, and blue ribbons tied to the birds of paradise and hydrangea. *Great people.* I pictured the kids splashing in the pool. *Great country.*

I heard the gate open and saw Mrs. James coming across the deck toward me. She was tall and generously proportioned and had an air of health and strength about her. It was noon and the March sun had come out strong. She squinted and held a flattened hand over her eyes.

"We were completely shocked at what happened to Mr. Asplundh," said Mrs. James.

I looked back at the house and estimated how much of the pool was visible from inside. There were plenty of windows, but most of them were behind the hedge of oleander or the big pines. I thought of Garrett in another part of the home, rinsing dishes and shooting video of the fireworks in the driveway while little Samantha snuck through the forest of adults' legs on her way to find her father. I saw the walkway down which she had come and I imagined where she would have stopped, her attention caught by the sparkling pool or maybe by the sight of her favorite doll floating in the warm, welcoming water.

"Is there a light inside the pool?" I asked.

"Yes," said Mrs. James. "It lights up the whole thing. Why?"

"Samantha's doll and the pool skimmer were found in the water after she drowned. There was some speculation that she fell in while trying to get the doll."

"The light would have made it show up on the surface," said Mrs. James.

I imagined the floating doll, illuminated from below. I wondered why, if it had been floating for some time, it hadn't made its way to the edge the way most floating objects do. If it had, Samantha could just have knelt down and picked it up. No need for the skimmer. No need to fall in. But apparently the doll had floated away from the deck. Just one more of the many small cogs that had meshed that evening to form the gear of tragedy.

"Are you here about Samantha or Garrett?" she asked.

"About everything," I said.

Cynthia James crossed her arms and took a small step backward.

"You haven't used the pool, have you?" I asked.

"No. Not warm enough yet. We didn't move in until December."

"Are you selling because it bothers you?"

She nodded. "I told Owen before we bought that I could never get used to it. It doesn't bother him. It doesn't bother the children. I've tried very hard, but what happened here bothers me, greatly. I had the old five-foot fence replaced with this eight-foot one before we moved in. I've hidden the key to that lock. The fence is wired with a very loud alarm. My children are forbidden to touch the fence or the lock. And I still have nightmares. When Mr. Asplundh was murdered, Owen finally caved in. We listed it Monday and we've gotten two offers already. I'm relieved. I can't wait to get out of here. This place is drenched in bad luck. The neighbor boy bothers my children. May I please have the key back?"

I handed it to her.

"Just make sure the lock is secure before you leave," she said.

I thanked her, knowing she would check the lock again after I had left. I glanced up to the window but the children were gone. I wandered the pool area. A mockingbird jeered at me from one of the big pine trees. I shot his picture and he stopped. Far above the mockingbird a vulture traced a lazy black circle in the blue sky.

I watched a young teenage boy clamber across a neighbor's yard and press himself close to the chain-link fence that divided the properties. Most of the fence was overhung with climbing jasmine but this boy had either found or worn away a spot between the fragrant white blooms. He wore red bathing trunks and nothing else. He was hunched, big-eared, clumsy.

"Who are you?" he asked.

"I'm Robbie."

"What are you doing?"

"Taking a few pictures. How about you?"

"That's where it happened. Samantha drowned."

"Yes," I said. "What's your name?"

"Jeremiah."

"Were you at home that night?" I asked.

"Uh-huh."

"See anything?"

"The fireworks were really, really good."

I looked back toward the former Asplundh house, over which the fireworks would have been visible, and realized that Jeremiah would have had a pretty good look at them from just about anywhere in his backyard.

"Where did you watch from?" I asked.

"Back there. Mom wouldn't let me go closer."

"Did you see Samantha?"

"She was really, really nice."

"Jeremiah!"

He flinched and turned. I saw the pronounced and crooked curve of his spine beneath his skin. Then he looked back at me with a dull annoyance on his face. A small woman stood in the sliding glass door of the house. She started across the patio toward us.

"I got to go," he said.

"Did you see her fall in the pool, Jeremiah?"

"Jeremiah!"

"No. I had to go to bed. I love those fireworks but I had to go to bed. Mom put me to bed before it was over. I heard sirens later."

The woman came down the sloping lawn, hands on her hips, head angled.

"Jeremiah, it is time for your nap."

"Yeah, uh-huh. This is Robbie."

"Ma'am," I said.

"You talking about Samantha again, Jeremiah?" the woman said.

"Uh-huh."

"He didn't see anything and he doesn't know anything and if one more of you insurance investigators or reporters or whatever you are comes around here I'm going to call the police."

"I am the police."

Jeremiah smiled crookedly as she shooed him away from the fence and got him headed in the direction of the house. He labored up the slope hunchbacked and bandy-legged and without self-consciousness that I could see. It looked as though his bones had been melted at birth, then hardened out of shape.

"I'm sorry," said the woman. "I'm his mother. It was horrible. Jeremiah really liked that little girl and she seems to have stuck in his mind in a way that very few things do. He's challenged, as you see."

"There's no need to apologize," I said.

"He didn't see her drown. None of us did. I guess each parent thought the other was with her. Do you suspect foul play?"

"No."

"Good-bye, then. Please don't question Jeremiah. He was in bed when it happened. It's all we can do to keep him in the present in a healthy way."

She raised a hand, turned and walked off.

I shot a few more pictures, locked the gate, pulled the lock hard three times, and left.

Abel Sarvonola rose slowly from his chair and shook McKenzie's hand, then mine. His skin was cool and he was stooped but there was an assessing gleam in his eye. His hair was white, with comb tracks fixed by wax. He wore the same loose black suit he'd worn a few hours earlier at the funeral.

"Please sit," he said.

He lowered himself stiffly back into his chair as his receptionist brought in coffee and bottled water. Sarvonola smiled at her but said nothing as she set out the drinks and closed the door behind her. His teeth were large and yellow.

We exchanged pleasantries about the funeral, the weather, and the privilege of living in San Diego.

"I know Garrett disliked my policies," he said suddenly. "We didn't agree on how certain things should be done. He wanted more money for Ethics, but we gave them all that we could, under the circumstances."

"He wrote about those disagreements in his investigation notes," I said.

Sarvonola nodded and stared at each of us in turn. He had the patience of a man used to being listened to.

"And I know about all that sex stuff he recorded—Fellowes, Mincher, Rood, and that prick Stiles—all of it. Even our little bond-rating friend from New York. Yeah, Garrett sat right there where you are and showed me some highlights. Made me wish I was young again. He asked me what I thought he should do with it. I appreciated that about Garrett. You could talk to him. He cared what you thought."

It was interesting that Sarvonola told us about the sex videos before we'd even mentioned them. How did he know we'd seen them?

"What was your advice?" I asked.

"I said first get the whoremongers together and show them the video. Tell them we can't have that kind of thing going on. Tell them if they do it again, they're fired—end of discussion. And if they squawk, threaten to tell the *Union-Tribune* why they got canned. That'll shut them up, believe me. Then break up that disc and flush it down the nearest toilet, which is out the door and down the hallway ten steps."

"Garrett wouldn't do that," said McKenzie. "He'd want to do more than just slap their wrists."

"True," said Sarvonola. "We had two very different opinions on what this city needs. Which is what you'd expect from an ethics investigator like Garrett and a policy maker like myself. Garrett wanted a legal solution—grand jury indictments, criminal charges, rolling heads. I can understand that. It has logic and the flair of retribution. But it would have dragged our city through the sewer. It would cost us hundreds of thousands of dollars to prosecute those men, it would dirty the face we show to the world, and it would slow the flow of dollars that keeps us all alive and healthy and happy. It would open the door to state or federal regulation, which is clearly unnecessary. For example, because of its scandals of years ago, the Los Angeles Police Department is now overseen by federal monitors. Ours is not. We will not let it be. We'll monitor ourselves. We'll take care of our own problems. In our city you good police are free to enforce the laws. We're America's Finest City, not America's Horniest City. In spite of what Mr. Asplundh's videos depict."

I thought about Abel's approach, and I pulled out a page I'd printed from Garrett's notes.

"What's that?" asked Sarvonola.

"Garrett wrote this," I said. "'*Think about it for one second, Stella. Sarvonola says no more money for Ethics. Just like there was no more money for fire protection while half the county burned and the firefighters didn't have enough batteries for their walkie-talkies. And don't forget we've got good honest city workers with a failing pension after some of them paid into it for thirty years. These are just more examples of the collapse that's coming, Stella. The crash that nobody will talk about.*' "

"He was a Boy Scout, an altar boy, and an alarmist," said Sarvonola. "San Diego won't crash."

"Why not?" asked McKenzie. "If we're spending more than we're taking in, then do the math."

"I have, and we'll just do what we've always done," said Sarvonola. "Raise taxes, cut services, sell off prime real estate holdings to developers for pennies on the dollar and float billions in bonds. Then we can afford to buy batteries and fill up the pension buckets that we've been emptying for years to balance the budget. It's boom and bust. Simple."

"That just makes the next generation pay for the mess," said McKenzie.

"So?" asked Sarvonola. "What are kids for?"

He smiled his large, yellow smile again.

"I should know—I've got eight children, twenty-four or -five grandkids, and six great-grandchildren. And do they care about San Diego's debt? Hell no. I'll tell you what they care about—it isn't debt, and it isn't batteries for walkie-talkies, and it's not some library full of outdated books when they can get everything they need online anyway, no—it's new stadiums and teams and really good parks and recreation programs. It's clean air and water and perfect beaches and high property values. It's plenty of good stores and discount warehouses. It's zoning out the useless and the unsuccessful and working with business that will bring in dollars. *Bring in dollars*. It's development, then redevelopment, then replanning, then rezoning, then more development all over again. That's prosperity. *Prosperity*. That's what I work for. That's what I represent—the policy of prosperity."

Sarvonola, as chairman of the Budget Oversight Committee, was afforded a rather nice office in City Hall. I looked through his window at the clear, sunny day. We were seven stories up. I could see some of the bay, and Point Loma beyond it, then the unhurried Pacific all the way to the horizon.

"What Garrett represented was the policy of honest government and honest business," I said. "Without that, everyone defaults to the lowest common denominator—they start thinking like you."

Sarvonola's dark eyes shone with apparent mirth. He smiled again. "Exactly, *exactly,* Detective. That's why we hired him and that's why it's such a tragedy he's gone. So let's just pick up the pieces and try to go on with the business of living our lives. That's what Mr. Asplundh would have wanted us to do."

"We pesky cops are paid to find out who killed him," said McKenzie.

Sarvonola sat back and stared at McKenzie, then at me. "Look, I'm sorry he got killed. I always liked him. We'd talked just a few days before. And I'm sorry his daughter drowned. So little and innocent—that's a tragedy. And I'm sorry for the wife he left behind, though I imagine she'll find a way to be well taken care of. In fact, she'll get some of his city pension someday, if she qualifies."

"If there's any money left in the pension," I said.

"We'll fill that pension fund back up," said Sarvonola. "You watch."

"Did you discuss those sex videos with anyone?" I asked. "Did you tell anyone about them?"

He narrowed his eyes at me. "You gotta be kidding. Garrett came to me for advice. I gave it. I knew he wouldn't take it. *He* knew he wouldn't take it."

No red squares.

"Why did he talk to you about what he'd found?" asked McKenzie.

"Didn't you notice? Because I'm the only heavy hitter who doesn't have at least one associate on Garrett's videos. The mayor? He's got Rood and Stiles. The chief of police? Fellowes and Mincher. Fire department, City Hall—all present and accounted for. But the Budget Oversight Committee? We're clean."

Sarvonola smiled as if for a camera.

"Did Garrett tell you exactly what he planned to do with the videos?" I asked.

"Naw," said Sarvonola. "He kept his cards close. He lobbied me for more money for the Ethics Authority next year. Said they needed phone-intercept hardware, more cars, a better phone system in the Enforcement building. Then we talked Chargers for a while, then baseball. You know, for having his knickers in a knot about what the city spent for the new ballpark, Garrett really liked the Padres."

"But you understood that Garrett was going to have to deal with those people in the video?" asked McKenzie.

"Of course I did. It was in his nature to deal with such people. I told him good luck if he wanted to bust them all, but it was the worst thing he could do for this city. And you know what? That got his attention. It bothered Garrett Asplundh because he was a good man and he loved this place and he understood that the damage done by a few fools doesn't stop when you toss them in jail."

"It's important to throw the right fools in jail," I said. "That's why we have the Ethics Authority."

Sarvonola looked at me as if I'd failed to understand something obvious.

"Trey Vinson said you introduced him to some of Jordan Sheehan's girls," I said. "You told him to have a good time with them and give San Diego a good credit rating when he got back home."

Sarvonola sat back, furrowed his brow, and looked at each of us in turn. "Horseshit."

"Not according to Vinson."

"You really want to talk about this?"

"We really do," I said.

"Trey Vinson is a pathetic little worm who couldn't get a date on his own in a thousand years. So I introduced him to some friends of friends."

"He's also married," said McKenzie.

"What do I care? You're missing the point, which is that Vinson's dates were all party girls. They were not professionals. They were not Jordan Sheehan's girls or anybody else's. They were young San Diego women out for a good time. They were our daughters and our sisters and our nieces. No money changed hands between Vinson and any girl on that video—none that I saw."

"Maybe it didn't change hands on camera," I said. "But somewhere it did. Somewhere along the line, Jordan Sheehan and the girls got paid. And since you're the one who told Trey Vinson to have a good time, you probably know exactly where and when and how much."

Three red squares of deception slipped from his mouth. When he smiled again, a dozen more wobbled out from between his big teeth and floated over his desktop.

"I never saw one penny of it."

Sarvonola stared at me again. I watched him behind the red squares, squinting menace into his eyes. I waited awhile and said nothing. Nothing annoys a liar more than silence.

"Not one penny."

"Did you see Garrett the night he died?" I asked.

"I hadn't seen him in a week."

The red squares had melted into space and no new ones spilled out to replace them. I waited again and watched Abel Sarvonola sit back and lock his arms across his chest.

Finally I looked at McKenzie and stood. "Thanks for your time, Mr. Sarvonola. We'll be in touch."

"Are you threatening me? I've told you nothing but the truth," said Sarvonola.

"You can lie to us all you want about paying Squeaky Clean and her girls," I said. "But I'd work on my presentation if I were you. Because if you lie in court it's called perjury and you go to prison."

"You're much worse than Garrett."

"Thank you."

Sarvonola squinted at me, eyes shining from deep within his heavy black brow. "Garrett was smart. He kept things to himself until he could understand the implications. But you two took what he found and lost control of it. You show it around to everyone. You leave yourselves open. You're dangerous to yourselves and everyone around you."

"Sounds like *you're* threatening *us* now," said McKenzie.

"I can't change the course of prosperity."

"Then enjoy the rest of your day," I said.

He worked himself up from the chair and extended a pale finger at me. His face was white and his back was bent.

"You're nothing but a mediocre detective who got thrown out of a building and landed on an awning instead of the sidewalk. You're not brave, you're lucky. You're not supposed to be alive. They promote you in order to create a hero. It shows how desperate they are."

I stood up straight and took a deep breath, as my father had taught me to do in the face of threat.

"And you're a parasite with a good shot at doing time for pandering and bribery," I said.

"The chief will hear about this."

"He'll hear about the girls you got for Vinson, too," I said.

"I will defeat you."

"Bring help," said McKenzie.

I spent the rest of the afternoon calling Hummer dealers in San Diego County. Since I believed I was looking for a white Hummer that still had the temporary tag taped to the windshield, I asked each dealer to go back three months to check sales. The normal time for the DMV to send the metal plates is more like eight weeks, so I left myself a cushion.

Seven Hummer dealers in San Diego had sold or leased a total of twenty-one new white Hummers between late last year and now. These included both 2004 and 2005 models. Two of the dealers asked if they could call back with the information.

Four of the sales managers and one owner were cooperative and gave me the names of the buyers or lessees. The others couldn't give out that information, though they both said that if I had a specific name they might be able to confirm a vehicle purchase or lease. One of the sales managers offered me a cash rebate of five hundred dollars and 0 percent "VIP" financing over five years on a new 2005 Hummer, "the most secure vehicle" I could ever drive.

None of the names of new Hummer drivers caught my eye. To the reluctant dealers I offered the names Fellowes, Mincher, Rood, Stiles, Jordan Sheehan, and Peter Avalos, but none of them were on the buy/lease lists. And I wasn't convinced that any of them had both the motive and opportunity to kill Garrett.

Fellowes didn't know that Garrett had him naked on tape until we told him. Mincher had half an alibi and did not strike me as capable of murder. Rood and Stiles were at the "exploratory fund-raiser" aboard the carrier *Midway*.

Jordan Sheehan and Chupa Junior claimed to have worked the Indigo that night from eight until midnight, which checked out. McKenzie had even tracked down the waitress, Dolly, who admitted to being with Chupa at his house from about 1:00 A.M. until noon the next day.

If Sanji Moussaraf was right, Garrett Asplundh had been shot dead at 8:52 that night, give or take the ten thrashing, bloody seconds it took him to rip off a fingernail on his killer's clothing.

I looked out the window at the falling evening and imagined Garrett dressed in his suit and good-luck blue necktie, sitting alone in his Explorer, parked in the rain where he'd proposed to Stella ten years before. I knew what he was thinking about: seeing Stella in just a little while and trying to rebuild the life they had shared before the drowning of their daughter. And I began to wonder if his murder was really connected to sex videos, Squeaky Clean girls, municipal-bond ratings, and corrupt city employees. From the beginning I had assumed it was, but by now I saw that Garrett hadn't *done* anything with what he knew. The meeting with the state attorney general? Maybe that was a motivation for murder, but who knew what Garrett would present to the attorney general and what he would withhold? Sarvonola understood that Garrett wanted to protect the city he worked for and loved, and Garrett's enemies must have known it, too. After all, Garrett Asplundh was one of them, one of *us:* a city employee, a man with problems and opportunities, a man of both power and weakness. Kill him on a hunch he was about to spill their secrets? Maybe, but maybe not.

I wondered if his murder was more personal than that.

My luck changed for the better on the drive home. I took a small detour to go past Sultra on the slim chance that Gina had driven back from Nevada and returned to work. I pulled over for just a moment. The salon blinds were open to the late afternoon and I saw a tall blonde at Gina's chair. This made my heart ache inordinately so I drove away. The detour landed me on Hawthorn Street where I passed a downtown car-rental company called Dream Wheels. I'd driven by it a thousand times. But I saw a new black Hummer on the lot and decided to stop and ask about a white one.

The Dream Wheels manager was a short, thick man named Reuben. His assistant was a striking, fortyish woman who introduced herself as Cass. They eyed me warily as I slid my detective shield back into my pocket. Cass excused herself and walked outside.

When I asked about a white Hummer, Reuben sighed. He tapped sharply on his computer keyboard, then nodded. Yes, he said, they had rented out a white Hummer at five-fifteen on the afternoon of March 8, the day of the murder. Oddly enough, it was returned that night after they had closed.

Odd indeed, I thought.

"Charles Hudson Black," he said. "He lives in Rancho Santa Fe. Go ask Cass about him. She did the rent. And tell you what—I'll print you a copy of this rental agreement if you can get patrol to drive past this place a little more often. People climb in here all the time. They touch my cars. Once they climbed over, hot-wired a Land Rover and tried to drive it through the fence and out of here."

"You've got a deal," I said.

I found Cass outside, smoking a cigarette and flicking the ashes down beside a Shelby Cobra. The rental cars shone brilliantly in the overhead lights.

"That's my dream wheel," I said. "If I could have any car ever made."

"I'd get a Maybach," she said. "The expensive one comes with a driver for a year. I'd boot him out of the car, do my own driving, and make him clean my house."

"Describe the guy who rented the white Hummer on March eighth. That was two Tuesdays ago, the last time it rained."

"Mid-forties," she said. "Chargers cap and shades. Cap looked new. Heavy plaid shirt—brown. A bushy mustache. Sunglasses. The kind of guy you'd see at a tailgate party at Qualcomm."

I saw the shape of a man move between the vehicles.

"What color hair?"

"The hat was pulled down tight but the mustache was brown with gray in it."

"How tall?"

"Six feet, maybe two-ten," said Cass. "My ex is six feet, two-ten, and this guy was about the same. Not fat. He had kind of a 'screw you' attitude."

"What did he say?"

"Nothing unusual. It was just the way he stood and looked at me."

I thought of Ron Mincher. The description could have been him, except he was almost twenty years younger than the man Cass had described and his mustache had no gray in it. I wondered if the brown plaid shirt and sunglasses could have hidden his youth. I wondered if he might have added some gray to his mustache. I wondered if the three brown wool fibers found in Garrett's Explorer had come from that heavy plaid shirt.

"What kind of pants and shoes?" I asked.

"Jeans, I think. Don't remember the shoes at all," said Cass.

"Did he say anything that you remember? Anything unusual or different?"

"I said it looks like rain tonight and he said he liked the rain but hated the humidity."

I thought of Mincher again. He'd said something like that when I talked to him outside headquarters that afternoon.

"How did he get here?"

"I'm not sure, come to think of it. I assumed a taxi. From the airport, I figured, or maybe one of the businesses around here. But I never saw the taxi."

"Luggage, briefcase, duffel, anything with him?"

"No. None that I remember."

I thought for a moment. I saw the surveillance camera tucked up under the eave of the building above us. "Is that a tape or closed circuit?"

"It's closed circuit until we close up for the day," said Cass. "Then we flip to digital record from the keypad inside."

"Fancy."

"You need fancy, with two million dollars' worth of cars here. You wouldn't believe the things people try to pull. Or maybe you would. But if you want the guy who returned the Hummer, forget it. The gate was locked. He couldn't have gotten in if he'd wanted to. So he parked it out on the street. The camera only picks up what's inside the lot, plus just a little."

"Was the Hummer muddy?"

"Yeah. He'd been offroading the damned thing."

"It's been washed several times since then?"

"Washed and rented several times," said Cass. "The Hummer is a real popular rental here, believe it or not. Talk about a pretentious, uncomfortable, overpriced, gas-guzzling piece of junk. You drive over a speed bump and things fall off. I mean, you may as well pay someone to drive behind you to pick up the pieces. I'll open up this black one if you want to see what they look like inside. I'll rent it to you, for that matter. Preferred rate."

Reuben came outside and gave me a printout of the rental agreement.

Cass opened the door to the black Hummer and I stood there for a long beat, admiring the quasi-military design of the interior. Reuben started back inside, then stopped and watched me.

"You didn't happen to find a Higher Grounds coffee shop bag in the white one, did you?" I asked. "When you cleaned it out that morning?"

Cass smiled and nodded. "Oh, a psychic cop. If you're so smart, tell me what was in that bag?"

"A stir stick and a wadded-up napkin."

She laughed. "And guess what was on the napkin?"

"Coffee?" I asked.

"Blood."

"A lot?"

"A little."

"You threw it away."

"What else would I do with a bloody napkin?"

I shook my head and smiled. I marveled at how a hopeless detour to see my wife had led me to evidence in the murder of Garrett Asplundh. I know a cop who had taken his daughter to Disneyland and recognized a rape suspect from a drawing done by our fine sketch artist, Kathy Iles. The guy was standing in line with his own daughter for Small World. He was arrested right on the spot.

"Will you give your description to a police artist?" I asked. "It could be a huge help."

Cass looked at me for a beat. "Okay. Send her down here, though. I've got a living to make. I can't be running all over town."

"I'll call you. And thanks for your help," I said.

"Get those patrol guys out here once in a while," said Reuben.

"Why don't *you* come back and check in on us?" said Cass with a smile.

"I'll do that."

I realized there was an outside chance I'd get something useful from the security tape. "Would you mind showing me the surveillance tape from that night?" I asked her.

"I told you, it only shows what's on the lot," said Cass. "He left the Hummer on the street outside the lot, on the other side of the fence, right there."

She nodded toward the street, then shrugged.

"But if the Hummer was left just outside that fence," I said. "Maybe . . . please, can we just take a quick look, fast-forward right up to that part of it?"

"There's not going to be a 'that part of it,' is what I'm saying," said Cass. "But come on, we'll try."

Cass was almost right. Back in the main office, she sat down at a computer and brought out her archived surveillance files for Tuesday, March 8. We found nothing on the disc until 10:20 P.M., when we saw the tires and about eight inches of lower body slide to a stop along the curb.

"That's it," said Cass. "That's the Hummer. Look, there's the mud on the bottom of the body panel, see?"

We watched the bottom of the door open and saw someone step out. All we saw were legs, from about the thigh down. Although the surveillance video was shot at night, it looked to me like the legs belonged to a man, and he was wearing jeans. His shoes shone in the light from the streetlamps. He was visible only for about three steps, as he headed west on the sidewalk, away from Dream Wheels.

"Well, slightly better than nothing," said Cass. "That was him."

We watched it again, then once more.

Mud on the body.

A man in jeans.

A flash of dark shoe leather.

"See anything useful?" she asked.

"No. Not really. Can I take this?"

She shrugged. "You sure want a lot."

I thanked her, then thanked her again. "You've really been a big help."

"Anytime."

Back in my car I used my cell phone to call Charles Hudson Black's home number but it belonged to a commercial nursery. His business number was a funeral home.

Funny.

I used my map to locate his street address in Rancho Santa Fe but there was no such street.

Not a huge surprise.

I called Records for a warrants check on Charles Hudson Black and gave them what I was reasonably sure was a false driver's-license number.

Sure enough, the number belonged to Susy Nguyen of Fresno, California.

Then I called Captain Villas and asked him to arrange for Kathy Iles to interview Cass of Dream Wheels and work up a sketch of the man who had rented the Hummer.

"You sound excited about this, Robbie," he said.

"First break I've caught in a while," I said.

"I'll set it up."

Next I called the Traffic captain and confirmed—for the second time—that Ron Mincher had worked the day shift on March 8 and clocked out at 6:10. I realized he could have rented the Hummer while on duty. It would have meant parking his patrol car, finding a place to change into street clothes, renting the Hummer, then leaving it somewhere nearby while he changed back into his uniform, got back into his prowler, and finished his shift. What, half an hour, if everything went right? I had an odd mental picture of Ron Mincher leaning forward toward a mirror while he added some gray to his mustache from a shoe-polish bottle with a sponge dispenser built into the top.

And again I had the tempting thought that Garrett's murder was not about the corruption he had found. Sure, he had collected enough evidence to sink a dozen powerful men, but what had he done with it? Nothing that I could see, except extorting some payback out of Steven Stiles and asking Abel Sarvonola's advice on how to proceed. True, he was set to outline his findings to the state attorney general's office the week following his murder, but the goal of the Ethics Authority—so far as I had come to understand it—was to dissuade the state from getting involved, not to encourage it. Stella had tried to speak for Garrett when she called his death not a murder but "a piece of work." But I thought now that she was wrong. I thought now that it was very much a murder and not a piece of work at all.

Then what was it about?

I sat in the dark and watched a big passenger jet come barreling down through the dark sky, lights blinking on its descent to Lindbergh Field. I thought of all the lights blinking in Las Vegas right now and I imagined a big marquee of clear bright bulbs streaked with the headlamps of the cars on the boulevard and a wisp of red hair from someone passing on the sidewalk below.

Maybe that's what Garrett Asplundh's murder is about, I thought. Something dark and private and contained within his heart.

I wanted to see the place where Garrett had been murdered because I'd never gotten a good look at it after dark. I picked up the 163, got off on Quince Drive and wound around to Laurel.

I found the dirt road and picked my way down toward the highway. When I reached a place where I could see where Garrett's Explorer had sat, I killed the engine.

Directly in front of me I could see the swale in which Garrett had parked and the gentle hillock down which he had driven to get there.

To my left was a very large and beautiful palm tree and to my right was a thicket of eucalyptus, the leaves flickering and flashing in the headlights on the highway. Beyond the swale towered the Cabrillo Bridge, lit and rising up into the night like one of the Roman aqueducts on which it was modeled. It looked like a great ruin from history protruding up from the lush greenery, something so strong and elegant that the centuries had accommodated rather than ruined it.

A man stood in the middle of the swale. At first I didn't see him in the flashing, strobelike headlights from the highway.

He was paying me no attention at all. He simply stood exactly where Garrett's car had been, then backed up a few steps and slowly turned. His arms were up and he was holding something to his face. It looked to me like he was shooting pictures, or maybe video.

A big rig roared toward me from the highway and I lost sight of the man in the blinding headlights. When the truck passed and I could see again, the guy was gone.

I got out and closed my door quietly. I took my flashlight from the trunk and eased into the eucalyptus grove. Through the pale trunks I could just make out the clearing where the man had been, ahead of me maybe fifty yards.

Then he stepped back into view.

I angled out from the trees and aimed the beam of my flashlight on him. "You there! Hold it there a second, will you?"

He looked at me, made some adjustment to the instrument he held in one hand, and relaxed his arms to his sides.

"You wait right there," I called out. "San Diego PD."

"Brownlaw?"

"That's right, who do we have here?"

"Walk over and find out."

It took me another few steps to recognize Samuel Asplundh. He'd changed from his funeral suit back into jeans and boots and a black sport coat.

An uncomfortable moment of silence passed between us. I felt the shadow of suspicion glide effortlessly over my heart.

"Come down here to pick up a scent?" he asked.

"That's right," I said. I watched the traffic flashing by. I looked up at the magnificent bridge lit in the darkness. I pictured Garrett Asplundh sitting right here in his Explorer in the rain, looking through the dripping passenger-side window as the Hummer drew up alongside him.

"What scent have *you* picked up?" I asked.

"Garrett wasn't surprised," said Samuel. "Garrett wasn't surprisable. He knew the guy. He rolled down the window to talk to him."

"The Explorer doors lock when you put the vehicle in gear," I said. My gut was telling me to share some information with Samuel, in order to get some back. "So Garrett would have to have hit the unlock button to let him in."

"He was shot from the passenger side?"

I nodded.

He looked at me, then back up the swale. "There was another vehicle?"

"White Hummer, new."

"Anyone see the shooter?"

"Maybe. Male, large. It was dark and raining."

Samuel reached into his jacket pocket and handed me a silver flask. "Johnnie Walker," he said.

"Black, like Garrett?"

"Black."

I unscrewed the top and sipped some. It reminded me of my night at McGinty's.

"And what about you, Brownlaw? What flavor do you get from this place?"

"I know it was special to them."

"Garrett proposed to her here," said Samuel.

"But I don't understand why he would come here," I said. "I don't see a reason for that, yet."

"Sentimental journey?" asked Samuel. "Garrett was a romantic guy. Flowers and poems and the little things a woman appreciates. Garrett was the kind of guy who would revisit a sentimental place because it would give him good luck. Really. He would. Back in high school he wore the same undershirt for all our league football games, but he wouldn't wash it between games. He would go back and back and back again to things that were important to him or that he believed in."

"They were trying to reconcile," I said. "That's what Stella told me. They were meeting in Rancho Santa Fe that night to lay some groundwork."

"Yeah," Samuel said quietly. "He loved her and then some."

Samuel was quiet for a moment.

"What happened to the blonde you brought to the Fourth of July party last year?" I asked. "I didn't see her at the funeral today."

He looked at me sharply, took another sip from the flask, and offered it to me. I shook my head and waited.

"I dumped her," said Samuel.

He stared at me as a river of red squares rushed into the darkness between us.

"I loved Garrett a lot," said Samuel. "We had our differences but anyone will tell you I loved and respected him. Hell, I adored him. I picked on him when we were young, but I protected him too. I watched out for him. And he watched out for me. Growing up, there was always this competition over everything—fastest bike, biggest wave, cutest chick. Until one day it all just fell into place—and we realized we didn't have anything left to prove. Just two brothers. You have a brother, Brownlaw?"

I shook my head.

"And now," he said, "I've got to see this through. I've got to make sure that the guy who did this is caught and punished. I had a dream the day I heard about it. In the dream I used Bureau resources off-hours to do some investigating on my own. I identified the person who did this and he resisted arrest. I shot him over and over again because it felt so fucking good. Funny part was, when I woke up I couldn't remember what he looked like or why he'd done this to Garrett."

"Maybe you should let me handle the investigation," I said.

"Maybe I should. The L.A. Bureau needs me more than the San Diego cops do. I always heard good things about you guys from Garrett. He was torn about leaving for Ethics. He was also exhausted, heartbroken, and drunk most of the time."

"He had made some enemies," I said.

"An Asplundh talent."

"I thought it was an execution at first. Now I'm not so sure."

"Something personal," said Sam.

I looked at my watch and offered my hand. Sam shook it.

"Let me know what you're thinking," I said.

"Back at you. I'm taking a couple of weeks off to help Stella with things."

"That's good of you."

"We're blood, Stella and I."

Which I found odd, because they weren't.

Driving home from the Cabrillo Bridge I decided to attend the San Diego Synesthesia Society meeting later that night. The decision came to me with instant clarity.

I reasoned that if my condition was part of the reason Gina had gone, other synesthetes might tell me how to minimize or disguise its negative effects. Using these techniques, maybe I could bring Gina back to me. I also wanted to know if my synesthesia would change over time, and if so, what I could expect. And I was just plain ready to talk to people who wouldn't think I was addled when I told them I could see their words.

I'd always worried that word might get back to the department if I attended a meeting, and people might assume that my brain wasn't working properly. But now, driving toward Normal Heights, I didn't care what people like Chet Fellowes or Roger Sutherland or Bryan Bogle thought of my brain. I was tiring of the bullshit—mine and everyone else's.

So I drove home with the same kind of eagerness I used to have, anticipating Gina. But as soon as I walked in, the new smallness of the house hit me again. No messages. Not even a hello from Vince and Dawn, or more pity from Rachel. Just as Uncle Jerry had experienced after the death of Aunt Melissa, the temperature of the house was much warmer than it should have been in March. I opened all the windows and checked the temperature on the thermostat—eighty.

I got the Synesthesia Society meeting information off the Web, then washed my face in the bathroom sink, put on a clean shirt, and headed right back out.

I'd read that synesthetes consider their condition a gift and that high numbers of artists, performers, and writers are synesthetic. The great painter David Hockney is said to hear colors as music. It is also said that Balzac wanted very badly to be synesthetic but was not. Although I'm not an artist, I do know that I'm a better detective now than before my fall, because I can see very clearly when someone, such as Carrie Martier or Abel Sarvonola, is lying.

I've also read that there is no such thing as synesthesia. Some researchers have claimed that synesthetes are simply victims of their own "overactive imaginations" or are perhaps suffering from the abuse of hallucinogenic drugs. This uninformed view has fallen out of favor. There is an entire department at the University of California, San Diego, dedicated to the study of this phenomenon, which leads me to believe that what I have is "real." There is an American Synesthesia Association, a UK Synesthesia Association, as well as an International Synesthesia Association. There are tests to see if you really have it. Several good books and many abstracts have been published on the subject, and many lectures have been given. I know for a fact that synesthetes don't invent what they see and taste and hear. We're not delusional. It's not that we see UFOs or Sasquatch or spirits of some kind.

The meeting was held at the community center in Hillcrest. The chapter president was Moira Handler, a hefty, fiftyish woman with short blond hair and sober gray eyes. There were twenty-three people there, ranging in age from around twelve to maybe seventy. Eighteen of them were women and fifteen of the women were left-handed. Snacks and drinks were arranged on a pair of long tables set up in the back of the room. Most were homemade. After some social chatter, the doors were closed, the synesthetes took their seats, and Moira went to the podium.

She welcomed the members and introduced the first visitor, Lillian, a young woman from north San Diego County. Lillian had found out about the group online but was not sure if she was genuinely synesthetic or not. She was unsteady and fawnlike in her blue jeans and a long, worn, burgundy-colored velvet coat. As she talked, I suddenly regretted being here and mentally concocted a story about coming to the meeting because my wife was pretty sure she was having synesthetic experiences but was too shy and uncertain to come here on her own. But I can't lie any better than I can cuss, so when it was my turn I stood and introduced myself and said that I'd come tonight because I'd begun experiencing synesthetic symptoms after an accidental fall. My voice wavered slightly and I wondered if anyone noticed. I focused my attention on Lillian, and tried to pretend that we were the only two people in the room.

Moira said she'd seen my fall too many times on television and was very happy that I had not only survived but was now "gifted." She said I was living proof of either "miracles or majestic good luck." A hearty round of applause followed. By the time the applause ended and I sat back down I felt okay again. I'd never been ashamed of who I was, and these people weren't ashamed of who they were, so what was the problem? I thought about people like Chet Fellowes and Roger Sutherland and Abel Sarvonola and realized that they were enemies whether I had synesthesia or not, and that if news of my attendance here tonight got back to them I was really no worse off. I was beginning to feel the same way about them that I'd felt about the muscular husband trying to rip me off for Gina's Hikari Cosmos styling scissors—mad and more than a little willing to do something about it.

Moira read the minutes from the last meeting and reported that the SDSS had $289 in the general fund. They had run up $26 in paper and postage for the March newsletter. Many members were behind on their annual dues, which were supposed to be paid by March 1. She glanced at me and said that yearly dues were $50, which included a Summer Solstice Party in the Bongo Room of the Outrigger Motel and discounts at Indy Tire & Wheel, courtesy of member Kris Shuttler's husband.

The evening's speaker was Darlene Sable, author of *Red Sax and Lemon Cymbals.* She described the book as a "straightforward telling" of her growing up synesthetic in San Francisco, California. Her mother was a piano instructor and her father a commercial pilot. From early childhood she remembered seeing music—certain colors would sweep through her vision when certain musical sounds were playing. Later she understood that specific musical instruments caused her to see specific colors: The saxophone was of course red and cymbals lemon yellow; violins were lime green, guitars magenta, and so on. Because of this she craved going to concerts, which her mother was happy to indulge.

By the time Darlene was five she knew that not everyone saw music like she did. She talked about this with her mother a few times but not with anyone else. Her mother said it was probably just a childhood thing that would go away. Darlene grew to be ashamed of it and desperately wanted to be normal, though it never interfered with her life in any way. To Darlene, live musical concerts were jubilant synesthetic extravaganzas almost beyond description—waves of colors and swells of sound rushing all around her, sweeping past her skin. She would leave the concert hall exhausted and elated.

At age eight Darlene began pretending that she no longer saw music. She developed terrible migraine headaches and ulcers. After two years of doctors and medications, she finally confessed to her mother that she was seeing music more vividly than ever. She began visiting a psychiatrist, and the headaches and ulcers gradually subsided. The psychiatrist was the first person to use the word "synesthesia" to describe her "talent" and encouraged her to develop and enjoy it. She had written the book to help others with synesthesia recognize their gifts and be proud. As an adult she had become a piano instructor like her mother and few things pleased her as much as sitting next to a young student and seeing the swells of crimson music flowing out of the instrument.

After the meeting Lillian and I were invited to join six of the members for coffee at the café next door. The inside tables were full so we sat outside in the brisk March night with our coats buttoned up and the steam rising from our cups. Most of the members described their various gifts for Lillian and me. One experienced just the opposite of Darlene Sable—she heard colors as music. Another experienced powerful tastes from certain spoken words. Most were pleasant and unexpected tastes, such as strawberries from the word "loyalty" and cumin from the word "archdiocese." But a few tastes were bad. The word "scrumptious" tasted faintly of a rotting tooth, while "chockablock" made her taste sulfur. Another saw the printed black letters in books or newspapers in varying vivid colors. *A,* for instance, was always yellow. *D* was always light green.

"Describe your gift," said Bart. He was a heavy, bearded man who had shaken my hand with exaggerated firmness when we were introduced.

All of the others went quiet. I told him about colored shapes being prompted by spoken words. By the emotions behind the spoken words, to be more exact.

"Example," he said.

"I see blue triangles from a happy speaker. Red squares come from liars. Envy comes out in green trapezoids, so 'green with envy' is literally true for me. Aggression shows up as small black ovals."

"That's not synesthesia," said Bart. "I've read every word ever written about the subject, and no one has ever established that a speaker's emotions can be visualized."

"They can," I said. "That's what happens."

"Maybe you should write an article, Mr. Brownlaw," said Moira. "The ASA would consider a piece, I'm sure."

Bart raised his eyebrows and sipped his coffee drink. Whipped cream came off on his mustache. He dabbed the bristles with a paper napkin.

"Have you taken the Reynolds?" he asked me.

"Reynolds?"

"Test. The Reynolds Test of Synesthesia. Obviously you haven't. It's in three parts: a basic questionnaire, Geography Test Eighteen—which of course has little to do with conventional geography—and the triad-solution section, which is just basically Form 1 RAT derivations by Mednick and Mednick. Ring a bell?"

I said no.

"I didn't think it would," said Bart. "Maybe you should find that test and take it, if you really want to make claims. There's a lot of misunderstanding about synesthesia. And a lot of bullshit."

"God, Bart," said Moira.

"What do you see coming from my mouth right now?" he asked me.

"Little black ovals. Quite a few of them."

"Aggression. Right, uh-huh. But what if I was really asking you these questions with a sense of humor in my mind?"

"Then I'd see orange boxes. You can't fake what I see. That's the synesthesia."

"That's parapsychology and crap," said Bart. "What did you really come here for, to find a date?"

I told him I was happily married.

"Hey, whatever," said Bart.

"Bart, come on," said Moira.

I watched the little black ovals pour from his mouth like some kind of plague. My heart was beating fast and I could feel the comforting flow of adrenaline in my blood. When I get angry, I see particularly well and my body feels light and quick.

"Thanks for not saying any more about my wife," I said.

Bart sipped his coffee and shook his head. "And what about you, shy Lillian, what kind of extraordinary talent do you claim to possess?"

She looked at him.

"None at all, you stupid prick," she said quietly. Then she stood. "Nice to meet the rest of you."

"I'll walk you out," I said.

"It's not necessary."

I walked her to her car. She said she couldn't believe that Bart would be "such a great big dork to complete strangers." She said she had worked with a guy like that once, a guy who wanted to expose everything she did as false.

We walked to the covered parking and she unlocked an old brown Toyota. She turned and leaned against the door. Lillian was slender and long-legged, with wavy black hair, freckles, and nice blue eyes. Her wine-colored velvet coat looked two hundred years old.

"Thanks," she said.

"You're welcome."

"Did that take a lot of self-control? I know who you are and what you do for a living. You could have hurt that guy, couldn't you?"

"Well, yeah, but that wouldn't have accomplished much."

She nodded and looked me in the eyes. She was a notch younger than me, mid-twenties maybe.

"So anyway," I said, "what kind of synesthesia do you have?"

"Oh, I'm still not sure." She bit her bottom lip with noticeable anxiety. "It's . . . well, it sounds weird, but what happens with me is faces make music."

"Oh, that's a good one."

She eyed me levelly. "It's only some faces. Not every face makes me hear music. But if they do, they make their own unique melody—every time. It's consistent."

"Are you a musician?"

She nodded and laughed quietly. "Yes. I can't wait to read Darlene Sable's book. It really sounded good, and she loves music as much as I do."

"Can you remember the melodies?"

"Oh, sure. I write them all out. Some I just hum into a recorder and transcribe them later because I have so many."

"You can hear a melody and write it as music?"

"Well, sure, Robbie, just about every musician can do that. I mean, it's how we read and write."

I thought about that. "That seems synesthetic to me. But I've never heard anybody say that writing music is synesthetic."

"Nope, me neither."

Lillian looked back toward the café. The group had dwindled to just three. Bart spread his arms and held forth. Lillian shook her head and looked at me.

"Well," I said. "That was nice until the end."

"Yeah," said Lillian.

"I like what you said to Bart. It was true and funny."

She shook her head. "Anyway. Well . . ."

"Have a nice night," I said. I wasn't in a hurry to end our conversation but I couldn't think of anything directly relevant to say.

"You, too," said Lillian.

"Really nice to . . . Have you always heard music with certain faces?" I asked. I knew I was just prolonging the good-bye, and she looked at me like she knew it, too. I felt a tug of betrayal of Gina but the words came out anyway. "Or is it new?"

She shook her head. "Yeah, it's a new thing. All new, all new. I was normal and then my brother was . . . It's a long story. Well, I guess I really should go."

"Drive safely."

"This thing only goes fifty."

"Buckle up anyway," I said. "Had the brakes checked lately?"

"Sure, yes."

"They're important."

"I mean, actually, I was normal until last year when my, well . . . when my brother, Rich, he was in Saudi with Global Thermal, and they, uh . . . well, he was one of those guys who— They beheaded him. And when I saw the picture there were these three men in masks and I got this really awful loud ringing in my ears and I kept seeing those three men in the masks over and over in my mind and I couldn't get them out no matter what I did, awake or sleeping, it was always those three men in the masks with this banner behind them with squiggly writing on it like snakes and this terrible sound of shearing metal and wind and it was so horrible I didn't sleep for two weeks and ever since then faces give me sounds and music and sometimes the music is really scary and fuck, I'm so sorry I brought this up."

She swung open the creaky door, slumped into the front seat, swept the elegant old coat onto her lap, then slammed the door shut and stared straight ahead. Six inches of red velvet remained outside the door.

I motioned for her to put the window down but she threw open the creaky door.

"Window's broke," she said.

"You can heal up," I said. I knelt and lifted the creased coattail back inside the doorjamb, then stood. "There's people you can talk to and things you can do and some prescription drugs that can help. You can't hold it all in. You could—"

"I've done all that." Lillian stood up and locked her wet blue eyes onto mine. "Look, I'm good now. I'm good. It just catches up with me sometimes. They took Richard, but Richard gave me music. *They took Richard, but Richard gave me music.* There. See? I know it's true. I can breathe deeply and control my own emotions. I am in control. In, out. There. Lillian controls Lillian. Masked terrorists do not control her. They bombed the bastards to smithereens a day later so what am I so upset about?"

She stared at me and breathed deeply, in and out, in and out. "I'm good. See?"

"Well, yeah, you're doing good now, Lillian."

"I'm a real pro."

"That's a wonderful gift your brother gave you."

"I don't want the gift," she said. "I want my brother."

"I understand."

"You got a wonderful gift when you hit that awning."

"I don't want the gift either," I said.

"I understand. Bring your wife to the Belly Up in Solana Beach and hear me sing some Sunday. I play evenings from six to seven to warm up the crowd for the stars. Call ahead to make sure I'm on. Sometimes I can't face a crowd."

"I'll do that."

"Thanks for walking me out."

I drove down my street just after ten and saw an unusual coupe parked across from my home. I was pretty sure it didn't belong to anyone in the neighborhood. I recognized it as a 1985 Thunderbird because my mother had driven one back in the early nineties.

I pressed the automatic garage-door opener and watched in my rearview as a woman got out of the T-Bird. She stood, looked around nervously, then started across the street toward me. Her sweater flapped in the glow of the streetlamps. She had something clutched to her chest.

Instead of pulling into my garage, I killed the engine and stepped out.

"Hello, Ms. Buntz," I said.

"Invite me inside," she said. She continued past me into the garage.

"Would you like to come in?"

I unlocked the door to the house, flipped on a light, and held the door open for Arliss Buntz. She was carrying a pale yellow tape player that looked old. When she walked past me, she smelled like lilac.

I stepped in behind her. A breeze had come up from the east and the house had cooled down nicely with the windows left open. I glanced at the answering machine but there were no messages. I motioned to the breakfast table and Arliss set her old tape player on it, but she didn't sit.

"What can I do for you?" I asked.

"Ethics Authority phone calls are randomly monitored and recorded," said Arliss Buntz. "This is done in accordance with our charter from the city. Director Kaven compiles, duplicates, and distributes the recordings on Fridays so that the chief of police, the mayor, the City Council, and other approved individuals can listen to them. As the head of Enforcement, John Van Flyke receives a copy every Wednesday. I catalog and store them. During a slow period this afternoon I listened to last week's tape and I ran across this conversation. You should hear it."

The player was old and faded, with oversize controls for the elderly and the function of each button written on it in Braille. She pushed the green "play" button.

I heard this conversation:

MAN: *. . . me.*

WOMAN: *Hello, Garrett.*

GARRETT: *How are you?*

WOMAN: *Scared.*

GARRETT: *We're all set then, for nine?*

WOMAN: *I'll be there.*

GARRETT: *I haven't looked forward to something like this in . . . ever.*

WOMAN: *Let's please just see how it goes.*

GARRETT: *I will. I'm going to. I feel like I'm crawling out of the dark.*

WOMAN: *It's just a date.*

GARRETT: *It's more than that.*

WOMAN: *I know. I never thought the darkness would break.*

GARRETT: *I love you, Stell.*

STELLA: *I love you, Garrett. Please don't drink tonight.*

GARRETT: *I haven't had a drink in two weeks. I'm in control, Stella. I told you I was, and I am. I'm going to the bridge before, just to say a prayer.*

STELLA: *Include me in it.*

GARRETT: *I'll see you soon.*

STELLA: *Please be careful.*

GARRETT: *"I'll come to thee by moonlight, though hell should bar the way."*

STELLA: (laughing softly) *Okay, Mr. Highwayman.*
GARRETT: *Okay, Bess, the landlord's red-lipped daughter.*
STELLA: *Hardly.*
GARRETT: *You'll always be that to me. Bye.*

There was a loud click, followed by silence. The recording was weak and had some static, but clear enough to hear. Because of the interrupted greeting at the beginning and the abrupt click at the end, I figured that Arliss had made it herself on the crude old machine, from the copy passed down by Kaven to Van Flyke.

"Play it again," I said.

Arliss rewound the tape and played it again.

"The time and date of each conversation is written down on a log that comes with the tapes," said Arliss. "At first this conversation caught my ear because it was Mr. Asplundh. Then I saw that it was recorded just hours before he was murdered."

I looked at her. She was lifting her chin in defiance but I could see the doubt in her old gray eyes.

"Nobody at Ethics knows you taped this for me?" I asked.

"I would be fired immediately."

I nodded. "But you trusted me."

"I trusted Mr. Asplundh because of his morals. I trust you because I have no choice. Someone heard this conversation. Someone knew that Mr. Asplundh would be at the bridge. Did you catch that? *'I'm going to the bridge before, just to say a prayer.'* He went there and was killed."

"Maybe he was followed there," I said.

Arliss Buntz hit the "eject" button, and the cassette tape clattered out of the player and onto my table.

"Garrett Asplundh?" she asked. "You have no idea how keen his senses were. He was not *followed.* He was betrayed. By someone who heard that conversation. Someone who knew which bridge he was talking about."

"Who is authorized to monitor Ethics Enforcement calls?"

"Kaven, the chief of police, the mayor, and each of the city councilpersons," said Arliss. "But don't forget the *unauthorized* ears that are always close by—there are all the office staff and aides to the councilmen, there are all the assistants and underlings to the chief, and the mayor's staff. There are secretaries and office managers and even janitors. There are scores of people with ears, Detective Brownlaw. And after Director Kaven collects and organizes the tapes, they are sent back down the chain of command to Van Flyke, the city attorney, and certain police department captains."

"Fellowes?" I asked.

"Yes, and Villas and Sutherland."

"What about Sarvonola?" I asked.

"Unauthorized," said Arliss. "And untrustworthy."

She lifted the tape recorder and held it against her chest. "I never thought that Mr. Asplundh should have been reconciling with his wife," said Arliss. "She brought out his weakness rather than his strength. With her he lost his reason and his sharpness. His heart went soft. I saw them together. I heard them talk. I know."

"Thank you."

"If I'm fired for this, I'll know who betrayed me."

"I won't betray you."

"It's out of my hands now."

I held open the back door for her. She marched through my garage toward the street, tape player held tight.

I watched her drive away and wondered at her courage and at her unusual devotion to Garrett Asplundh.

I called Stella, got a busy signal, and tried again a few minutes later. I apologized for calling on the day her husband was buried, especially so late, but told her I had an important question or two for her.

"Ask them," she said.

"It has to be face-to-face, Mrs. Asplundh. I'll explain it then."

"Make it Stella," she said. "Meet me at Higher Grounds. People keep calling. I'd love to get out of this apartment for just a few minutes."

I made a copy of the tape, then opened the floor safe and stashed the original. At first the old familiar disbelief swept over me when I saw again that all of Gina's jewelry was gone. Then came the familiar spike of anger, followed by the idea that I could bargain her back to me if I could only figure out what to offer her.

But by the time the safe lid clanked shut I realized I would never get her back. The idea came with sudden, awful finality. I hadn't felt helpless since my fall, but a terrible helplessness swept over me again. I felt as if I had been shrunk down and locked in the safe, where I could do nothing but wait.

24

Higher Grounds was crowded and a little loud. I looked at the people who worked there and wondered who had served the driver of the Dream Wheels Hummer the night of the murder. I was looking forward to walking in with Kathy Iles's sketch and finding someone who had seen our man.

We got coffees to go and walked down Fourth. Stella had traded her funeral dress for jeans, a long sweater with big pockets, and a red baseball cap. She looked pale and hollow, much as you would expect of a woman who had just buried her husband. I felt the same way myself.

I told her that I'd gotten an interesting tape recording in the mail.

"I want to hear it."

"My car's right there."

I played the tape once, then again.

She stared straight ahead through the windshield.

"You told me about that conversation once," I said. "Now tell me again."

"March eighth," she said. "Around four-thirty. I was at home and Garrett was at his desk. It was . . . just exactly what it sounds like. Two people trying to lay the past to rest and create a new future."

I rewound the tape. I thought that if someone had monitored the Asplundhs' four-thirty conversation, he would realize that Garrett would soon be alone and vulnerable under a bridge in the dark. Figuring that driving his own vehicle there might be too risky, the killer had taken a taxi down to Dream Wheels and rented the Hummer at five-fifteen.

But the name of the bridge had never been mentioned. It would have to be someone who knew their story and their attachment to the Cabrillo Bridge.

She looked at me. "How would they know *which* bridge?"

"You told your friends about the bridge because it was romantic. Assume that Garrett did the same. Friends tell friends, stories get repeated. Enemies hear things. Enemies collect things. Years pass. Anybody could know, Stella."

She closed her eyes and let her head roll back against the rest. "Okay. Say that's what happened. Someone knew the story and the bridge. Someone used that conversation to kill Garrett. Why would they send a tape of it to you?"

"They're either trying to confuse me or trying to help," I lied.

I saw the red squares hovering in the space between us. I didn't want to lie to Stella, but I had Arliss Buntz to consider.

Stella opened her eyes. "This tape doesn't really surprise me. For the last few months, I've felt watched and listened to. It's been very strange."

"Where?"

"On the street. In my car. Even in my home. Crazy? Maybe. Maybe some of Garrett's paranoia rubbed off on me."

"Have you ever seen anyone watching or following you?"

"No," she said. "But I've felt as if I've made him turn his face away, like he knows I'm feeling watched and he stops. Like I've just missed seeing him. Garrett and my landlord are the only people I even told about it. The landlord lives on the ground floor of the building. I figured he could, you know, keep an eye out."

"Is this watcher a man?"

"I think so."

"You should have told me a lot sooner."

She gave me an odd look, part strength and part surrender. "I didn't want you to think I was losing it. Now I don't care if you think I'm losing it."

I ejected the tape from the player.

"Come up to my apartment," she said. "There's no reason we have to sit in a cold car."

Stella put the tape in a player. She tossed her baseball cap on a chair and we sat at opposite ends of the big purple couch with the gold piping. There was only a corner lamp on, and one distant light from the kitchen, and it was strange to sit in the near darkness and listen to Stella Asplundh talk to her dead husband.

She played the tape again.

Then again.

I thought of "The Life and Death of Samantha" and how I had watched it over and over, unable to pull myself away but not sure why.

GARRETT: *Okay, Bess, the landlord's red-lipped daughter.*

STELLA: *Hardly.*

GARRETT: *You'll always be that to me. Bye.*

"You know what is most difficult right now?" she asked. "Garrett was my own husband, and I've got no idea *why* someone would kill him. Do you know how confusing that is? To not even know why? I wish there was one logical killer. One clear reason. One understandable event."

"Garrett had videodiscs made by prostitutes," I said. "They showed city leaders and cops and businessmen with the girls."

"Oh, Jesus."

"Some of the men are influential. Even powerful. I thought at first that Garrett had probably stepped on the wrong toes. Like you said, he had plenty of enemies."

"But now?"

"I'm not so sure. You said he didn't tell you much about his work."

"Few specifics," said Stella. "He told me, for instance, that there was a prostitution problem in the city that nobody was acknowledging. I knew he was involved in some aspect of that."

The telephone rang again and Stella excused herself to answer it.

Oh, hello, Mom. . . . Oh, no, I'm glad you called. . . . I was just talking with Detective Brownlaw. . . . Yes. . . . Okay, I will. Bye, and I love you, too. . . .

Stella came back and sat on the couch.

"I want to ask you about people that Garrett may have mentioned. How about Jordan Sheehan?"

"No," said Stella.

"Chupa Junior?"

"No."

"Carrie Ann Martier?"

Stella shook her head.

"Abel Sarvonola and Trey Vinson?"

"I know of Sarvonola, of course. But not Vinson."

"Chet Fellowes?"

"Not much anymore," said Stella. "We used to be friends with Chet and his wife, but the four of us drifted apart after Samantha."

"Ron Mincher?"

"No."

"Did Garrett ever talk about someone he'd really love to take down? Someone he just couldn't stand?"

Stella thought about this for a while. "No. But he didn't fully trust his own director. He thought that Kaven was too tight with Sarvonola and the mayor and the supervisors, that Kaven would let them . . . well, stretch their ethics a little too far for Garrett's taste. Apparently Kaven wasn't overwhelmed with the idea of hiring Garrett. He thought Garrett was better off staying a cop. John Van Flyke was the one who brought him aboard. Garrett and John saw themselves as the good guys lined up against the corrupt legions. I mean, they'd joke about it, but I know they saw themselves as fighting the good fight. And they always put up a united front for the Ethics Authority. Garrett would never have dissed Kaven behind his back."

"Like the soldiers who see the action while the generals stay above it all."

"That was my take."

"But you and Garrett thought enough of Kaven to invite him to your home."

She thought for a moment. "We had a wonderful social life. Even though everyone thought he was tough and uncompromising, Garrett loved his friends. He was ferociously loyal. And oddly trusting, too, for a man with a job like his. We had a wide variety of friends—people from the PD, people from the school district where I was a counselor. I had old college friends from swimming, and Garrett had boyhood friends who were still very close. He made friends all the time. He became friends with the guy who serviced his car—he was at the memorial today. One summer Garrett came back from Montana with a young fishing guide who was having some problems. The kid stayed with us for a month and Garrett got him a job on one of the charter boats out of Point Loma. He was there today, too."

It's always interesting to see a side of someone you never knew was there. I thought about Garrett Asplundh's odd mix of suspicion and generosity, morality and forgiveness, humility and superiority.

"Did you know about Garrett's National City apartment?"

"He told me about it. But not exactly where it was."

"Did you know that a young woman named April Holly has been living there since late January?"

"No," said Stella. "I did not. Someone named April came to the funeral."

I told her the story about April's scrape with prostitution and Garrett's entry on the white horse. I told her that April said there had never been any sexual contact.

She listened without interrupting and was quiet for a long while.

"Well," she said finally, "I'm not surprised at that, really. Before Samantha he was trusting and generous with people. We let one of his nephews live with us for a year because he was having trouble at home. We took in a neighbor boy once because his parents were separating and his home life was in a shambles. I mean, Garrett brought home stray animals. After Samantha, though, all that trust reversed itself. I'm glad to know that some of it came back, with this April girl."

"Explain."

"He'd always been a drinker, but then he began drinking very heavily," said Stella. "He became worried that something was going to happen to him. He became obsessive about locks and alarms. About varying his travel routes and schedule. About phones and bugs and tape recorders. About my safety. He would worry about every single thing that I did. He got worse and worse. I couldn't live with him like that. It was like being strangled. I took this place in September, barely eight weeks after Samantha. He got the apartment in Hillcrest and a month later the one in National City."

"Was this about the time you began to feel watched and listened to?"

She looked at me. "I began to sense it in August, not long after Sam died. And I know what you're thinking. But it wasn't Garrett, stalking or spying on me. I knew what it felt like to be watched by him. It was different. It was someone else."

I thought about that, wondering if she could really tell her husband's invisible gaze from someone else's. I wondered about Garrett's fears becoming hers. I remembered reading of a mental disorder in which one person's delusions came to be "shared" by another.

"So the Seabreeze was his antidote to his paranoia?" I asked.

"Yes, he said so himself. And it seemed to work. He was visibly relieved when he rented it. It made him feel safe. If the girl has been there since late January, it makes some kind of odd sense. Garrett had just begun to heal by then. He was trying to get back to being the man he'd once been. The old Garrett would have taken her in."

I told her that according to April, Garrett had been at the National City apartment between seven-thirty and eight that night—he had left it less than one hour before Sanji Moussaraf had seen the flash. According to April, Garrett had come down to National City to "check up on her."

"She said he'd come by almost every day, or at least every other day, just to make sure she was okay," I said.

We sat in the dim room for a while without talking. I wondered how many hours of the last week Stella Asplundh had spent doing exactly this.

The phone rang again. She let the caller start to leave a message, then picked up.

Oh, Sam. Yes, I'm doing well. . . . What about you?

She listened for a long while without saying anything. Then she told Sam she loved him, too, and that she would call him in the morning.

When she came back I asked her if she'd ever noticed a woman wearing gold earrings in the shape of a crescent moon with a small sapphire resting inside the curve.

"Never. Why?"

I explained what we had found in the Explorer and that it looked like it could have been ripped off in a struggle.

"It's hard enough to imagine a man doing that to another human being," said Stella. "Let alone a woman."

"Did Garrett have a lover?" I asked.

Stella shook her head. "I would be very surprised. I'd think you would have uncovered her by now. No, Garrett was devoted to me. I say that with pride in him, not ownership or arrogance."

"How did you meet, you and Garrett?"

She looked at me and smiled very slightly. I was struck again by her unusual beauty, compromised though it was by tragedy, murder, and grief.

"I met Sam Asplundh in a restaurant bar in Los Angeles. I was finishing up my master's, student-teaching at the time. We dated twice, and then he made the mistake of arranging a double with his brother. I was in Garrett's pocket by the end of the night, though I had the good sense and manners not to show it to anyone, including Garrett."

I thought of my own headlong fall for Gina.

"Sam have hard feelings?" I asked.

"Just a little, maybe. He married and divorced."

"The woman from the Fourth of July party?"

She nodded, remembering.

"Was Garrett's light blue necktie special to you?" I asked.

"He wore it on our wedding day. Was he . . . when he . . . ?"

"Yes."

"God," Stella said softly. I believe that she shuddered though I couldn't see much more than her profile, backlit by the kitchen light.

She went to the tape player, rewound, and hit "play." Their scratchy, poorly recorded voices issued through the apartment like the soundtrack to an old TV show. I could almost picture them as they talked that day, four-thirty in the afternoon and the dark clouds gathering outside for the night's rain.

GARRETT: *You'll always be that to me. Bye.*

"Who's Mr. Highwayman?" I asked.

Stella came back and sat. "He's a dashing robber who's in love with Bess, the landlord's black-haired daughter. He's got lace at his chin, and a coat of claret velvet, and his rapier and pistol butts twinkle in the starlight.

And he rides off to rob the travelers and swears that if the cops really press him, he'll hide out and come back to her the next night by moonlight, though hell should bar the way. It was Garrett's favorite poem when he was a boy. He memorized it as a child and he'd recite it to me. It's beautiful. It's quite long. Listen:

The wind was a torrent of darkness among the gusty trees,
The moon was a ghostly galleon tossed upon cloudy seas,
The road was a ribbon of moonlight, over the purple moor,
And the highwayman came riding—
Riding—riding—
The highwayman came riding, up to the old inn-door.

I heard her voice evaporate into the sound of the traffic on the street below.

"Does he make it back with the loot?" I asked.

"They're betrayed by a jealous hostler. It costs them their lives."

"It sounds good," I said.

"It's romantic and tragic."

I said nothing but I could tell she was looking at me.

"You've had your share of tragic," she said.

"Everyone does if they live long enough."

"Do you talk about what happened?" she asked.

"I don't enjoy it."

"I understand that. I watched the fall on TV. I knew that you had lived, or I wouldn't have been able to watch it. I can't really describe how it made me feel. Terrible. Then relieved. Then very hopeful. It made me see that not everything ends in death and tragedy."

"I'm glad you felt hope," I said. "It cuts through the darkness better than anything, doesn't it?"

I heard tires squeal down on the street. I thought of being trapped down in the bottom of that floor safe where Gina's jewelry used to be.

"Do you mind talking about Samantha?" I asked.

"I don't enjoy it either," said Stella.

Neither of us said anything for a long moment.

"What was it like?" she asked. "The fall?"

The image of Vic Malic's grimace as he held me close came to my mind's eye. I didn't want it, but there was nothing I could do to get rid of it. I also smelled the gin on his breath and saw the flames lapping at the window as he spun me around and around. I felt the first thrilling terror of being alone in the air, high up and attached to nothing.

"It seemed to take a long time," I said. "I thought about a lot of things. At first I tried to will myself to stay up, but that didn't work. Then all these things raced by in a kind of code that ran much faster than memory or thought. It was as if my total experience on earth were being condensed and played back for me. I wasn't really worried about dying. I was more worried about . . . well, more practical things. Like exactly when would I hit, and which bones would break, and how long it would be before I saw Gina again. That's the most I've ever told anyone about it, except for Gina."

"She's your wife?"

"Yes."

"Are you two happy?"

"I can't tell you how much."

I went to the window and looked down through the blinds. I'm always somewhat relieved when I look out a window and see that I'm up less than six stories. A group of young women was crossing just then and I thought of Gina trying to jaywalk in front of the Rock Bottom nightclub. I marveled at how large a part chance played in life: the chance that brought Gina and me together on the same street at the same time, the chance that Samantha's doll would float into the middle of the pool and she would climb a fence without being seen.

"Have you ever watched the film that Garrett made about Samantha?"

"No," said Stella. "Garrett told me he was making it. And I sat down with him once but could only watch just a few seconds. He mailed me a copy but I never played it."

"I've seen it. It's difficult. She was perfect."

"I don't think I could watch it," she said. "See, Garrett . . . Garrett and I had very different reactions to what happened. Garrett wanted to preserve and possess—images, clothes, belongings, her room intact, exactly as it was. For almost six months, I did too. I collected and organized and preserved. Then I saw a white fire. The fire told me to let go. To give up trying to keep my daughter. It told me to forgive and remember, but not to dwell. It told me that if I buried myself with the objects of her life I would never be able to believe in her death. So I let go of most of her things. I allowed only a . . . reasonable number of her photographs in my home. I unburied myself. And the strangest transformation took place. When I was able to surrender Samantha's life, I found a measurable quantity of peace. Garrett went deeper the other way. Later, coming from the opposite direction, he found the same peace that I had found."

From the window I saw the women on the street go into an Italian restaurant. I wondered what it would be like to be single, with friends, and going out for eleven-fifteen drinks in the Gaslamp.

"I guess you've seen the video of your fall many times," Stella said.

"I've never watched it."

"Why not?"

"I think it might scare the piss out of me. Sorry for the language."

"Your language is fine."

Through the window I saw another jet heading down to Lindbergh Field. I thought of the lights in Las Vegas again and wondered where she was.

"That's interesting we've both got videos we won't watch," said Stella. "Videos of the most important things in our lives, and we don't want to see them."

"I think ignoring certain things is good," I said. "I don't think people need to know everything."

Her telephone rang again, startlingly loud in the high-ceilinged old room. It was a relief from having to talk about the Las Palmas. I still felt Malic close to me. I could still smell his breath.

Stella went into the kitchen. I could see her in the faint light as she picked up the phone. I heard without listening.

Hello? Oh, John. . . . I'm feeling okay tonight, considering. You? Yeah, yeah, I know. I loved your words today about Garrett, I wanted to tell you again. . . . Oh. . . . Oh, I didn't know that. Sure, I'd like to have it. . . . Okay. . . . Okay. . . . Okay. . . . I will. Good night.

Stella set the phone in its cradle and came back to the couch.

"Sorry. That was Van Flyke," she said. "I left my memorial pamphlet at the grave site. He's been a big help, but sometimes I think he's taken this worse than I have."

"Why do you think that?"

"He calls almost every day to make sure I'm okay, but he's a wreck himself. I think he's developing a crush on me. Under all that bossy cool, John's got a good heart. He thought the world of Garrett. He treated Garrett like a big brother, even though John's a few years older. I thought all that came across in the eulogy today."

"I did, too."

"So many people have offered help, gone out of their way for me," she said. "Mom and Dad have been here for me. Samuel's willing to do what he can, though he's hurting, too. Abel Sarvonola's trying to expedite the pension. The chief wants to create a memorial in Garrett's honor. Sutherland and even Chet Fellowes have offered to take care of any financial or even household things that might need seeing to."

"It's nice when people surprise you."

"Some surprises aren't so nice. I understand why Garrett disliked Erik Kaven. He didn't say one word to me until today. No call. No letter of condolence. No flowers sent to the chapel. He said nothing to the media about Garrett's murder. Today he spoke to me just before he left. He looked at me as if I'd killed him myself and he said, 'We must all look within ourselves at times like this.' That's all. End of statement. Like, if I looked far enough inside myself I'd find the murderer."

I wondered how Kaven had risen to the directorship of the Ethics Authority on such a meager spirit. I thought of his shameless stare and his disheveled appearance. I wondered if underneath it—as underneath the dismissive arrogance of John Van Flyke—there was actually a decent guy with no idea how to express himself. I was not convinced there was. In my twenty-nine years of experience, I have found that most often people are exactly what they appear to be.

In the near dark I watched her move across the room to the stereo again. The tape quickly rewound then whined to a stop. I stood and went to the door.

"You can keep the tape," I said. "I made it for you."

"Thank you."

"I'll get this guy."

"I know you will."

I looked at the two dead bolt locks and the chain lock on Stella's door, then closed it and took the stairs down. The east breeze had turned warm and I could feel spring advancing. I slung my jacket over my shoulder and walked through the Gaslamp to Salon Sultra and wondered when I would get it through my head that she didn't work there anymore. I sat on a bus-stop bench opposite the salon and watched the occasional car roll by. I wondered when Vince Brancini would call.

I drove back to Normal Heights wondering if making Stella Asplundh a copy of that tape was the right thing to do. I put myself in her shoes and asked myself if I would want a tape of my last conversation with Gina. Yes, certainly. Then I asked myself if I would listen to it.

I wasn't certain of that at all.

McKenzie and I stood in the shade of the Dream Wheels building late the next morning, while sketch artist Kathy Iles finished with Cass. Our St. Patrick's Day temperature was supposed to hit eighty degrees by the afternoon.

Kathy is an exceptionally good sketch artist because she makes the subject look like a real person instead of a generality or type. I'm sure you've seen sketches, or Identikit drawings, that don't quite look like real people. Kathy won't settle for that. I think her secret is how calming she is, how "okay" she can make things seem, even though many of the people she interviews are victims of terrible crimes. She takes her time and gets details that other artists miss because the witnesses are so upset. Kathy's a big, easygoing woman and she's very sensitive to people's mood changes. She became a police artist because her mother was killed in a botched convenience-store robbery by a man who was never identified and never caught.

"Sorry," she said as we stood in Cass's office and looked at the fresh sketch. "The hat, the sunglasses, the mustache. He looks more like a disguise than a man. This isn't one of my best."

"It's what he looked like, though," said Cass. "You got him, really, you did."

"Well, thanks," said Kathy.

Her rendition of Hummer Man showed a heavy-faced, blue-collar guy who, just as Cass had suggested, might be found on the back of his pickup truck at a Chargers tailgate party at Qualcomm Stadium. The sunglasses and thick mustache hid much of what might have been revealing. Kathy was right: This was not her best. Her Hummer Man was vague and generic.

Physically, the man in the sketch looked a little like Mincher, but Mincher was still too young. And Mincher had an affable, southern attitude about him that didn't fit Cass's "screw you" description of Hummer Man. Unless, of course, Mincher was a talented actor.

I learned that Hummer Man was right-handed, which was something I'd forgotten to ask Cass myself.

Kathy had also gotten Cass to remember that Hummer Man's fingernails were neatly trimmed and clean, in possible contrast to his overall appearance as a workingman. His hands looked smooth. I thought of Hummer Man's new Chargers cap, the clean fingernails and smooth hands, and his superior attitude.

Then I thought of the surveillance tape that I'd seen, and the flash of shoe leather. What kind of shiny shoes would a working fellow be wearing on a drizzly, soon-to-be-rainy day?

It seemed wrong. I wondered if we were looking for a real workingman or for a guy who had tried to seem like one.

"Maybe that's exactly what we're looking at—a disguise," I said.

"I did think there was something phony about him," said Cass. "Just . . . *off*. He looked like a regular person trying to look like a famous person trying not to be recognized. Or something like that."

Back at my desk I found a message that Assistant Chief Dale Payne of the New Orleans PD had called. I called him back.

"I've got everybody who came through the annex to claim those guns," he said. "That includes us, Sheriffs, feds, everybody. I got badge and phone numbers. Took some doin'. So here goes. Maybe this'll help you find out who walked out of here with my Model 39."

I typed out the name, rank, and organization of each person who was present at the annex weapons release. Just as I had thought, the NOPD had not let Lieutenant Darron Wight handle the weapons transfer alone—he'd been assisted by Officers Clay Strunk and Gloria Escobedo. I was partly expecting to hear Ron Mincher's name but was glad I didn't. None of the six names were familiar to me.

I left messages for three of them, but the other three I managed to get live. I explained in brief, concise terms that I was looking for someone who had lifted a murder weapon that day in New Orleans.

The first two told me with condescending patience that of course everybody had signed in—it was procedure. Bob Cramer of DEA hesitated, then was pointedly uncooperative. He said he wasn't in the habit of giving out the names or whereabouts of DEA agents to "local law enforcement."

I scratched the names off the list with increasingly bold sweeps of my pen, but I circled Bob Cramer.

I sighed and looked out the window at sun-drenched San Diego, still winter in America's Finest City.

After lunch McKenzie and I left headquarters with a half-inch stack of wanted posters and a half-inch sliver of hope. Before making copies of the posters, we had scanned the picture to an SDPD flyer form with our department seal and WANTED FOR QUESTIONING at the top, and a description of the unidentified subject at the bottom.

First we stopped at the Ethics Authority Enforcement Unit building. The Little Italy sidewalks were busy with pedestrians enjoying the sunshine and I could smell the bread and garlic from the restaurants. Arliss Buntz looked at us when we walked in, then began straightening her desktop. Her ancient, near-green sweater hung on a coatrack by the stairwell and there was a very small vase of California poppies beside her telephone.

"Come on up," said Van Flyke. He stood over us, looking down from the second story.

"Well, go on up," said Arliss.

I closed the door and played the tape of Garrett Asplundh's last conversation with Stella. Van Flyke listened with a frown, his head slightly cocked.

"Where did you get this?" he asked.

"Our friends in law enforcement," I said.

Van Flyke shook his head in disgust. "Some of the stuff that I have to put up with in this city. They create the Ethics Authority to watchdog the city, and what's the city do? It watchdogs the Ethics Authority."

"The conversation took place at four-thirty on Tuesday the eighth—the day Garrett was killed," I said.

Van Flyke nodded but said nothing.

"Whoever heard it could know that Garrett was going to be down at the Cabrillo Bridge that night," said McKenzie.

"He doesn't say what bridge," said Van Flyke.

"If you knew Garrett well, you knew what bridge he was talking about. Did he ever tell you about it?"

"He proposed to her there."

"When did you get your copy of this tape?" I asked.

"Yesterday," he said. "Always on Wednesdays, unless Kaven forgets and drags his feet. These tapes aren't of high interest to us in Ethics. We think it's demeaning to be taped and monitored in the first place. Especially by the mayor and you people."

McKenzie took one of our new "Wanted for Questioning" flyers from her briefcase and showed it to Van Flyke.

"Looks like you with a mustache," she said.

"I'm a Dolphins man," he said.

McKenzie held a flyer up toward him for comparison. She raised her eyebrows and Van Flyke smiled and shook his head.

"He's better-looking than you," said McKenzie.

"Most men are," said Van Flyke. "What they don't have is my vibrant personality. Tack your poster to the wall behind Arliss's desk and everybody who comes through here will see it."

"We'll leave a few on the downstairs table too," said McKenzie.

"Great," said Van Flyke. "And do me a favor—tell your bosses over at the PD to keep their noses out of Ethics Authority business. They want to pass around tape-recorded conversations, they can bug their own people."

Erik Kaven said that he "irregularly" monitored and recorded Ethics Authority phone calls but he did not listen to the conversation between Garrett and his wife. He was not prone to spying on his own employees. Certain other individuals had access to the monitoring equipment and could have eavesdropped while the conversation took place or perhaps replayed it later from the tape. He said the policy of monitoring Ethics Authority calls was "asinine" and he was firmly against it, but because such practice was included in the Ethics Authority charter, he had to play by the rules.

"It was the mayor and council's idea," said Kaven. "It's their way of keeping us under their political thumb. They want ethics, but they don't want ethics with teeth."

I thought of what Stella had said, how Garrett distrusted Kaven because of Kaven's coziness with Sarvonola and the business interests of San Diego.

"You were against hiring Garrett, weren't you?"

He eyed me. "I thought he'd be better off as a cop, but the decision was up to Van Flyke. I direct the Authority. I don't dictate. And don't bother asking me to let you hear any more Ethics Authority tapes. You want Ethics Authority property, go to court and come back with a warrant. Or talk to all your blameless captains—you can probably get anything you want from them."

"We've already got some paper," said McKenzie. She brought out another flyer. "Looks like you."

He took and studied it. " 'Wanted for Questioning' . . . What kind of a face is that? Looks like a costume. What put you onto this guy? What's his story?"

"Get some paper and we'll talk," said McKenzie.

Kaven smiled. Behind his gunslinger's mustache his teeth were white and straight. "Fine. I don't want to know. I know too much already."

Over the next four hours we drove to three television studios, six radio stations, six newspapers, and three magazines. We could have just faxed the sketch to each of them, but in my experience a personal appearance helps get attention.

We were greeted with gravity and furrowed brows at each stop and we got assurances that our sketch would be aired, published, or—in the case of radio—described, by everyone we talked to. With each sketch we included a press release about the Garrett Asplundh murder.

At five that afternoon we were finishing up with the city-run community centers, all of which feature bulletin boards for local, allegedly nonprofit announcements. Among the flyers for natural-childbirth classes, baldness therapies, free kittens, gem and mineral shows, herbal weight-loss programs, haiku workshops, and nonmedical treatments for sweaty palms and poor eyesight, we tacked our "Wanted for Questioning" flyers of Hummer Man. He looked brusque and lowbrow in the optimistic mix of self-improvement schemes, educational programs, and free pets.

By the time we rolled back into headquarters it was almost dark and still seventy degrees. We had ten flyers left. I put a few of them in my briefcase and gave the rest to McKenzie. She began scanning one into her computer to post it on our PD Web site and send it out as a jpeg to some of the watchdog Web sites that are helpful to law enforcement.

Chet Fellowes eased into the Homicide room, shoulders sloped and arms long. He put both hands on my desk, leaned over, and turned to face me.

"We're set for Eden Heights at midnight," he said. "You found it, you can come along for the fun if you want."

"Cortez, too?"

"Cortez, too. And wear your vests. People like Chupa Junior go well with body armor."

"You talk to Villas?" I asked.

"Of course I talked to Villas."

"Then we're in."

"You can ride in one of the tactical trucks with my people," said Fellowes. "We'll have two. I looked over the location yesterday. We'll have some men waiting out back by that pool house. That's going to be the emergency exit when Chupa spots us driving up."

"All right. Thank you, sir."

He leaned closer and whispered. "The video that Garrett had, with our guys and the girls on it. It hasn't gotten out, you know? You've kept it in-house, haven't you?"

"I turned it over to Professional Standards," I said.

"But you made a copy, right?"

"No, sir. Why would I?"

At times like this I'm glad that people can't see the lies tumbling out of my mouth like I can see theirs. But I always wonder if, maybe in some other way, they can.

"There's going to be a shitstorm when the VIPs get popped at Eden Heights tonight," said Fellowes. "Cops, pols, fire, businessmen—everybody gets pulled into the net. Bad for us. Bad for the city. Can you handle that?"

"I can handle that."

"Because you're not like some people. I mean, you don't *want* our city to look bad, do you?"

"I like it the way it is."

"Meet us down by the sally port at midnight."

He slapped a heavy hand on my shoulder and went to McKenzie's desk.

McKenzie left the station a few minutes earlier than usual. She had a dinner date with Hollis Harris and needed to have it wrapped in time to get her back here by twelve for our raid on Eden Heights. I smiled and was pleased that it would take McKenzie and Hollis four or five hours to have dinner. McKenzie read my thoughts and looked away.

I thought of all the endless dinners that Gina and I had made together from magazine recipes in our home, spacing the courses between love-making and letting the cooking and eating become part of the love, or the love become part of the cooking and eating—a dizzying series of desires we built and rebuilt together with the windows open to the breeze and the TV turned down low and the answering machine taking all calls and me praying my pager or cell wouldn't go off and take me away to deal with criminals.

McKenzie had looked somewhat tired but happy ever since she first went out with Harris. Her complexion and attitude seemed less severe. She had told me that he had the fastest mind she'd ever known and was coming along nicely as a recreational handgunner. He had shown an interest in sporting clays, which McKenzie had never shot. She said they were planning to try clays together and wondered if Gina and I would like to do it, too. I'd told her that would be great—I'd get with Gina and see when she was free. I found it disappointing that after five years of marriage I was lying about my wife, while after one week of dating, McKenzie was able to make plans with and speak honestly about her boyfriend.

I stayed late at headquarters, then stopped by Higher Grounds on my way home. The first two employees I talked to were pretty sure they had worked that night, but neither remembered seeing the man on my poster. The second two were pretty sure they had not worked that night, and neither of them remembered seeing him either.

Then an extremely pale girl with lucid green eyes took one look at the flyer and lifted her brilliant gaze to me.

"I waited on him," she said. Her badge said "Miranda." Her hair was white. "That's not a great sketch, but I recognize the guy. He came in about eight-thirty. I remember thinking his sunglasses were overkill cool, because it was dark and rainy."

"Tell me what happened," I said.

"He ordered a medium decaf with cream," said Miranda. "I remember thinking that was a good thing for him to order. He looked nervous."

"How could you tell that?"

"His hands were shaking."

"Had you seen him before?" I asked.

"Two or three times. But . . . he was different that night."

"Different how?"

"I'm not sure. I can't say exactly how."

"Did he say anything to you, besides ordering the coffee?"

"Not one thing," said Miranda. "He looked off to the side when he paid, like he didn't want to see or be seen. He paid with two dollars. That's when I saw his hands shaking. He left me the forty cents for a tip."

"What kind of voice did he have?"

"I don't remember. I'm visual, not aural."

"Did he ever take off the sunglasses?"

"No."

"Would you recognize him if he came in again?"

She smiled and shook her head as if dealing with a child. "I'm an art student. I've got twenty-ten vision. There's only one thing I can really do well, and that's *see*. I'd recognize him."

I wrote my cell number on the back of five business cards and gave one to her.

"I'll keep an eye out," she said. "Two, actually."

Then I handed the others to the employees one at a time.

"Cool."

"Cool."

"Cool."

"Cool."

"I saw you on TV," Miranda said, studying me with her perfect green eyes. "I'm glad you lived."

"Thank you. That's nice of you to say."

"It made me thank God for my life."

"Me, too. Can you think of anything else about this man you saw?"

"No. I'm sorry I can't tell you how he was different. It's not that I didn't see him clearly, it's just . . . I'm sorry. He was just not the same as when I'd seen him before."

A pale fog was drifting through the valleys surrounding Eden Heights. The last of the streetlights cast its muted round glow as we headed up into the hills.

I thought of Garrett Asplundh's favorite poem, as recited by Stella:

The road was a ribbon of moonlight over the purple moor . . . .

I pictured Hummer Man again and hoped we might buy some more luck with our "Wanted" poster. What Miranda had told me was apt, interesting, and a little chilling. But it wouldn't do me a lot of good unless he went back to Higher Grounds when she was there or until I could match a suspect's DNA with that in the saliva from the lid that Sanji Moussaraf had given me, inadmissable as that might be.

It was twelve forty-five by the time we left headquarters in the tactical SUV, a black-and-white Suburban heavy with lights and bristling with antennae. It's an impressive vehicle. Eight of us were crammed inside: Fellowes and two detectives, all in street clothes, and three uniforms. Mincher had been plucked from duty in traffic, no doubt by Fellowes, and he sat quietly at the wheel, devoted to the road, saying nothing to me or McKenzie.

Everyone had armor. Fellowes seemed especially uncomfortable in it, and in fact the vest looked too small for his long torso. I wear an older, Kevlar II vest made by Point Blank, which fits me very well and is highly rated, though weighty and no longer considered cutting edge.

Behind us were four cruisers and two slickbacks, with a total of twelve armed and armored officers. Four of them were females from Vice; two were female patrol officers. It's easier for women to arrest women because there is less likelihood of excessive force or groping accusations, though sometimes women peace officers have trouble subduing a violent suspect alone. Bringing up the rear were two transportation vans and four uniforms to take the girls and the johns directly to jail.

I turned to watch one van, two cruisers, and two unmarked cars pull to the roadside, then bump off into the darkness. They would use county-maintained fire roads and come in the back way. According to Fellowes, they would get to their destination sooner than the rest of us. They would park as close to the back of the Tuscan mansion as possible, then move on foot and take positions around the backyard and pool house.

The rest of us would divide into two groups, roll right up, and block both ends of the house's circular front driveway. Some of us would spread out on foot to cover side doors and windows. The rest of us would go in, serve our warrant, and start cuffing people. Fellowes would do the knocking and talking, though I suspected we might end up breaking down the front door.

I looked out at the moon, a curve resting on its back in the gauze of fog and darkness. McKenzie checked her Glock, then holstered it and snapped the strap. I was aware of my grandfather's Colt 1911 A1 up against my ribs.

Fellowes told us what they'd found out about the brothel. He told us that his Vice detectives had discovered that the Eden Heights house was actually owned by a Los Angeles–based financier who had never occupied it. It was managed by Sorrento Property Management and rented out month to month to Preferred Financial Services for seven thousand dollars. Preferred Financial Services was a company owned by Jordan Sheehan & Associates, Investments. There was no formal rental agreement on which her name appeared.

"I hope she didn't smell us out," said Fellowes as we slowed for the off-ramp. "She isn't stupid."

I figured that Fellowes had made sure she smelled us out, or we wouldn't be marching in right now. I figured that Jordan Sheehan was far, far away from Eden Heights at this moment, likely at Indigo, where she would be seen and remembered. I figured that she had arranged to let Chupa take this fall. I figured that Fellowes would not be telling the press who the actual renter of the Tuscan behemoth really was. I didn't think we'd find much of the A-list here tonight, but rather the second-echelon johns who actually paid for their Squeaky Clean fun.

"I hope I can cuff her myself," said McKenzie. She leaned forward toward Fellowes as she said this, stepping on my toe with her duty boot to let me know that she understood Jordan had taken the night off.

We all had extra plastic wrist restraints, which are quickly accessible inside a belt or waistband. Two of our officers would carry video cameras to record the procedure. We wanted a clear record to help establish our case and to protect us from the storm of criticism that can come when police actions are questioned. Of course, our behavior had to be perfect, which can be difficult when people are screaming, running, or resisting arrest.

At least we wouldn't have to pull off to the side of the road and wait for someone with the gate code to come in or out of Eden Heights. Fellowes had gotten the code from Liberty Ridge Protection, the private security company that maintained the gate to Eden Heights.

We waited while Mincher punched in the code. The elaborate wrought-iron gate swung open and the Suburban rolled forward. We started up the road slowly so the others could catch up. A moment later Mincher kicked the big Suburban into a trot, and we headed up the hill.

We passed down the wide street and through the handsome neighborhood. It was like driving through a life-size travel brochure for a Mediterranean paradise. I saw the Tuscan mansion up ahead, its fountain throwing streams of water into the air, the windows aglow with muted light, and the sharp reflections coming off the cars parked along the big circular drive.

McKenzie leaned forward, then sat back and took a deep breath. We knocked fists for luck. Chupa Junior stood on the porch in a swatch of light, took one look at us, then vanished inside.

"We've been made," said Fellowes.

Mincher punched the Suburban to the far entry and swung sideways to block it. Two cruisers pulled up around us to seal it off. I glanced back to the first entry and saw our cruisers and slickbacks throttling the entrance, doors swinging open.

We trotted up the drive, Fellowes leading the way. The blue water splashed in the fountain and I could smell the damp sage from the hillsides. Our video shooter flared off to the side and kept pace with us, camera rolling.

Captain Fellowes knocked three times, waited a few seconds, and knocked again. Standing on the driveway behind him I saw a light come on upstairs, then another. Doors slammed. Voices touched the walls inside.

Fellowes signaled. Mincher and another officer slammed the battering ram into the fancy door. The brass burst off the wood, the door twisted open like something wounded, and Fellowes stumbled inside.

I heard shouting from the back of the house. Fellowes and three men ran down the foyer then branched off to the left. McKenzie and I followed but went right. A door slammed open in front of me and a young man shot out, saw us, and ran the other way. He wore a suit but carried his shoes and socks. Behind him tumbled a barefoot young woman with her dress almost on, her hair in her face, and a wild glint in her eyes as she tried to follow him down the hall.

I charged past the woman and caught up with the john halfway across the game room, yelling at him to stop. He didn't, so I brought him down. We crashed hard into the leg of a billiards table and I could hear the balls clack apart up on the felt but I swung the guy's wrists behind him and put a tie around them. He did not meaningfully resist. I ran back to find McKenzie in control of the girl, who was cuffed and demanding to see her lawyer immediately.

Two of our uniforms appeared to escort our suspects to the transport van.

More shouting from the back of the house then, but I couldn't tell what was being said. In a suite off the hallway McKenzie and I surprised a couple still trying to get enough clothes on to run away. The man was middle-aged and plainly terrified. The girl was a very young Latina in a red slip. Her hair spread into a shiny black fan as she tried to sprint past me for the door. McKenzie took her down and they spit and argued in frightening Spanish while I let Middle-Aged put on his pants and shirt.

Suddenly the lights were out. A woman screamed upstairs, and a man yelled. A gun went off somewhere in the back of the house—a small-caliber handgun, .22 or .25 was my guess.

Two more quick pops rang through the chaos. A man screamed in pain. Middle-Aged broke away from my grip and ran down the hall.

I yelled at him to stop but he didn't. I saw his silhouette round the end of the hallway and head for the game room. I clambered in behind him, remembering where the billiards table was but miscalculating the jukebox location. I crashed into it, managing to stay upright. The French doors stood open at the far end of the room. I could see the faint moonlight outside and the shimmer of the pool on the window glass. Middle-Aged blundered outside and headed right.

I identified myself and ordered him to stop one more time. I caught up with him out by the pool house and took him down hard. He broke my grip with a nice turn of his wrist and struggled back to his feet. He made the spiked fence and I slammed into him as he tried to climb over, then fell to the ground and rolled once. He writhed away from me again. I picked myself up and clawed after him. But instead of running he stopped, planted his feet, and swung for my face. I leaned away from the blow and used his momentum to take him down again. I drove a knee into his back and used all my strength and weight to get his wrists together and finally cinch the plastic tie tight.

I stood up panting and really noticed what was going on around me for the first time.

The plan had worked. Our back-side interceptors were now marching off the girls and their johns two and three at a time. The lights on the cruisers bathed the scene in alternating flashes of red and blue and yellow, and the headlights of the transport van and the slickbacks cut through the scene with high beams powdered by the fog.

I recognized the San Diego fireman from one of Garrett's videos. I recognized another face, though I still didn't know his name. Carrie Ann Martier, wrapped in a white terry robe, looked at me as one of the Vice officers marched her past.

"Hi, Robbie,"

"Hi, Carrie."

"Help me out here, will ya?"

"I would if I could."

"All I did for you?"

"I'm cuffed too, Carrie."

Then the wall exploded. A huge, headless shape blasted through a ground-floor French door, caught its foot on the broken glass, crashed to the patio, and rolled once. It came to its feet like a big, heavy cat and lowered the protective sport coat from its face. Chupa froze. He looked at me and at the other cops, then swung his immense arms and legs into rhythm and powered his way across the backyard toward the fence. He was limping badly. A Vice detective tried to tackle him but Chupa lifted him over his head and threw him into the pool. Another one climbed onto Chupa from behind but the big man shrugged him off. Another Vice detective drew down on him and yelled for him to stop but Chupa was already at the fence. A uniformed officer approached with his gun drawn but Chupa turned away from him and started climbing the fence topped by the elegant points.

I didn't think he could do it. The fence was six feet high and built on an embankment. But he had already locked each of his big fists onto a spike, and he had more than enough strength in his arms to hoist his body toward the top. He hooked one ankle over the top horizontal railing. I could see the blood running off his shoe.

Then I saw Fellowes stumble through the broken French door, followed by Mincher. They looked at Chupa and lifted their already drawn weapons.

"Down from the fence!" yelled Fellowes. "He shot an officer! Officer down inside!"

"Bullshit, man, I got no gun!" yelled Chupa.

Someone fired over Chupa's head and ordered him down. He had found a precarious balance, his feet stable on the top railing, his body bent over and wobbling. His big mask of a face glared down at us.

Another warning shot rang out into the night, humming into the darkness of the hills behind the house.

"Get down from that fence!" Fellowes yelled. "You are under arrest! You are under arrest!"

"Got no fucking gun, man. What's wrong with you?"

Chupa let go of the spikes and stood. He raised his great arms for balance and his sport coat flared out, giving him a billowing grace. He began to gather and shift his weight for the jump down but the bloody foot either slipped or gave way, and he fell back down inside the fence and hit the ground with both feet. He was breathing heavily now, huge legs straining to keep him upright, his hands gripping the iron railings behind him.

Two officers moved closer, guns drawn.

"He's armed!" yelled Fellowes.

Chupa found his balance. "Bullshit, man, I got no gun!"

"Drop the gun!"

He smiled. "I got no gun!"

"Drop the gun!"

And that was when Chupa whipped the pistol from inside his coat.

I drew down in an instant but it didn't matter.

Chupa didn't get off the round. A roar of gunfire collapsed him to his knees. He looked hapless and surprised. He fired one crazy shot into the air and another fusillade dumped him onto his face on the embankment. His back heaved and the blood gushed out through the bullet holes. He lifted his head, squinted out at us and into the flashing lights, then lowered his face to the grass and shuddered.

By 1:30 A.M. someone had found the main circuit breaker and turned it back on.

By 2:00, all of the johns and girls had been taken downtown. A small bunch of neighbors had gathered outside the driveway, and the fog had thickened.

By 3:00, the Coroner's van had taken away the body of Chupa Junior.

By 4:00, Roger Sutherland and his Professional Standards Unit had confiscated the video cameras used to record the scene, completed their measurements and calculations of the crime scene, conducted interviews relating to the shooting death of Chupa Junior, and ordered all SDPD personnel to refer press and media questions to his office.

As it turned out, one of Fellowes's Vice officers—Swanson—had gone down with a gunshot to the chest, but his armor had done its job. Mincher had witnessed the shooting: Chupa Junior had produced a small handgun from the pocket of his jacket and caught the officer as he burst into an upstairs suite.

McKenzie and I stood out back. The transport vans and cop cars were gone but the pool lights made the water bright and the yard lights issued a soft glow in the fog.

"You okay?" I asked.

"My nerves are shot and I'm sleepy."

"Me too."

Fellowes came from the house, slouching his way over to us.

"There you are," he said.

"Here we are," said McKenzie.

"I hate swimming pools," said Fellowes. "They remind me of Samantha Asplundh. Take a walk with me, will ya?"

We followed him back inside the house, then upstairs. As I climbed the stairs behind him I understood that Fellowes, as directed by Sarvonola, had tipped off his influential friends so they wouldn't get busted that night—Rood, Stiles, Vinson. And that he was covering his own and Mincher's tracks by raiding the brothel. I understood that he had let Squeaky Clean get through the net so she could set up shop somewhere else. Jordan's girls would take the fall for her—Carrie Ann Martier and the others. And I understood that we had killed a man who may or may not have taken a shot at a Vice officer, as witnessed by a traffic cop on the take along with Fellowes. I felt a deep sickness in my guts, like nothing I had felt before.

He motioned us into one of the suites. I saw that the door had been broken down.

The room was quite large. The furniture was leather and the carpet was dark and thick. Gas logs burned in the fireplace. One wall was a huge, mirrored walk-in closet. The bed was tossed—black satin sheets and pillows.

Mincher was there, leaning against the entrance to the bath. Two Vice detectives stood across from him and two more stood by the window.

"Shut the door," said Fellowes.

Mincher shut the door. Fellowes went to the window then turned to McKenzie and me.

"You two should understand something," he said. "We don't know what happened to Garrett. Leave Vice out of it. We have our hands full with our own problems. Clear?"

"One of your problems was Garrett," said McKenzie.

"No. He never said one word to us about anything he was doing. We had no problem with Garrett until you showed up. Listen, you fuckin' crusaders—this is my turf. I allowed you to come along tonight so you would see what happens on it."

"We saw," I said.

"This was nothing."

"Tell Chupa that," I said.

"Dirtbag deserved what he got," said Fellowes. "Ask Mincher. He saw it."

Mincher shrugged. But he didn't look at McKenzie or me.

It was sunrise when I got home, the second all-nighter I'd pulled in one week. My ears were ringing and I felt slow and stupid.

I walked around my house with an exhausted eye, like a tourist too tired to care. I made frosted strawberry toaster pastries then sat for a while at the yellow table in the breakfast room and looked down at the scores of indentations and scratches and nicks that five years had brought to the cheap pine tabletop. While I traced with a fingertip the codes of my life with Gina, I wondered where she was and what she was doing. It was time for her father to tell me. You don't leave five years of marriage with hardly a word to the man who loved and cared for you the best he could. Vince didn't want her to do that. I wasn't going to let her, though I had no idea what either of us would say.

I knew there were bigger problems in the world than why my wife had left me, so I thought about all of the corrupt and self-serving men and women who were conspiring to make San Diego their own. Why didn't they care about this wonderful city? I was ashamed that there were men in my department who were so easily bought for a little flesh, a little cash, a little power. And I felt bad for the young guys like Mincher who tried to do the right thing but got in over their heads and couldn't get out. The others you could understand: Sarvonola, a career manipulator in love with his own power; Rood and Stiles, politicians with grandiose appetites and even bigger senses of entitlement; Jordan Sheehan, a brazen retailer of youth and innocence, in love with money; Trey Vinson, a weakling in a powerful company; Peter Avalos, a vicious, dead hood who hadn't finished tenth grade; the Squeaky Cleans, a battalion of pretty young women who wanted all the nice things right now; and a city full of guys eager to contribute to their desires a few hundred dollars at a time.

Which led me to Garrett Asplundh, who had found his way to the dark middle of all this, tried to get his bearings and labored under the tremendous weight of knowing. His old department had been compromised and used. His city was in the hands of gamblers and fools. His daughter had drowned. His heart had been broken, then begun to heal. The woman he loved more than anybody on earth was willing to take him back after nine months of hell. And I saw him sitting there alone in the dark and rain by Cabrillo Bridge, thinking of everything that he was going back to, everything he could have again. Like he could get up on that bridge with Stella and let it carry them away from a disastrous past to a future of promise.

I left messages for McKenzie and Captain Villas, then lay down on our bed with my clothes on.

Six hours later, just past noon, I felt the vibration of the cell phone on my belt. I had been dreaming of a distant land with good rivers and was not so sure I wanted to be called away. I sat up and answered it.

"Bob Cramer, DEA Miami," he said.

"Oh, boy."

"Sorry about that last call. Look, I've been thinking about your question, Detective. About who was present at the evidence transfer in New Orleans that day. At first I thought it was none of your business who was there from DEA. We impound and process a ton of weapons every year, especially here in Miami. You're not DEA. We don't open our books to local cops."

"I heard all that the first time." I wished I was back in the distant land.

"But it bothered me," said Cramer. "It wasn't sitting right. So I had some talks with my people here, to see if I could help you without breaching DEA rules and regs. You wouldn't believe the levels of bureaucracy here, or maybe you would. Anyway, I got things smoothed out."

"Good. I'm listening."

"My partner that day was John Van Flyke. But he signed in, like everybody else. That's what he says. I remember him making motions on the log with his pen. I didn't stand there and look over his shoulder, but it sure looked to me like he was signing in."

My scalp went cool. "New Orleans PD has no record of him being there," I said.

"Look, Detective, Van Flyke is a good man and he had a spotless record with us. He was there. But there's bound to be a reasonable explanation for this. If the Property Annex can lose a nine-millimeter autoloader, they can lose a sign-in sheet, right?"

I didn't tell Cramer that the sheet wasn't missing. The only things missing were a gun and John Van Flyke's signature.

"When did you talk to him?"

"An hour ago. I told him San Diego PD was making inquiries. I didn't name names."

"Thank you."

I called McKenzie and gave her the news. She met me outside the Ethics Authority Enforcement office half an hour later. So much for her trip to Jackson Hole.

We walked into the drafty old room and Arliss Buntz told us that Van Flyke had taken the rest of the day off.

"He has vacation time coming," she said.

"Did he leave right after the call from Cramer?" I asked.

She nodded. "And he asked me to remove the 'Wanted' posters from the lobby. He said your sketch was *useless.*"

Outside, I dialed the cell number that Van Flyke had given me on our first interview.

"Brownlaw, why didn't you just ask me if I was in New Orleans that day?" he said. "I fetched more weapons for DEA than you guys see in a year. Cramer bother to tell you that?"

"More or less. But if you signed in, why isn't your name on the sheet?"

"Police ineptitude? San Diego PD lets a murderer walk out of the courthouse. New Orleans can't keep track of guns or paper. I think most of you cops must originate down near the bottom of the gene pool."

"Did you lift the Model 39?" I asked.

"No. And I didn't shoot anybody either. You'll have to work a little harder to close your case, Brownlaw."

No colored shapes came out to greet me. I'd never seen them during a phone conversation. I wanted to see Van Flyke's answers for myself.

"We need to talk face-to-face," I said. "I've got a few questions."

"Monday okay?"

"Right now."

"Fine. I'm at a sushi bar in La Jolla, into my first martini, my first helping of salmon sashimi, and looking forward to the rest of my Friday afternoon away from Ethics, the San Diego PD, Erik Kaven, and Arliss Buntz. I just met an interesting woman. You're welcome to join the party. So is Cortez. But I'm not going to move one inch from this stool."

In the background I heard what sounded like faint music and the muted tones of restaurant activity.

"I'll be there in thirty minutes."

"Sushi on the Rock, Girard Avenue. The salmon is the best I've ever had."

I aimed my Chevrolet toward Interstate 5.

"You're not really thinking Van Flyke, are you?" asked McKenzie.

"I'm just thinking."

She was quiet for a moment.

"I don't see any reason why he'd kill his friend," said McKenzie. "What on earth does that get him?"

I'd been asking myself that question since Cramer called, and I kept coming up with the same answer. The answer came from somewhere inside me that was disturbing and seldom visited. "It gets him a shot at Stella."

I merged into the freeway traffic, feeling McKenzie's stare on the side of my face.

"No," she said. "It was business, Robbie. It was something Garrett knew. It was something he was going to do."

"Why can't it be personal? Van Flyke moved all from Florida a few weeks after Samantha drowned, to be here while the Asplundh marriage collapsed.

He hired Garrett. Every time Garrett or Stella turned around, there he was. His office is just a few blocks from Stella's apartment. Maybe those are Van Flyke's eyes she's been feeling for so long. He saw the reconciliation coming and he saw a chance to cancel out Garrett forever. He didn't listen to the *tape* of Garrett's last conversation with Stella—he heard it live from his office in that hollow old building. Sound carries so easily there, haven't you noticed?"

McKenzie nodded but said nothing for a long moment. "That's ugly stuff, Robbie."

"Very."

"Okay, if you want to do ugly, then what about his dear brother, Sam?" asked McKenzie. "You told me he was the one who discovered Stella. Then Garrett took his big find away from him. The blonde finally ditched him. Samuel was at the party when Samantha drowned. He was probably also at lots of other Asplundh family events. So every time Garrett or Stella turned around, there was Samuel, too. He lives close enough to drive down and stalk her around town. He's a Bureau guy, so, hell, he could have her apartment bugged with hidden cameras, right?"

"I thought of that," I said. "But a brother? No. My blood won't let me believe it."

"I don't believe it for a second either, Robbie. I'm still thinking business. Business, dollars, and the people who run this city. I'm thinking that Garrett had the videos and they couldn't let him act on them. That would ruin everything, from City Hall to Wall Street. The rulers can't let it happen."

"Okay," I said, "Tell me who and how."

"Kaven," she said. "If you stuff all that hair up under a Chargers cap and put on a pair of shades, you got Hummer Man. He wouldn't even need to fake the mustache."

"Why shoot Garrett?"

"Garrett's set to spill to the attorney general. He's holding out on his own director, because Garrett thought Kaven was too friendly with Sarvonola—even Stella knew that. If you can't see Kaven pulling the trigger, then try this: Maybe he and Sarvonola dumped the job on Fellowes, who got Mincher to do the dirty work. Both Fellowes and Mincher got caught on tape with the Squeaky Cleans, and Sarvonola had seen it, right? So he's got plenty of leverage. And Mincher's got no alibi for that night."

"But Cass at Dream Wheels made Hummer Man for mid-forties. Mincher's twenty-six."

"Age is tough to estimate, Robbie, when a face is covered up like that."

Everything she said was welcomed by my head but rejected by my guts.

"I like Van Flyke best," I said.

"You've got some dark spots inside, for being such a nice guy."

I shrugged and gunned the Chevy down the on-ramp.

Van Flyke wasn't at Sushi on the Rock. I checked the men's room then asked the hostess about him. He had left shortly after taking a brief phone call—about one o'clock. He paid with cash for a mixed sushi platter and three martinis. There was no woman seated near him. He was serious and unfriendly and she had seen him furtively inspecting what appeared to be a small vial, which she assumed to be insulin because she was a type 1 diabetic who still injected herself manually.

When we stepped back outside into the mild March sun, I called Van Flyke's cell and got a recording. I had just clipped the phone back on my belt when I felt it agitating my side again.

"Detective Brownlaw? This is Miranda at Higher Grounds Coffee Pub. The man who bought the coffee from me that night in the rain? He just walked past our window here and got into a big white car with an antenna on the roof. I was right—I've seen him in here several times *without the shades, the mustache, or the hat.* That's why he looked so familiar but so different that night. Because he usually wears a suit, and that's what he had on just now. He had one arm around this pretty woman, a brunette. She was a little wobbly—drunk, maybe. He kind of helped her into the car. I've seen her around here a bunch of times, too. I couldn't tell if she was struggling or if he was keeping her on her feet."

My heart dropped. Stella.

"You're positive it's him?"

"Positive."

"Did you get the car plates?"

"I couldn't get close enough without calling attention to myself. I'm pretty sure it was a Ford."

"Which direction did they go?"

"North on Fourth Avenue."

"Give me your phone numbers, please."

She gave me her work, home, and mobile numbers.

I punched off and looked at McKenzie. "Hummer Man and Stella just got into a white car with an antenna on the roof, then headed north on Fourth. Try to get Stella on her cell."

We scrambled into the car and I hooked a U-turn on Girard against the traffic. While McKenzie tried to get through to Stella, I got Dispatch to issue a computer alert for a white sedan with a roof antenna, possibly a Ford, last seen headed north on Fourth Avenue toward Broadway. I gave a description of the driver and identified his companion as Stella Asplundh. I said that she may have been abducted. I requested that officers stop and hold the man for questioning.

"Consider him armed and dangerous. I think he killed Garrett Asplundh," I said.

"Copy, Robbie. You want SWAT and ABLE?"

"ABLE" stands for Airborne Law Enforcement—we've got four choppers and one fixed-wing aircraft in our department. The choppers have scopes on board that can read a license-plate number from the sky and infrared sensors that can see the body heat of runaway suspects and locate them for officers on the ground. They're awesome tools for us.

I told dispatch to get SWAT assembled and ready to roll on a code eleven and all four of the choppers into the air as soon as possible.

"You mean both choppers," she said.

"I said all four."

"Only two of them work. Sarvonola and the budget crunch, you know."

"Christ. Over and out."

I gunned the Chevy through posh La Jolla, back toward Stella's apartment in the Gaslamp Quarter.

The landlord let us in. Nothing looked unusual. No sign of a struggle. No sign of anything at all.

"Let's see if our sharp-eyed friend at Higher Grounds recognizes a mug of John Van Flyke," I said.

"I'll call sweet Arliss," said McKenzie.

Ten minutes later I stood at Arliss Buntz's desk, looking down at a blown-up print of the picture used on John Van Flyke's city-issued photo ID. Arliss also gave me the license-plate numbers for his white Ford Crown Victoria and his home address on Coronado.

"Is Mr. Van Flyke diabetic?" I asked.

"If he is, he kept it from his employers," said Arliss.

I handed the photograph to Miranda at Higher Grounds.

She looked at it and nodded. "It's him."

We continued north on Fourth, just as Van Flyke had done. I saw four patrol units still slowly cruising the area. And I spotted two unmarked detective Delta units, drifting like sated sharks, but I knew these guys would be quick to depart at the next hot call. Both of our ABLE choppers were in the air. I saw one stream across my windshield toward the ocean as I continued north and another hovering over the 163 where it spills into downtown. I knew that their best chance of spotting the car was already gone. I cursed unskillfully. McKenzie glowered out the window.

I drove past McGinty's on India Street where Garrett sometimes drank. Then I passed through the intersection of Hawthorn and Kettner where the festive St. Patrick's Day marbles had spilled in time to get into the tire of Garrett's Explorer. Then I drove down Kettner past the Ethics Authority Enforcement Unit, where Garrett had been employed. Then back onto Hawthorn and past the shining vehicles of Dream Wheels. Finally back to Higher Grounds in the Gaslamp Quarter.

I knew it was illogical to cruise the area again, but it was the only thing I could think to do while my mind tried to spin a web of comprehension around what was happening.

What was Van Flyke going to do with her?

I called Coronado PD for backup.

Van Flyke's house was tucked away on Astrid Court in Coronado. The neighborhood was older, with tree-lined streets, neat lawns, and a quiet blush of afternoon sunlight on it.

The house was a wood and glass two-story. The wood was stained almost black and the windows were darkly smoked. The angles were sharp and concealing. In the middle of the front yard stood an enormous magnolia tree, its leaves waxy and sleek. The house seemed to be hiding behind it. A detached garage sat to the right.

"Ethics pays about the same salaries that we do," said McKenzie. "How'd he afford that?"

"Maybe he rents it."

"It looks a lot like him. Tight-assed and grim."

I unsnapped my holster strap and got out.

We kept an easy pace down the sidewalk. Two Coronado PD uniforms and two plainclothes fell in with us. A newspaper sat on the driveway. I picked it up—Friday's *Union-Tribune*—and checked the mailbox, but it was empty.

"His name is John Van Flyke," I said to the others. "He's abducted a woman and he's probably armed."

"Who is he?" asked one of the plainclothes. "What's he do?"

"He's with the San Diego Ethics Authority," I said.

"No shit?"

"None. Be careful, guys," I said. "He's a capable man."

We walked past the big magnolia tree toward the dark angles of the house. There was a planter by the front porch but it had no plants or flowers in it, just a private security sign poked in and leaning at an angle. The porch was shaded and the front door was solid wood except for a peephole. There was no welcome mat.

I dropped the paper near the planter, knocked twice, and stood to the side. A moment later I rang the doorbell. I heard a distant chime but that was all. I knocked again, harder, and waited.

I stepped forward and to the right and peeked quickly through one of the sidelights that ran up either side of the front door. I made out the foyer, a coatrack, a high-backed bench, and a mirror before pulling my face out of there. Too good a target. I went to the other side of the door and did it again. I saw that the foyer opened up to a room diagonally divided into shade and sunlight. I saw a sofa and a chair.

I tried the door but it was locked. Then I drew my sidearm and turned to the Coronado cops.

The four men drew their weapons. McKenzie's was already out and ready.

"We'll take upstairs," I said. "You guys get the ground."

I kicked the door open on my first try. An alarm wailed to life. I spun away and the officers went in yelling. Then McKenzie and the plainclothes. I went last, my vision clear and my muscles buzzing with adrenaline.

The light inside was good. I followed the barrel of my Colt through the foyer and down the hallway, then right. I climbed the stairs through a slant of sunlight. I made the landing and swung the gun left to right while everything jumped at me: a doorknob, a wall sconce, a tree limb wavering just beyond a smoked window. The alarm was screaming in my ears as I pivoted into the master bedroom.

Empty. Bed made.

McKenzie barged in behind me. I heard the breath catch in her throat, watched the steady sweep of her barrel across the room. "Shit," she said quietly. "That would have been nice."

"Too easy."

A few minutes later one of the Coronado detectives called the security company and got the alarm turned off. Twenty minutes after that we had searched the house and the garage and the grounds and found no one and no evidence that Van Flyke had committed even the smallest crime.

"Where did he *go*?" asked McKenzie.

I'd been asking myself that question since Miranda had confirmed Van Flyke as the man who'd gotten into the car with a woman who was almost certainly Stella Asplundh.

Where had he taken her? Why hadn't our patrol cars and ABLE come up with such an obvious car? It had been approximately two and a half hours since the abduction, and the white Crown Victoria, so punctually pinpointed by Miranda of Higher Grounds, had vanished.

I didn't think he'd made it out of San Diego County—not in a law-enforcement vehicle that could be spotted easily from the air or ground.

I didn't think he'd even made it out of the city. He'd simply parked the car out of sight, where it wouldn't seem too unusual, and let us scurry around all night looking for it.

He had chosen someplace close. Someplace private. Someplace he could take and conceal Stella and the car.

"What about Garrett's apartment?" I asked.

The front door of Garrett's apartment was unlocked. An empty bottle of scotch lay in the middle of the living room floor. There were fast-food wrappers on the kitchen table.

The bed was torn apart, and the sheets were marked with blood. An empty syringe and needle lay on the nightstand by the clock. A piece of wadded duct tape stuck with long brown hair lay in a corner of the bedroom, in full view of the scores of images of beautiful Stella and Samantha looking out from the walls.

The garage was empty.

So we drove, radio up loud and windows half open and my optimism following the gas gauge down from full. It was a slow Friday night so far: minor collisions, a domestic call on Banker's Hill, a possible assault at a bar on Front Street, a drunk and disorderly in Hillcrest. One of the ABLE choppers cut across my field of vision on its way over the dark baseball stadium. I wondered if Stella Asplundh would be able to withstand what was happening to her now.

We flashed the patrol units and got flashed back. We pulled over and talked a couple of times. Some unmarked Deltas joined us. The ABLE choppers drifted overhead. A frustrated irritability sets in when an entire metropolitan police force is looking for one vehicle, one man, and can't locate either. We were understaffed and underfunded but doing what we could. Everybody was griping but nobody was throwing in the towel.

Ten became midnight. Midnight became two. Two became four, and I realized that in just a couple of hours the sun would be rising on Saturday morning. I gassed up the Chevy while McKenzie washed the windshield. We got drive-through breakfast sandwiches, then candy bars from a convenience store.

We cruised in a slow, expanding circle through the many beautifully named parts of San Diego: Mission Bay and Midway, Loma Portal and Uptown, Linda Vista and Old Town, Middletown and Centre City. Then through Sherman Heights and Logan Heights, Golden Hill and Grant Hill, South Crest and Shelltown. Then up through Rolando to Tierrasanta and Allied Gardens, Grantville and Kensington, Crown Point and Mission Valley. As a child I had traced my finger and read these names on my father's Thomas Guide, intrigued and impressed. I had loved Shelltown and Logan Heights and Rolando long before I could tell them apart.

I even showed McKenzie the place in Normal Heights where the dog had cornered me in the juniper bush when I was a boy, and the cop had run off the dog and taken me home. That was twenty-three years ago. I still remember the officer's name—Bob Hoppe. The juniper bush was still there, bigger and even more twisted than I remembered it.

The sun was rising on Normal Heights when Captain Villas called on my cell phone.

"Robbie, ABLE just picked up your car north on 79, out in east county. It's Van Flyke's Ethics sedan, no doubt. Our guys made a pass, nailed the plates, and backed off. You can have it if you want, but the Sheriffs will get there a lot faster than you will."

"Get the Sheriffs on alert and in position," I said. "If Van Flyke stops, take him. Until then let him think he's alone and let him get to where he's going. We're rolling now."

"He's alone," said Villas. "No woman."

"She might be in the trunk," I said. Or dumped somewhere on the long trail from downtown to east county.

"You want Emergency Negotiations Team?"

"Send them."

"We can go code-eleven SWAT," said Captain Villas. "We'll use Secondary Response and the Snipers."

"Get them ready," I said. *"Tell them she might be in the trunk."*

"Got it. Talk to ABLE on the Mobile Data Terminal, and Van Flyke can't intercept on his radio."

The Saturday-morning traffic was light. We picked up the 8 east and I hit ninety all the way to State 79. ABLE kept long-distance visual contact and they messaged us every few minutes on the MDT. Van Flyke was coming up on the little mountain town of Julian. He was holding a steady sixty miles an hour and he hadn't stopped yet. If he'd spotted the chopper he wasn't letting on.

He didn't stop in Julian. Instead he picked up Julian Road, bound west for the tiny village of Clear Creek.

"Clear Creek burned in '03," said McKenzie. "I don't think there's much left of it."

I remembered the newspaper photographs of tiny Clear Creek, known locally for its wineries, a cafe specializing in apple pies, and an old hotel once allegedly favored by Gable and Garbo. Several vineyards were reduced to rows of stumps and ash. The adobe Clear Creek Hotel had been gutted but remained standing and vacant. It was built to look like an old California mission, around a central courtyard. In the newspapers it had looked ruined, but somehow noble, too, the burst windows staring out from the blackened inside like the eyes of a blind man.

We tore north on 79, up through the greenery of the hills, then into the black expanse left by the fire. I glanced out at the skeletons of the trees and the rocks burned black. It looked like a charred moonscape. There were shoots of green grasses, though, and the beginnings of regrowth down low in the center of the burned trees, so you could see that life was going to win. It would just take time. I wondered if Stella's life would win out, too. We charged past Cuyamaca Reservoir and the little lake cabins that had been so mercilessly razed, climbing in elevation as we neared Julian.

The MDT screen jumped to life with a message from one of the ABLE choppers:

"Delta Eight, white four-door has stopped in Clear Creek. Looks like the old hotel. We've got him in our glasses. He just exited the car and he's looking up at us."

"We're less than five miles out," I said to McKenzie. She tapped the message onto the keyboard.

We slowed through the quaint mountain town of Julian. Gray clouds hung low over the mountains, snagging on the jagged pines. We picked up Julian Road east and I gunned it for Clear Creek.

Again we entered a world blackened by the 2003 fire. Although there was green grass and some regrowth, most of the tree trunks were just lifeless spires reaching for the gray sky. The verdant grass and brush had burned back to reveal rocks and boulders, and I wondered how long it must have taken all this life to flourish, only to be scorched to death in a few short minutes of fire.

The MDT screen blipped to life again:

"Delta Eight, he's got the trunk open now and he's lifting out a body. Confirm, a woman's body. He's got it up over his shoulders now and he's going toward the hotel."

"Is she alive, you dumb-ass?" asked McKenzie, as she typed.

A moment later the answer was on our screen:

"Dead or unconscious. SWAT is still twenty minutes out. Paramedics are about two miles behind you right now."

A smoke-blackened sign for the Clear Creek Hotel flashed by on my right. I swung the Chevy into the turn and started down the narrow asphalt road toward the hotel. The forest was dark and close, and the soft gray sky hung down like the belly of a cat.

"Why did he bring her here?" asked McKenzie.

"He must have run out of ideas," I said.

"Or gas. There's the building."

I pulled off the road and stopped.

"We can wait for SWAT," she said. "This is what they do best."

"Stella's up there."

"She could be dead, Robbie."

"I'm going in."

"Then I'm going in with you."

"Follow me. Stay in the trees."

We got out and began picking our way through the forest of black trunks. Sometimes I could see the three-story adobe hotel ahead of us, sometimes it was blotted out by the scorched trees. The world smelled of ash, and the branches left sooty streaks on our clothes and hands and faces.

Ahead I could see a clearing on one side of the hotel. Beyond the hotel was the remains of a vineyard. The vines were just stumps, and the uprights formed diminishing rows of black crosses all the way up a gentle hillside.

"Stay here and watch me," I said. "If I wave you off, use the MDT to get ABLE out of here. Then work your way back the way we came, cross the road past the car, and go into the hotel from the front. I'm going to try to talk him out of there. If he starts shooting or something, just call in the troops and stay down."

"Got it. Robbie, goddamn, be careful."

I moved through the trees toward the hotel. Above me a jay squawked and jeered, jumping from one charred branch to another. I made no attempt to be quiet, but I did try to keep at least one large tree trunk between me and the hotel windows. I stopped just short of the clearing. From behind a tree I looked up at the burned-out windows while I drew my grandfather's old Colt.

"John!" I called. "Robbie Brownlaw here!"

Nothing. So I yelled again.

A moment later Van Flyke's face appeared in the lower-right corner of a tall third-floor window. It looked small and white within the black cavern of the building. He was about a hundred feet away. It would be hard to hit him with my .45, and easy to miss.

"You're worse than a tick, Brownlaw."

His voice carried well in the silence, as if the great ashen aftermath were starved for sound.

"Is Stella alive?"

"Where's your partner?"

"Jackson, Wyoming. Is Stella alive?"

"Doing what?"

"Skiing with Hollis Harris. Is Stella alive or did you kill her?"

"Oh, of course she's alive. Very relaxed. Filled with morphine, breathing nice and deep."

"We've got SWAT and paramedics and backup on the way. Come on down and make things easy on yourself."

"No. I'll hang on to her as long as I can."

"Damn, John, don't you think you've put her through enough?"

"After Cramer called I knew I only had a few hours."

"Whose blood is that on the bed at Garrett's?"

"Stella stabbed me with a nail file."

I pulled back behind the tree and waved off McKenzie. I watched her turn and begin picking her way through the stinking remains of the burned forest. Then I leaned back around to see Van Flyke, my weapon still in hand.

"What's the deal, John?" I asked. "What are you trying to accomplish here?"

"I didn't get to plan this part. I ran out of time."

"What happened to you? What made you do all of this?"

His face disappeared from the window. I tried to see McKenzie through the forest but couldn't. Then Van Flyke was back in the lower-right corner of the window again.

"The first time I saw Stella," he said, "it changed me, instantly. Everything went upside down and backward. It got worse and worse. I never should have come to the Fourth of July party. I never should have interviewed for the Ethics job. If I'd just stayed in Miami, I might have been all right."

"What really happened to Samantha?"

Van Flyke's face remained in the window but he didn't say anything. It was hard to see his expressions clearly but I thought I saw a kind of puzzlement on his face. Beyond the old hotel the black vineyard crosses marched up the hill amid the scorched vines.

"I didn't think it could happen."

"What could happen?"

"I tossed the doll into the middle of the deep end when everybody was watching fireworks," he said. "It was one of those moments we talked about in my office, where everything changes in an instant. It was an impulse. A speculation. I didn't think that what I had imagined would actually happen. Then, a few minutes later I walked past the pool and saw that it really *was* happening. I only had a few seconds to decide. I decided to do the most terrifying thing I'd ever done—nothing. The sounds were quiet but awful, and nobody could hear except me. I knew that I'd sold my soul to the devil for Stella. It was worth it."

I looked back for McKenzie and saw nothing but dead trees. "Can Stella talk now? Can she say something?"

Van Flyke's face vanished from the window. A moment later he was back.

"She's still knocked out."

"Is she alive?"

"I told you she's alive," said Van Flyke. "I never wanted to hurt her. When you came up with the recording of the conversation between Garrett and her, I knew it was only a matter of time before you realized I'd heard half of that conversation while it happened. I knew what bridge he meant. I just needed a good vehicle to take me in and out of there, so I wouldn't be seen in my own car."

"You drove the Hummer down to the bridge and parked next to him and . . . what? Did you knock on the passenger-side window?"

"Sure. I waved through the glass. I smiled. He frowned at me like 'What the hell are you doing here?' but he hit the door-unlock button just the same. I swung open the door and put the gun in his face. Took all of about four seconds from the time I rapped on the window."

So there it was. Garrett was murdered by a man he thought was his friend as he sat in his car in the rain and looked out at a bridge that was his past and his future. It had gone down pretty much as we had reconstructed it, though the shooter was not who we expected. A shudder broke over me like a towering, cold wave.

"Why the earring, John?"

"Why not? I knew you'd find out about Squeaky Clean when you looked into Garrett. Jordan dropped it at a party. I picked it up to give it back to her but I thought I might use it for something someday. Speculation again. Then, when I imagined what would happen down there by the bridge, I thought I'd throw the earring into the brew."

"The backing had fallen off so you got a different one."

"I bought a cheapie thrift-store earring with the same kind. I figured if you got far enough to compare backings, you'd wasted plenty of valuable time."

"Yes," I said. "Some."

"But the call to Cramer is what sank me, Brownlaw. Why did you do that? Why not check the log to see who signed in at the Property Annex that day and just leave it at that? I mean, years had gone by. Anything could have happened to that gun."

"I'm stubborn," I said.

"You sure that partner of yours isn't on her way up here?"

"I talked to her just an hour ago. She's in Wyoming with Hollis Harris. Scout's honor."

"I never planned to hurt Stella. But she's mine now, and I'll kill her if I have to. Don't make me do that."

"You don't have to," I said. "Nobody has to kill anybody. But SWAT's going to be here any minute. They'll surround you with sharpshooters and wait you out. You'll get hungry and cold while they eat and drink coffee. That's news-at-eleven stuff, John—cameras and everything? That's for losers. You're better than that. Come on down. I'll drive you out before the cameras even get here."

Van Flyke's face disappeared for a moment. I tried to see McKenzie through the burned forest. I saw nothing alive but a bright blue jay peering down at me like a prosecutor. Then Van Flyke was back. "I thought we could make the Arizona border before it got too hot," he said. "Figured there was just enough air in the trunk."

"The chopper got you," I said.

"Then all the way back to Florida. I'd have kept driving."

"You're kind of stuck now, John."

He was quiet for a minute but his face remained in the tall window, low and right.

"You really see her for what she is, don't you?" asked Van Flyke. "I could tell when you came to the restaurant that day. How you looked at her."

"She's got something rare," I said.

"She sure does."

"My wife has it, too," I said.

"So, Brownlaw—I'll leave her here if you let me get to my car. I'd rather die in a high-speed chase than from a sniper."

"Deal," I said. "But you have to show me she's alive. I'm not trading for a corpse, John."

His face vanished again.

A few seconds later, Stella was in the window. Van Flyke was behind her, his wrists jammed under each of her armpits, either holding her up or holding her steady—it was hard to say which. He had a big automatic in his hand. Stella's head lolled to one side, then seemed to find upright balance for a moment, then swung heavily to the other. In that brief attempt at balance, I could tell that she was alive.

I realized that if McKenzie were to come through the door to that room right now, she'd be unable to shoot Van Flyke without shooting Stella too, unless she was good enough to get him in the head.

"She can't stand up," said Van Flyke. "I overdid it."

"She looks fine to me," I called out. "Put her down, John. You're free to get back to your car. Put her down!"

Suddenly the ABLE helicopter appeared in the middle distance, hovering low over the crosses of the vineyard and raising a black cloud. Van Flyke couldn't see it from his window, but he could hear it. I looked through the trees to the road behind me and saw the flash of metal and paint as the SWAT trucks piled to a stop behind my car.

I could tell by the angle of Van Flyke's head that he had seen them, too. He dropped Stella. I brought up my Colt and aimed at him. He turned quickly away and I heard the four quick pops beneath the roar of the advancing helicopter. Van Flyke backed up and sat on the sill, arms out as if for balance. Two more pops and he slumped out of the window and cascaded three floors down, landing in a fatally shapeless heap.

McKenzie appeared in the window, gun in hand, looking down at Van Flyke, then to me.

I sat with Stella for a while in the hospital that evening. I had the feeling she wanted me to stay and was talking to keep me there.

Her right eye socket was purple, her eye was swollen almost shut, and there was a three-stitch cut on her brow. She wasn't sure how it had happened, but she did remember trying to drive a fingernail file into Van Flyke's back and being hit in the face for her trouble. She had clear memories of the first part of her abduction, followed by hazy recollections, courtesy of the Valium-morphine cocktail he had injected into her. She had attacked him two or three times. He had struck her. He had choked her unconscious at least once. He had kissed her forcefully and seemed to be preparing to rape her, then stopped and apologized. He had cursed and talked to himself a lot. He had not seemed sure what he was trying to accomplish.

McKenzie came by around seven. She looked just as drained and suspicious as she had looked after the officer-involved-shooting interviews we gave to Captain Sutherland and his Professional Standards team. She brought a yellow rose in a slender vase and set it next to the plastic water pitcher on Stella's rolling tray. Stella offered her a very small nod and that was all.

After the hospital I got drive-through food and took it home. I called McKenzie and we talked for quite a while.

The aftermath of a fatal shooting is a tricky thing. You think you're okay with what you did, and then you feel tremendous doubt that you did the right thing. You tell yourself there was nothing else you could have done. But you wonder. You think about all of the life you've taken away—the weeks and months and years that you've denied someone. You feel guilty for being alive, then angry about the guilt. You build yourself back up, one thought at a time, until you believe again that you did the right thing, and you remind yourself that you agreed to take this responsibility when you were sworn to serve and that you were the tool in what happened, not the cause. This is what you have to believe in order to go on. I shot and killed a man in the line of duty when I was very young. He had a knife, out and ready. He was three steps away from me and coming fairly fast. He had threatened to kill his girlfriend, then himself, and then he came at me. He had a long history of mental illness. They called it suicide by cop. It happened down in Logan Heights when I was on patrol. I was twenty-two, and he was twenty-five. He was baby-faced, blond-haired, and blue-eyed. His name was Duane Randolph. I thought about him on the way down from the Las Palmas.

On the phone that night, McKenzie covered her pain with bravado. She was eager to put the shooting behind her but I knew it would keep coming back. The counseling that the department gives us really helps, though it takes time. McKenzie talked awhile about Hollis Harris and how his world was bytes and gigs and jets and toys, and hers was crooks and guns and take-out food, and what sense was there in mixing the two?

"Maybe good sense," I said.

"I love him," she said.

"Then there you have it."

"Not everyone ends up happy like you and Gina," she said.

"You did the right thing today, McKenzie. You were alone up there and it wasn't easy. You did the job. You got her out of there alive."

McKenzie was quiet for a while. "How about you, Robbie? You okay?"

"I'm good."

I watched the TV without sound until late. I fell asleep right there on the couch and dreamed of men falling from bridges and buildings into rich green jungles.

Late Sunday afternoon I called Vince. He sounded brusque and bothered and said he'd have to call me back. Ten minutes later he did, and his voice was changed.

"Sorry, Robbie," he said. "Dawn and I been at it again about this. Look, Gina's got a place of her own right here in Las Vegas. Nice little apartment. I'm going to give you the address but I need your word you won't do something stupid, you won't get loud or something with her. She's my girl and I can't let that happen."

"I can't get loud with Gina, Vince. You know that by now."

"Maybe you two can work it out. Dawn says no, but what's she know? Two people are two people. They find their own ways of doing things."

"Thank you."

He gave me the address. I wrote it down and stared at it: 414 Villa Bonterra, #B-303, Las Vegas.

I had just enough time to hit the Horton Plaza mall for a new suit. I had to buy one as is so I could put it on a few hours later, but I'm a forty-four tall, so it wasn't hard to find. All of the forty-four tall trousers were too big in the waist but the salesman said safety pins and a snug belt would do the trick. The suit was navy wool and expensive. I got a new white shirt and a light blue tie in honor of Garrett Asplundh. A pair of new black shoes. When I got home I turned the trouser cuffs under and used duct tape to hold them in place. I looked in the mirror, tried to get the safety pins right, examined the finished product, and shook my head.

Dream Wheels opened at nine the next morning. I rented a silver Porsche 996 Twin Turbo because Gina had always wanted one. Cass said the new suit was sharp and my date was lucky. The car cost me nine hundred dollars for one day. I felt powerful and potent. I now understood why Garrett Asplundh had rented fancy cars and purchased expensive clothing to impress Stella.

I made the Las Vegas city limits in five hours and eight minutes. I was stopped by the California Highway Patrol and proffered my law-enforcement ID, which is a cheap trick when you're driving a rental car over ninety. The CHiP looked over the Dream Wheels registration while telling me about a brother-in-law in National City who had season tickets for the Pads. He told me to cool it and get to Vegas alive. Heading into town I felt like a TV-show detective with my cool suit and killer car and the casinos wobbling up to greet me through a mirage of crisp desert air.

I found the B building of the Palacio Toscana apartments and drove the perimeter of the carports but didn't see Gina's car. The apartments were salmon-colored and new, with faux shutters swung back from their windows. There were flowers along the walkways. The Palacio Toscana smelled of fresh asphalt. I parked in the shade and spread a newspaper across the steering wheel. The afternoon was sunny but not hot.

An hour and fifteen minutes later Gina's little blue coupe bounced off the street and into the lane of carports. I lifted the newspaper and watched her over the headlines, and she drove past me without turning. She swung wide right, then pulled hard left into her space.

As I walked toward her across the black asphalt she got out of her car. I could tell by the sudden stop of her head that she recognized me. I waved and couldn't keep myself from smiling and walking faster. I remembered that there had been times like this when she'd run to greet me.

She had on a pretty blue sundress and blue shoes. Her hair was drawn into a ponytail that rose from a jeweled tube atop her head, then spilled over like a wild orange fountain.

"I'm not here for a scene," I said.

"You shouldn't be here at all. Nice car."

I looked at her for a moment. "You take my breath away, Gina."

"That's why this is so difficult."

"Should we talk inside?" I asked.

"Okay."

Her apartment was upstairs. It had a view of buildings A and C, and the swimming pool, and a grassy park with a big pavilion for shade. A couple about our age sat in the shade of the pavilion, kissing unhurriedly.

I saw from the bland tan harmonies of the interior that Gina had rented the unit furnished. I looked at her. She was bright and radiant and as out of place as a ruby in a bowl of oatmeal.

"What?" she said.

"I miss you."

"I miss you, too."

How disappointing, to watch the red squares of dishonesty pouring out of Gina's mouth. I watched the colored shapes flow toward me, then slide over a rounded edge, like water going over a fall.

I remembered times when she'd meet me at the front door when I came home from work and actually pull me inside.

Gina took a deep breath and looked down at the tan carpet. "Here. Have a seat."

I sat at one end of the tan sofa and Gina sat at the other.

"How's work, Robbie?"

"It's good."

"Catch any bad guys lately?"

"One."

"Do you still see the shapes when people talk?"

I nodded. "Kind of wish I didn't. It just seems to get in the way."

She looked down.

"Do you know what you're doing?" I asked.

"Yes."

"Can you explain it to me?"

"I can try." She crossed her pale legs and folded her hands in her lap.

"I came here for a new life. I think there must be more."

"More *what*?"

"More everything. I know that sounds really shallow but I'm aching inside for something I can't see and can't identify and can't touch. But I know it's there. It's right there, just past my ability to understand. Just out of reach of my words."

"I'd be happy to help you look for it."

"It's something I want to do alone. I'm sorry, Robbie. I fell out of love with you. I was planning to call. I'm going to file the papers and I don't want anything—you can have it all. I don't want it to be expensive for either of us."

I could barely formulate a reply. Something inside me took over the task of communication while my heart withered and died.

"Everything we have is community property," I heard myself say.

"But I don't want any of it. Not one thing."

She bent her face to her hands and the orange fountain pitched forward. She reached up, yanked out the jeweled ornament and her lovely hair spilled down. She put her face into her hands again. Her back heaved but she made very little sound.

"Got another guy?"

She shook her head and her back heaved faster.

I sat for a while, feeling the rhythm of her crying relayed to me through the couch springs and the frame and the cushions. Because her face was buried in her hands, I was able to stare at her, as I'd been wanting to do for some time. I can't accurately describe her beauty in that moment, but to me it was unique and entire. I wanted to take her in my arms until the tears stopped but I understood that they wouldn't. I could smell them from where I sat, the same humid perfume of the Sonoran thunderstorms that sometimes towered over and burst upon Normal Heights early Septembers when I was a boy.

"Was it something I did?" I asked. "Or didn't do?"

She shook her head again.

"I know I've got my faults."

"No, you're perfect. You really are."

We sat without talking for a long minute or two. During that silence my thoughts organized themselves and I could tell that my heart was not dead, just wounded. A great relief began to spread inside me.

"Look at me," I said.

She uncovered her face, wiped her tears and held me with her bloodshot green eyes.

"I've never told you this before, Gina, but I lost something in the fall, some kind of purchase or traction that other people have, and I used to have. What I have now is the opposite of those things. I'm not even sure what to call it—the power to let go, maybe. Because, you know, at the very end of that fall, that's what I did. I just let go. I gave up and I understood that my own life was out of my hands. I never told anybody that, because I was too busy being a hero. Heroes fight all the way down. They never give up. So I wasn't really a hero at all. But now I see that sometimes letting go gets you just as much as fighting does. I don't know why that's true, and I can't explain it, and it goes against everything I was taught. There was only one thing I knew I'd never let go of, and that was you. But I'm going to do it now, Gina. I can't keep you. I can't give you what you need, because I don't know what it is. So good-bye. Please don't worry about me. I'll start over."

I stood and took a step and sat down close to her. As the cushion under me compressed with my weight, the cushion under Gina lightened with her departure, and she swept around the end of the couch and ran into the bathroom. The door slammed and the lock clicked.

I stood, as my parents taught me to do when a woman enters and leaves the room. I looked around the apartment once. I lifted my nose to gather in the smell of her. I locked her door from the inside and tugged it closed behind me.

A week later I gave closed-session testimony to the San Diego Grand Jury. They had assembled at my request. I told them what Garrett Asplundh had discovered in his work as an Ethics Authority investigator, and I documented it with his reports, his sex videos, and my own discoveries. Talk about a hush falling over a room. I was thanked and told that I might be asked to testify again to the grand jury and perhaps subsequently in a court of law. Two days after that, I was back in the grand jury room again, this time with McKenzie and Captain Villas, going over the evidence in more detail.

I met with Carrie Ann Martier for lunch one day down in Seaport Village. We sat outside in the spring sun and watched the tourists go by. I told her that trouble was brewing and she would be a part of it. I told her that if she wanted to leave town and save herself from the theater of a trial, I wouldn't stop her.

"You've got my bare ass on DVD with all those clowns," said Carrie. "That's my testimony, and thanks for the tip-off. I missed two days of work for the pinch up at Eden Heights, so I figure I've done my duty."

"Got enough for a down payment on the Hawaii place?" I asked.

"I'm about eleven thousand shy," she said. "Want to loan it to me? I can work it off. First night's free because you're a good guy. You'd be one happy man till I paid you off."

"You think like a whore," I said.

She smiled, a little coolly.

In mid-April the indictments started coming down—Anthony Rood and Steve Stiles, Fellowes and Mincher, and of course Jordan Sheehan. The headlines in the *U-T* were three inches high. There were more news crews downtown than there were for the Super Bowl back in '03.

It was interesting to see not only who fell but who escaped.

By the end of that month, Jance Purdew issued a "stable" rating for San Diego municipal bonds. In spite of the turmoil brewing in our fine city, Trey Vinson had come through with a one-word rating that would save us scores of millions of dollars in interest payments over the years. I wondered if he had rated us "stable" in spite of being caught on video with a Squeaky Clean or because of it. The news media editorialized about the importance of "cleaning house" and how such painful diligence had already given San Diego a fresh new face on Wall Street.

Abel Sarvonola and the Budget Oversight Committee had glowing things to say about the new rating and San Diego's future. The mayor unveiled a budget that would include funds for a new library and eighteen new patrol cars for us, without raiding the pension fund. That same week the Padres did a big trade with New York, which brought us two badly needed medium-length relief pitchers and stole the headlines from Sarvonola and the mayor, which is exactly what everybody wanted. Our city loves sports.

On behalf of Garrett, I went down to the National City apartment one evening and checked in on April Holly.

April had gotten a shorter haircut since I'd seen her at the funeral. Her wavy dark hair framed her face smartly and she looked even more like Stella Asplundh than before. She said SeaWorld was treating her just fine. She liked the people she worked with and had changed her major to biology in order to become a dolphin or killer-whale trainer someday. She told me that the first time she'd seen the Shamu show at night, she had realized what she wanted to do with her life.

Later I went to Miranda's show at the Zulu Grill in Ocean Beach. It wasn't a formal show. She had hung her twenty paintings around the restaurant that morning, and I sat with her at the bar that night as the patrons came and went.

Her paintings looked solid and humorful. She had taken the time to get the lighting on them right. Each work was a bright jewel that occupied its small space with surprising depth and authority. The longer I looked at them, the more comedy I saw taking place between the muscled men and curvy women on Miranda's audaciously colored beaches. In one a surfer knelt in front of a seductively posed young woman. The woman was working her hands through her flowing yellow hair, ignoring him, and the surfer was scratching his head as he looked out at the waves. To me it was an illustration of the perfect disconnection between people who are together in a nice time and space.

"I like that one," I said.

"Me, too," said Miranda. "They're both so lost and right for each other, but they don't know it."

Miranda sat beside me at the bar with a small stack of business cards she'd made up on a computer, but she couldn't screw up the courage to introduce herself to the diners and drinkers, as the manager had suggested. She drank three quick mai tais and smiled at me goofily. A few minutes later she took a deep breath, slid off her barstool, cards in hand, and introduced herself to two couples sitting at a booth in the corner.

By ten she'd made the rounds of the entire restaurant and the bar. While she was talking to four loud guys sitting near the exit, I called over the bartender, paid the tab, and told him not to let her leave the restaurant drunk. I made sure he saw my shield. I was reminded of my first date with Gina and Rachel and the fact that I had refused to let them buy alcohol because of their ages.

Oddly enough, two nights later Rachel herself was sitting on my front-porch bench when I got home from picking up fast food. She stood as I came up the walkway. She was dressed beautifully and was noticeably perfumed. On the small wooden table in front of the bench were two glasses of red wine and an open bottle.

We sat on the bench. The wine was exceptionally good and Rachel let me know that it had cost eighty dollars. She also let me know that she had talked to Gina and that Gina was doing well. Gina had told Rachel about our good-bye. Rachel felt terrible for me, but she knew that "the seeds of pain can grow into wonderful things."

We shared the fast food and Rachel laid her head on my shoulder for a while. Then she pecked me on the cheek and stood. "Call me if you want, Robbie."

"I'll do that."

"Good. Just so you know, I asked Gina. She said I was free to do this. She wants both of us to be happy."

Another piece of my heart chipped away. "That's nice."

"Life is long, Robbie."

"Mostly."

Stella moved back to Northern California early that summer. We talked a few times before she left. She gave me Garrett's fishing gear, which included a split-cane fly rod that Garrett's father had given him.

Her eye healed up nicely but I can't vouch for the rest of her. Every word she said and every movement she made seemed to come from huge effort. It was like she was saying and doing things for the first time. You can't get back what was taken away from Stella Asplundh. You can't replace. You can only move on and make a life again. You can look back but not too long, and forward but not too far.

McKenzie talked to Stella much more than I did before Stella left San Diego. In McKenzie's opinion Stella would be okay. Stella had strength, empathy, generosity, anger, and a deep well of loss and sadness.

"It's more than a lot of people have inside," said McKenzie.

After drinks at the Grant one evening, Erik Kaven offered me John Van Flyke's old job as head of Ethics Authority Enforcement. Kaven said I'd have plenty of latitude to sniff out corruption and four investigators to help me go after it. I turned it down because I already had the job I'd always wanted to have. And who knew—maybe someday I'd be able to shoo off a mean dog and drag some little boy out of the bushes and give him a ride home in my car.

One night I got out the tape that Gina had made me, of my fall from the hotel. I set it on the VCR in the living room while I tried to straighten up the place a little, glancing at it as I came and went.

Late that night, after cleaning the house and going to McGinty's for dinner and a glass of wine, I slipped the tape into the machine and hit play.

It was brief but very dramatic. The cameraman had shot the video from across the street, probably not far from where I'd been eating my lunch. But thanks to a powerful zoom lens, the old Las Palmas took up most of the screen. Flames lapped from the open windows while the smoke billowed into the sky.

I knew which window to watch. I could see Vic Malic crouched there, screaming down at the people on the street. His voice had something helpless in it, which is what fooled me into thinking I was going to help him rather than be attacked by him.

For a minute Vic vanished from the window and I knew that he had stood and come at me.

I pictured his drunk and insane face, smelled the gin fumes pouring from his mouth, felt the power of his wrestler's grip on my body, saw the gasoline can in one corner, saw the small hotel room spinning around me once . . . twice. . . .

And then I watched myself fly out. I had been dressed in chinos and a white shirt and a light-colored jacket that day, so I showed up well against the darker brick of the Las Palmas. I saw my early struggle for purchase in thin air, the craning of my neck, and my hands clawing at the sky. I saw that odd moment of stillness, followed by a woeful acceleration down. My arms and legs pumped furiously as the bricks sped up behind me. I looked like a many-legged insect. I folded open onto my back, leveling and looking up at the window from which I'd been thrown, and I saw on video what I'd seen in life: Vic Malic staring down at me with a surprised look on his face.

I recognized the point—it was between the third and second stories of the building—that I realized there was nothing I could do to slow or stop my fall, and I looked up into the sky and let go. I saw my body relax and I saw my back arch gracefully, though I don't remember relaxation or grace when it was happening.

Right after that I must have blacked out.

I watched myself slam into the awning and chute through the bottom of it feetfirst and greatly slowed, like a mummy sliding from a conveyor belt, for the last ten feet of my journey. Even with my fall broken so effectively, I still hit the sidewalk with a tremendous whack that I don't remember.

The crowd closed over me and a moment later Vic Malic spilled from the front door and joined them.

I rewound and watched the tape one more time. I'm not sure what I was expecting to discover.

I didn't want to see my moment of surrender because I had come to be ashamed of it in light of being made a hero. But I could see exactly where I was in the sky when I realized the drastic truth of my predicament and let go. Religious people might tell me I found God. Nonreligious ones might say I found a "higher power." Atheists might tell me I had just awakened to the great, pure aloneness we all share.

After watching the tape twice, I could see my fall in all of those ways. With time to reflect, things take on meaning. But at that moment I wasn't thinking of meanings at all. I was just a hopeless man hoping for the best. A man so scared his brain finally shut down.

When I saw what he had gone through I wasn't ashamed of him anymore.

McKenzie married Hollis Harris that June in Jackson, Wyoming. Harris flew in over two hundred friends and family members, put us all up in five of the very nicest hotels in that pretty little city.

McKenzie was indescribably beautiful in her lacy white dress, with her black hair back in an elegant swirl that somehow disappeared within itself. She had her makeup done by a professional and the results were extraordinarily impressive. I'd never known she had such stunning eyes.

Neither McKenzie nor Hollis came from wealthy families—in fact, they were both lower middle class—so there was a very pleasing eccentricity among the attendees. Everyone seemed giddily happy to be there. I saw some very odd and very old clothes. One of McKenzie's older brothers had a prison tattoo on the back of his thick neck. Hollis's best man had been his best friend since they met in kindergarten. He was an extremely thin, bespectacled stutterer who had a heck of a time with his toast and whose rented tuxedo pants suddenly slipped to his ankles while he was dancing with McKenzie. The crowd roared and a massive and intense red blush covered his face, but he was smiling.

McKenzie had told me some months earlier that Hollis's parents had died in a car crash when he was ten, and while I watched him dance with his bride with the splendor of the Grand Tetons as a backdrop I wondered at the great loss that had helped propel him to great achievement. His son was smart and talkative and had just turned six. We had a nice discussion about Bionicles, a line of ingenious and popular toys, one of which he carried around with him during the long, loud reception. When it was my turn to dance with McKenzie I told her she looked very nice without a gun.

The only downside of the wedding was that I had been forced to confess Gina's departure. I tried to put "positive spin" on it by saying that we'd both left the door open in case we wanted to go back. I fooled no one. People began looking at me a little differently, though since my fall from the Las Palmas people had always looked at me differently, so I was used to it.

I had no one to impress.

I knew it was time to start over again.

I flew home the next day, a Sunday, and that evening drove to the Belly Up in Solana Beach to hear Lillian, the synesthete, sing.

The house was nearly full, which is saying something, because the Belly Up brings in some very good, big-name entertainment. I was obviously not aware of Lillian Smith's substantial local reputation. I got a seat up close, probably because I was alone.

When Lillian walked onstage I found myself clapping and cheering along with everyone else. She looked larger onstage than off, with the gleaming white guitar strapped over her shoulder, the shiny high black boots, and the same long wine-colored velvet coat she'd worn to the Synesthesia Society meeting back in March. The stage lights crisscrossed over her and bounced colors off her glossy black hair. She squinted out at the audience as she prepared for her first song and I think she recognized me, though the nice smile could have been for anyone in the room, really.

She had a wonderfully expressive voice. It was high and pure but had a little roughness on its way up and down the notes. The colored geometrical shapes that poured out around her microphone were brilliant and profuse as tropical flowers. The more she sang the more they filled the air around her. Back in the old days, I might have reached out to move the shapes aside but they don't annoy or fascinate me like they used to. Now they're just part of what is. I'm learning to ignore them if I want to.

I sat and listened and let my mind wander, which is what it does when I hear music, or sermons in church. In the middle of her second song I became aware that she was looking at me. After that I had the odd feeling that she was singing only to me, much as I had paid attention only to her when I spoke at the San Diego Synesthesia Society meeting. It was a pleasant feeling.

Lillian's songs ranged widely in topic, from a young girl's relationship with her aging mother to a young woman who gets her heart broken but won't admit it to a song called "Carefree Blonde," in which the singer names her rivals after hair dyes, such as "Platinum Bounce," "Cornsilk," and "Urban Angel." This song was funny and sarcastic, and many people sang along with the chorus.

While her songs filled the room with emotions and the shapes and colors flowed forth from her mouth, I tried to say good-bye to Gina once and for all. But you can only say good-bye to something that big a little at a time. So I said another small good-bye and I knew again in my heart that it was time to start over. I wasn't the man for her. I thought I could change, but I never knew what to change into. I had done all I could do: I had fallen.

After the show I took a walk through the parking lot, then the nearest side streets. I located Lillian's battered brown coupe parked under a streetlamp. I could hear the distant roar of the waves on the beach and see the downy threads of June fog riding by on the breeze. I decided against waiting for her and walked down by the beach for a while, but when I came back the car was still there.

I crossed my arms and leaned against it.

She came through the fog in her wine-colored coat, her guitar case in one hand. Behind her one of the large bouncers rolled a dolly with her monitors and another guitar case and a blue plastic milk crate filled with cords and plugs.

"Hello, Robbie," she said.

"Hello, Lillian."

"Want him to get lost?" asked the bouncer.

"He's okay," said Lillian.

"Pop the trunk, Lil," he said.

She unlocked the car, bent inside, then stood up straight again. With the boots on she was almost as tall as I was. In her stage makeup she looked older than she had before, and the age looked good on her.

"How have you been?" she asked.

"Really good. You?"

"Good, too. Still seeing voices?"

I nodded. "I really don't mind. You kind of get used to it. Still hearing faces?"

She studied me a moment. "Yeah. I read about you and the grand jury," she said.

"It had to happen."

"Where's your wife?"

"Las Vegas. It was over when I met you. I just didn't believe it then."

She eyed me with frank distrust.

The trunk slammed and the car rocked. The bouncer came over, hugged Lillian, and glared at me. Then he turned and aimed the empty dolly back toward the nightclub.

"Take a walk?" she asked.

"That would be great," I said.

"Talk to me, Detective Brownlaw," she said.

"About what?"

"Anything you want."